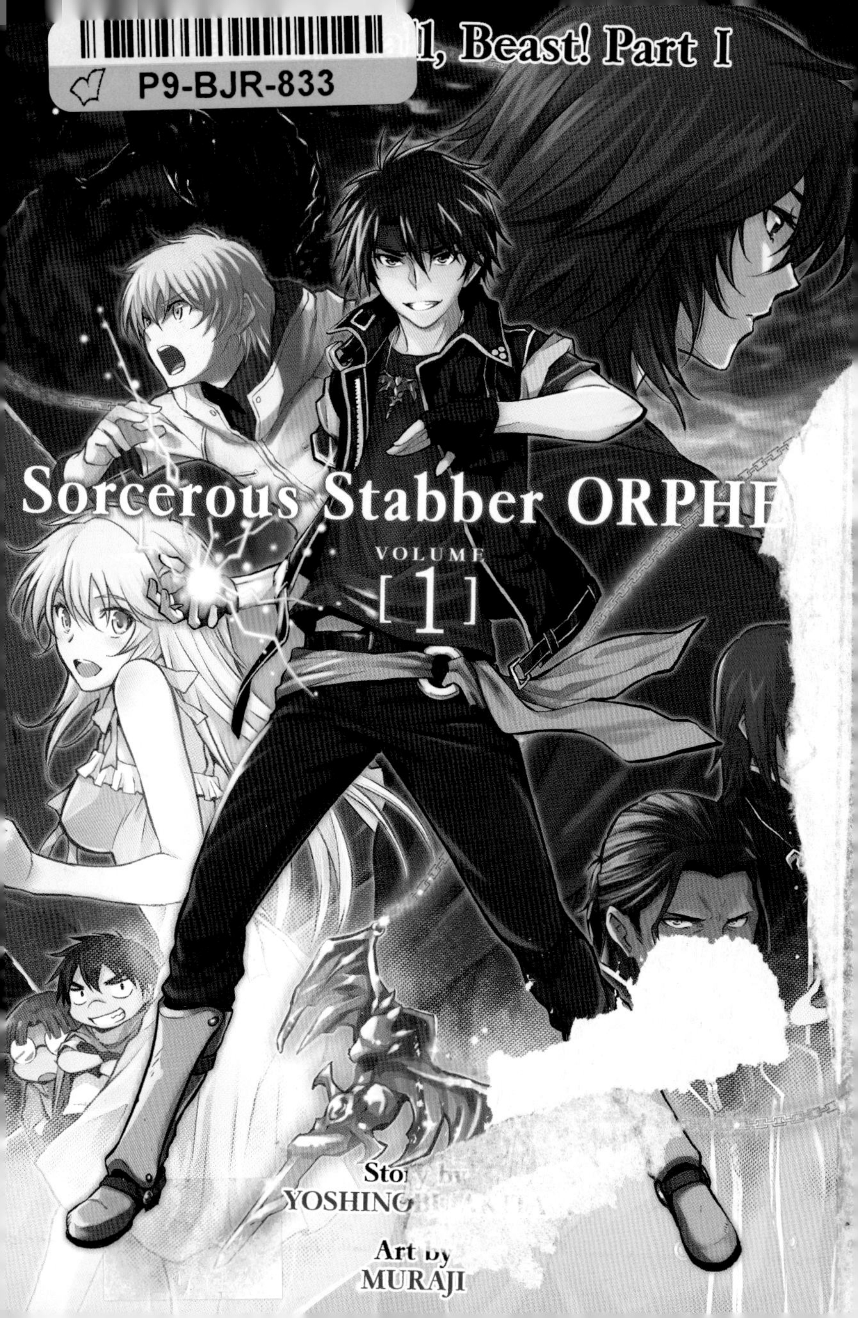
ll, Beast! Part I
Sorcerous Stabber ORPHE
VOLUME
[1]
Sto
YOSHINO
Art by
MURAJI

Sorcerous Stabber ORPHEN

CONTENTS

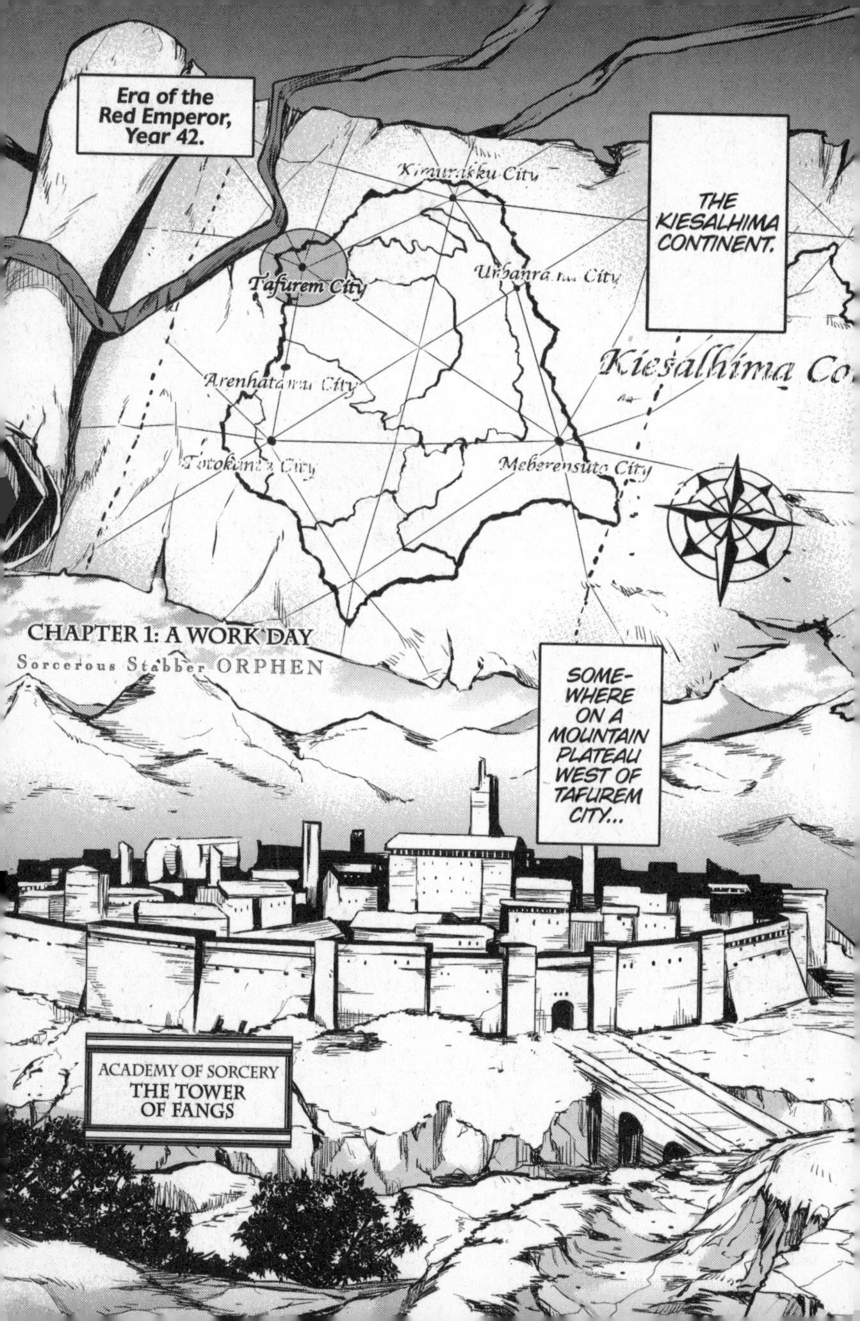
THE KIESALHIMA CONTINENT.
Era of the Red Emperor, Year 42.
Tafurem City
Meberensuto City
CHAPTER 1: A WORK DAY
Sorcerous Stabber ORPHEN
SOME-WHERE ON A MOUNTAIN PLATEAU WEST OF TAFUREM CITY...
ACADEMY OF SORCERY
THE TOWER OF FANGS

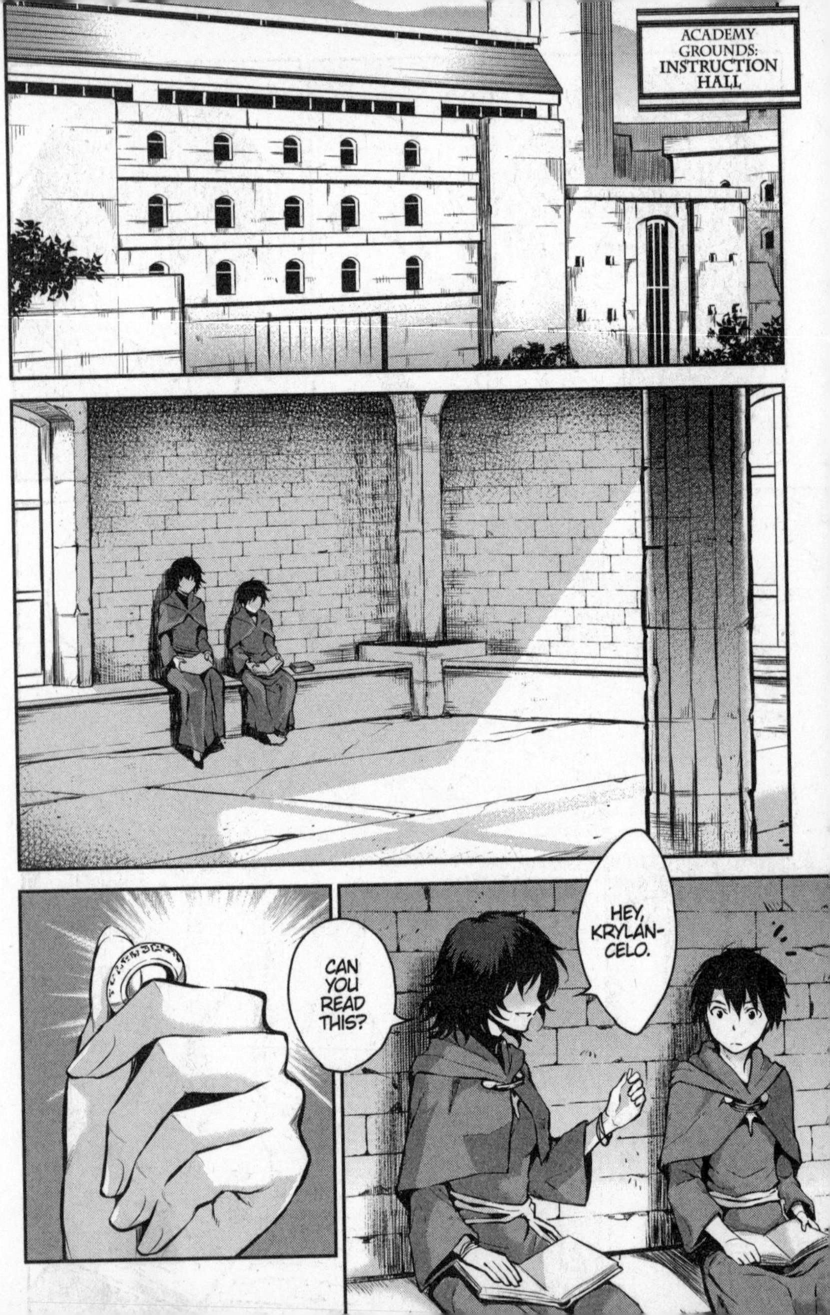
ACADEMY GROUNDS: INSTRUCTION HALL
HEY, KRYLAN-CELO.
CAN YOU READ THIS?

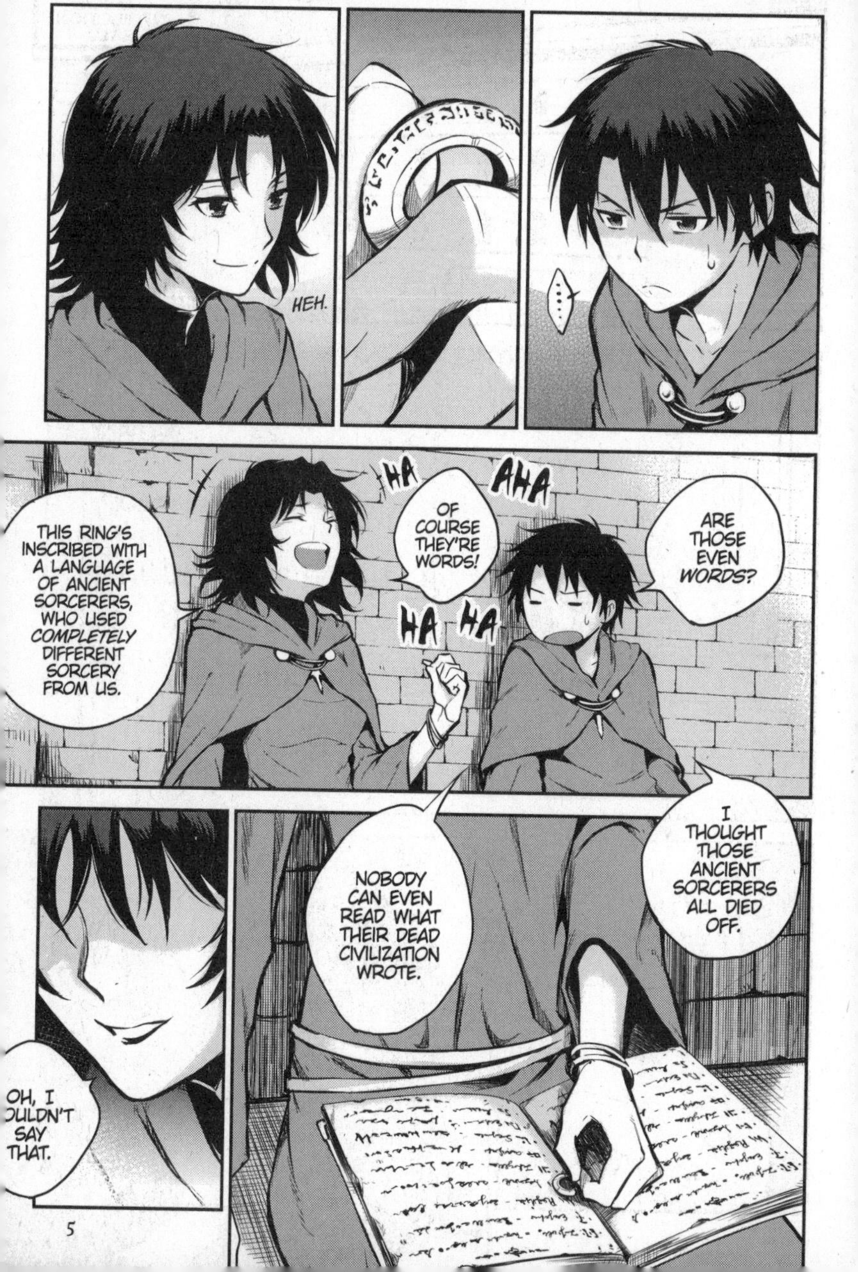
...
HEH.
ARE THOSE EVEN WORDS?
AHA
HA
OF COURSE THEY'RE WORDS!
HA HA
THIS RING'S INSCRIBED WITH A LANGUAGE OF ANCIENT SORCERERS, WHO USED COMPLETELY DIFFERENT SORCERY FROM US.
I THOUGHT THOSE ANCIENT SORCERERS ALL DIED OFF.
NOBODY CAN EVEN READ WHAT THEIR DEAD CIVILIZATION WROTE.
OH, I OULDN'T SAY THAT.

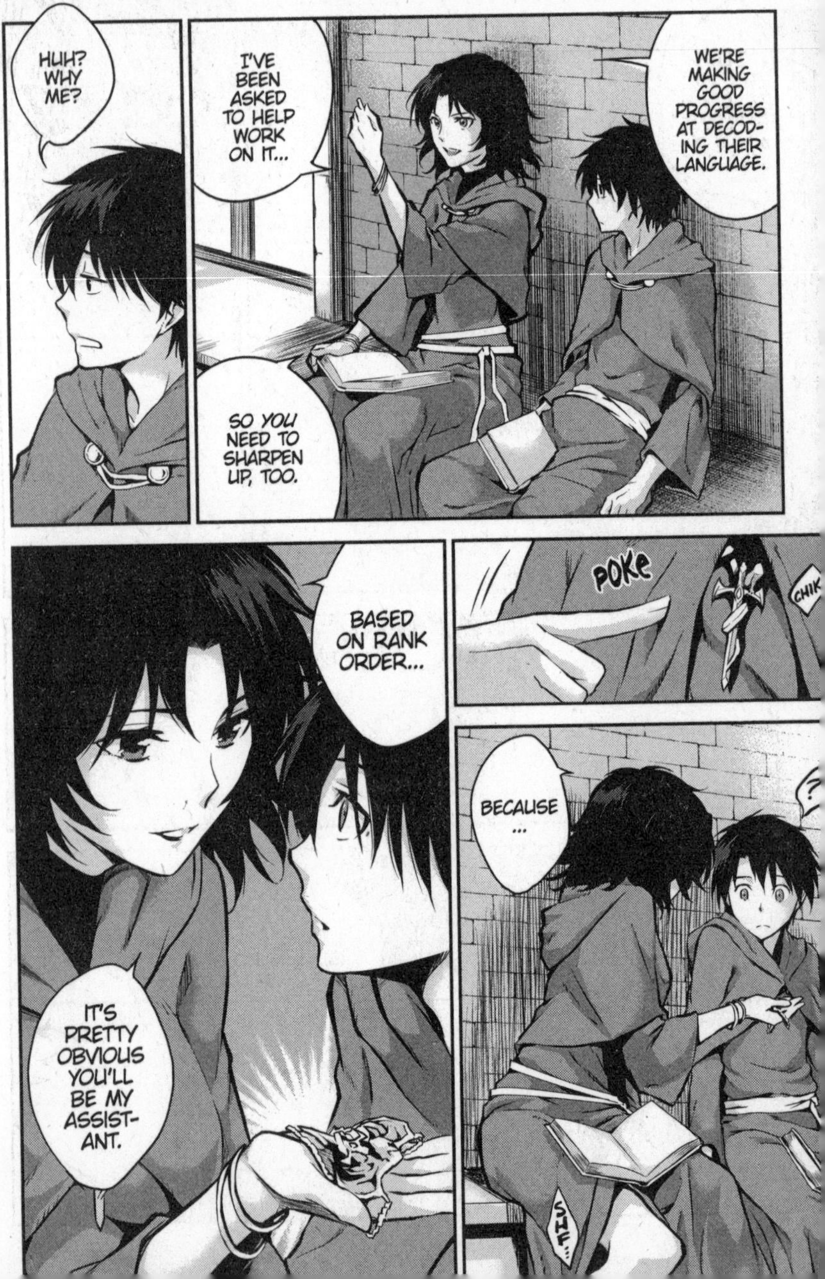
WE'RE MAKING GOOD PROGRESS AT DECOD-ING THEIR LANGUAGE.
I'VE BEEN ASKED TO HELP WORK ON IT...
SO YOU NEED TO SHARPEN UP, TOO.
HUH? WHY ME?
POKE
CHIK
?
BECAUSE ...
SHF...
BASED ON RANK ORDER...
IT'S PRETTY OBVIOUS YOU'LL BE MY ASSIST-ANT.

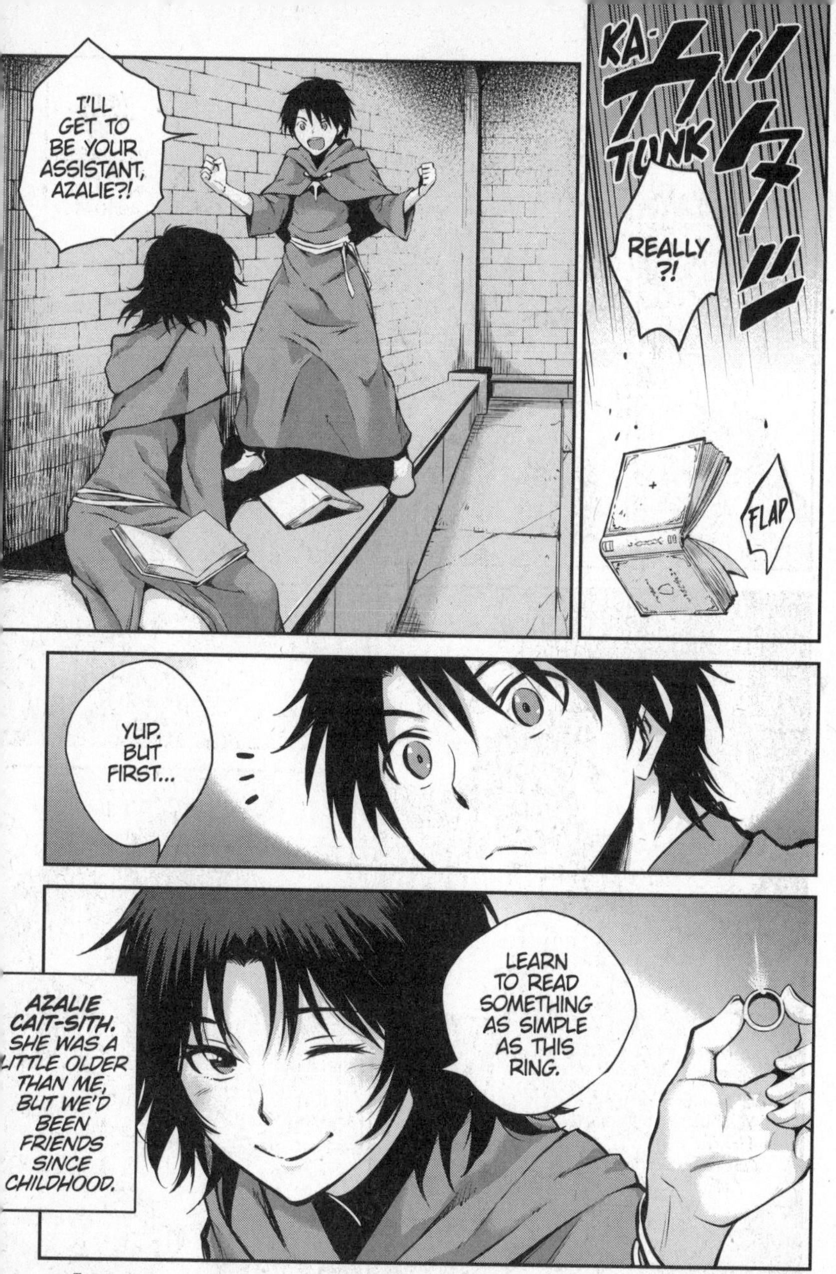
KA-TUNK
REALLY?!
FLAP
I'LL GET TO BE YOUR ASSISTANT, AZALIE?!
YUP. BUT FIRST...
LEARN TO READ SOMETHING AS SIMPLE AS THIS RING.
AZALIE CAIT-SITH. SHE WAS A LITTLE OLDER THAN ME, BUT WE'D BEEN FRIENDS SINCE CHILDHOOD.

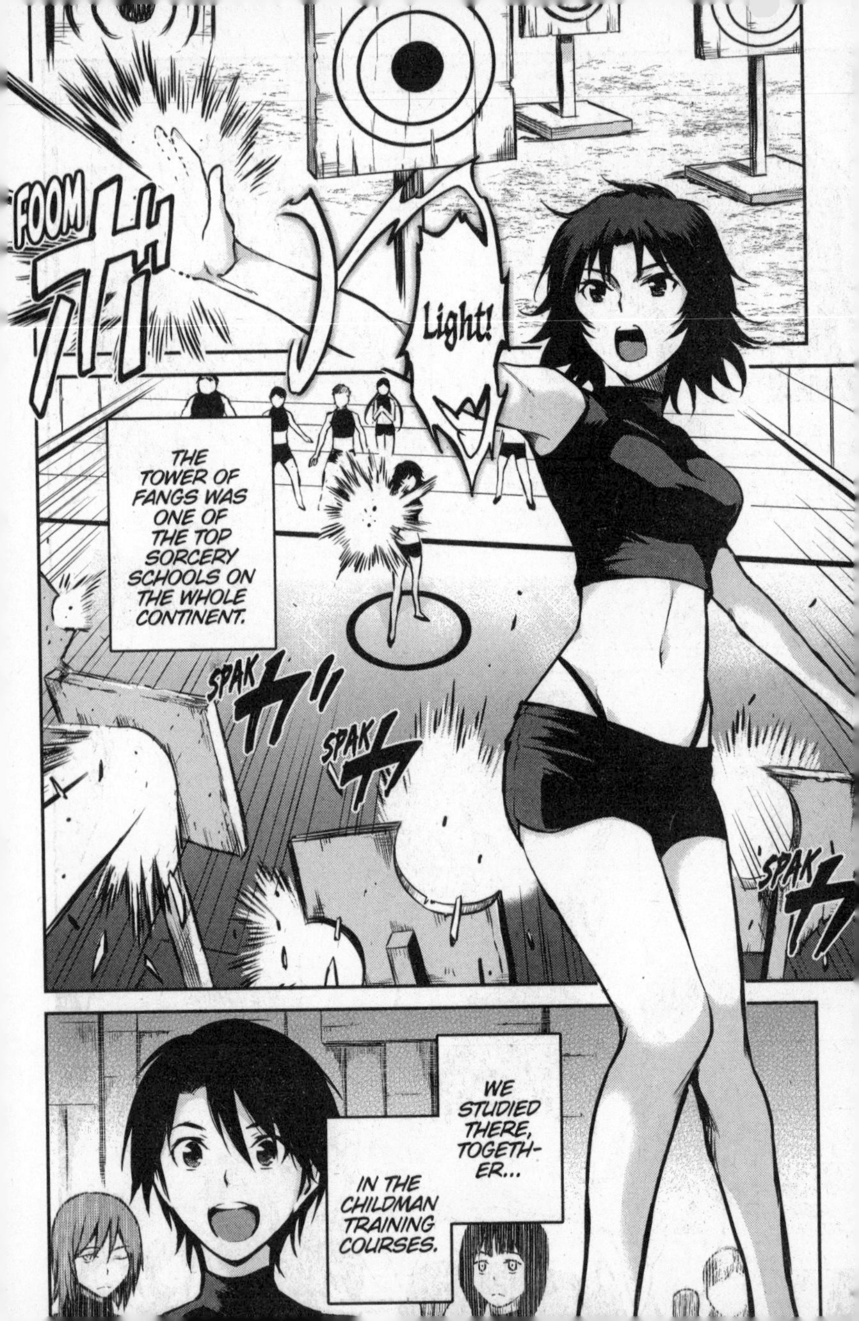

Light!
FOOM
THE TOWER OF FANGS WAS ONE OF THE TOP SORCERY SCHOOLS ON THE WHOLE CONTINENT.
SPAK
SPAK
SPAK
WE STUDIED THERE, TOGETHER...
IN THE CHILDMAN TRAINING COURSES.

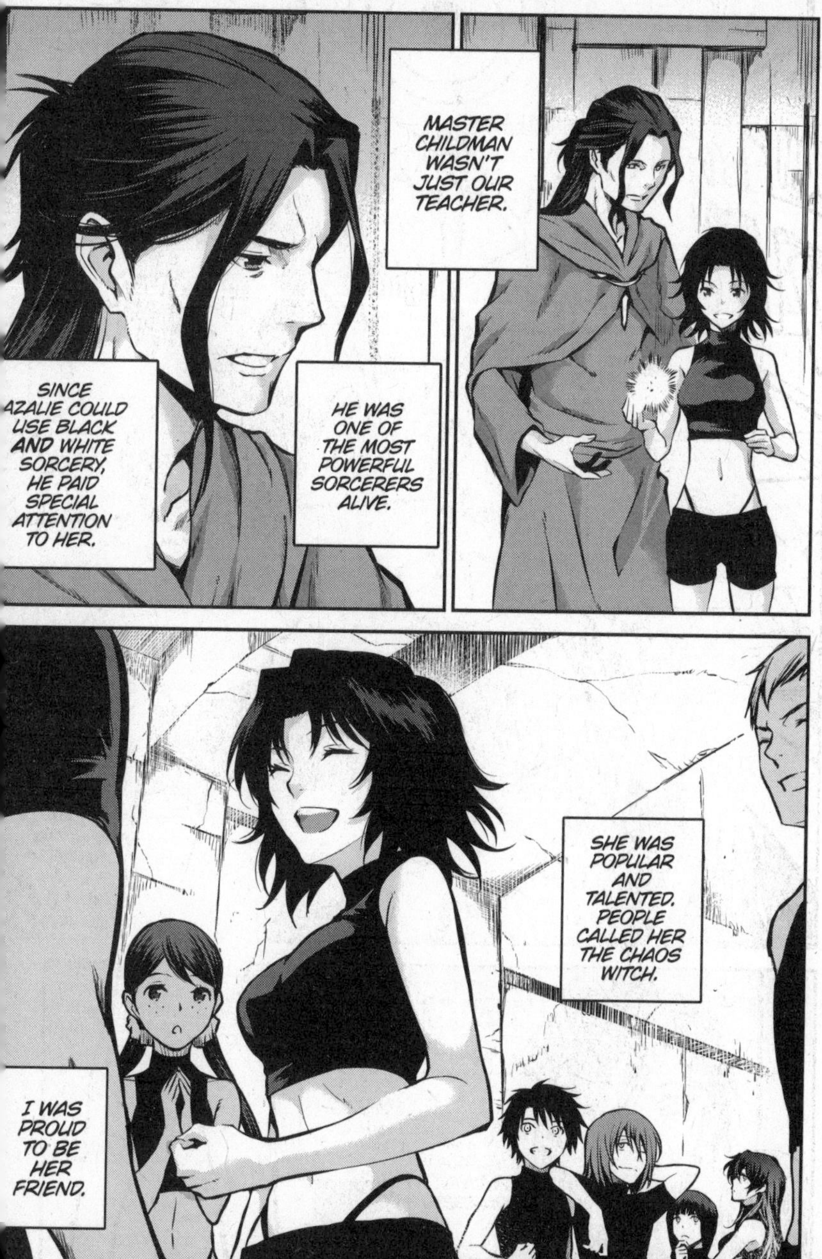
MASTER CHILDMAN WASN'T JUST OUR TEACHER.
HE WAS ONE OF THE MOST POWERFUL SORCERERS ALIVE.
SINCE AZALIE COULD USE BLACK AND WHITE SORCERY, HE PAID SPECIAL ATTENTION TO HER.
SHE WAS POPULAR AND TALENTED. PEOPLE CALLED HER THE CHAOS WITCH.
I WAS PROUD TO BE HER FRIEND.

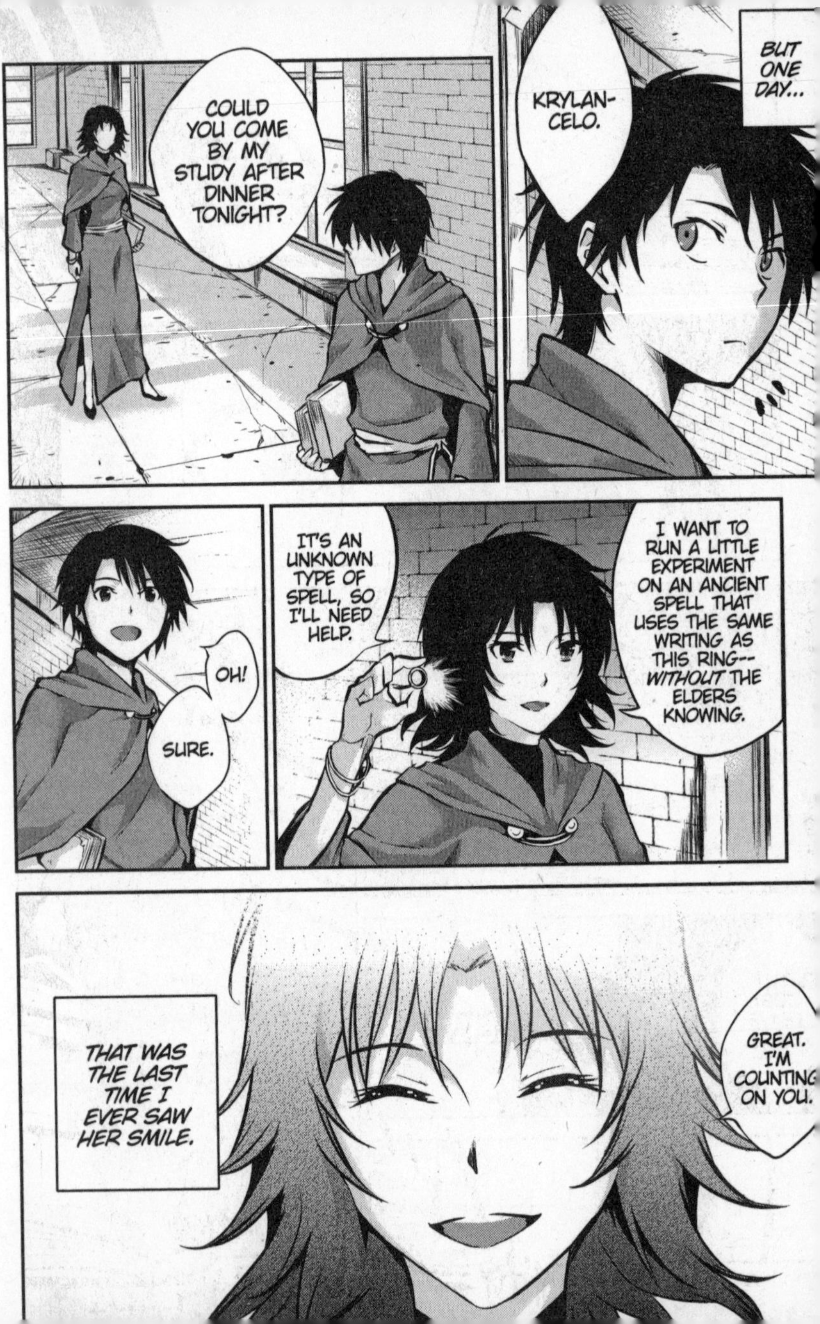
BUT ONE DAY...
KRYLAN-CELO.
COULD YOU COME BY MY STUDY AFTER DINNER TONIGHT?
I WANT TO RUN A LITTLE EXPERIMENT ON AN ANCIENT SPELL THAT USES THE SAME WRITING AS THIS RING-- *WITHOUT* THE ELDERS KNOWING.
IT'S AN UNKNOWN TYPE OF SPELL, SO I'LL NEED HELP.
OH!
SURE.
GREAT. I'M COUNTING ON YOU.
THAT WAS THE LAST TIME I EVER SAW HER SMILE.

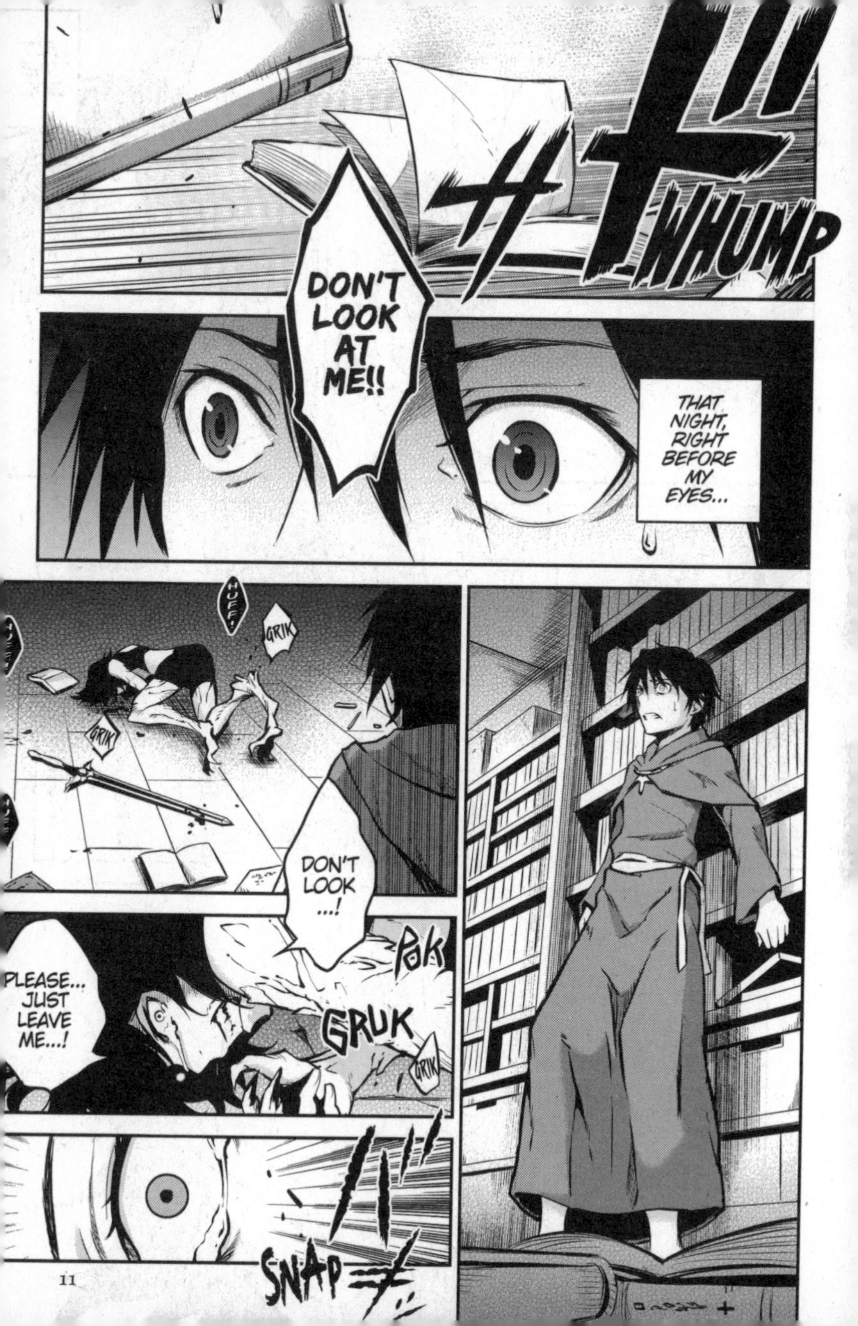
WHUMP
DON'T LOOK AT ME!!
THAT NIGHT, RIGHT BEFORE MY EYES...
HUFF!
GRIK
GRIK
DON'T LOOK ...!
POK
GRUK
GRIK
PLEASE... JUST LEAVE ME...!
SNAP

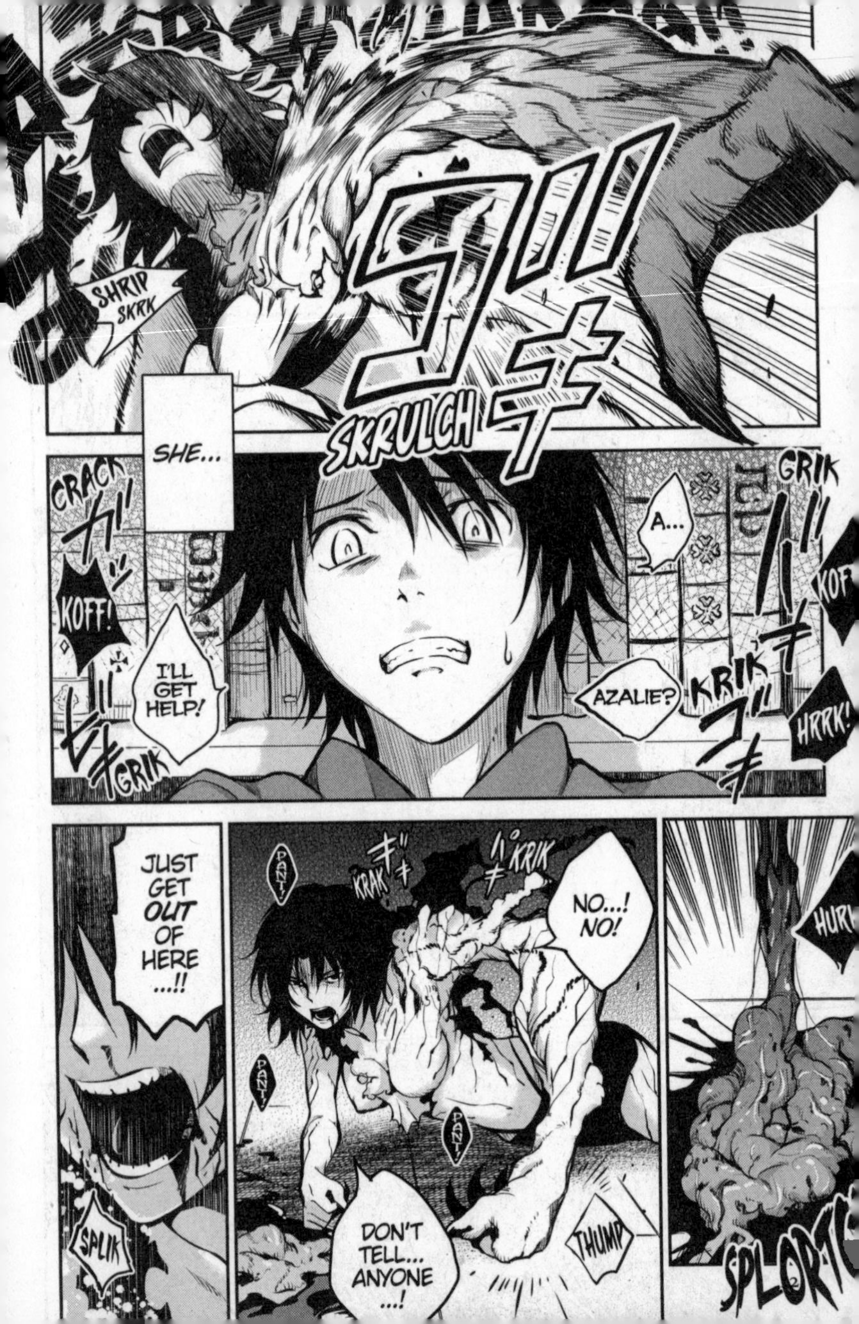
SKRULCH
SHRIP SKRK
GRIK
KOF
HRRK!
A...
KRIK
AZALIE?
SHE...
CRACK
KOFF!
I'LL GET HELP!
GRIK
NO...! NO!
KRIK
KRAK
PANT!
PANT!
PANT!
THUMP
DON'T TELL... ANYONE ...!
JUST GET OUT OF HERE ...!!
SPLIK

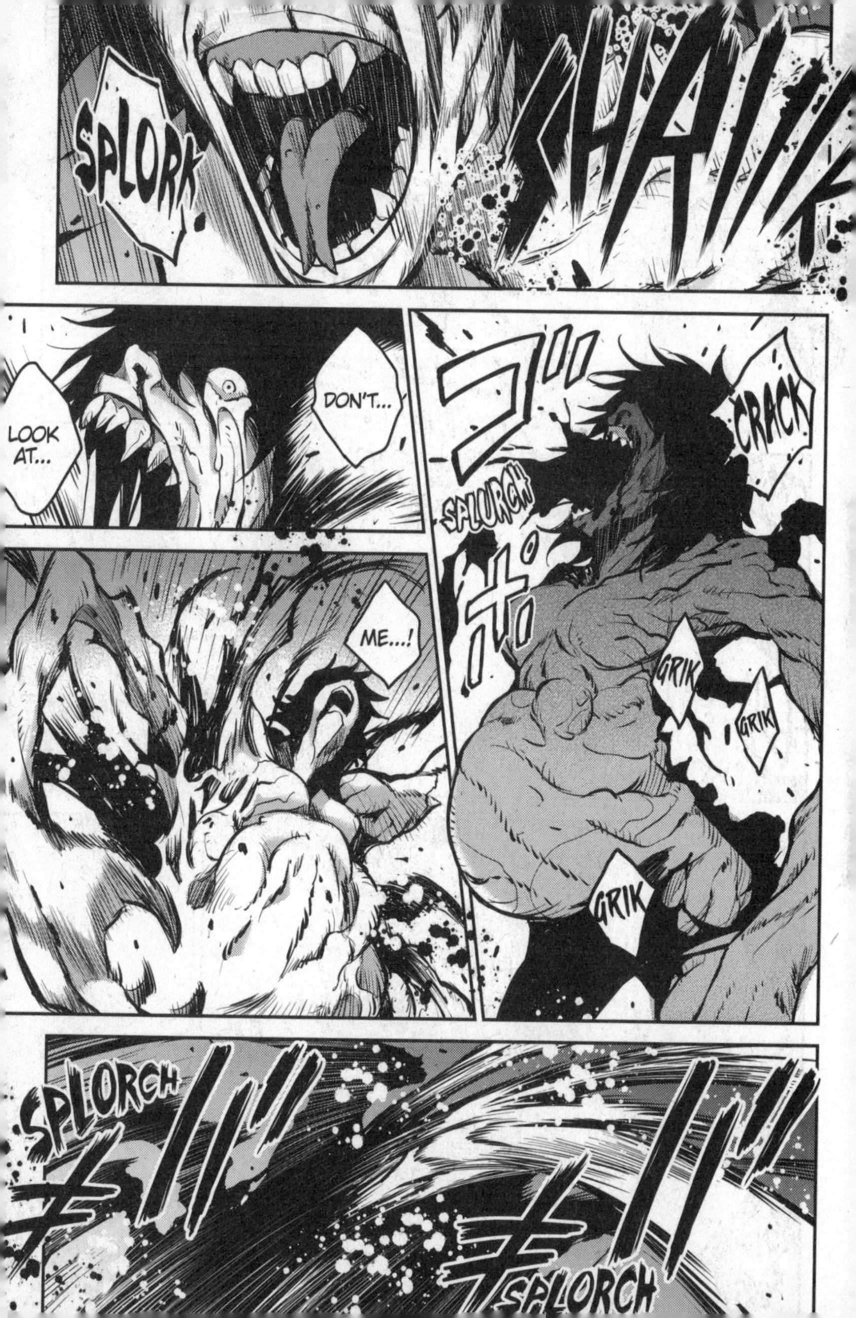
SPLORK
CRACK
SPLURCH
GRIK
GRIK
GRIK
DON'T...
LOOK AT...
ME...!
SPLORCH
SPLORCH

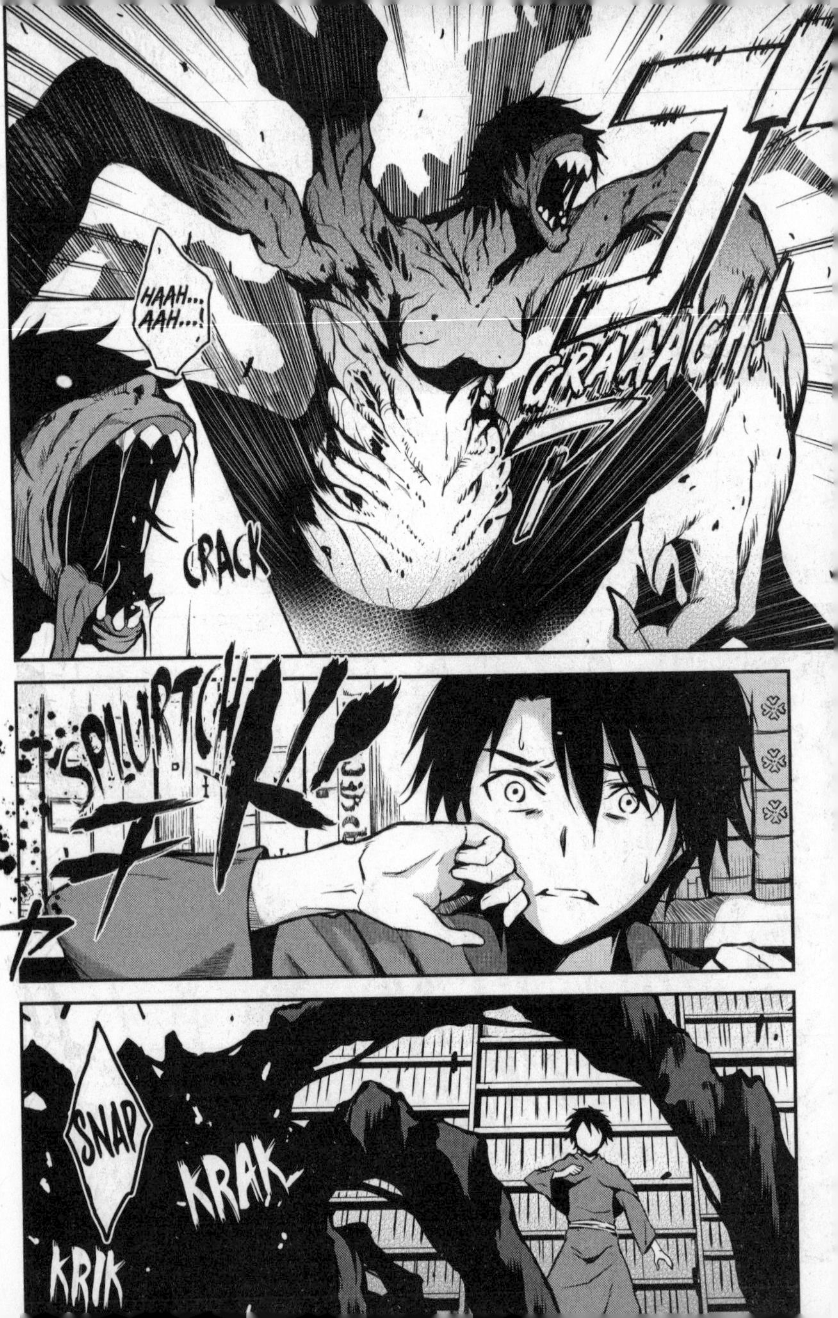
GRAAAGH!!
HAAH... AAH...!
CRACK
SPLURTCH!!
SNAP
KRAK
KRIK

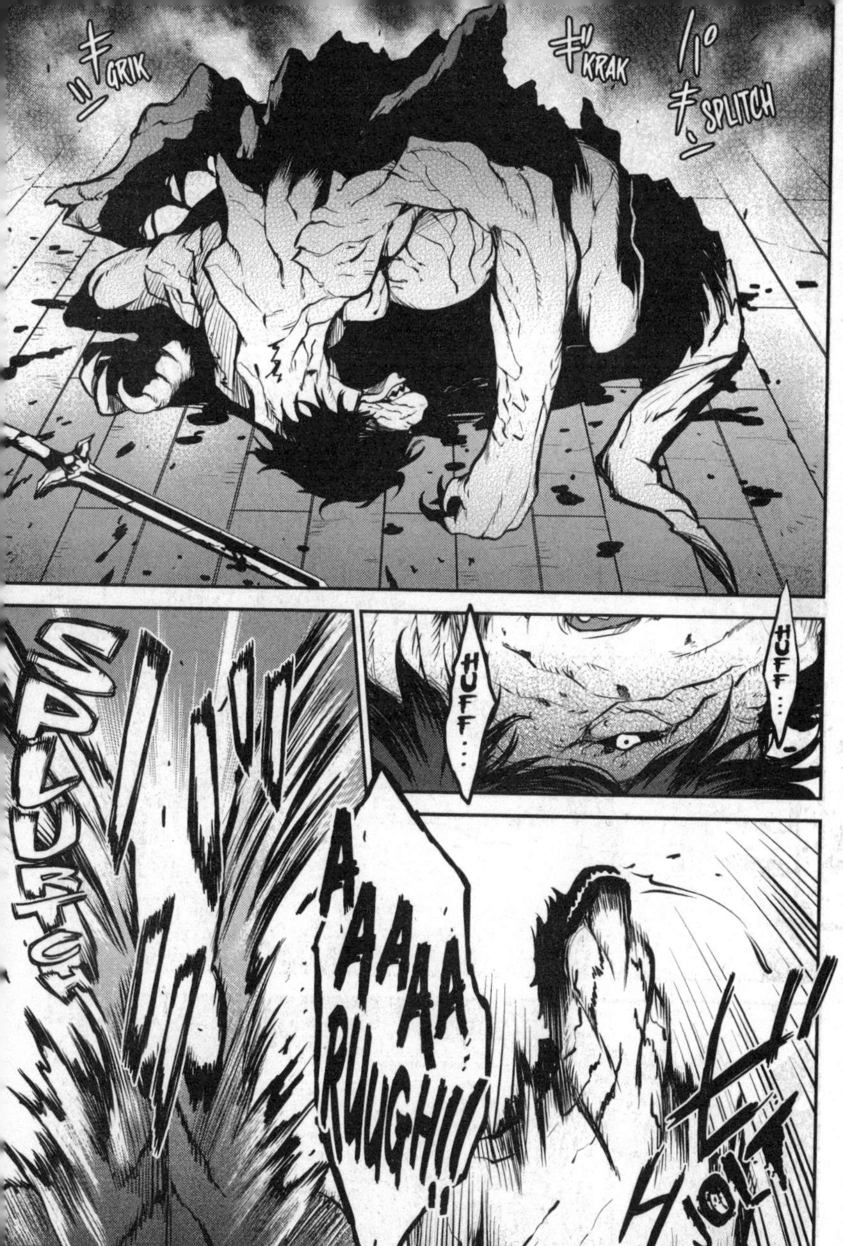
SPLITCH
KRAK
GRIK
HUFF...
HUFF...
SPLURTCH
JOLT
AAAAAA RUUGH!!!

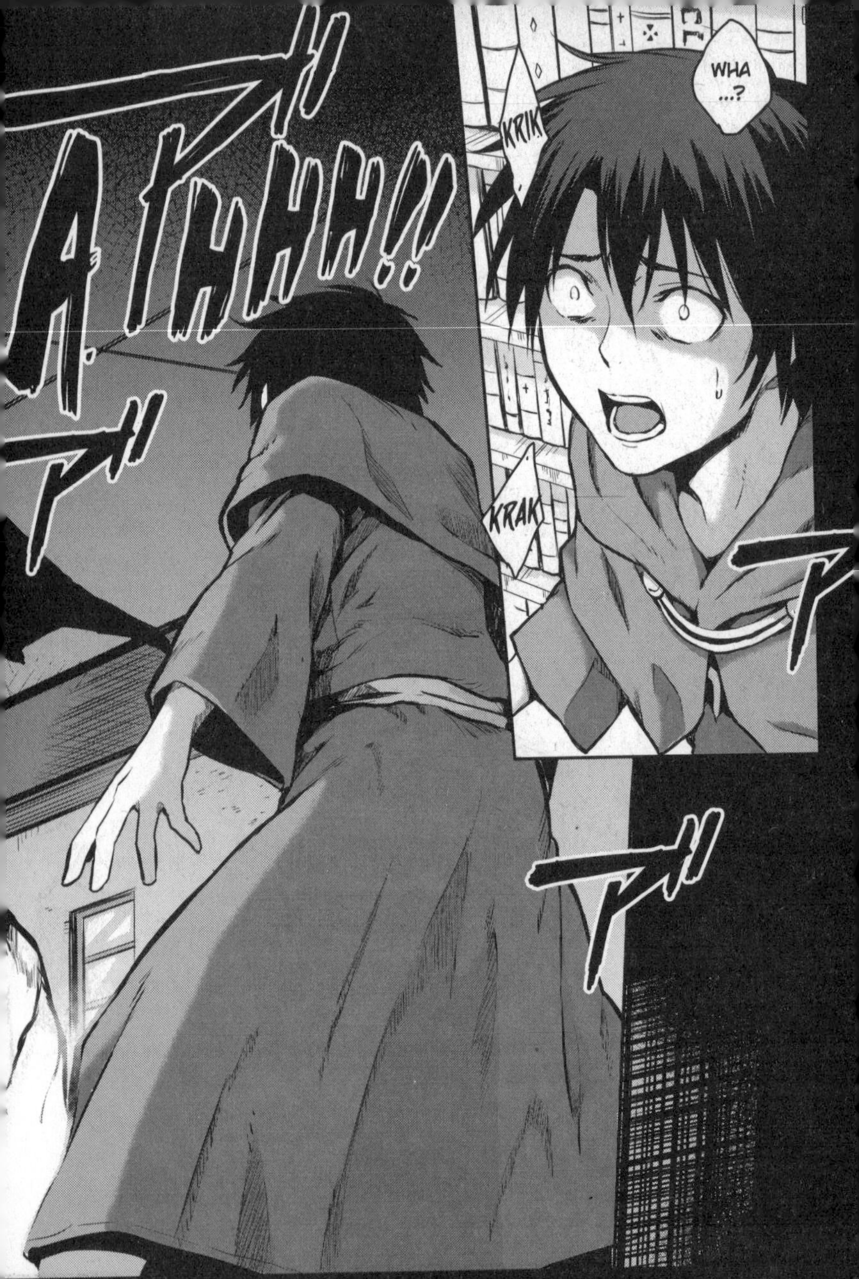
KRIK
WHA ...?
KRAK

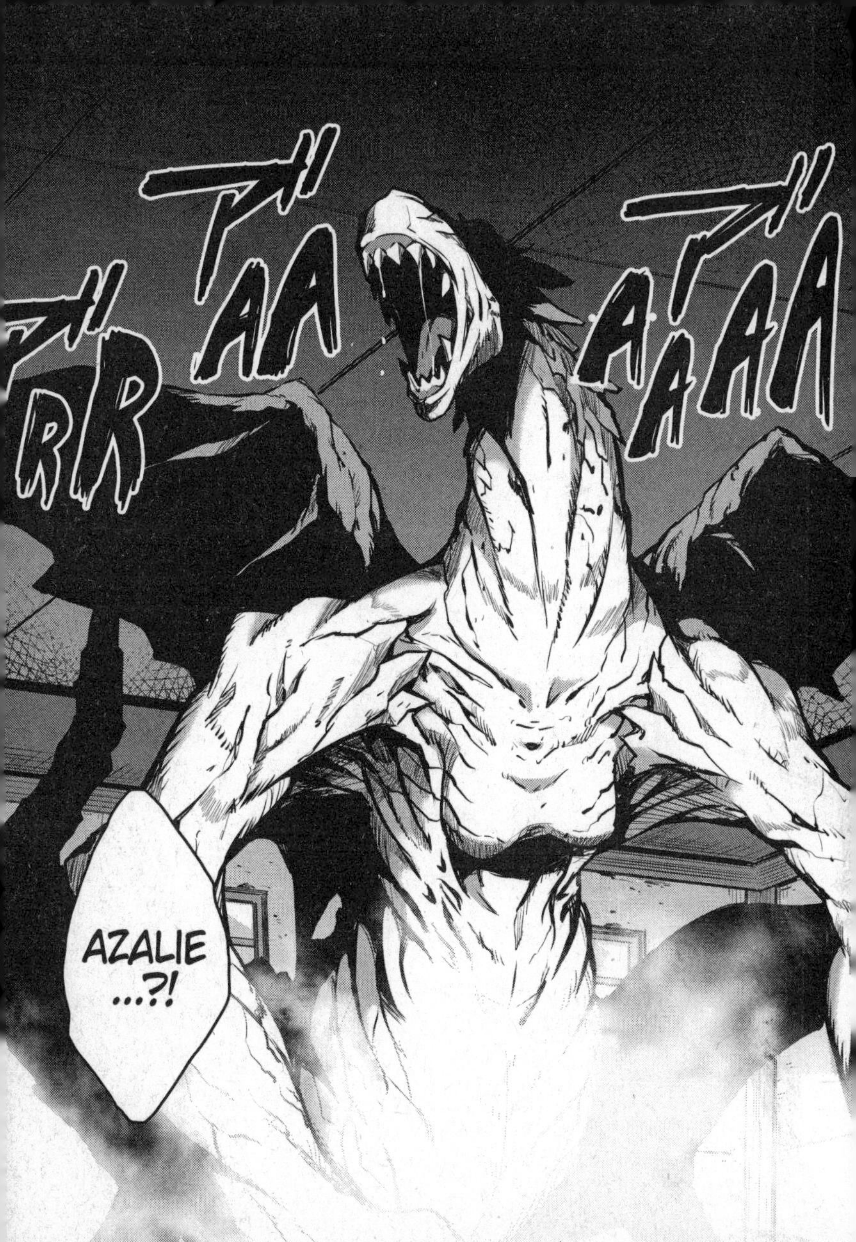
AZALIE ...?!

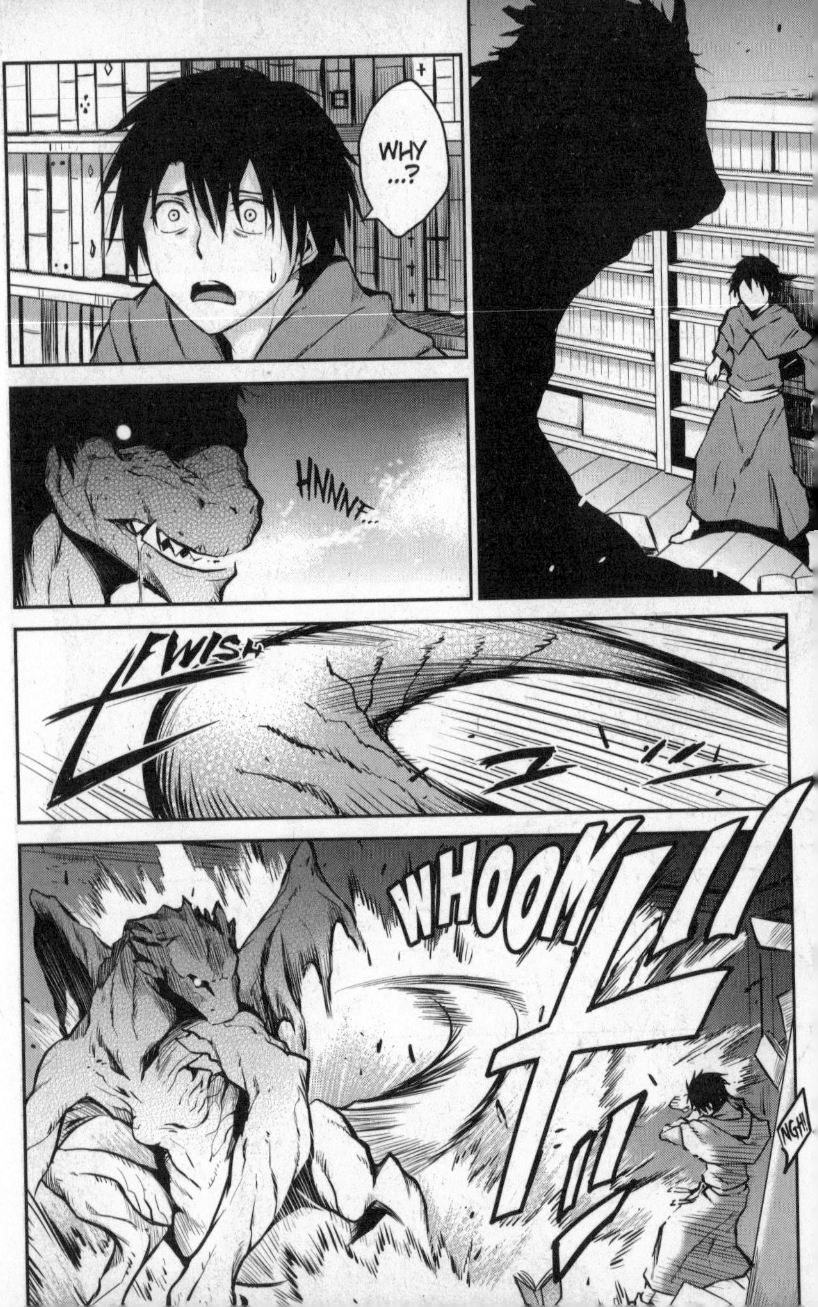
WHY ...?
HNNNF...
FWISH
WHOOM
NGH!

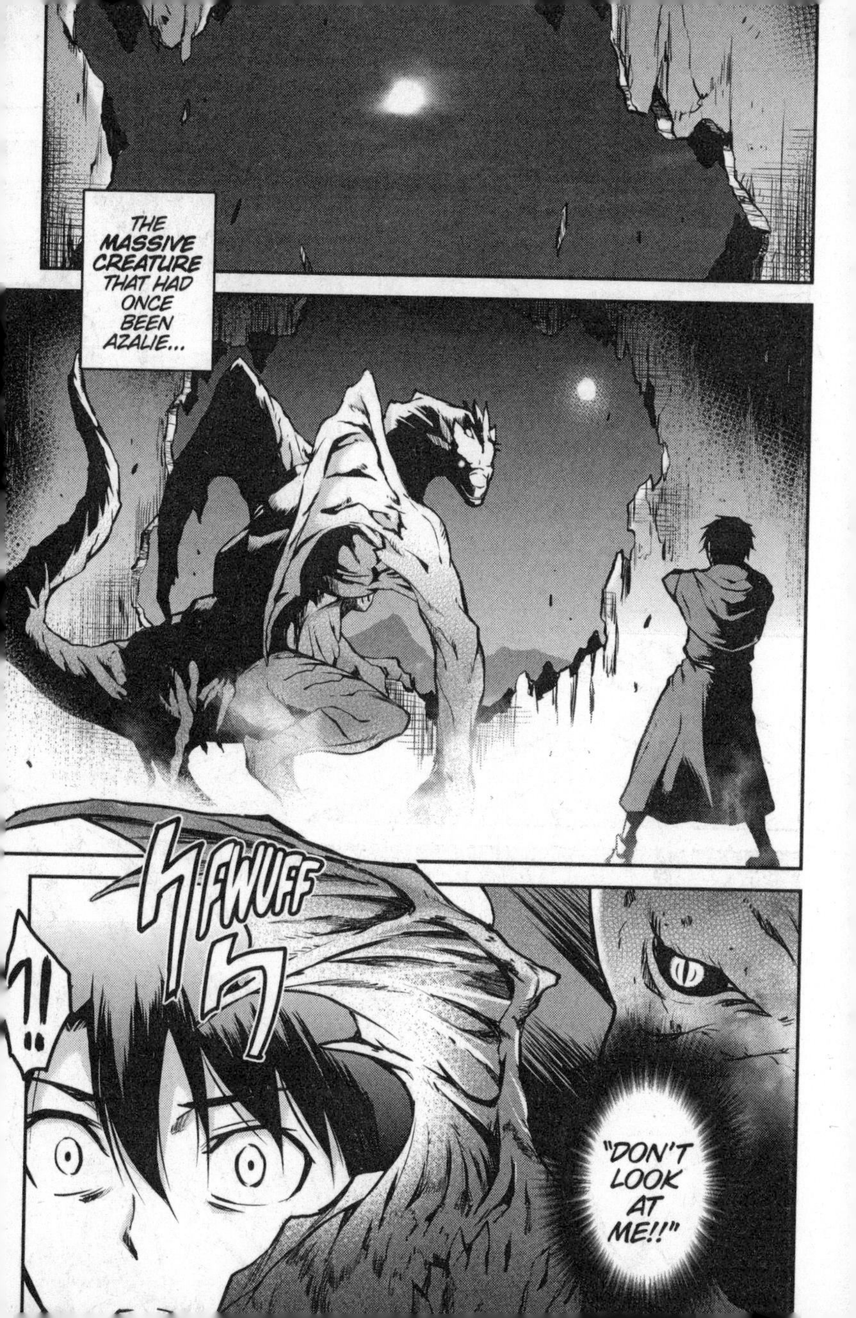
THE MASSIVE CREATURE THAT HAD ONCE BEEN AZALIE...
FWUFF
!!
"DON'T LOOK AT ME!!"

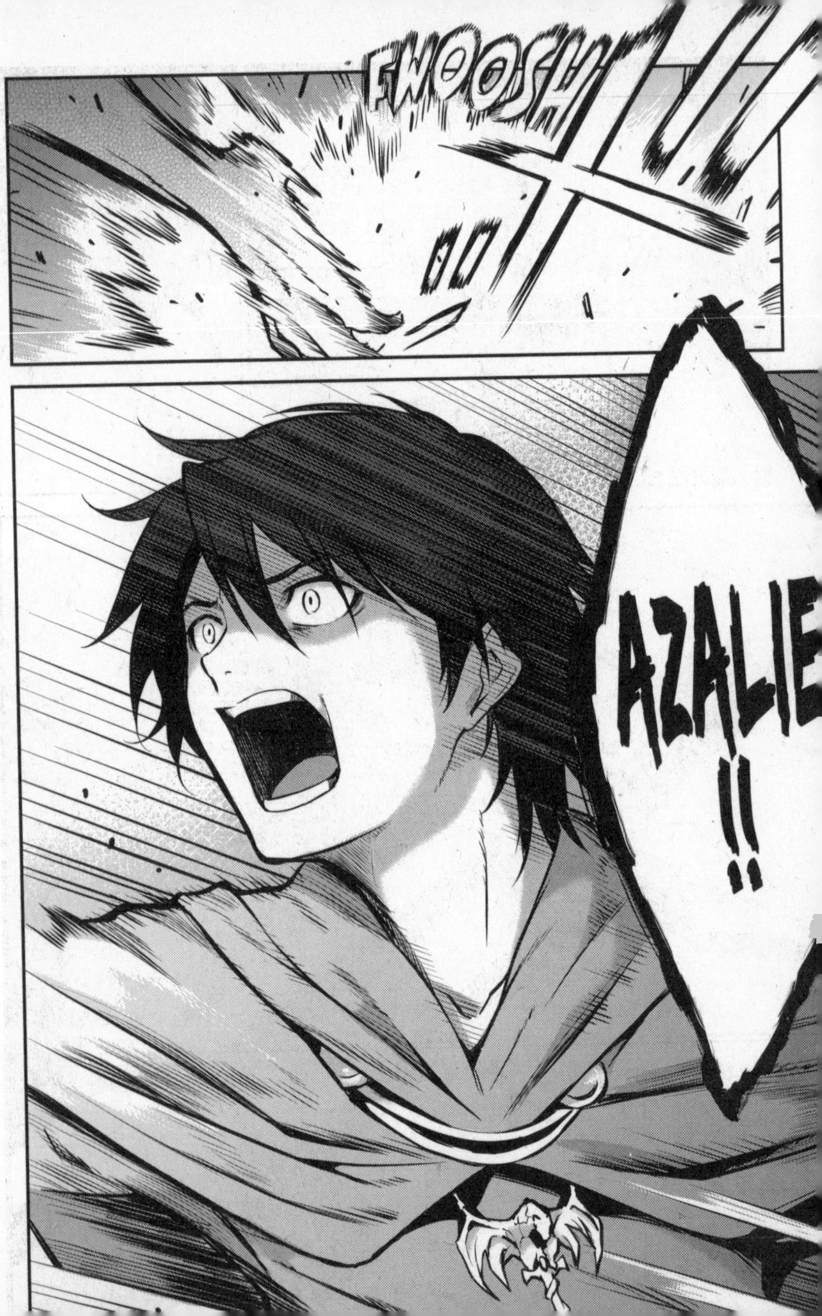
FWOOSH
AZALIE!!

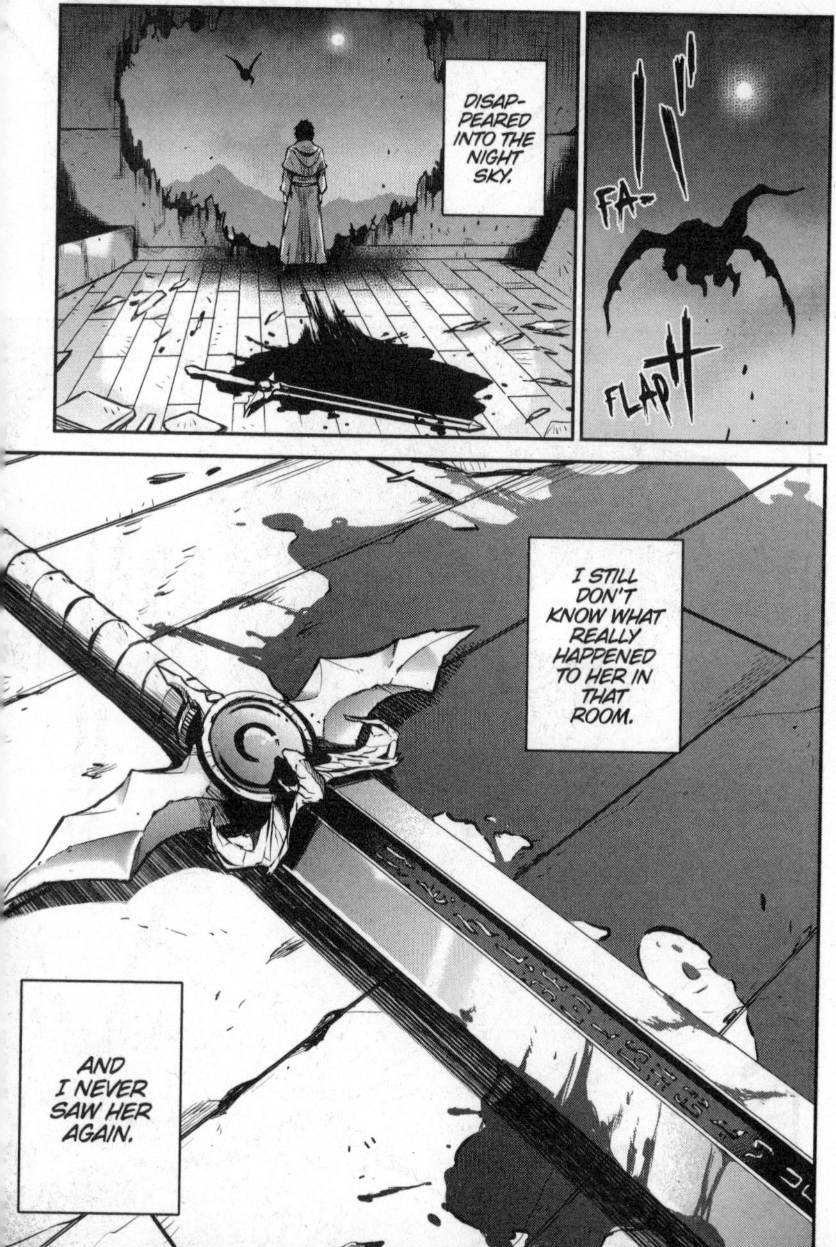
FA-
FLAP
DISAP-PEARED INTO THE NIGHT SKY.
I STILL DON'T KNOW WHAT REALLY HAPPENED TO HER IN THAT ROOM.
AND I NEVER SAW HER AGAIN.

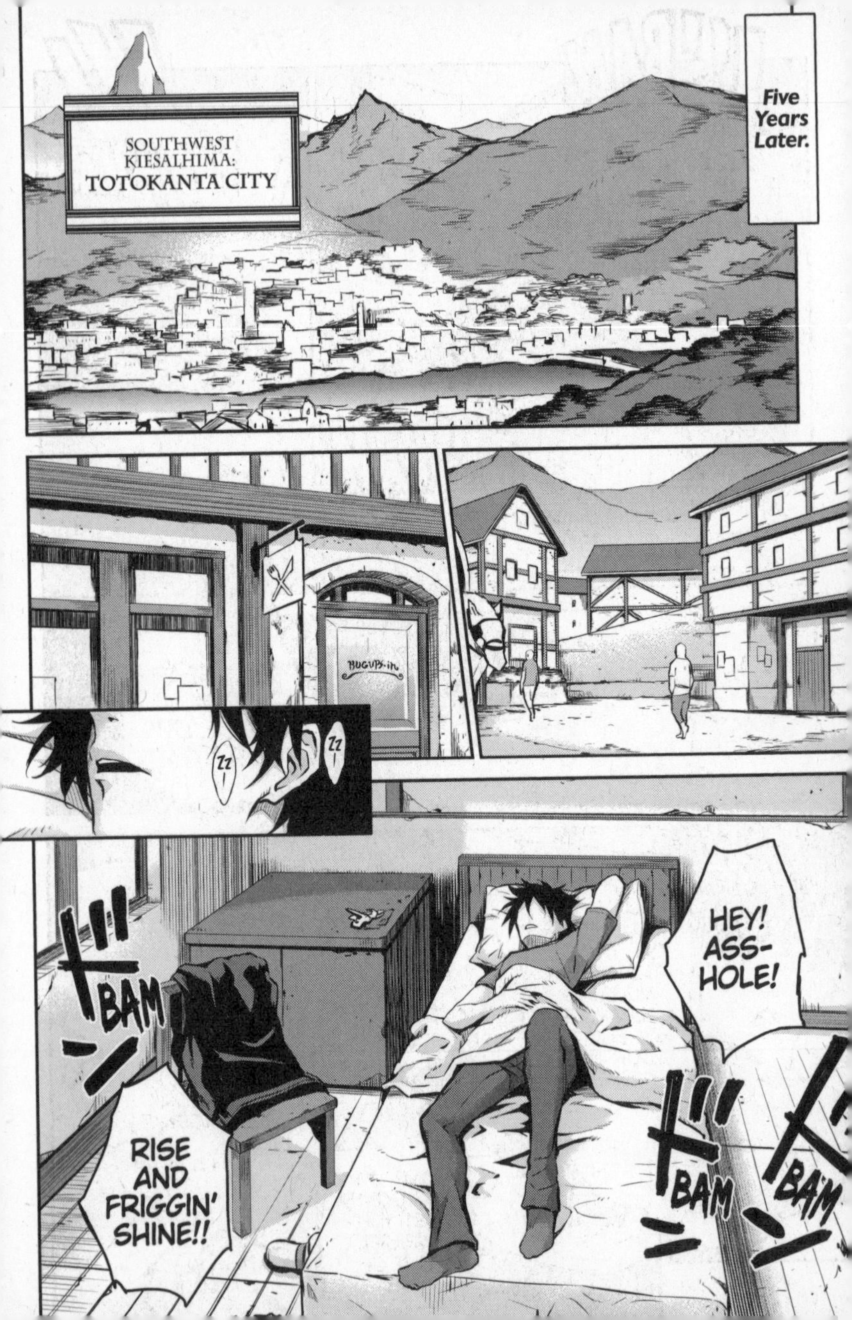
Five Years Later.
SOUTHWEST KIESALHIMA: TOTOKANTA CITY
Zz
Zz
HEY! ASS-HOLE!
BAM
BAM
BAM
RISE AND FRIGGIN' SHINE!!

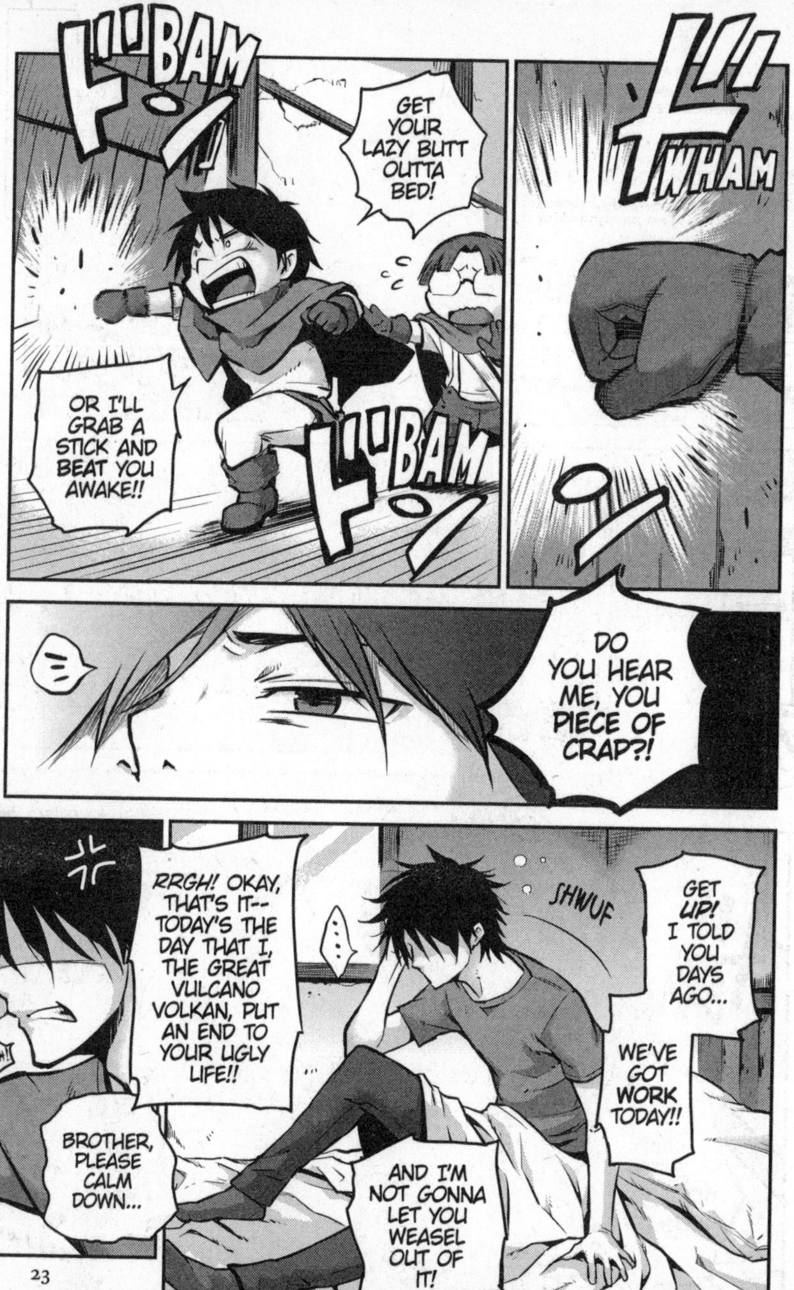
WHAM
BAM
GET YOUR LAZY BUTT OUTTA BED!
OR I'LL GRAB A STICK AND BEAT YOU AWAKE!!
BAM
DO YOU HEAR ME, YOU PIECE OF CRAP?!
GET UP! I TOLD YOU DAYS AGO...
SHWUF
WE'VE GOT WORK TODAY!!
AND I'M NOT GONNA LET YOU WEASEL OUT OF IT!
RRGH! OKAY, THAT'S IT-- TODAY'S THE DAY THAT I, THE GREAT VULCANO VOLKAN, PUT AN END TO YOUR UGLY LIFE!!
TCH!
BROTHER, PLEASE CALM DOWN...

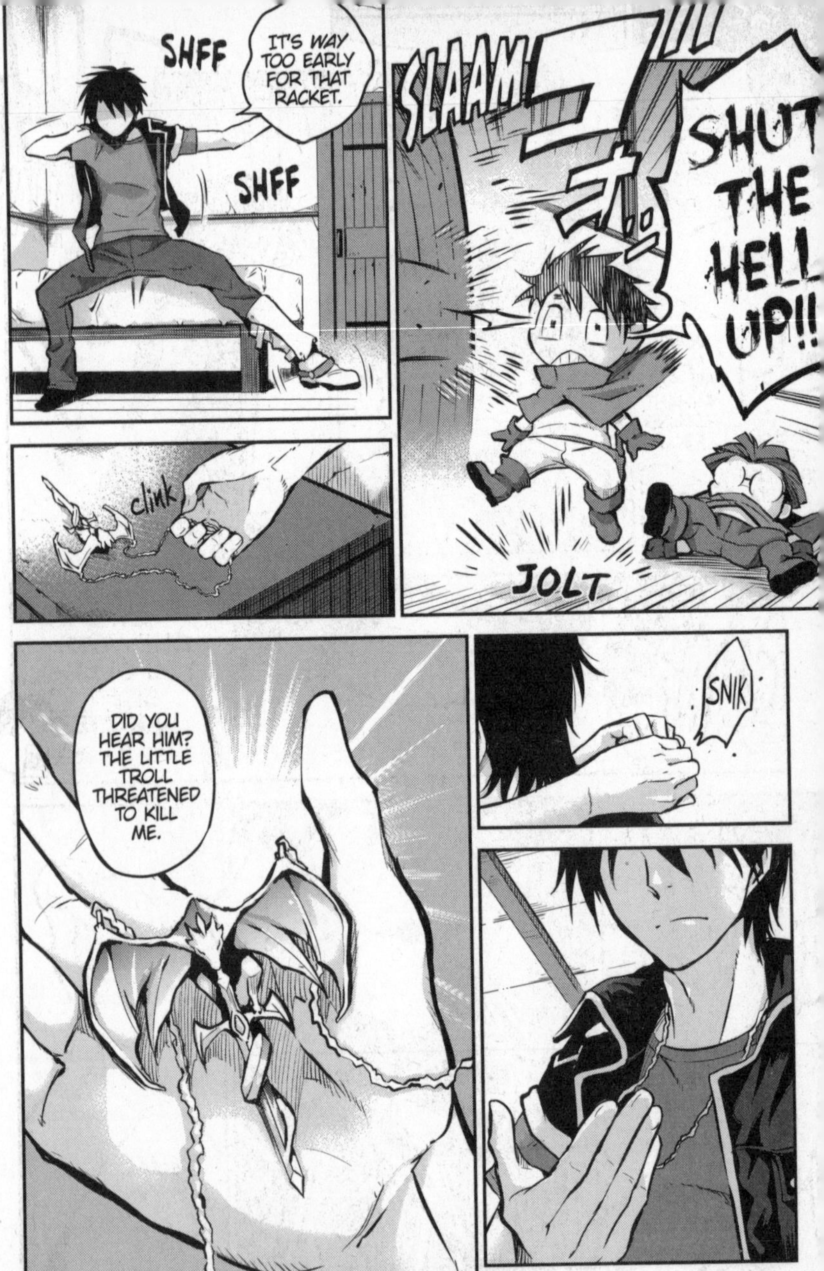
SLAAM
SHUT THE HELL UP!!
JOLT
SHFF
IT'S WAY TOO EARLY FOR THAT RACKET.
SHFF
clink
SNIK
DID YOU HEAR HIM? THE LITTLE TROLL THREATENED TO KILL ME.

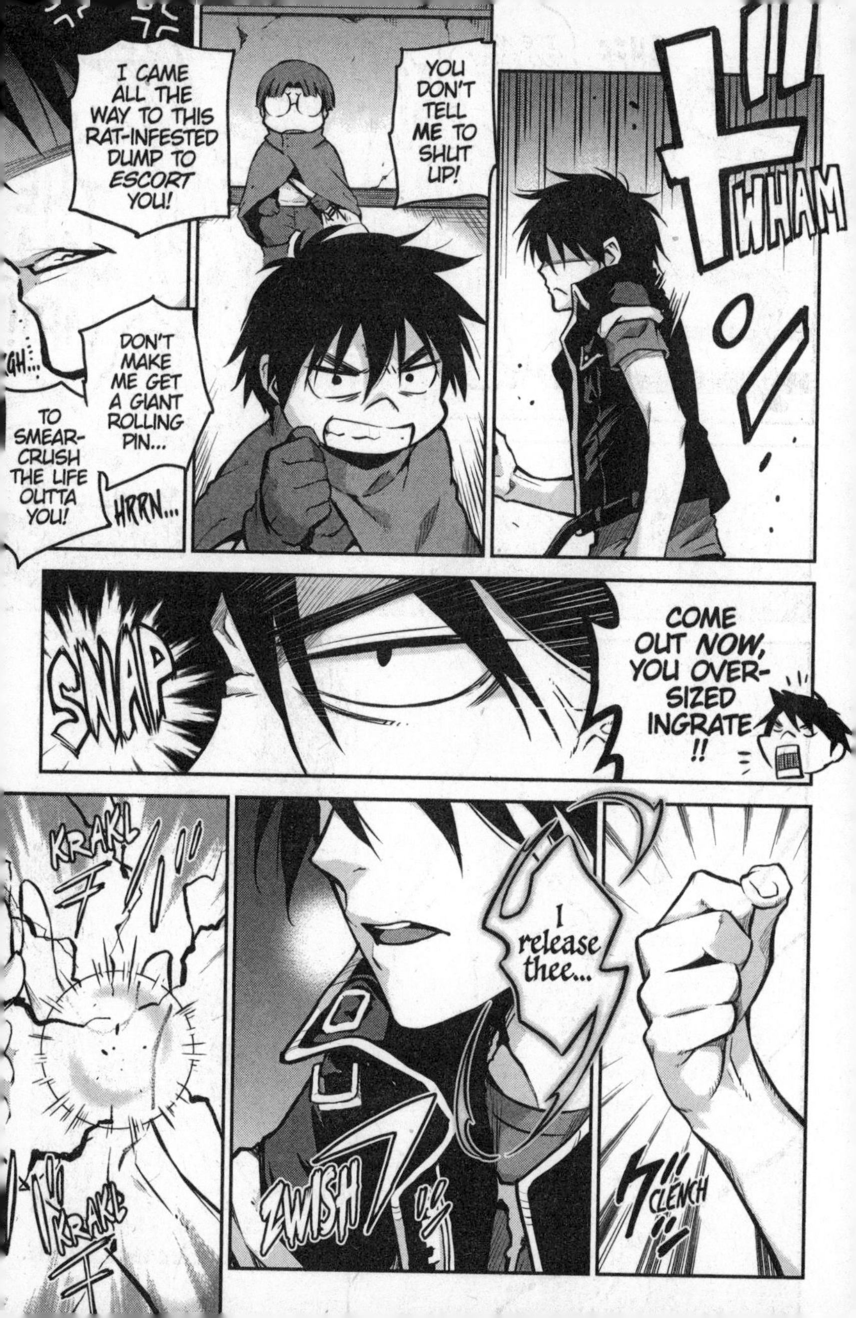
WHAM
YOU DON'T TELL ME TO SHUT UP!
I CAME ALL THE WAY TO THIS RAT-INFESTED DUMP TO ESCORT YOU!
DON'T MAKE ME GET A GIANT ROLLING PIN...
HRRN...
GH...
TO SMEAR-CRUSH THE LIFE OUTTA YOU!
COME OUT NOW, YOU OVER-SIZED INGRATE !!
SNAP
CLENCH
I release thee...
ZWISH
KRAKL
KRAKL

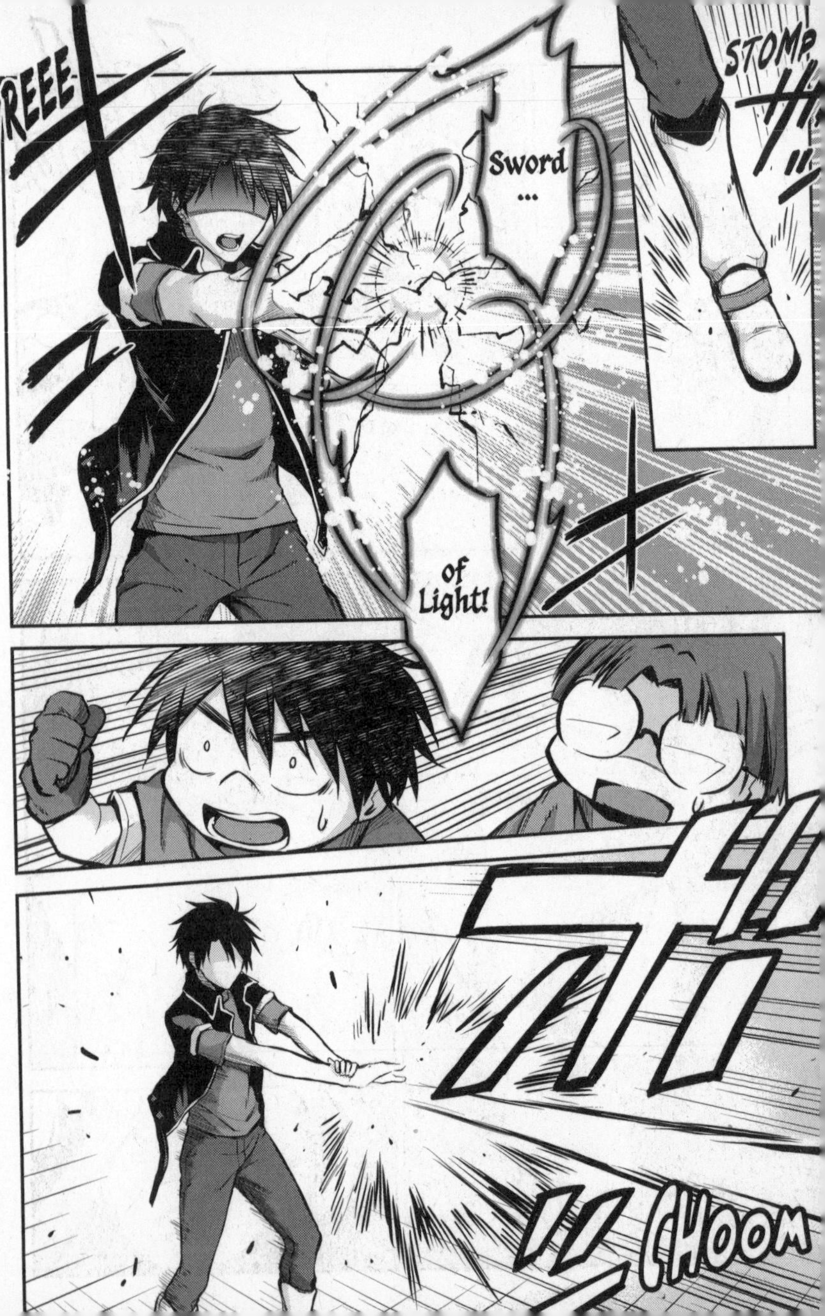
STOMP
VREEE
Sword ...
of Light!
CHOOM

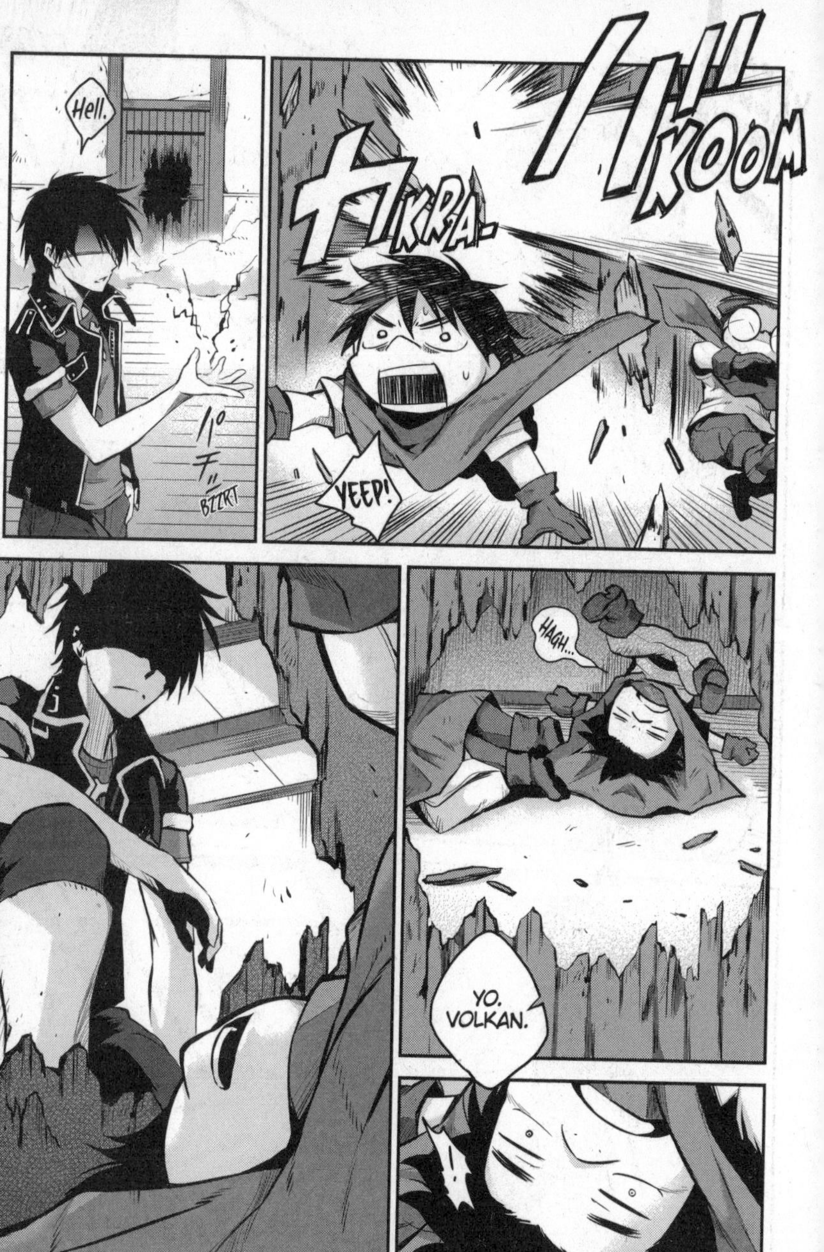
KOOM
KRA.
YEEP!
Hell.
BZZKT
HAGH...
YO. VOLKAN.

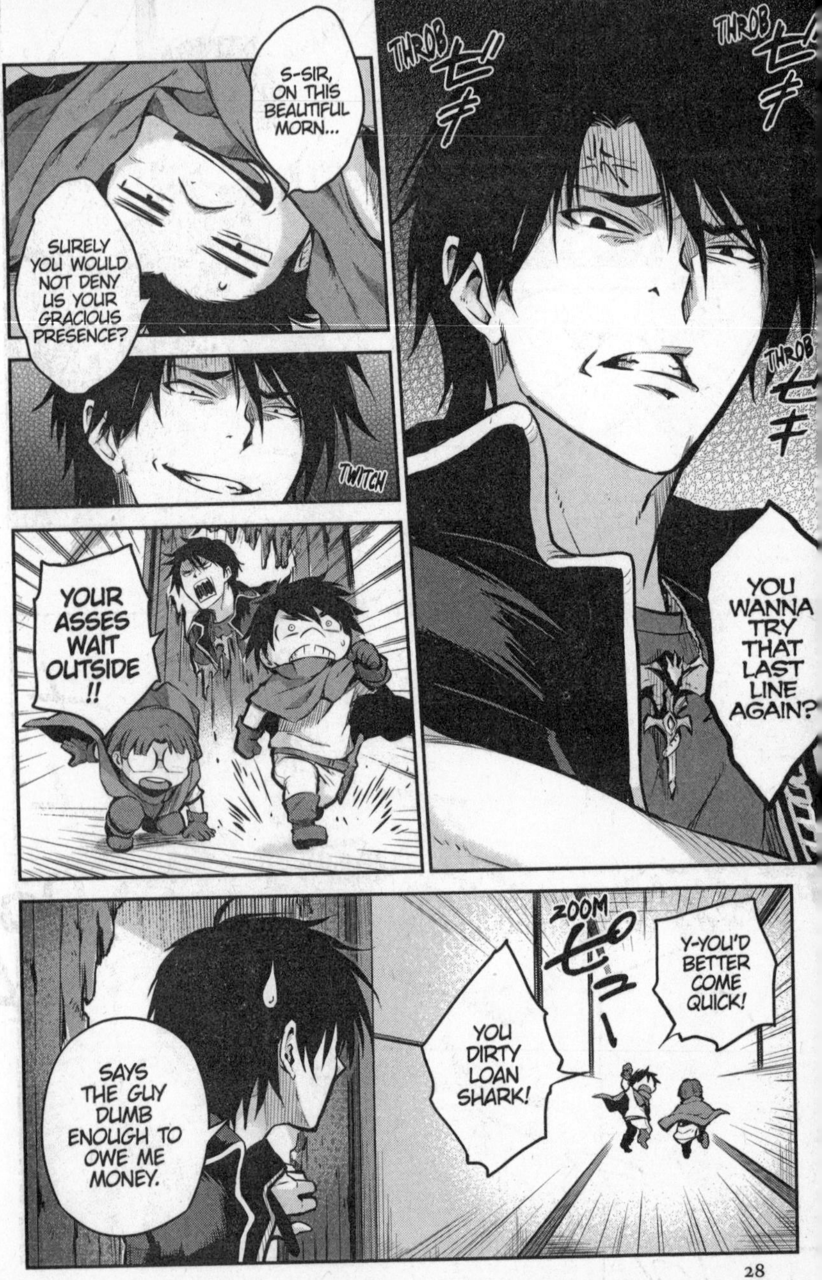
THROB
THROB
THROB
YOU WANNA TRY THAT LAST LINE AGAIN?
S-SIR, ON THIS BEAUTIFUL MORN...
SURELY YOU WOULD NOT DENY US YOUR GRACIOUS PRESENCE?
TWITCH
YOUR ASSES WAIT OUTSIDE !!
ZOOM
Y-YOU'D BETTER COME QUICK!
YOU DIRTY LOAN SHARK!
SAYS THE GUY DUMB ENOUGH TO OWE ME MONEY.

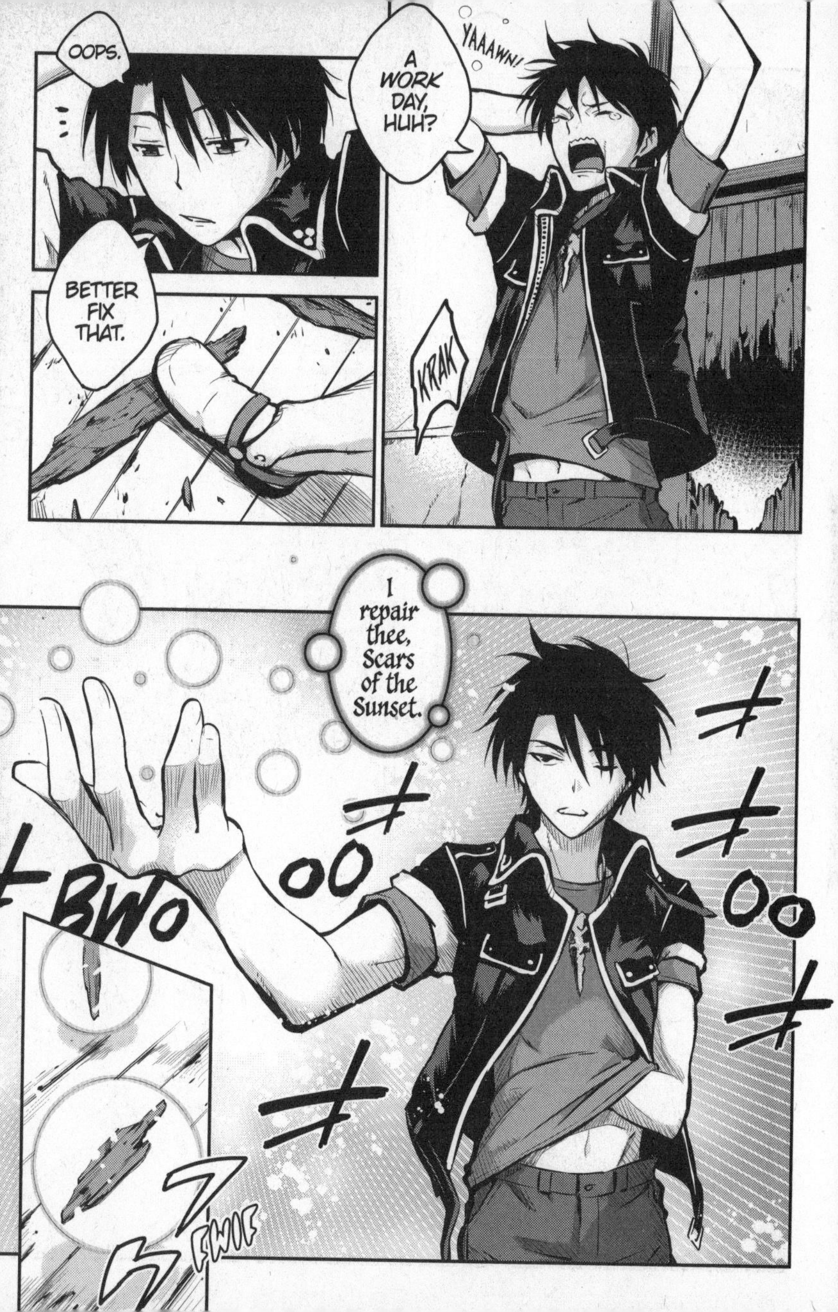
YAAAWN!
A WORK DAY, HUH?
KRAK
OOPS.
BETTER FIX THAT.
I repair thee, Scars of the Sunset.
BWO
OO
OO
FWIF

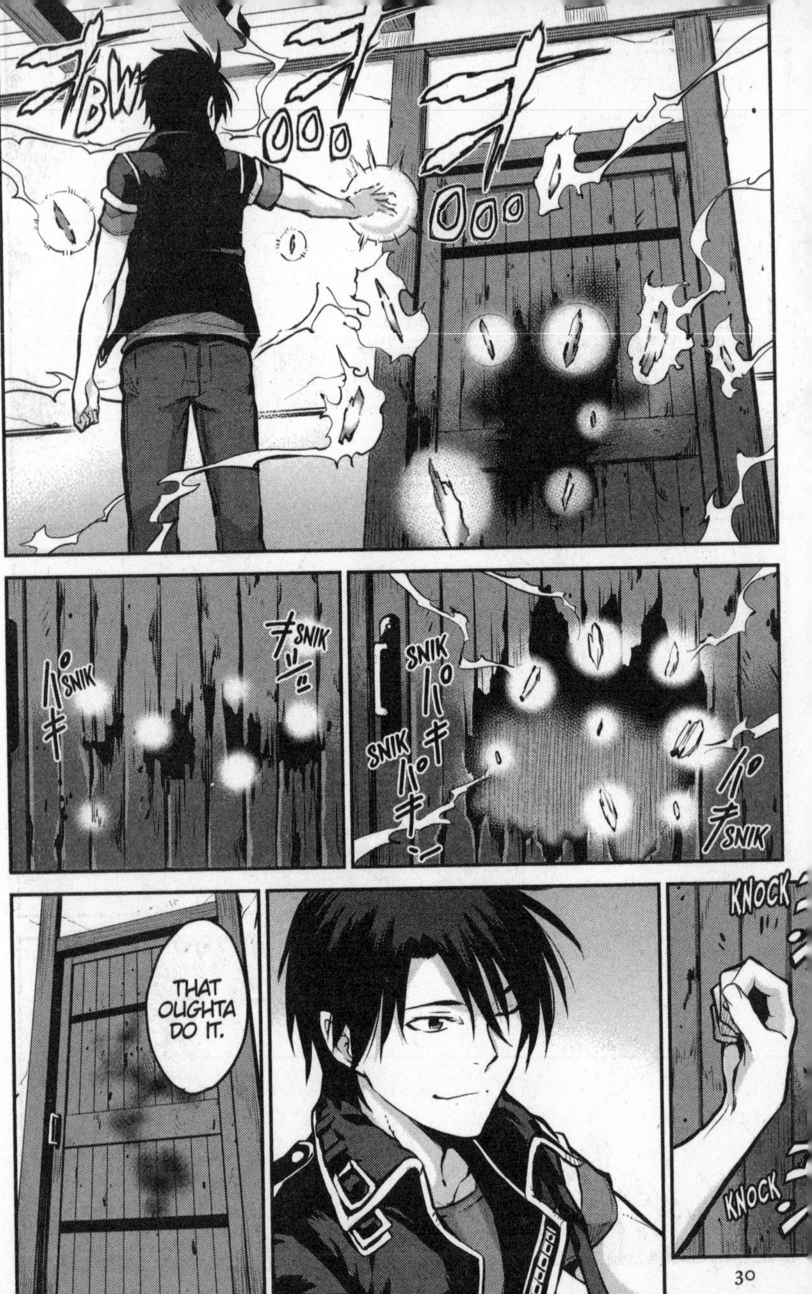
BW
OOO
OOO
SNIK
SNIK
SNIK
SNIK
SNIK
KNOCK
KNOCK
THAT OUGHTA DO IT.

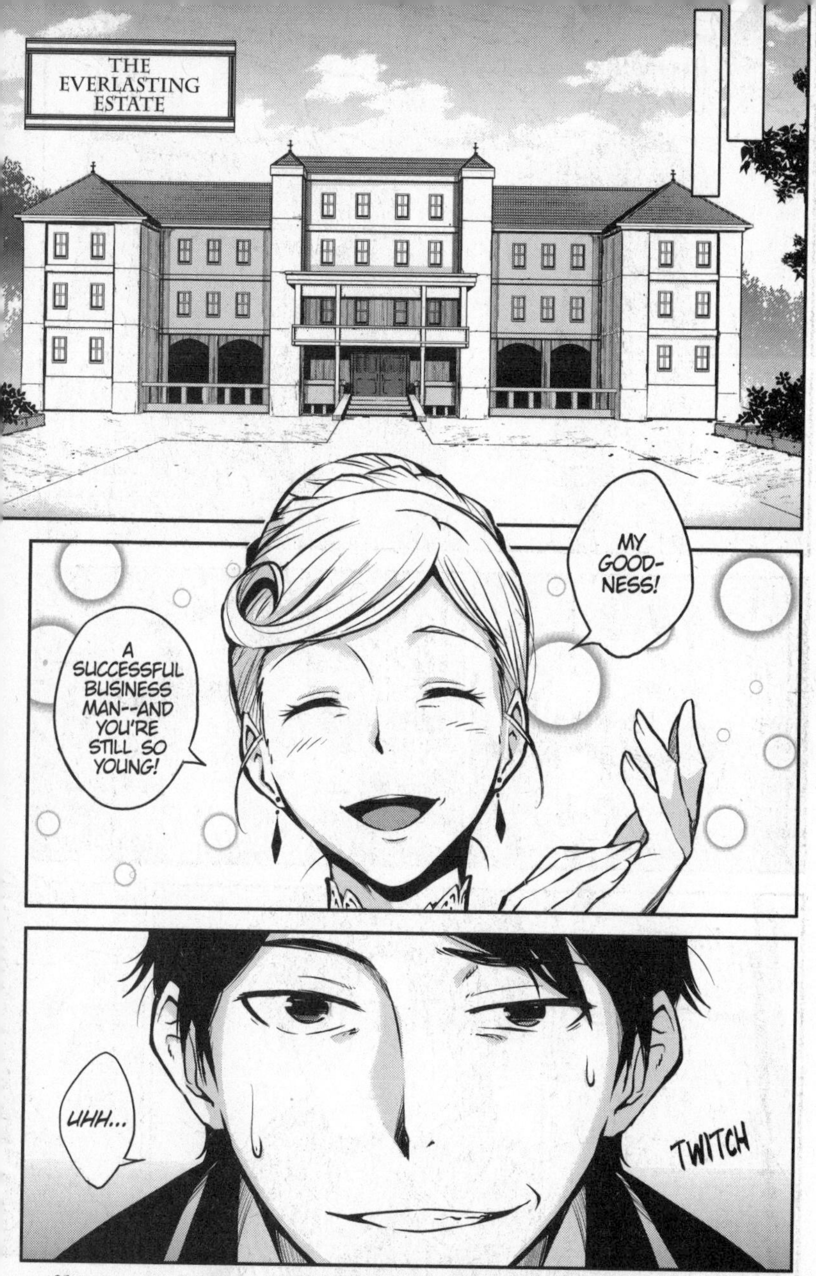
THE EVERLASTING ESTATE
MY GOODNESS!
A SUCCESSFUL BUSINESS MAN--AND YOU'RE STILL SO YOUNG!
TWITCH
UHH...

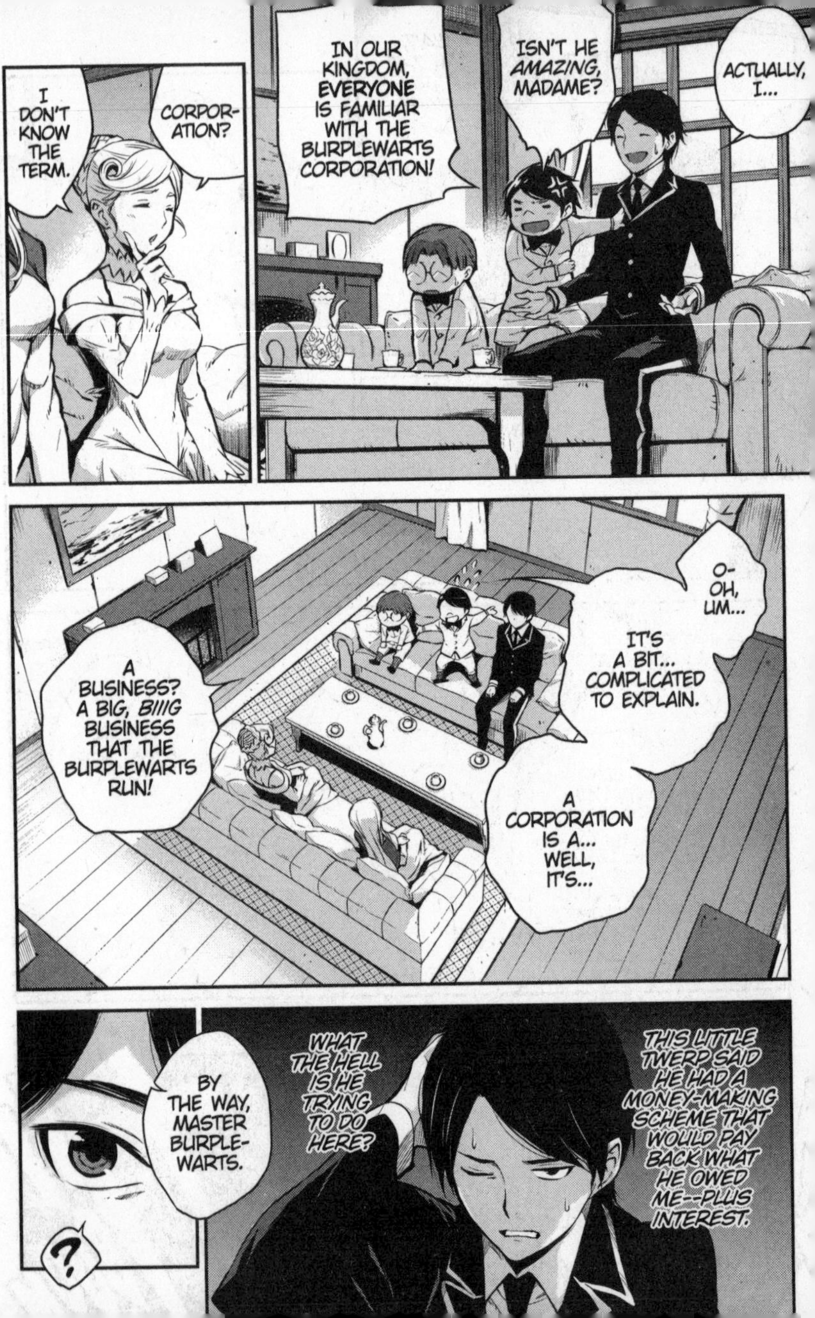
ACTUALLY, I...
ISN'T HE *AMAZING*, MADAME?
IN OUR KINGDOM, EVERYONE IS FAMILIAR WITH THE BURPLEWARTS CORPORATION!
CORPOR-ATION?
I DON'T KNOW THE TERM.
O-OH, UM...
IT'S A BIT... COMPLICATED TO EXPLAIN.
A CORPORATION IS A... WELL, IT'S...
A BUSINESS? A BIG, *BIIIG* BUSINESS THAT THE BURPLEWARTS RUN!
THIS LITTLE TWERP SAID HE HAD A MONEY-MAKING SCHEME THAT WOULD PAY BACK WHAT HE OWED ME--PLUS INTEREST.
WHAT THE HELL IS HE TRYING TO DO HERE?
BY THE WAY, MASTER BURPLE-WARTS.
?

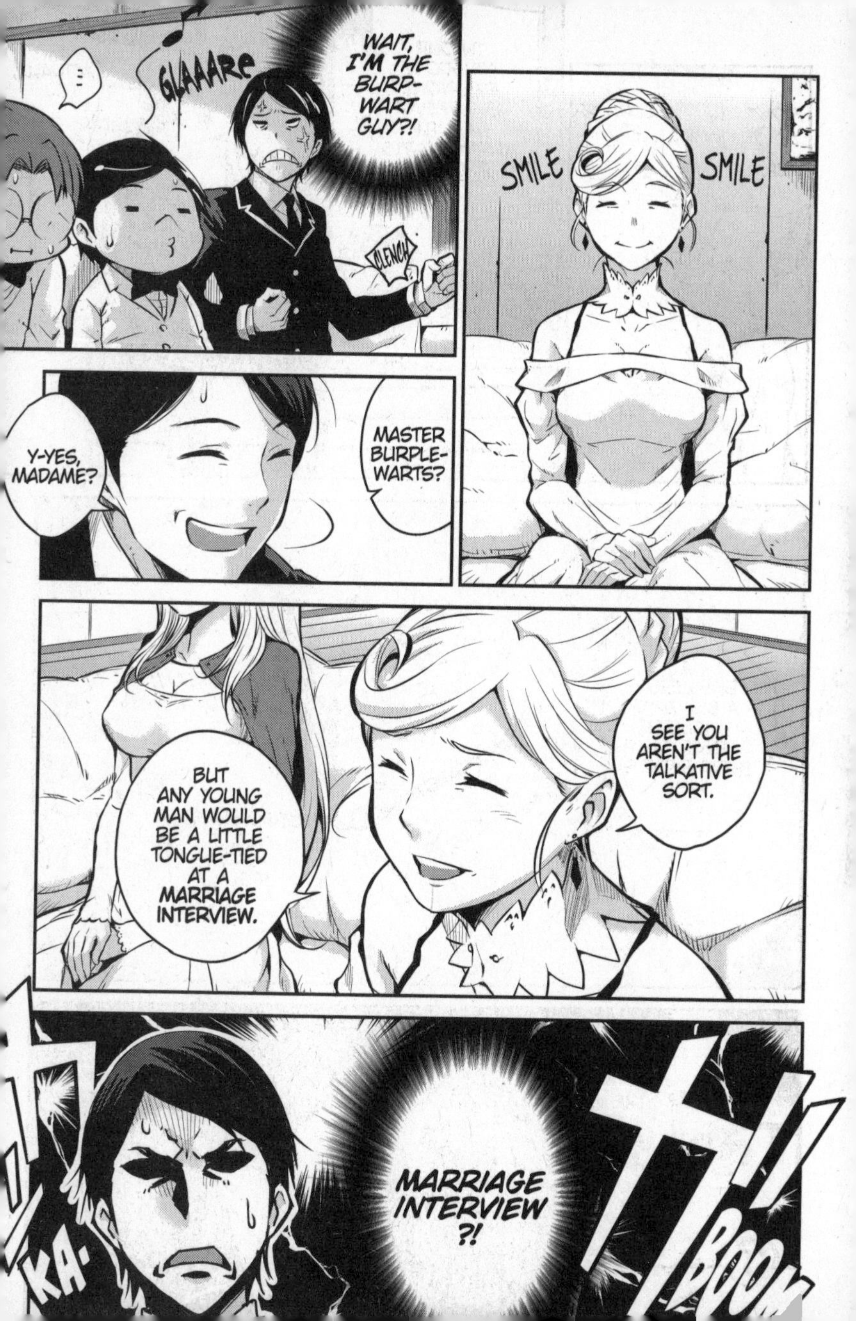
SMILE
SMILE
GLAAARE
WAIT, I'M THE BURP-WART GUY?!
CLENCH
MASTER BURPLE-WARTS?
Y-YES, MADAME?
I SEE YOU AREN'T THE TALKATIVE SORT.
BUT ANY YOUNG MAN WOULD BE A LITTLE TONGUE-TIED AT A MARRIAGE INTERVIEW.
BOOM
MARRIAGE INTERVIEW ?!
KA-

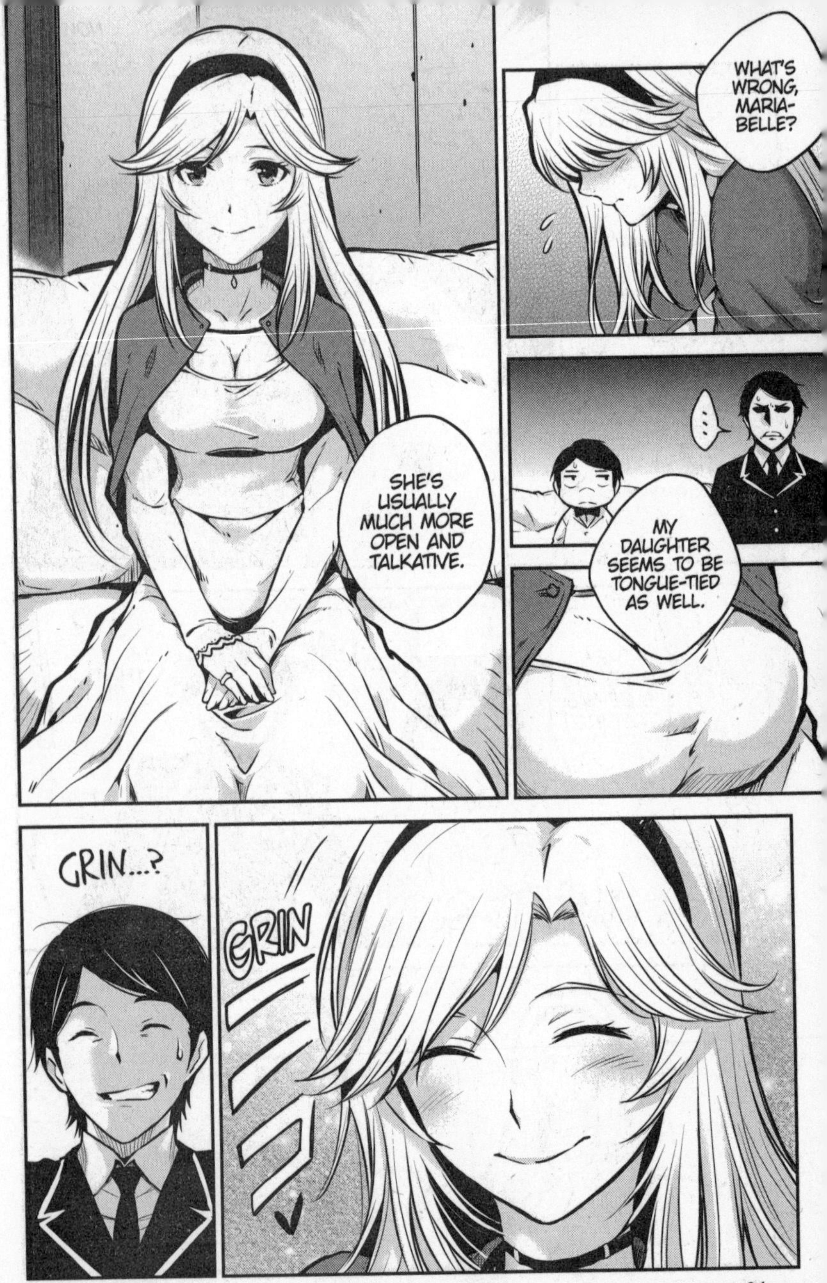
WHAT'S WRONG, MARIA-BELLE?
...
MY DAUGHTER SEEMS TO BE TONGUE-TIED AS WELL.
SHE'S USUALLY MUCH MORE OPEN AND TALKATIVE.
GRIN
GRIN...?

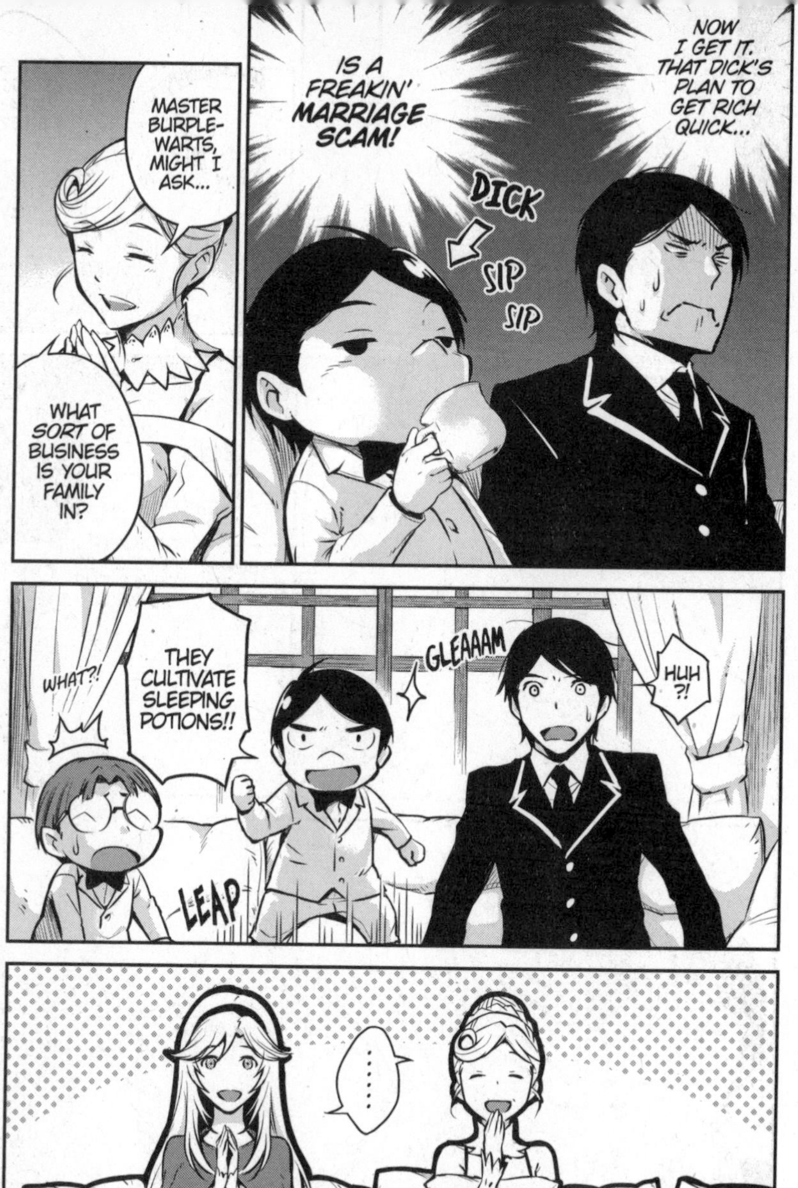

NOW I GET IT. THAT DICK'S PLAN TO GET RICH QUICK...
IS A FREAKIN' MARRIAGE SCAM!
DICK
SIP
SIP
MASTER BURPLE-WARTS, MIGHT I ASK...
WHAT SORT OF BUSINESS IS YOUR FAMILY IN?
HUH ?!
GLEAAAM
THEY CULTIVATE SLEEPING POTIONS!!
WHAT?!
LEAP
......

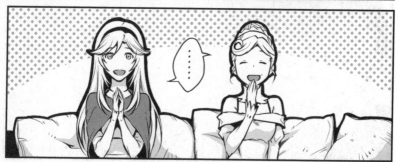

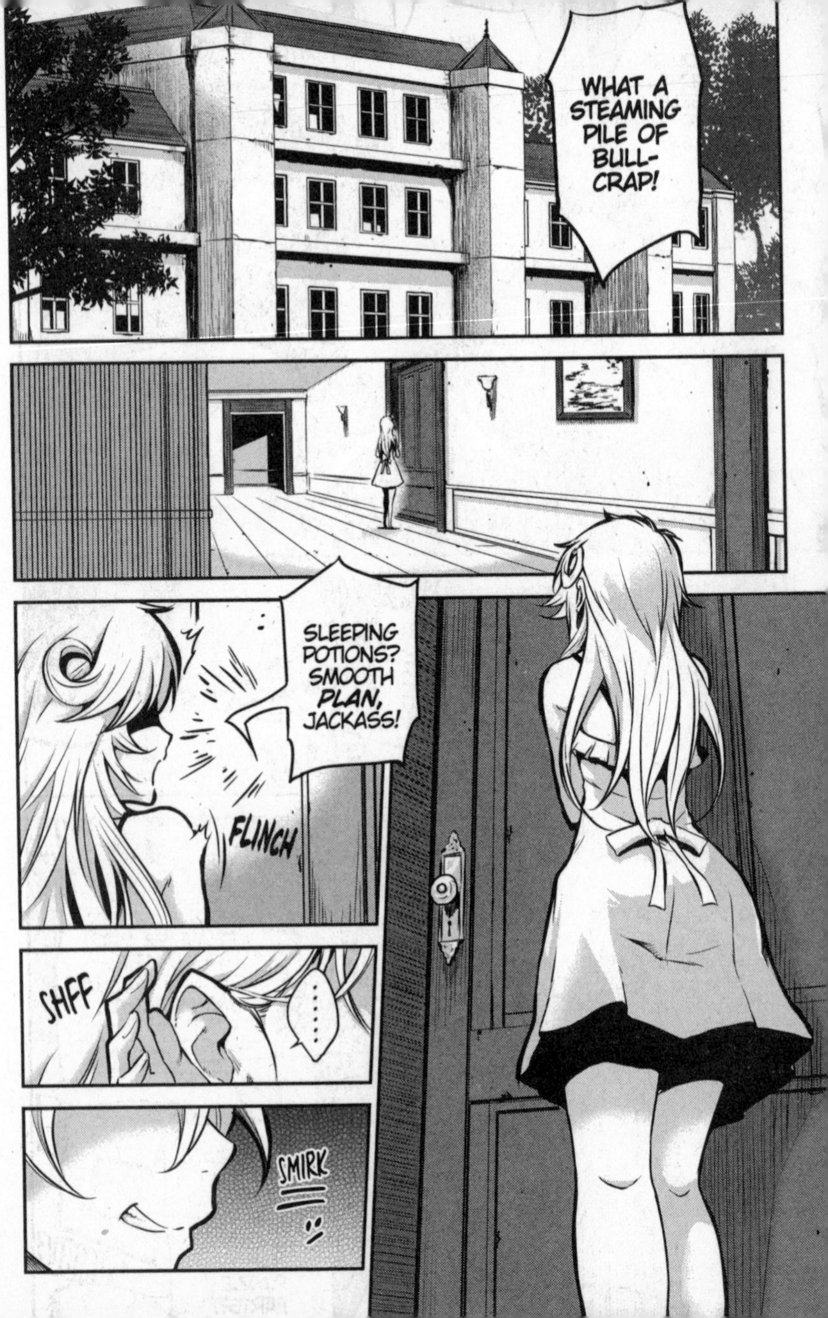
WHAT A STEAMING PILE OF BULL-CRAP!
SLEEPING POTIONS? SMOOTH *PLAN,* JACKASS!
FLINCH
......
SHFF
SMIRK

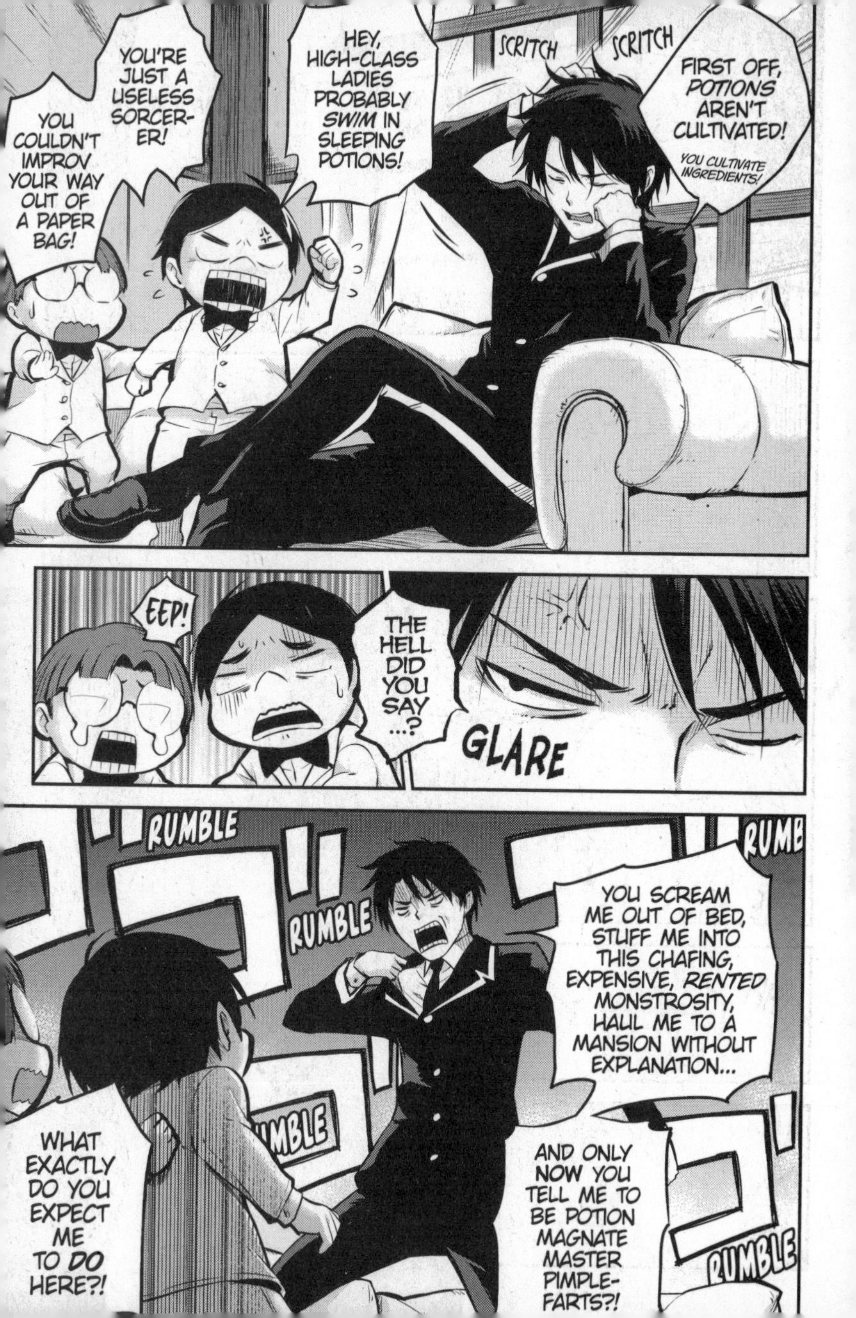
SCRITCH SCRITCH
FIRST OFF, *POTIONS* AREN'T CULTIVATED!
YOU CULTIVATE INGREDIENTS!
HEY, HIGH-CLASS LADIES PROBABLY *SWIM* IN SLEEPING POTIONS!
YOU'RE JUST A USELESS SORCERER-ER!
YOU COULDN'T IMPROV YOUR WAY OUT OF A PAPER BAG!
GLARE
THE HELL DID YOU SAY ...?
EEP!
RUMB
RUMBLE
RUMBLE
YOU SCREAM ME OUT OF BED, STUFF ME INTO THIS CHAFING, EXPENSIVE, *RENTED* MONSTROSITY, HAUL ME TO A MANSION WITHOUT EXPLANATION...
RUMBLE
AND ONLY NOW YOU TELL ME TO BE POTION MAGNATE MASTER PIMPLE-FARTS?!
UMBLE
WHAT EXACTLY DO YOU EXPECT ME TO ***DO*** HERE?!

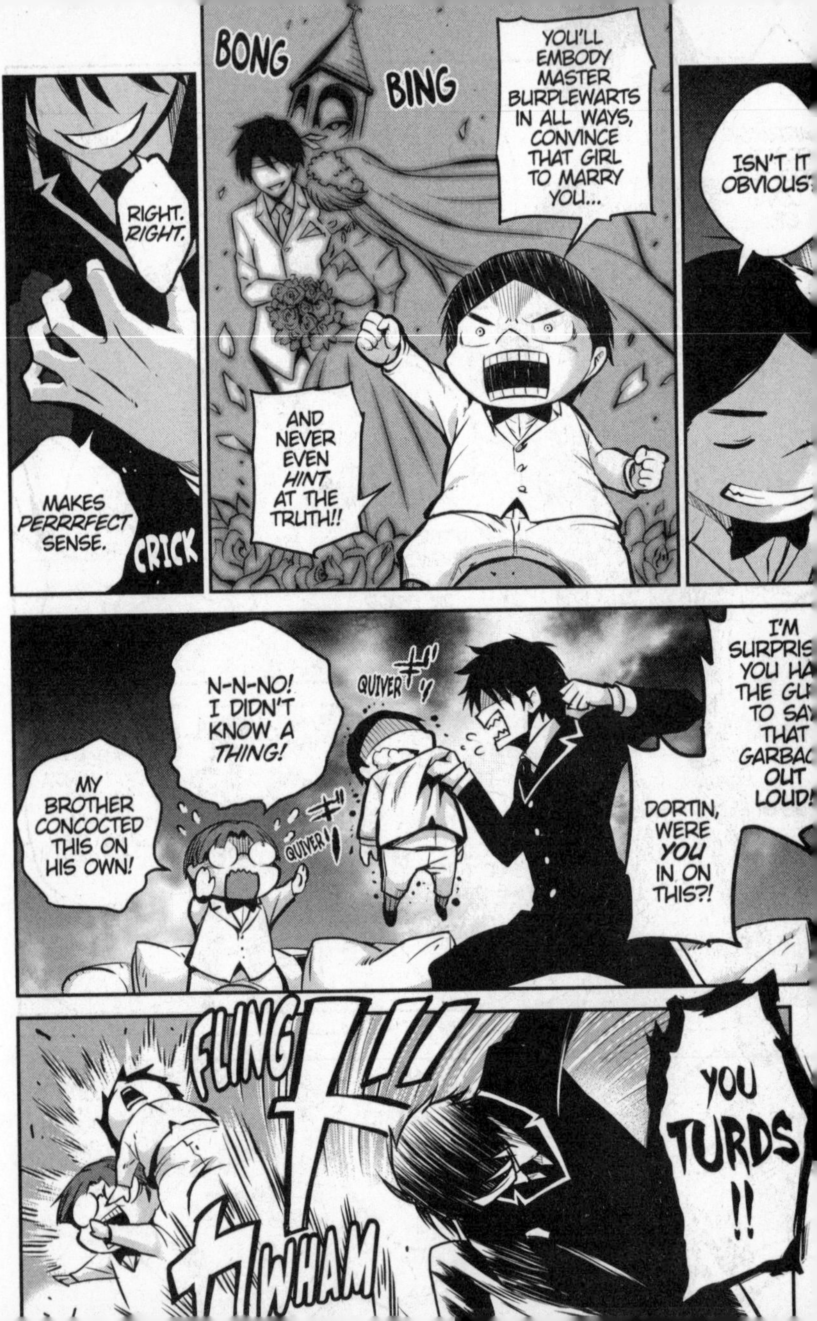
ISN'T IT OBVIOUS
BONG
BING
YOU'LL EMBODY MASTER BURPLEWARTS IN ALL WAYS, CONVINCE THAT GIRL TO MARRY YOU...
AND NEVER EVEN *HINT* AT THE TRUTH!!
RIGHT. *RIGHT.*
MAKES *PERRRFECT* SENSE.
CRICK
I'M SURPRIS YOU HA THE GU TO SA THAT GARBAG OUT LOUD!
DORTIN, WERE *YOU* IN ON THIS?!
QUIVER
N-N-NO! I DIDN'T KNOW A *THING!*
MY BROTHER CONCOCTED THIS ON HIS OWN!
QUIVER
YOU TURDS!!
FLING
WHAM

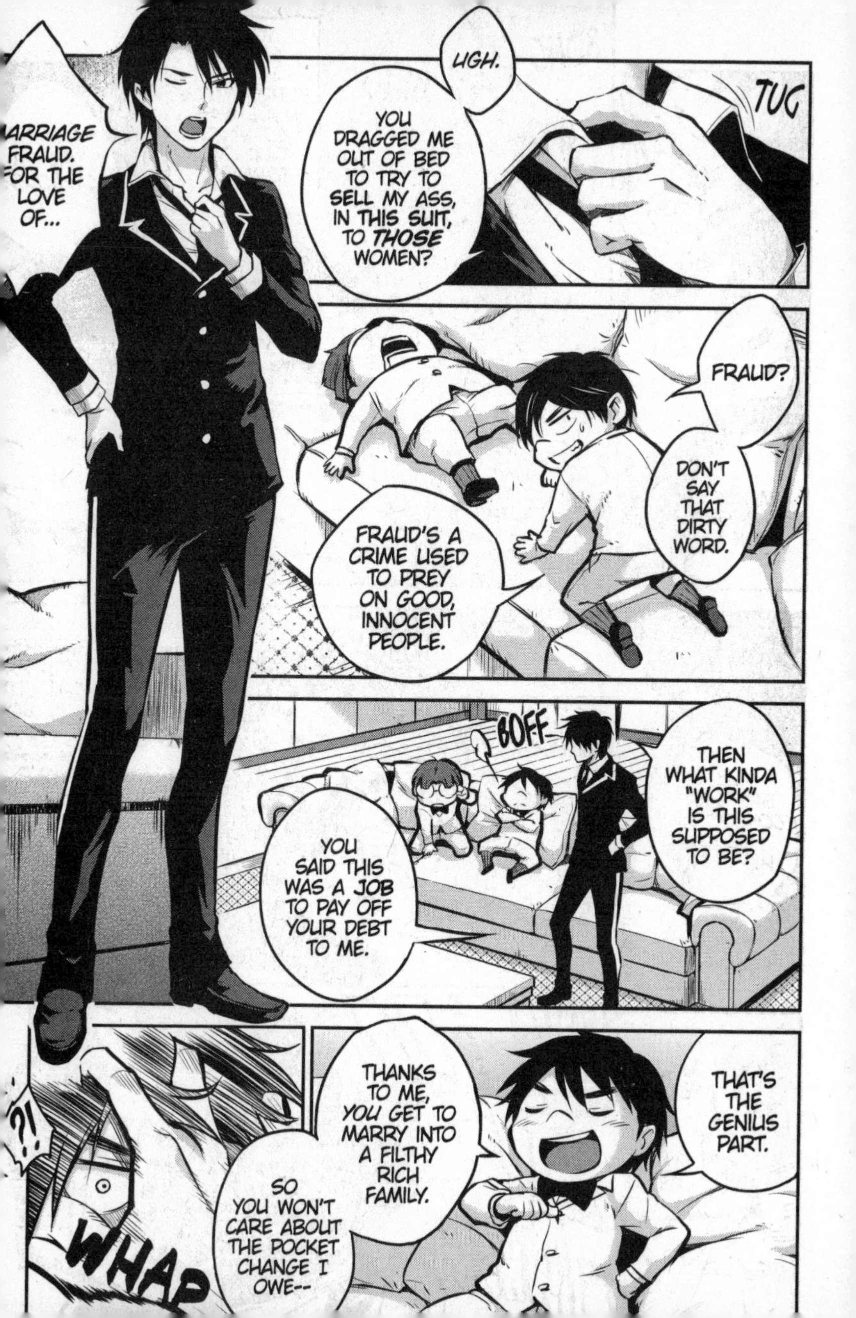
TUG
UGH.
YOU DRAGGED ME OUT OF BED TO TRY TO SELL MY ASS, IN THIS SUIT, TO *THOSE* WOMEN?
FRAUD?
DON'T SAY THAT DIRTY WORD.
FRAUD'S A CRIME USED TO PREY ON GOOD, INNOCENT PEOPLE.
THEN WHAT KINDA "WORK" IS THIS SUPPOSED TO BE?
BOFF
YOU SAID THIS WAS A JOB TO PAY OFF YOUR DEBT TO ME.
ARRIAGE FRAUD. FOR THE LOVE OF...
THAT'S THE GENIUS PART.
THANKS TO ME, *YOU* GET TO MARRY INTO A FILTHY RICH FAMILY.
SO YOU WON'T CARE ABOUT THE POCKET CHANGE I OWE--
?!
WHAP

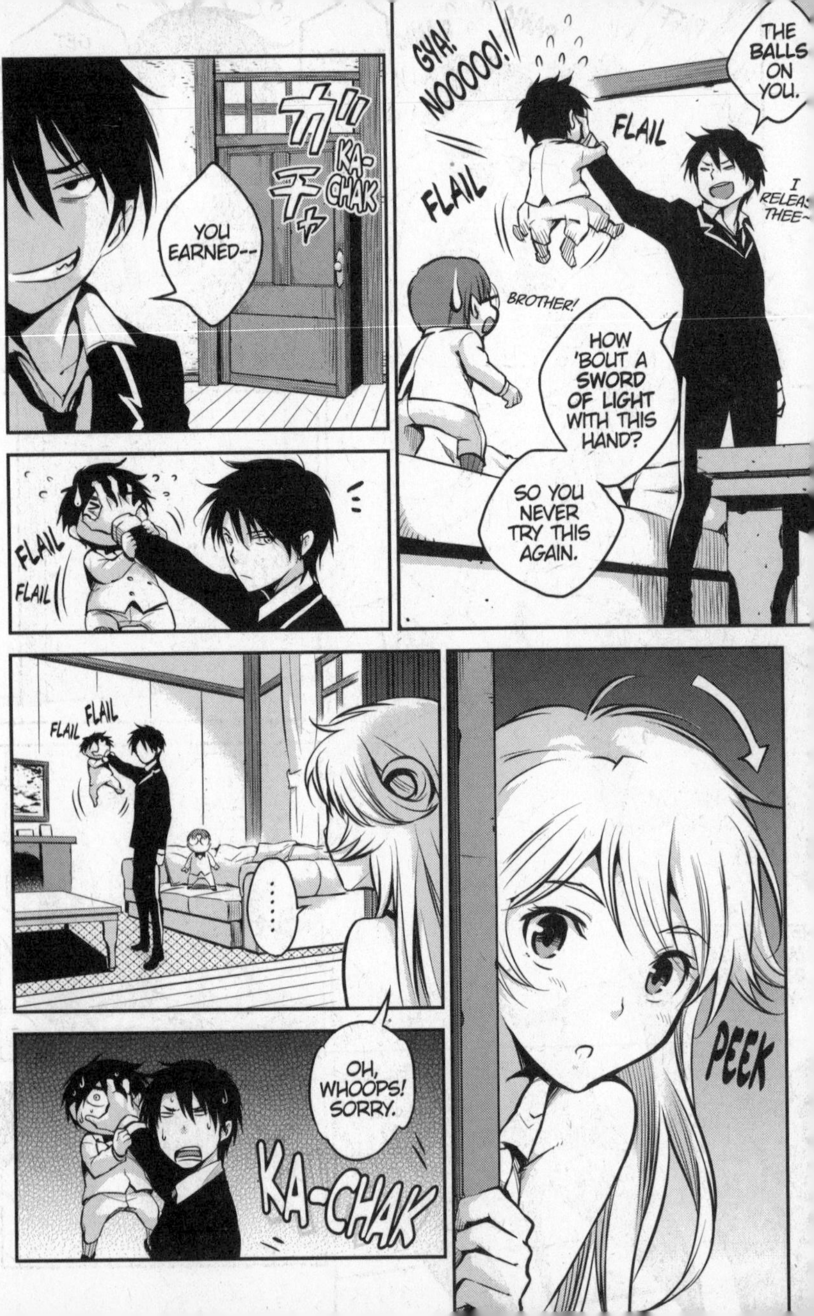
THE BALLS ON YOU.
GYA! NOOOOO!!
FLAIL
FLAIL
I RELEAS THEE~
BROTHER!
HOW 'BOUT A SWORD OF LIGHT WITH THIS HAND?
SO YOU NEVER TRY THIS AGAIN.
KA-CHAK
YOU EARNED--
FLAIL
FLAIL
PEEK
FLAIL
FLAIL
......
OH, WHOOPS! SORRY.
KA-CHAK

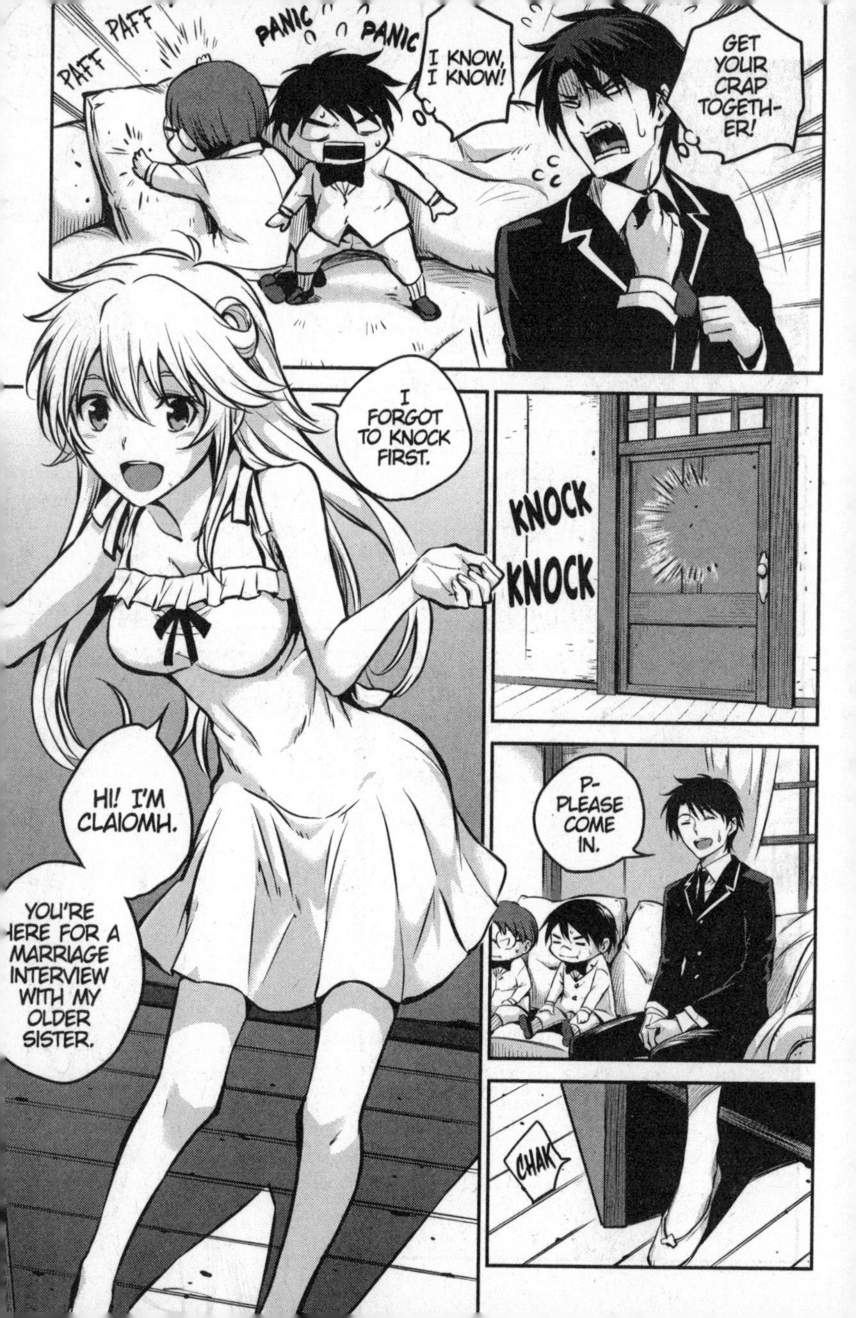

GET YOUR CRAP TOGETHER!
I KNOW, I KNOW!
PANIC PANIC
PAFF PAFF
KNOCK KNOCK
P-PLEASE COME IN.
CHAK
I FORGOT TO KNOCK FIRST.
HI! I'M CLAIOMH.
YOU'RE HERE FOR A MARRIAGE INTERVIEW WITH MY OLDER SISTER.

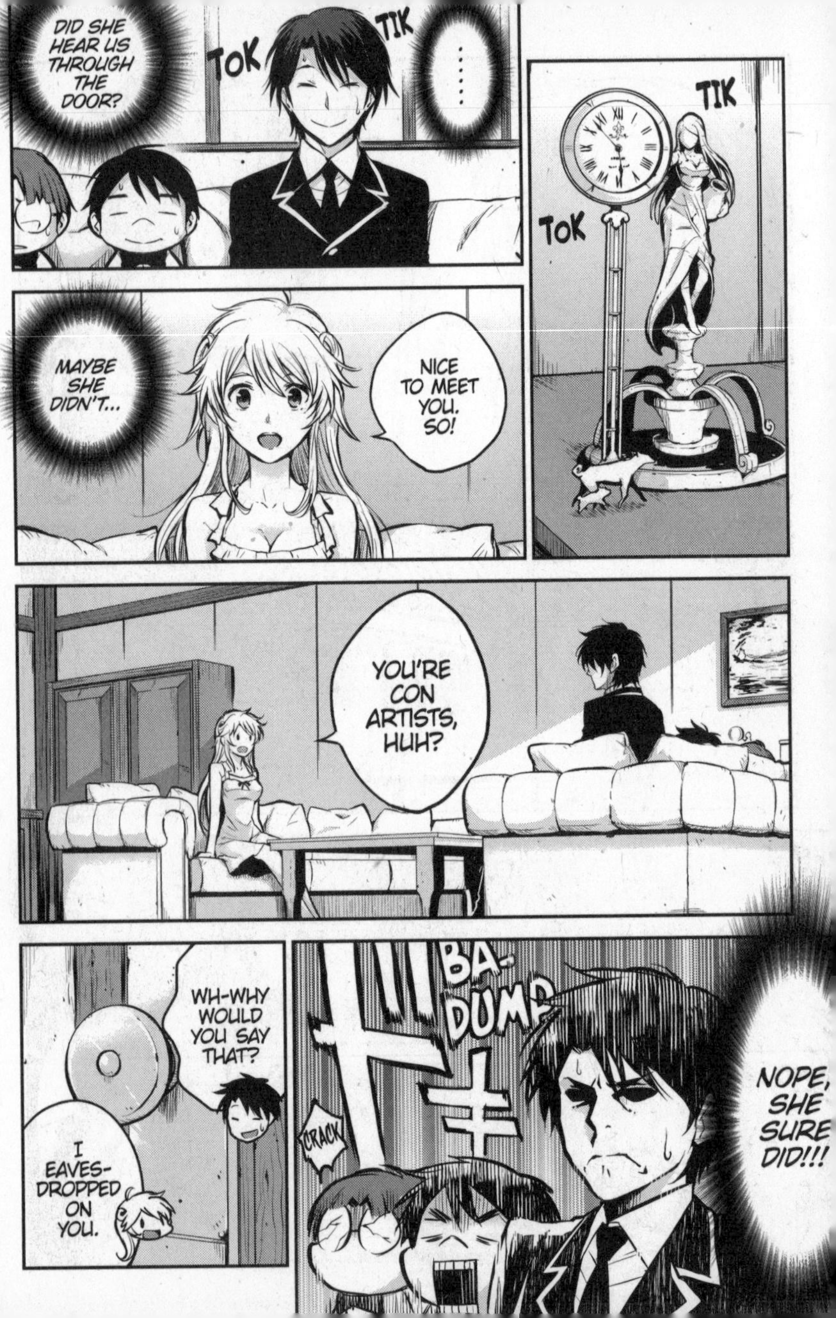
TIK
TOK
TIK
......
TOK
DID SHE HEAR US THROUGH THE DOOR?
NICE TO MEET YOU. SO!
MAYBE SHE DIDN'T...
YOU'RE CON ARTISTS, HUH?
BA-DUMP
CRACK
NOPE, SHE SURE DID!!!
WH-WHY WOULD YOU SAY THAT?
I EAVES-DROPPED ON YOU.

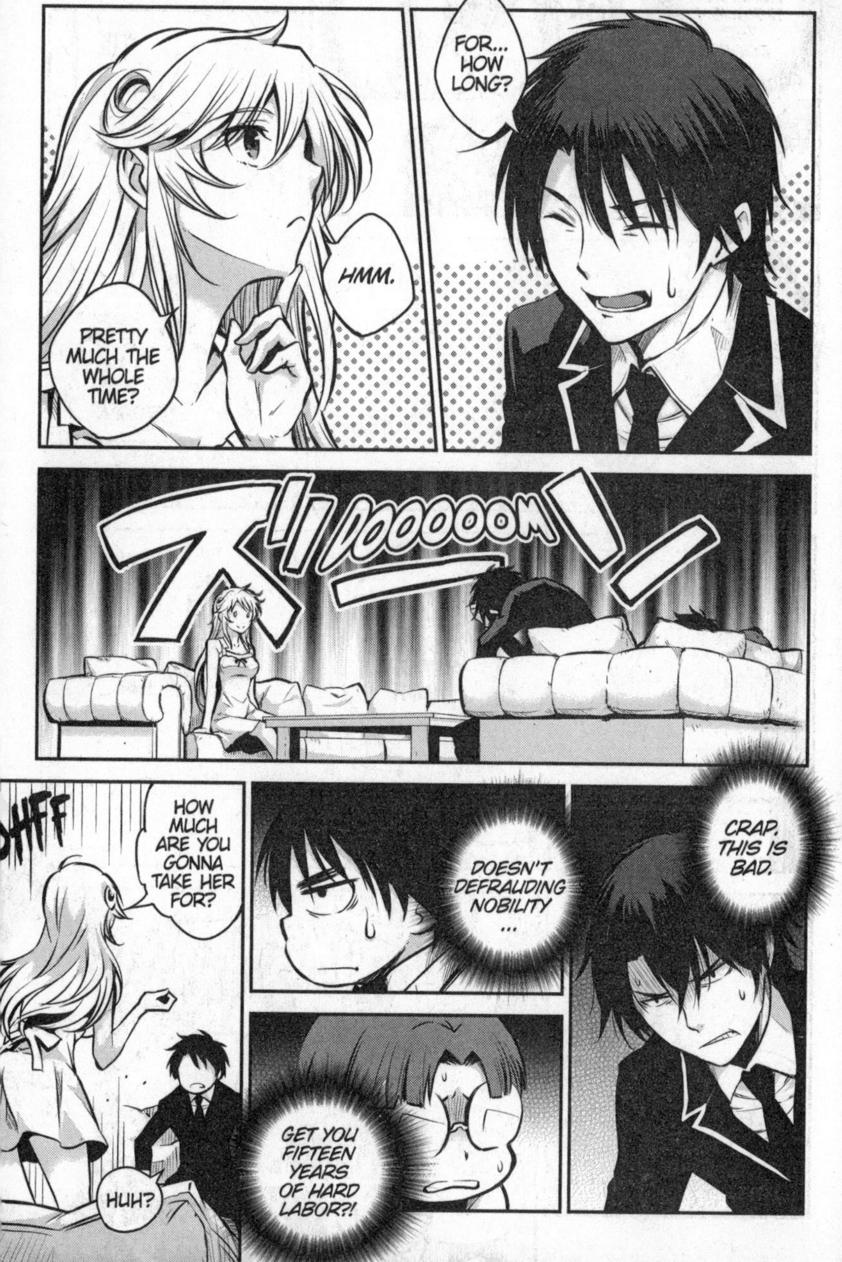

FOR... HOW LONG?
HMM.
PRETTY MUCH THE WHOLE TIME?
DOOOOOM
CRAP. THIS IS BAD.
DOESN'T DEFRAUDING NOBILITY ...
GET YOU FIFTEEN YEARS OF HARD LABOR?!
HOW MUCH ARE YOU GONNA TAKE HER FOR?
HUH?

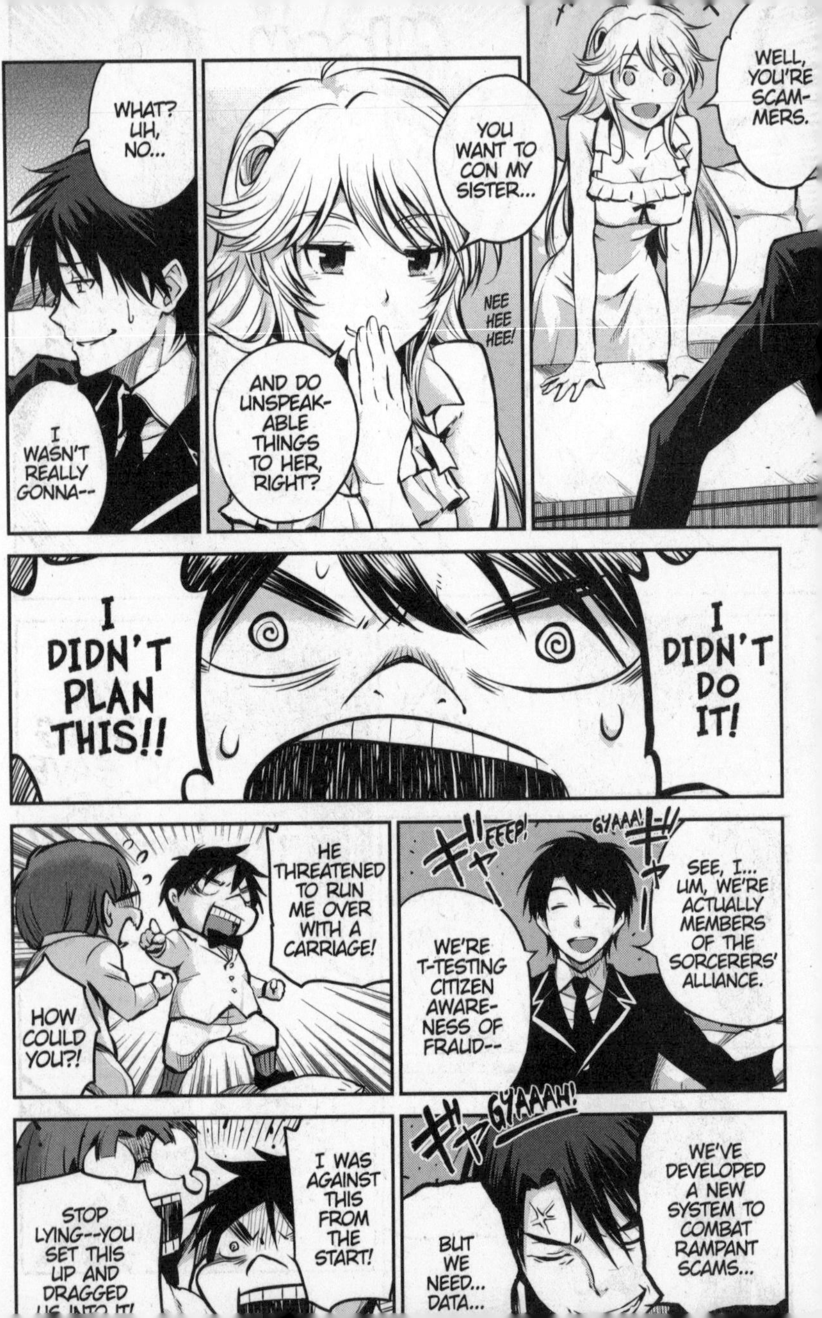
WELL, YOU'RE SCAM-MERS.
YOU WANT TO CON MY SISTER...
NEE HEE HEE!
AND DO UNSPEAK-ABLE THINGS TO HER, RIGHT?
WHAT? UH, NO...
I WASN'T REALLY GONNA--
I DIDN'T DO IT!
I DIDN'T PLAN THIS!!
GYAAA!
EEEP!
SEE, I... UM, WE'RE ACTUALLY MEMBERS OF THE SORCERERS' ALLIANCE.
WE'RE T-TESTING CITIZEN AWARE-NESS OF FRAUD--
HE THREATENED TO RUN ME OVER WITH A CARRIAGE!
HOW COULD YOU?!
GYAAAH!
WE'VE DEVELOPED A NEW SYSTEM TO COMBAT RAMPANT SCAMS...
BUT WE NEED... DATA...
I WAS AGAINST THIS FROM THE START!
STOP LYING--YOU SET THIS UP AND DRAGGED

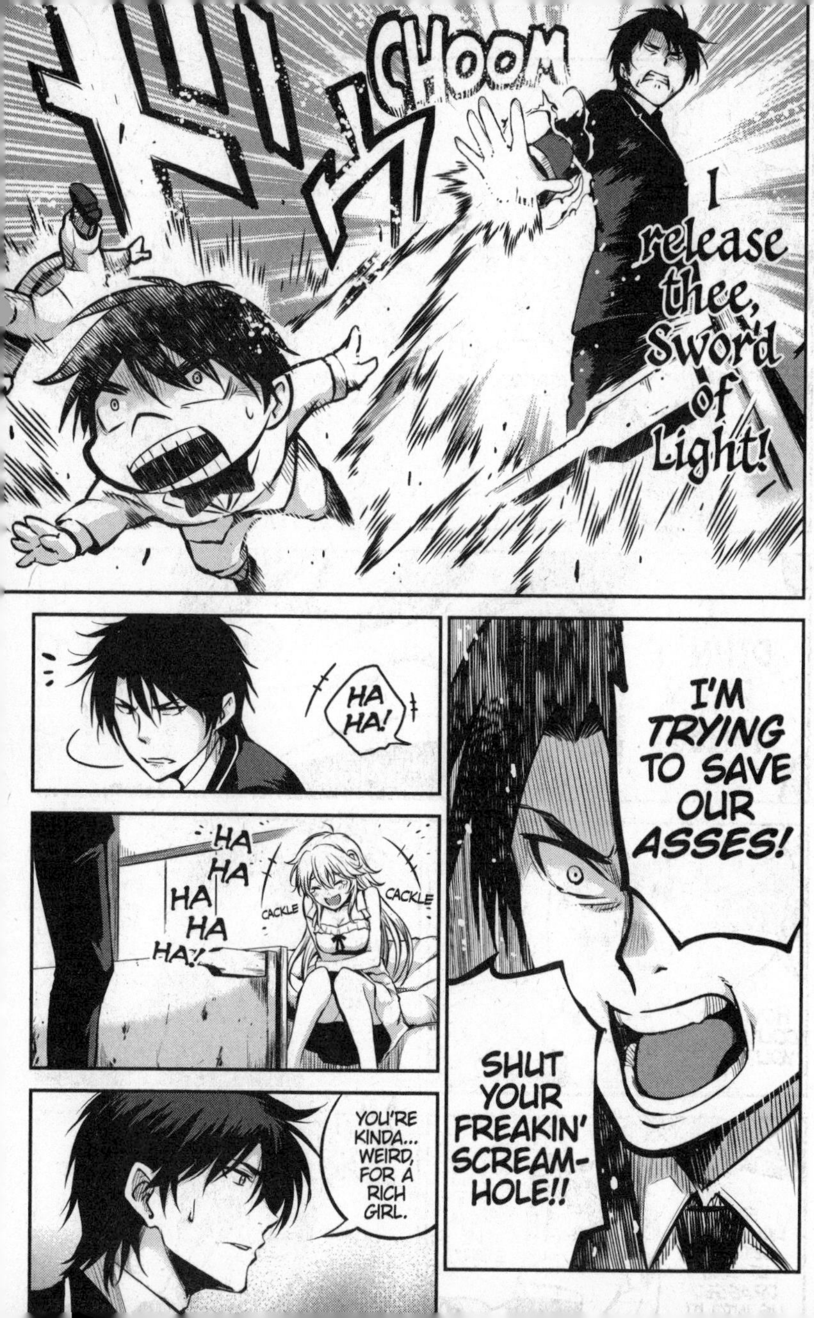
I release thee, Sword of Light!
CHOOM
I'M TRYING TO SAVE OUR ASSES!
SHUT YOUR FREAKIN' SCREAM-HOLE!!
HA HA!
HA HA HA HA HA!
CACKLE
CACKLE
YOU'RE KINDA... WEIRD, FOR A RICH GIRL.

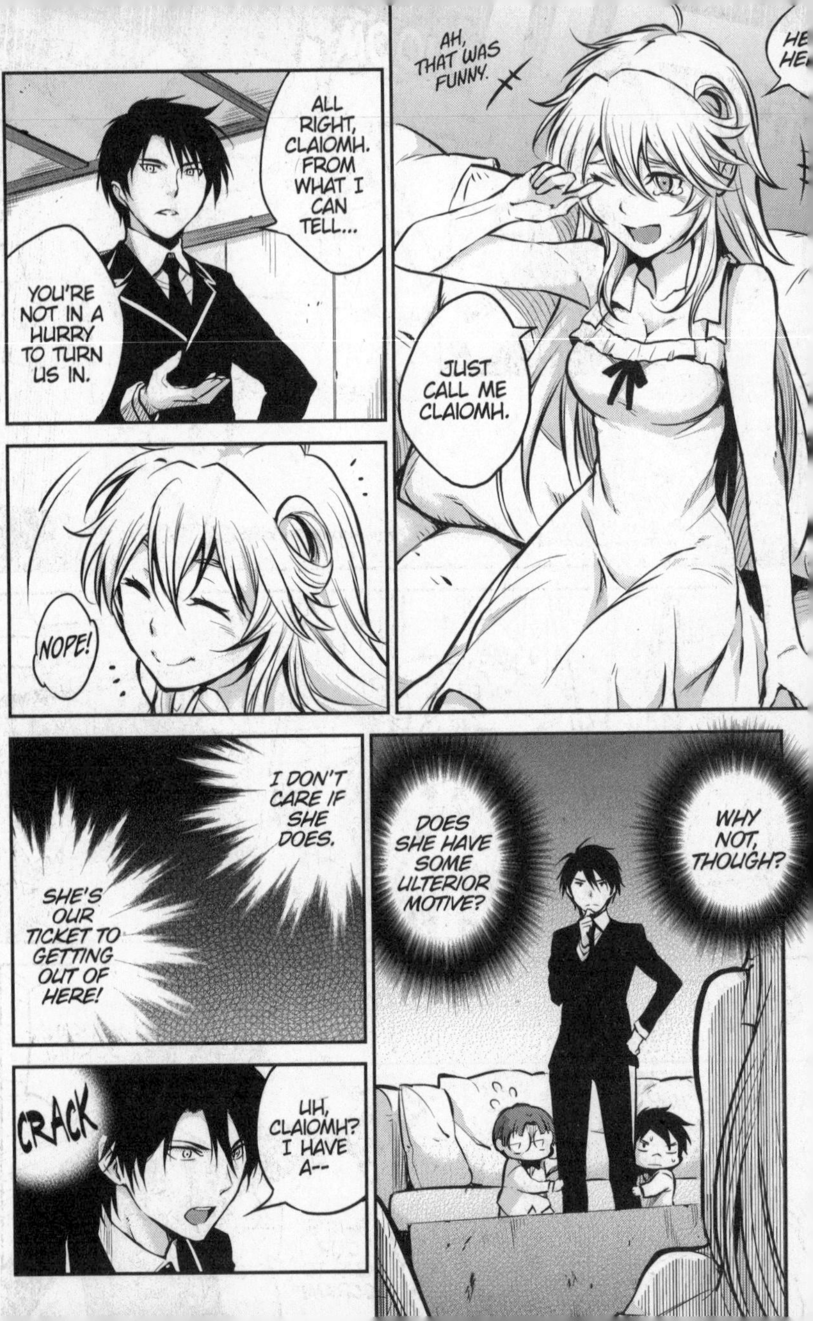
HE HE
AH, THAT WAS FUNNY.
JUST CALL ME CLAIOMH.
ALL RIGHT, CLAIOMH. FROM WHAT I CAN TELL...
YOU'RE NOT IN A HURRY TO TURN US IN.
NOPE!
WHY NOT, THOUGH?
DOES SHE HAVE SOME ULTERIOR MOTIVE?
I DON'T CARE IF SHE DOES.
SHE'S OUR TICKET TO GETTING OUT OF HERE!
UH, CLAIOMH? I HAVE A--
CRACK

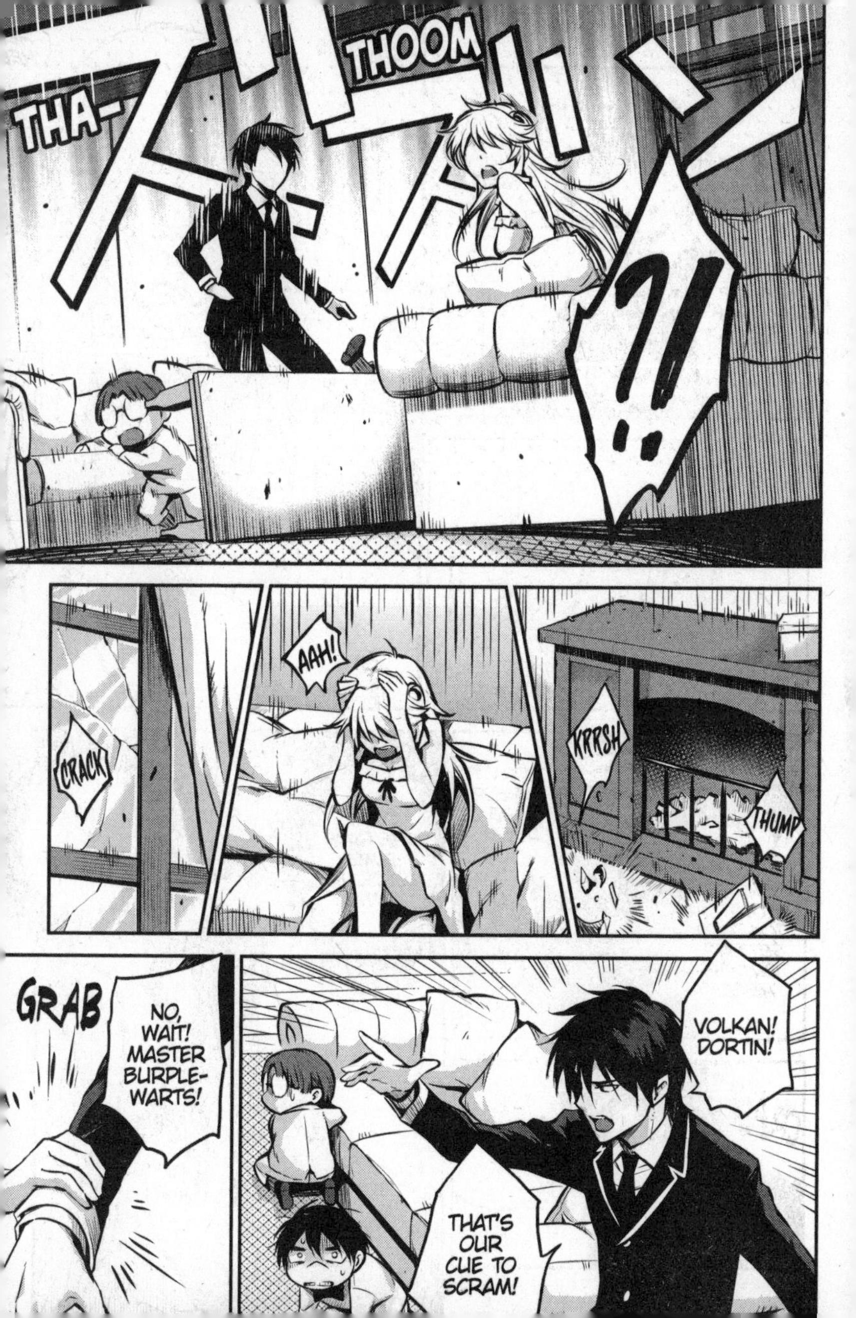
THOOM
THA-
?!
THUMP
KRRSH
AAH!
CRACK
VOLKAN! DORTIN!
THAT'S OUR CUE TO SCRAM!
NO, WAIT! MASTER BURPLE-WARTS!
GRAB

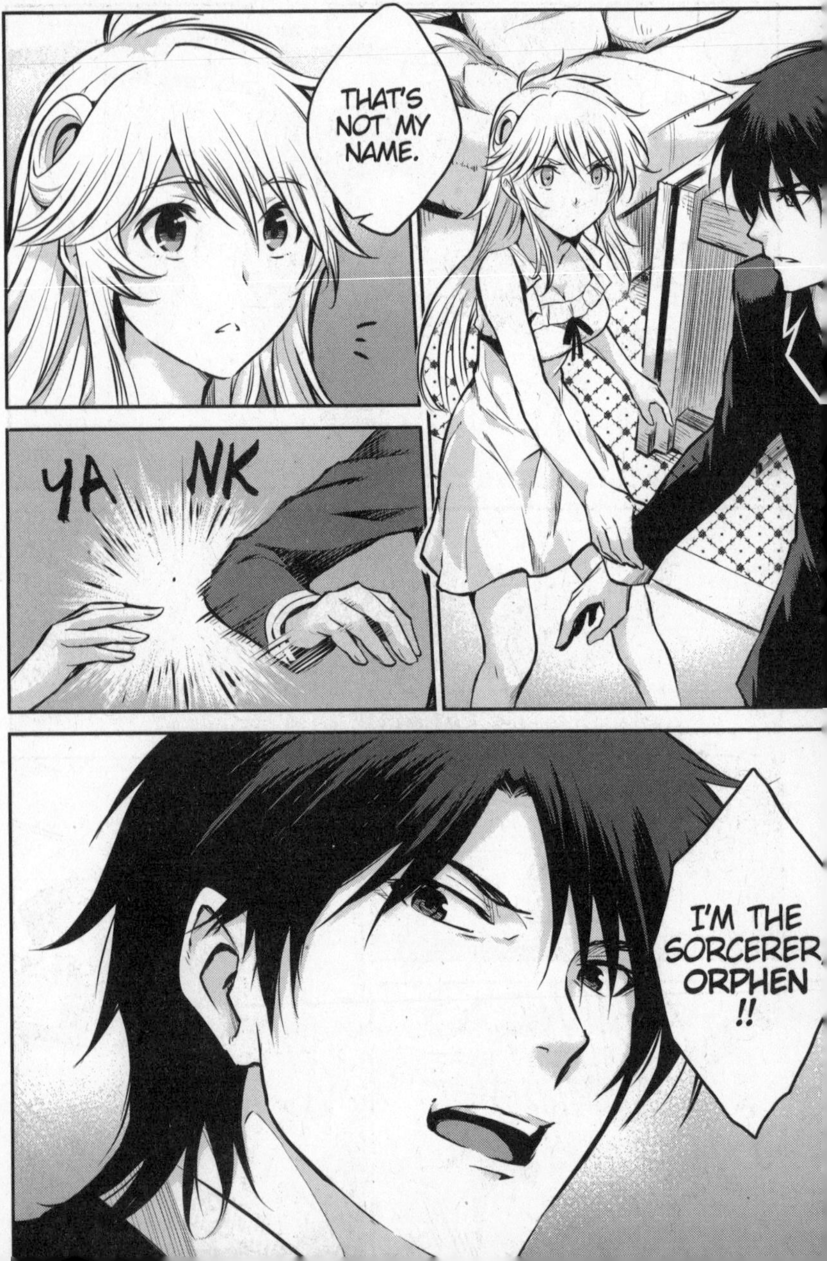
THAT'S NOT MY NAME.
YANK
I'M THE SORCERER ORPHEN !!

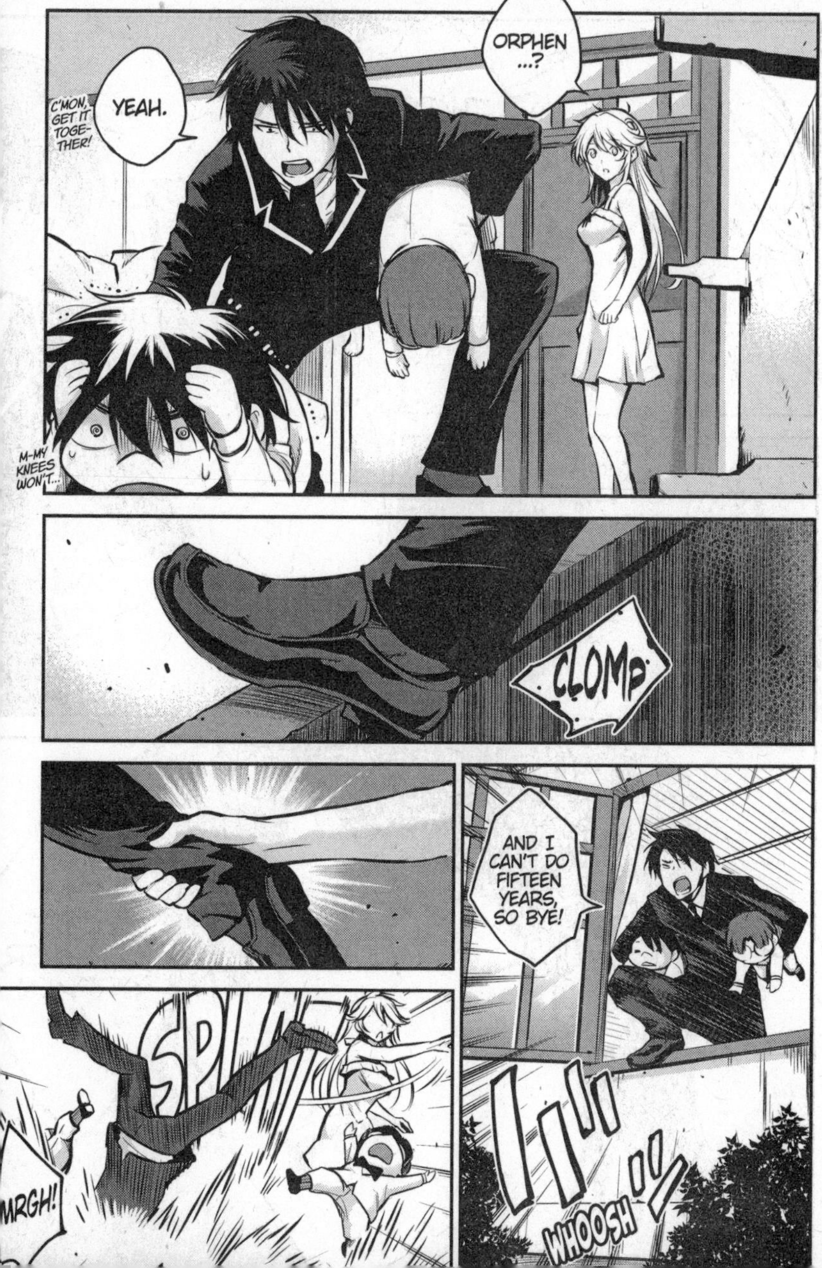
ORPHEN ...?
YEAH.
C'MON, GET IT TOGE-THER!
M-MY KNEES WON'T...
CLOMP
AND I CAN'T DO FIFTEEN YEARS, SO BYE!
WHOOSH
MRGH!

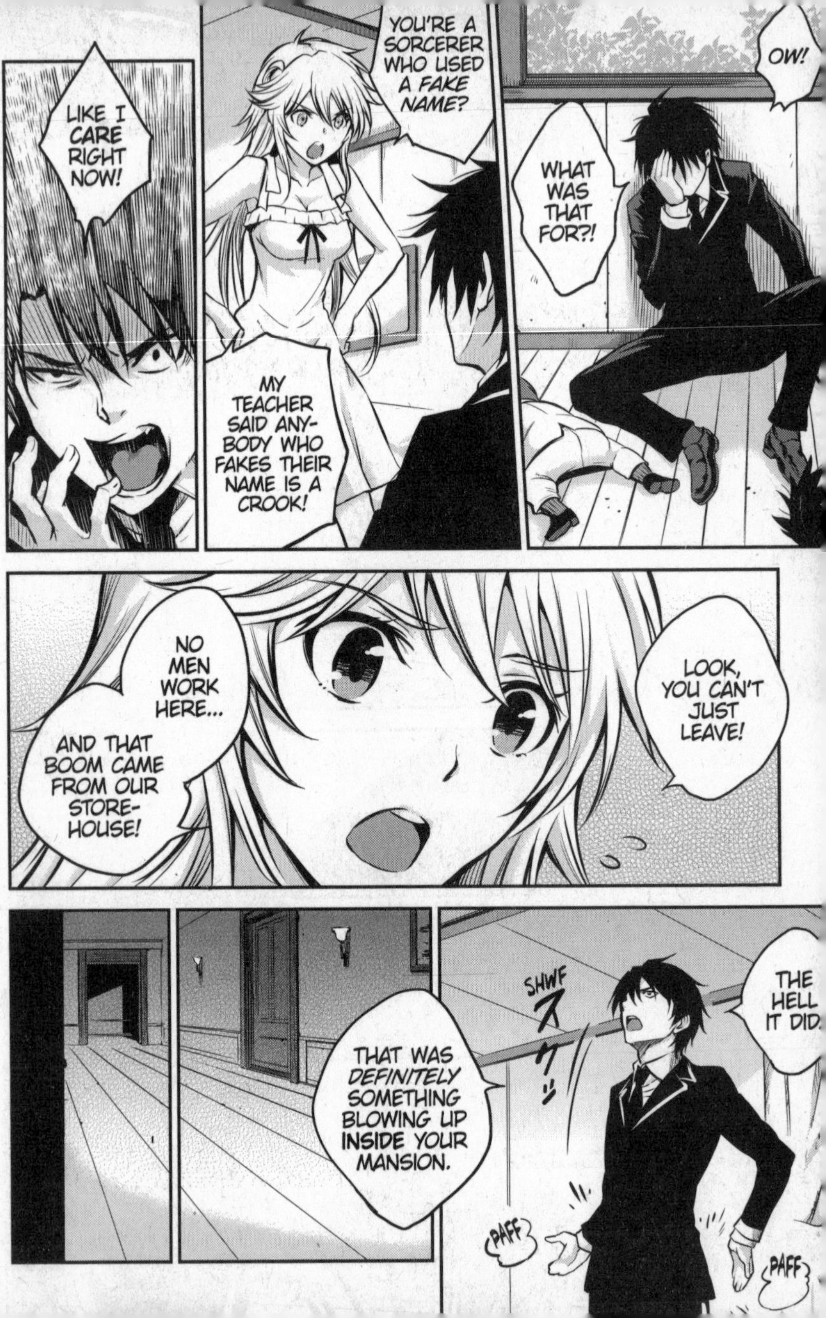
OW!
WHAT WAS THAT FOR?!
YOU'RE A SORCERER WHO USED A FAKE NAME?
MY TEACHER SAID ANYBODY WHO FAKES THEIR NAME IS A CROOK!
LIKE I CARE RIGHT NOW!
LOOK, YOU CAN'T JUST LEAVE!
NO MEN WORK HERE...
AND THAT BOOM CAME FROM OUR STOREHOUSE!
THE HELL IT DID.
SHWF
THAT WAS DEFINITELY SOMETHING BLOWING UP INSIDE YOUR MANSION.
PAFF
PAFF

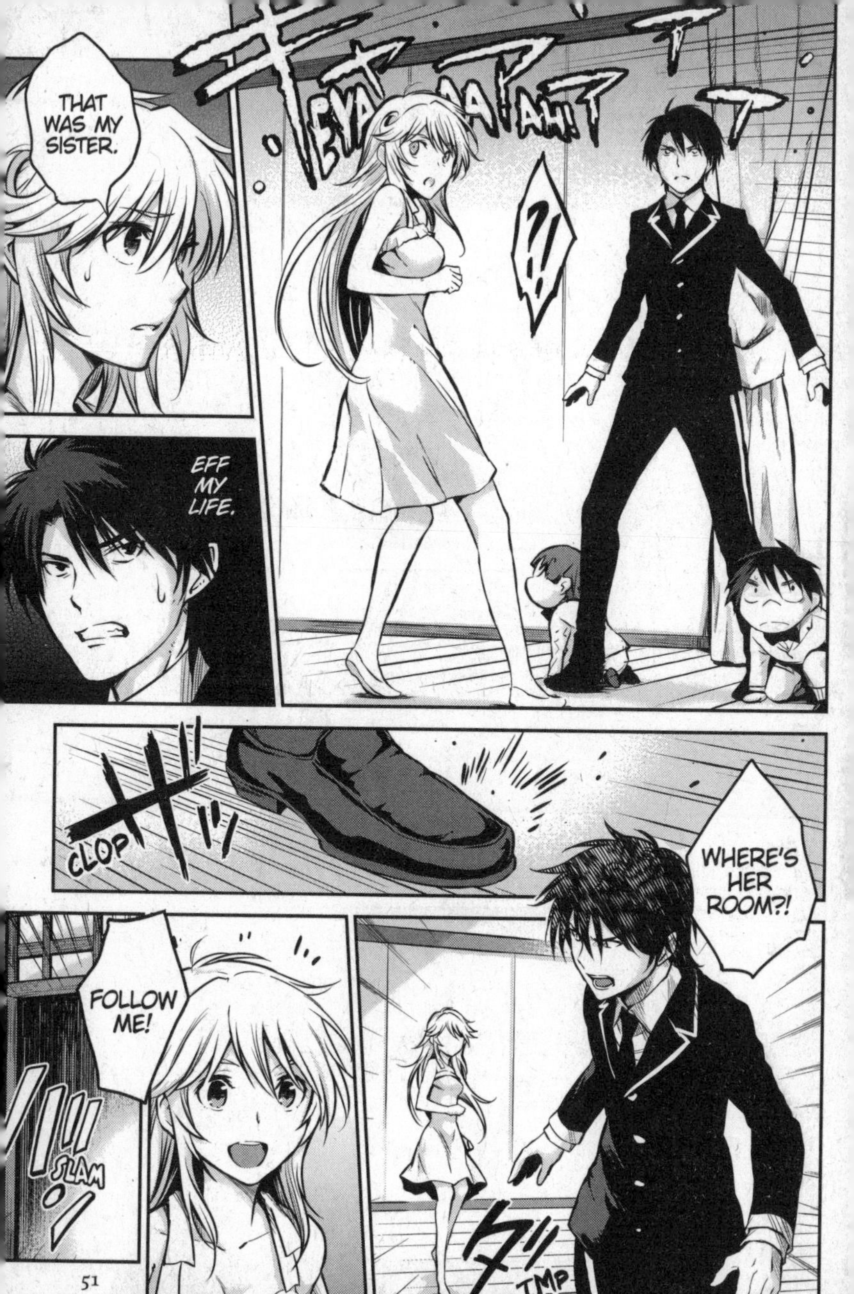
EYAAAAH!?
?!
THAT WAS MY SISTER.
EFF MY LIFE.
CLOP
WHERE'S HER ROOM?!
TMP
FOLLOW ME!
SLAM

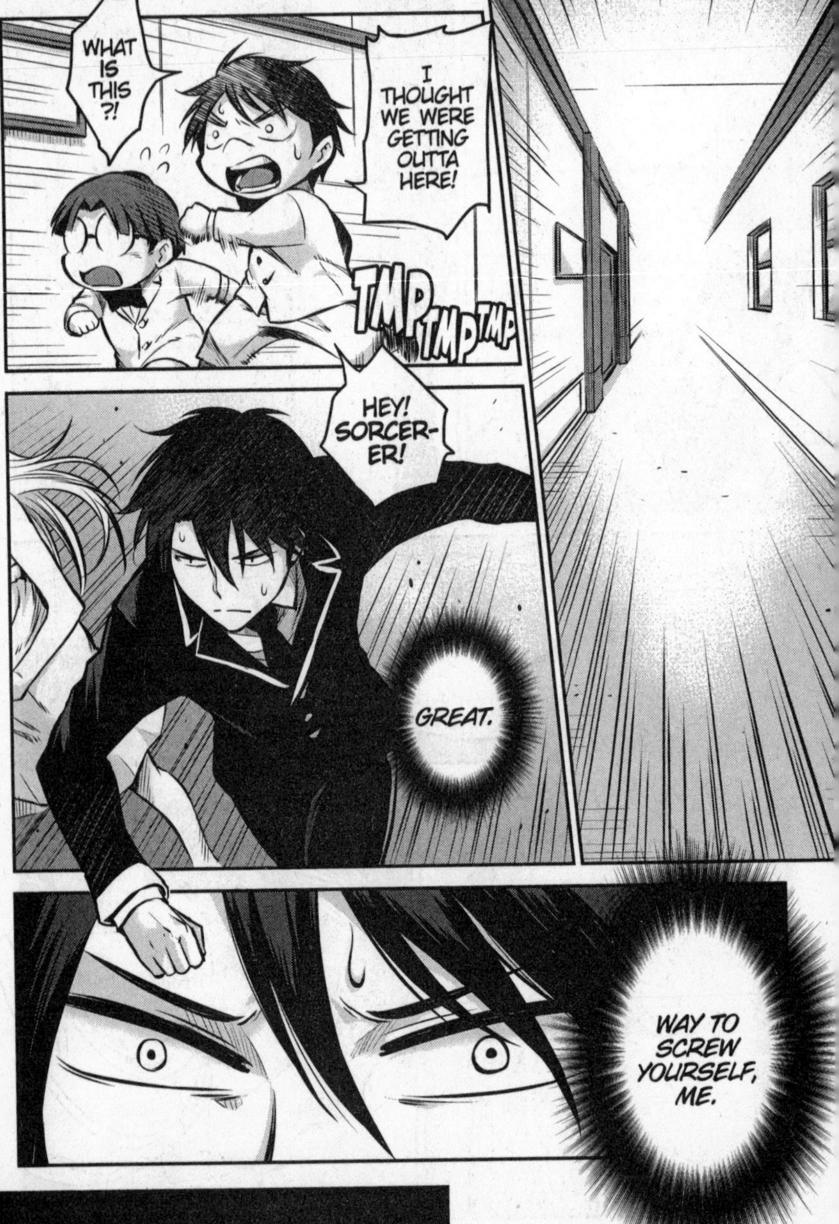
I THOUGHT WE WERE GETTING OUTTA HERE!
WHAT IS THIS?!
TMP TMP TMP
HEY! SORCER-ER!
GREAT.
WAY TO SCREW YOURSELF, ME.

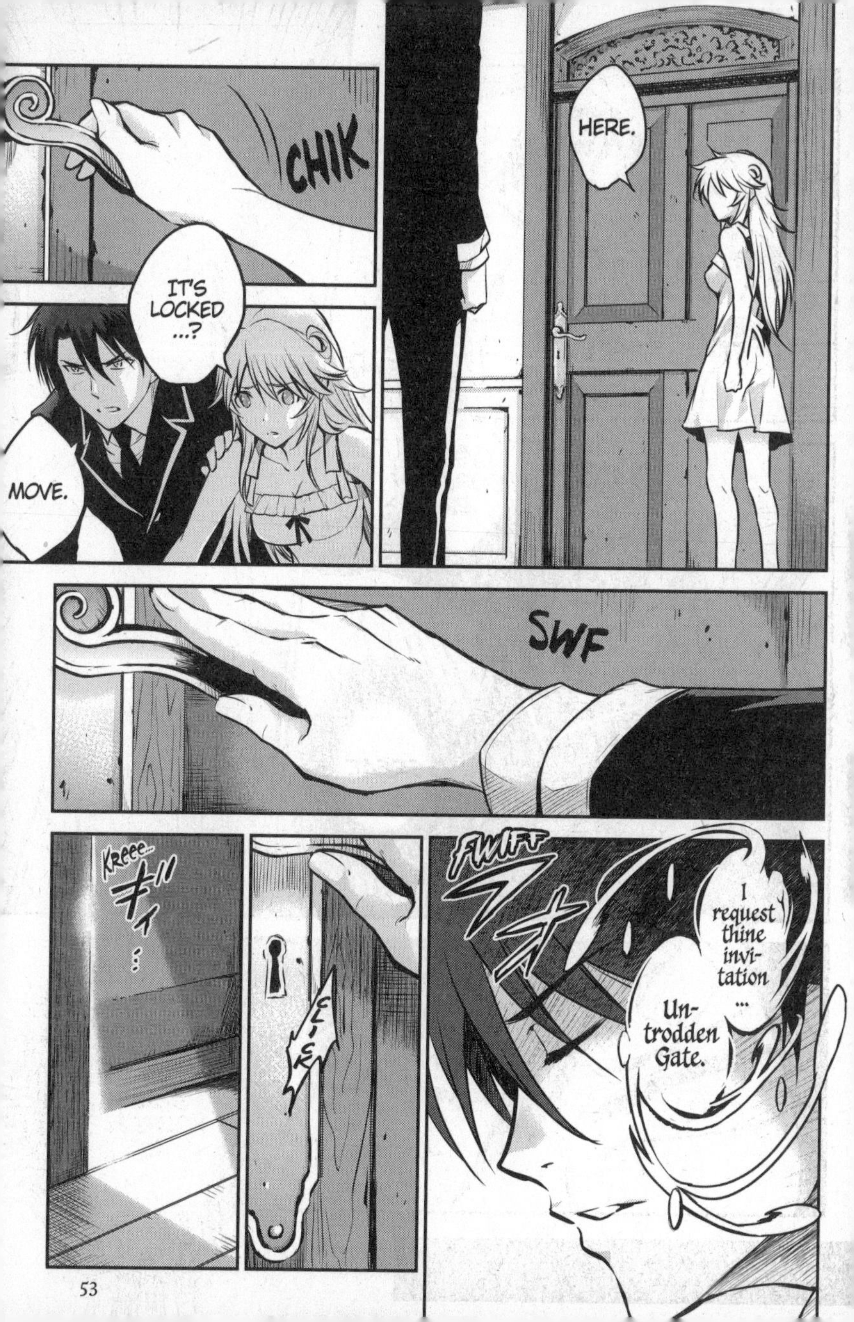

HERE.
CHIK
IT'S LOCKED ...?
MOVE.
SWF
FWIFF
I request thine invitation...
Untrodden Gate.
CLICK
Kreee...
ギィ...

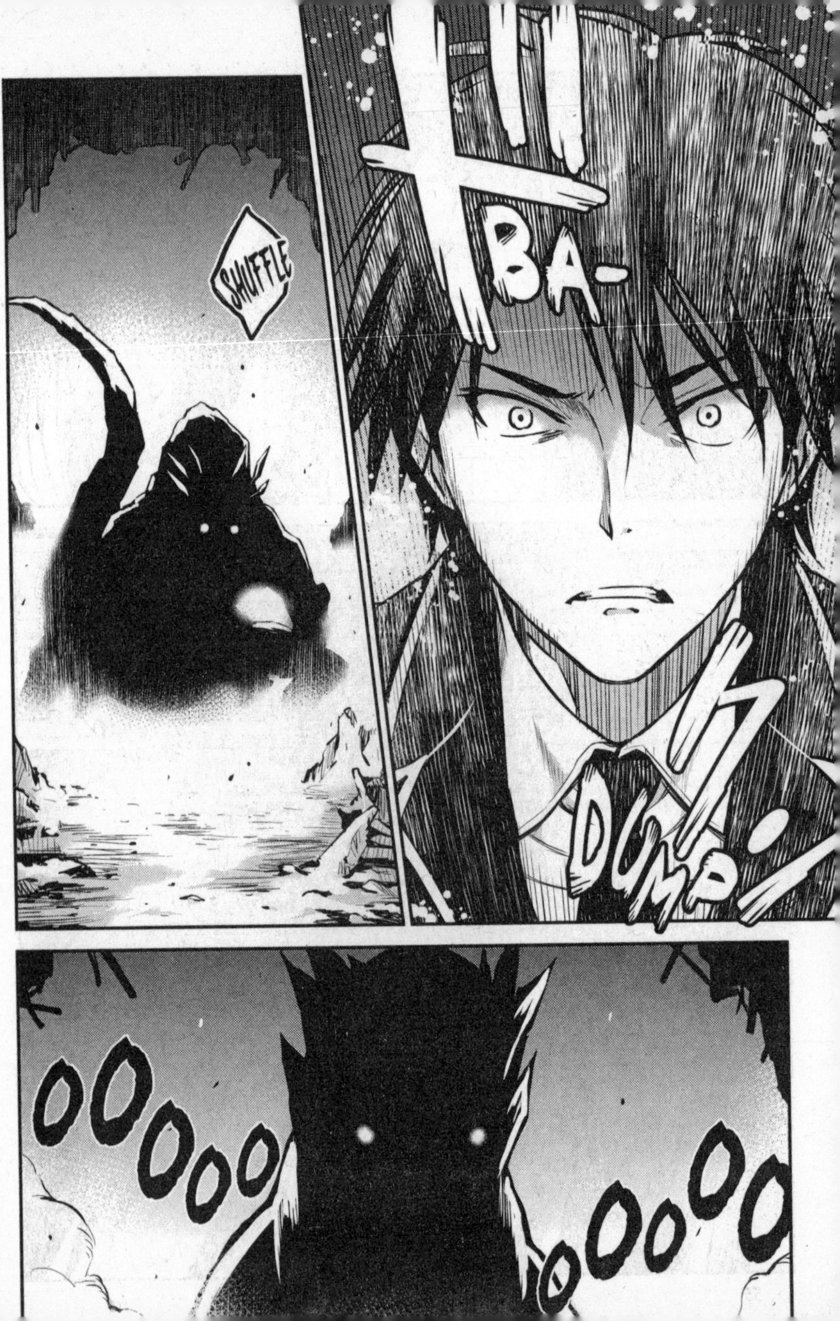
BA-
DUMP!
SHUFFLE
OOOOOO
OOOOOO

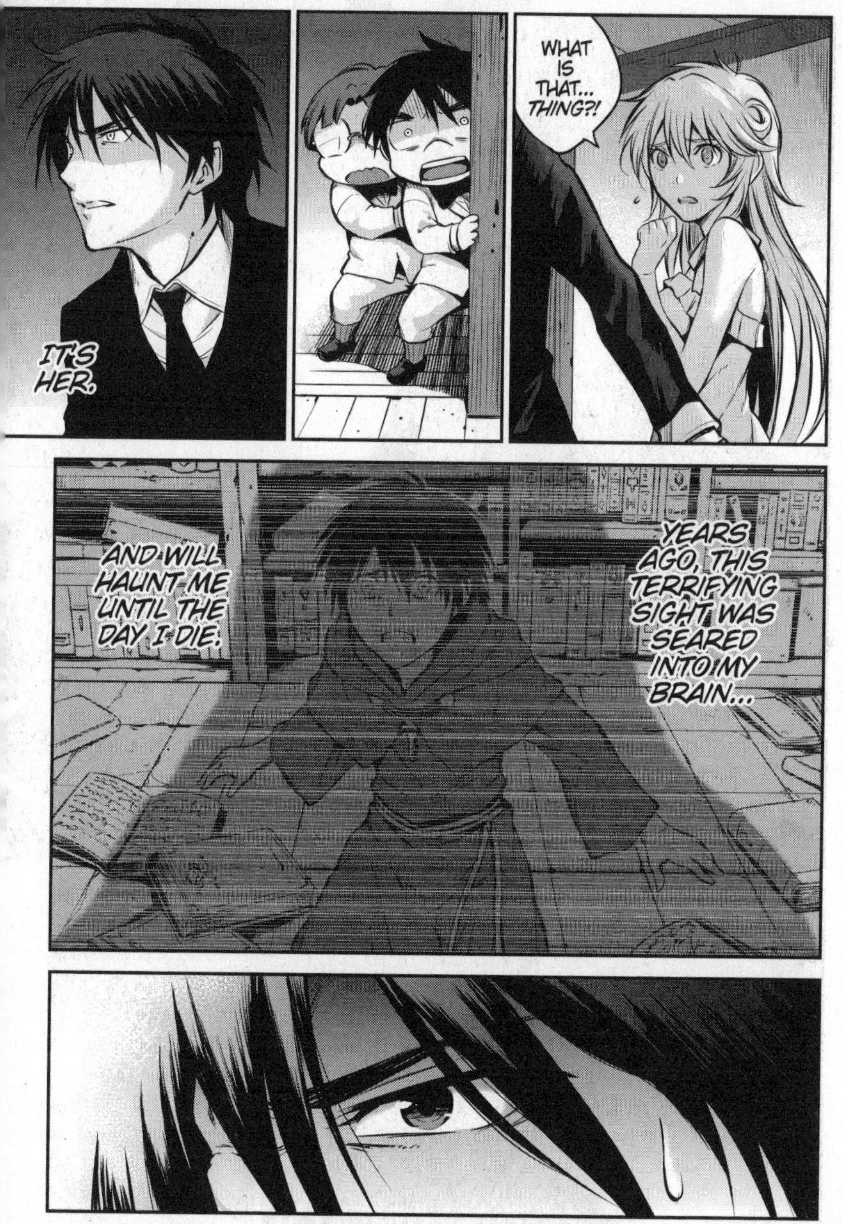
WHAT IS THAT... THING?!
IT'S HER.
YEARS AGO, THIS TERRIFYING SIGHT WAS SEARED INTO MY BRAIN...
AND WILL HAUNT ME UNTIL THE DAY I DIE.

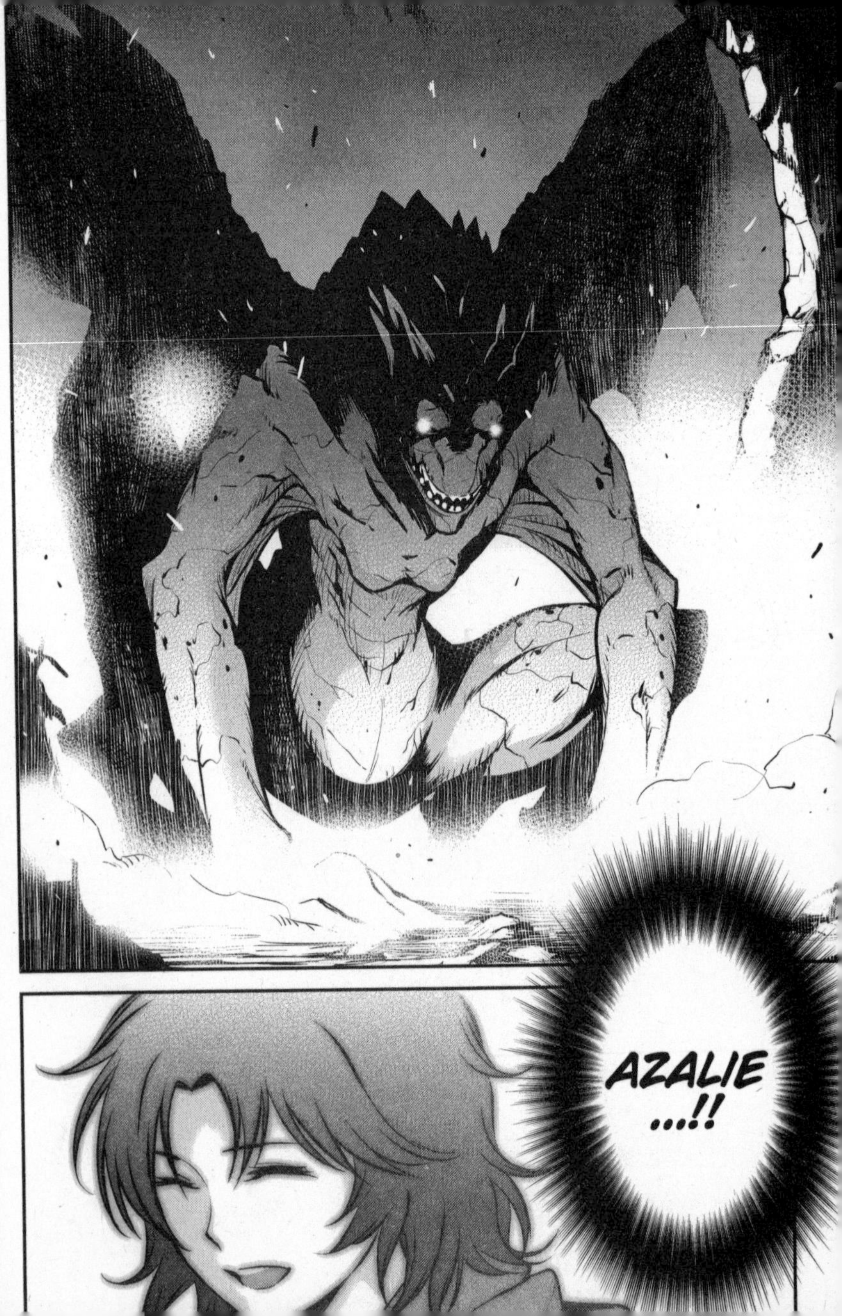
AZALIE ...!!

Sorcerous Stabber ORPHEN

CHARACTER DESIGNS ①: ORPHEN

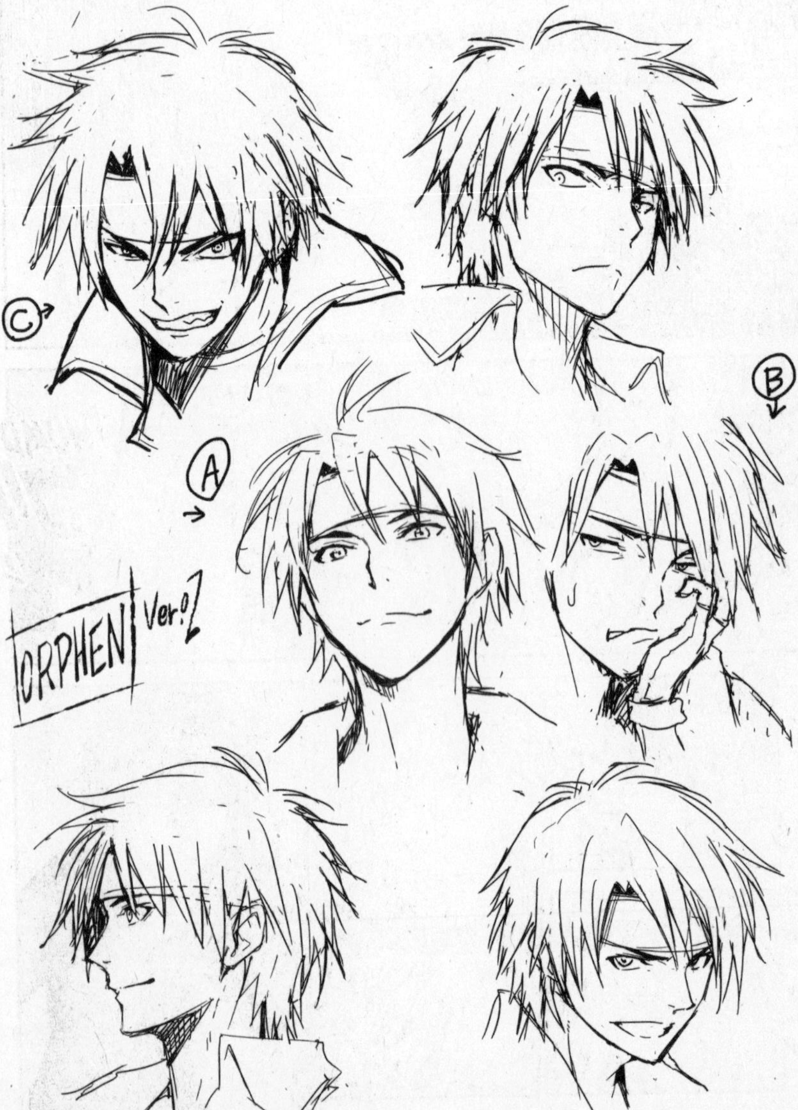
C
B
A
ORPHEN
Ver.2

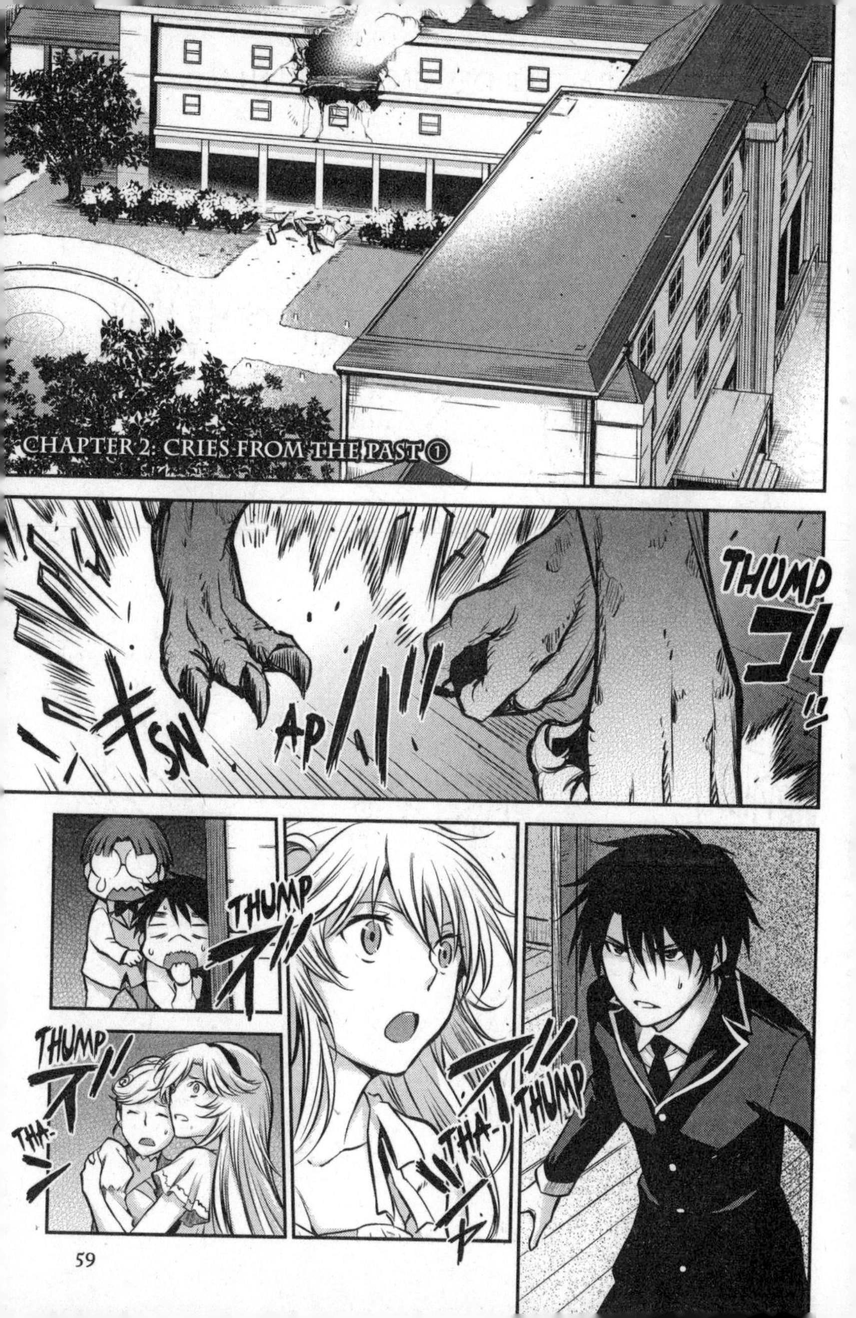

CHAPTER 2: CRIES FROM THE PAST ①
THUMP
SNAP
THUMP
THA-
THUMP
THUMP
THA-

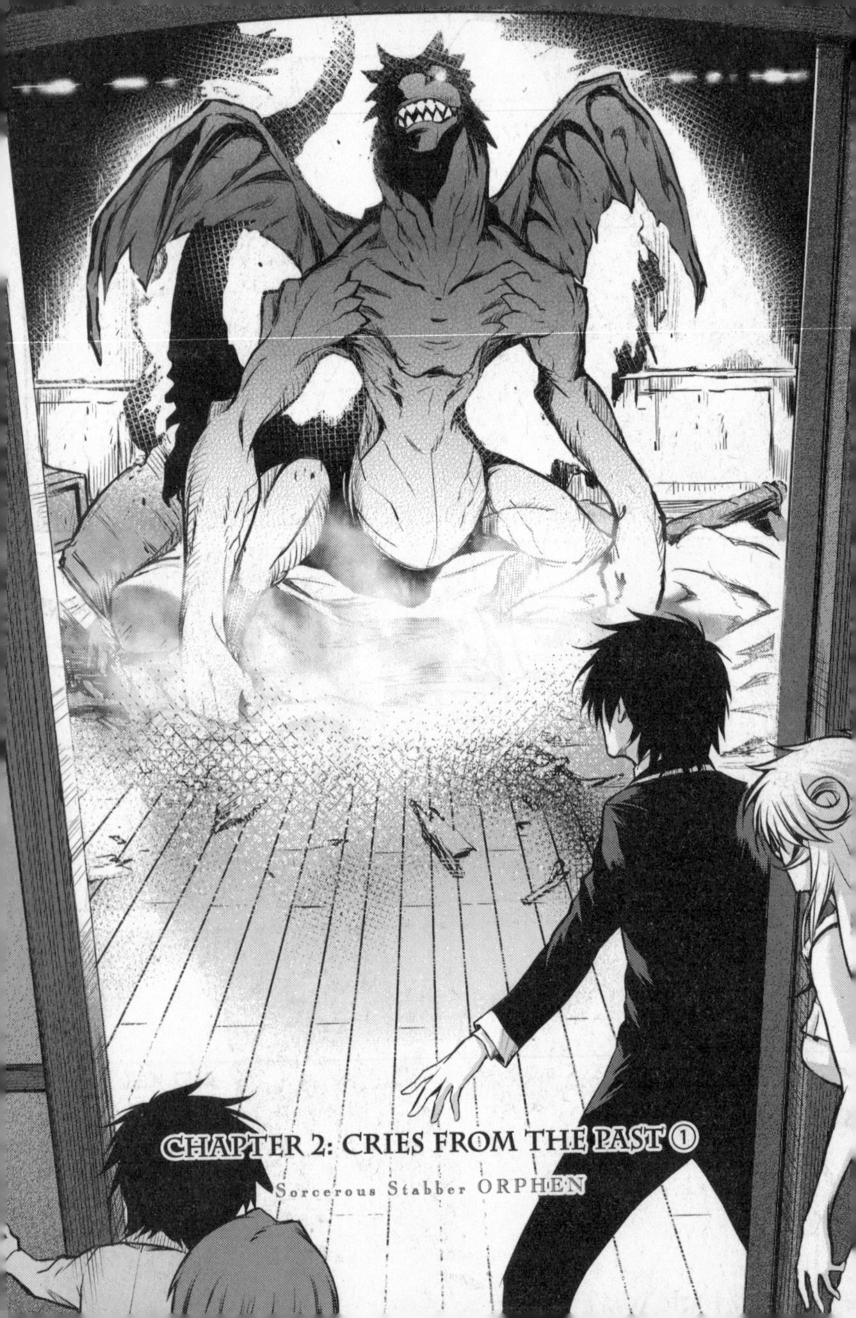
CHAPTER 2: CRIES FROM THE PAST ①
Sorcerous Stabber ORPHEN

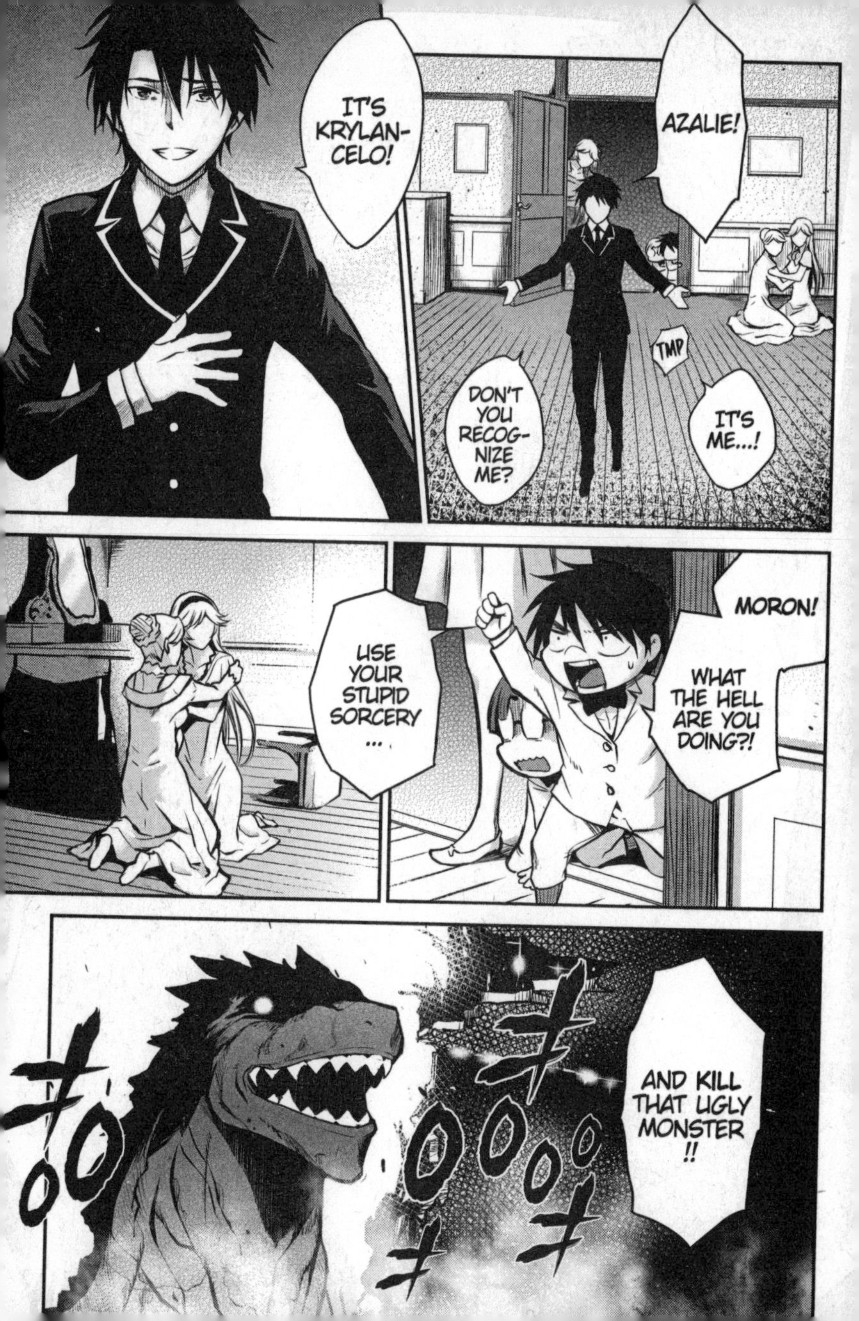
AZALIE!
TMP
IT'S ME...!
DON'T YOU RECOGNIZE ME?
IT'S KRYLANCELO!
MORON!
WHAT THE HELL ARE YOU DOING?!
USE YOUR STUPID SORCERY ...
AND KILL THAT UGLY MONSTER !!

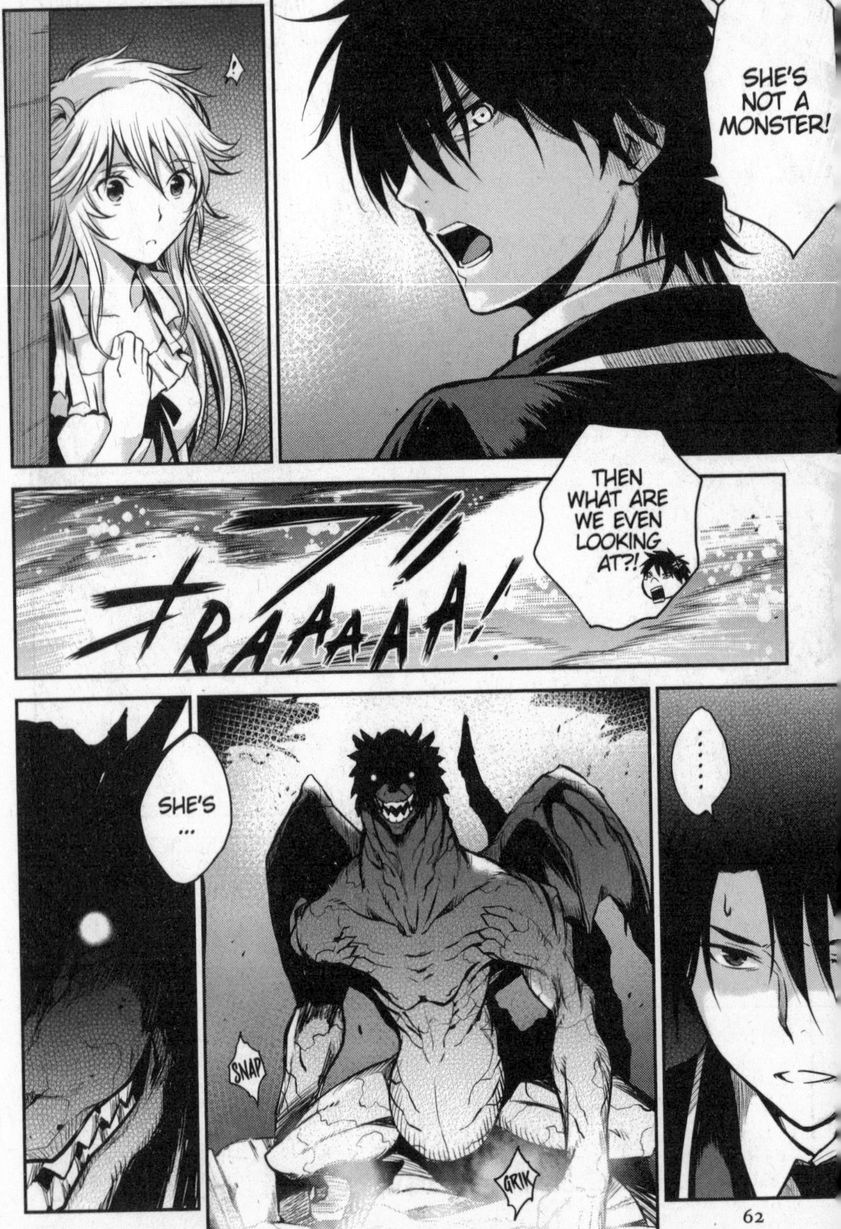
SHE'S NOT A MONSTER!
!
THEN WHAT ARE WE EVEN LOOKING AT?!
RAAAAA!
......
SNAP
GRIK
SHE'S ...

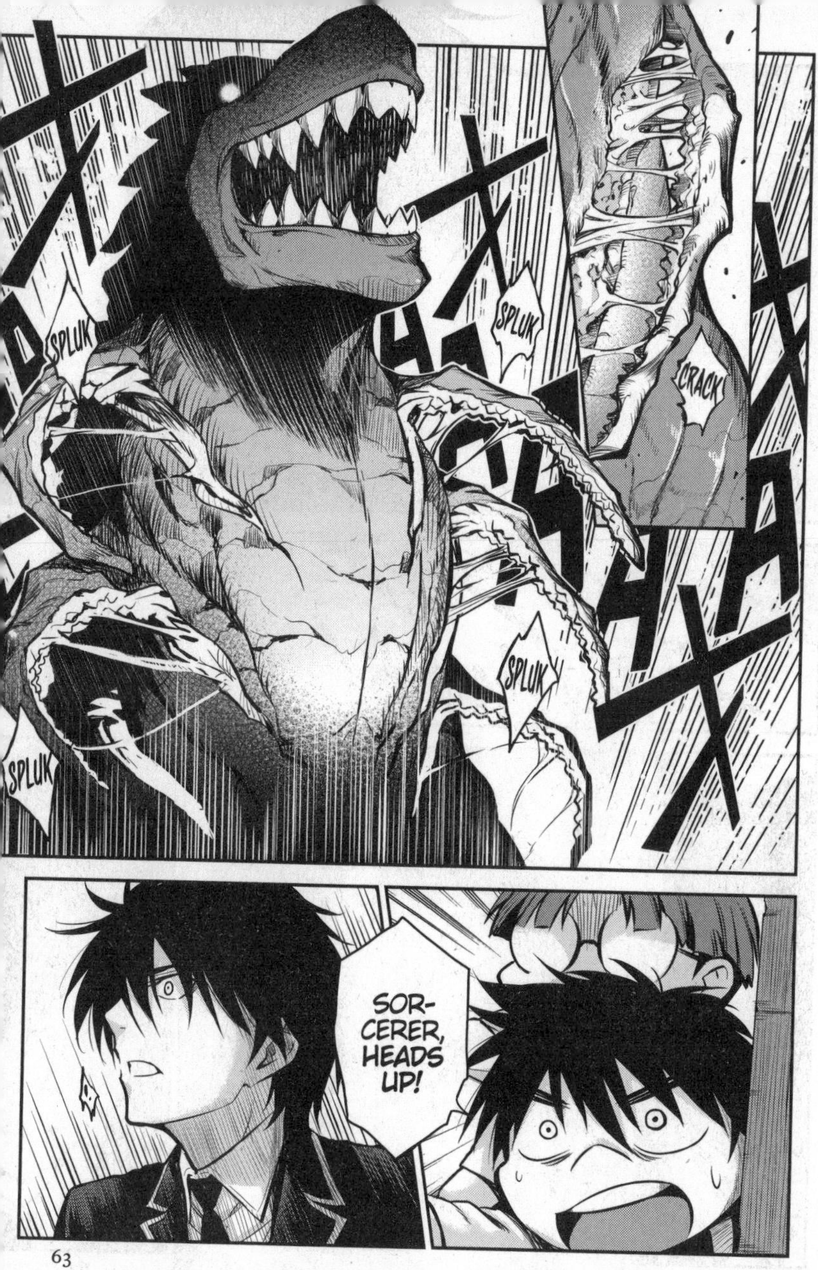
CRACK
SPLUK
SPLUK
SPLUK
SPLUK
SORCERER, HEADS UP!

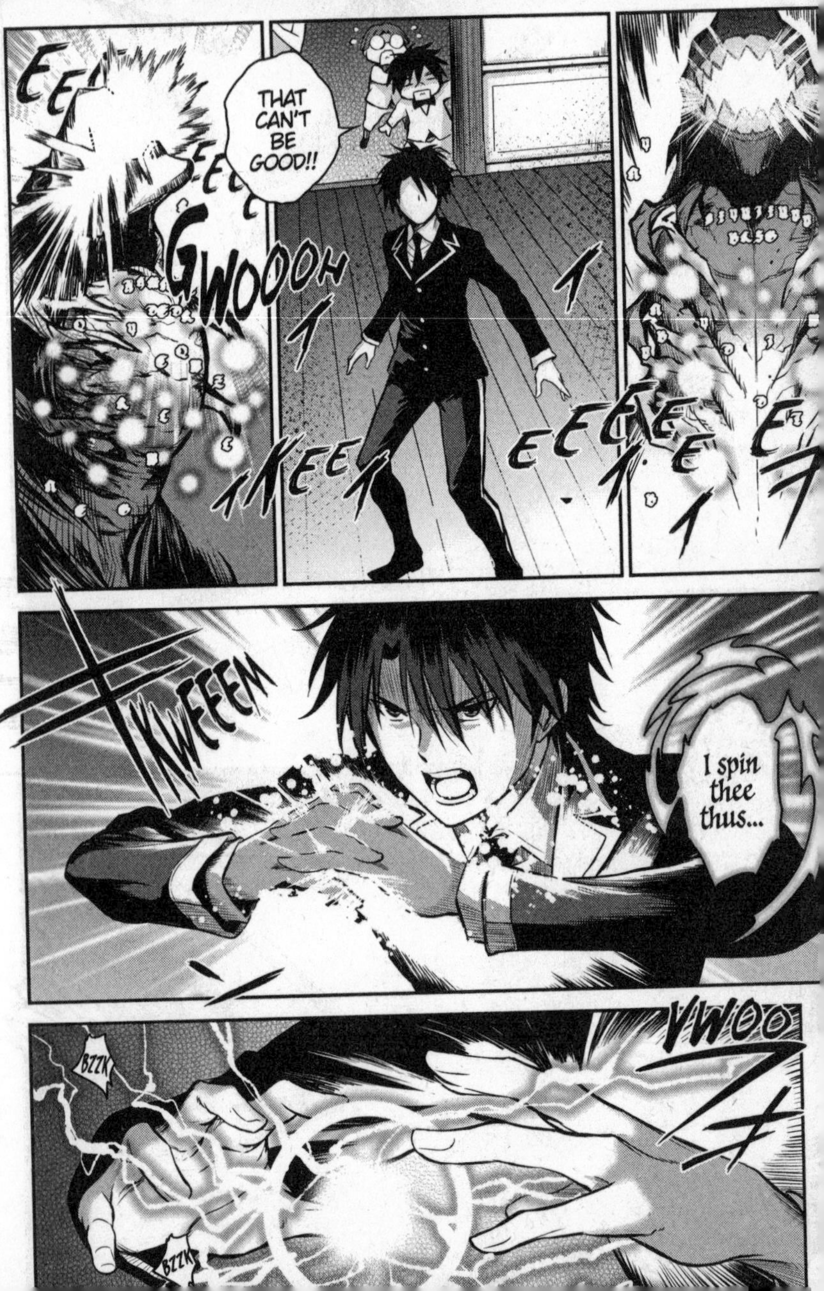
THAT CAN'T BE GOOD!!
GWOOOH
I spin thee thus...
KWEEEM
VWOO
BZZK
BZZK

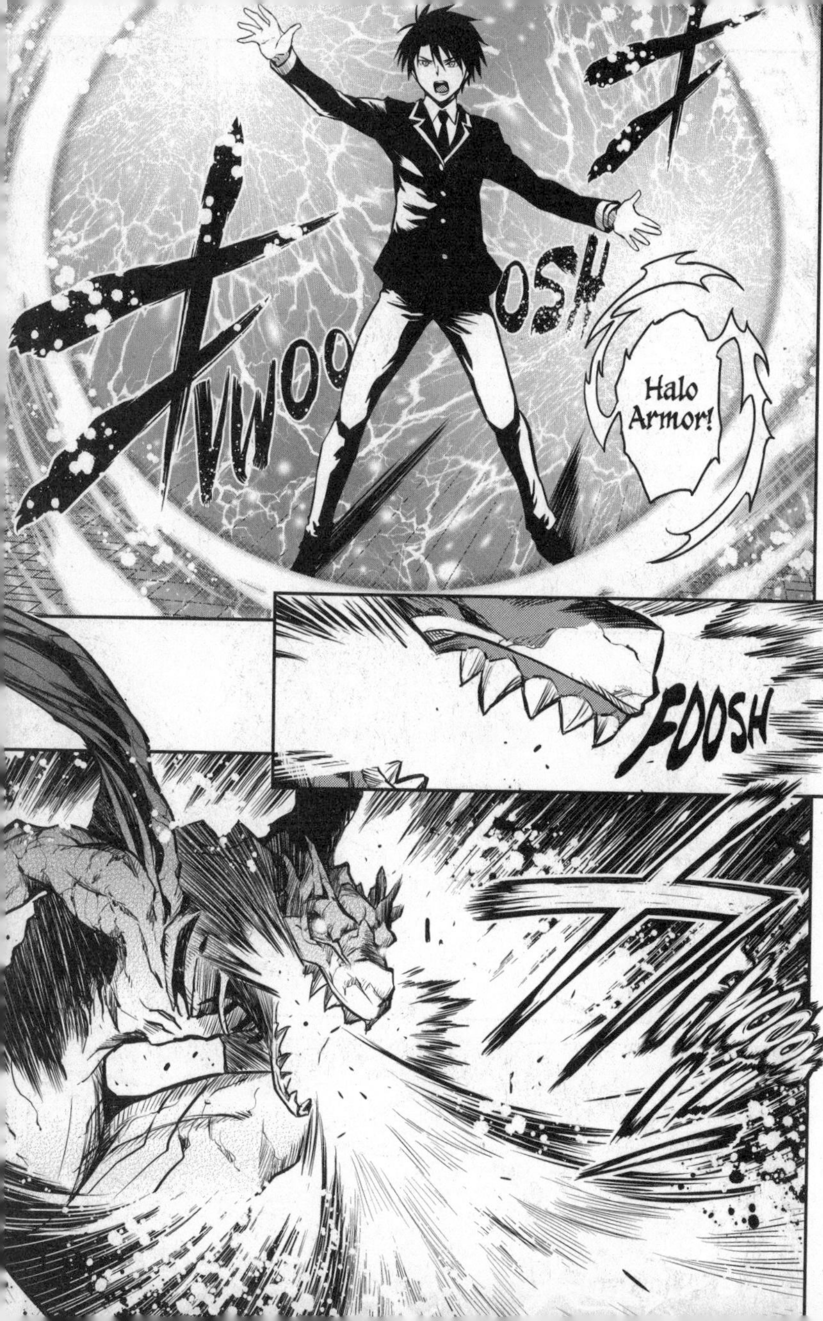
Halo Armor!
VWOOOSH
FOOSH

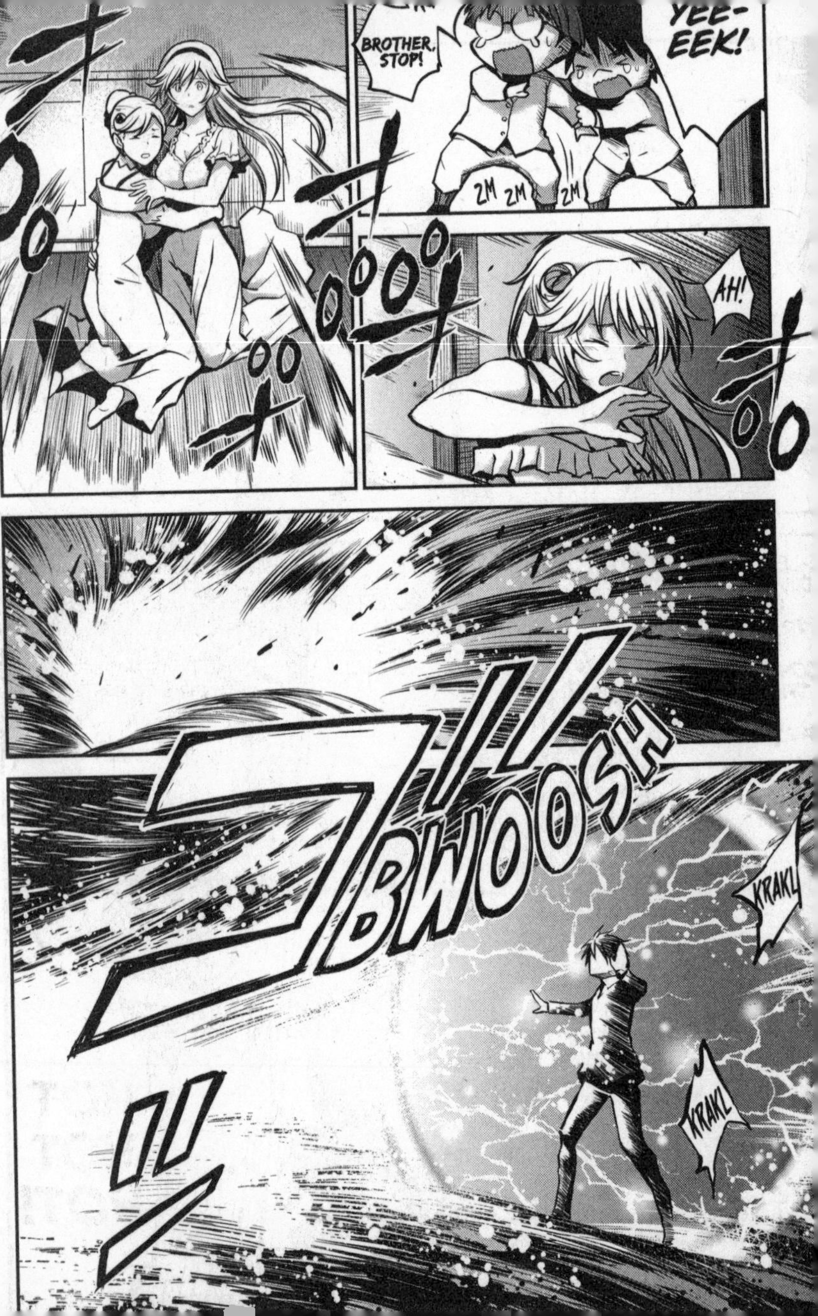
YEE-EEK!
BROTHER, STOP!
ZM ZM ZM
AH!
BWOOSH
KRAKL
KRAKL

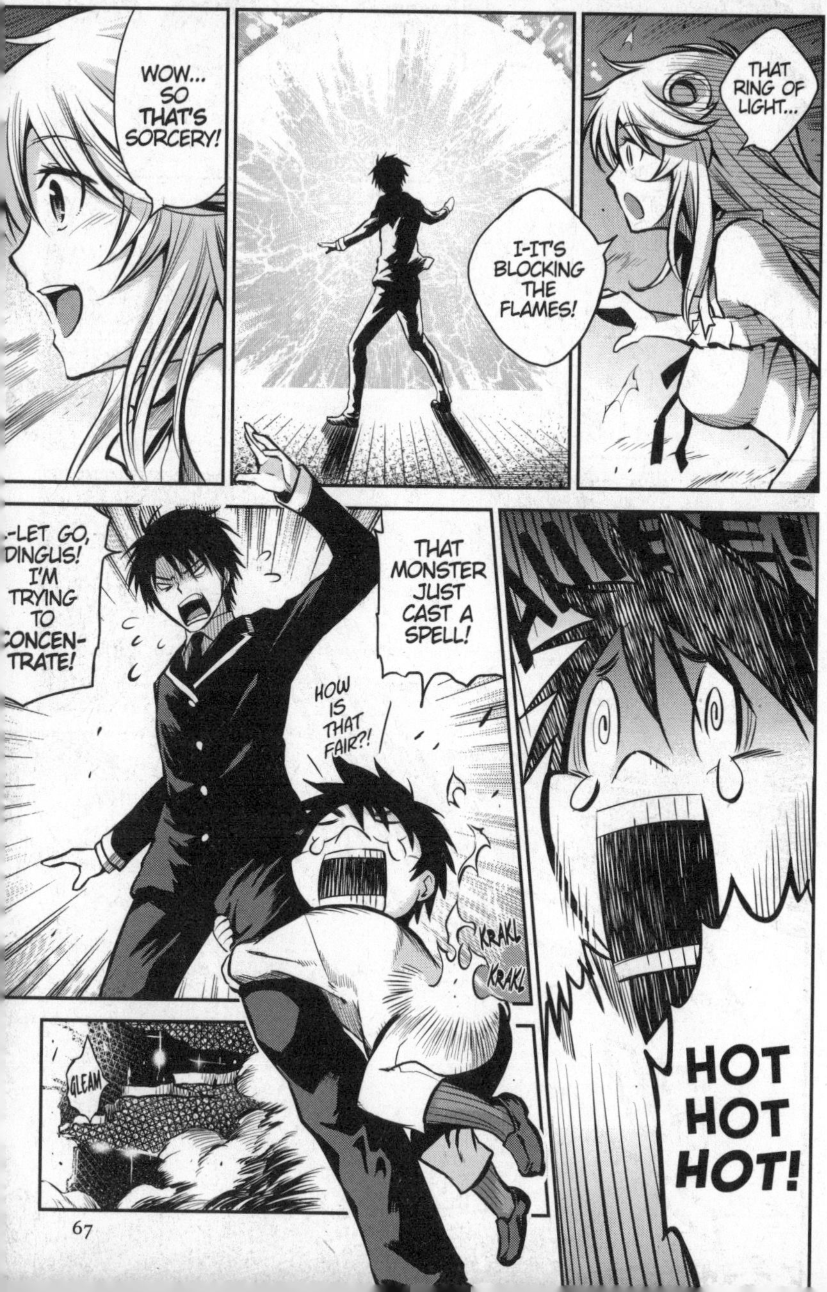
THAT RING OF LIGHT...
I-IT'S BLOCKING THE FLAMES!
WOW... SO THAT'S SORCERY!
HOT HOT HOT!
THAT MONSTER JUST CAST A SPELL!
HOW IS THAT FAIR?!
-LET GO, DINGUS! I'M TRYING TO CONCEN-TRATE!
KRAKL
KRAKL
GLEAM

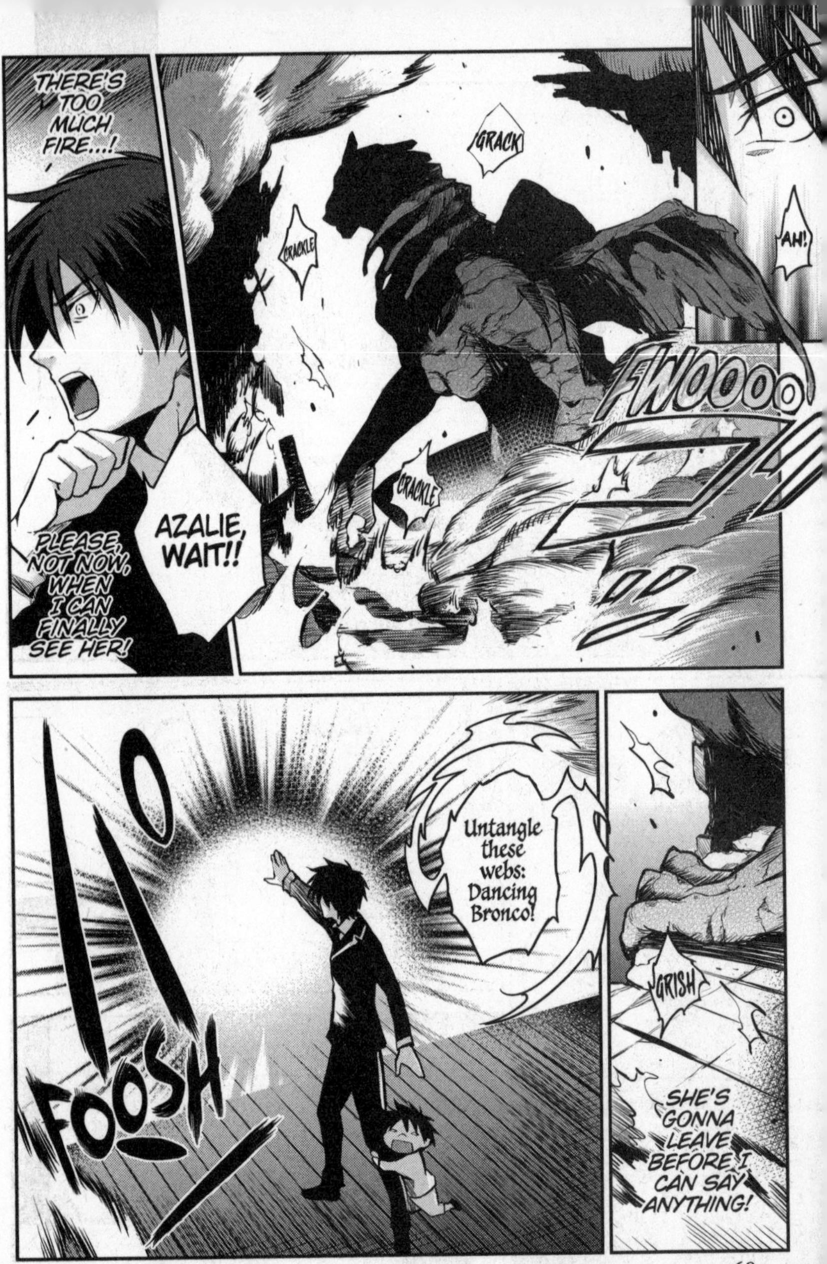
AH!
GRACK
FWOOOO
CRACKLE
CRACKLE
THERE'S TOO MUCH FIRE...!
AZALIE, WAIT!!
PLEASE, NOT NOW, WHEN I CAN FINALLY SEE HER!
GRISH
SHE'S GONNA LEAVE BEFORE I CAN SAY ANYTHING!
Untangle these webs: Dancing Bronco!
FOOSH

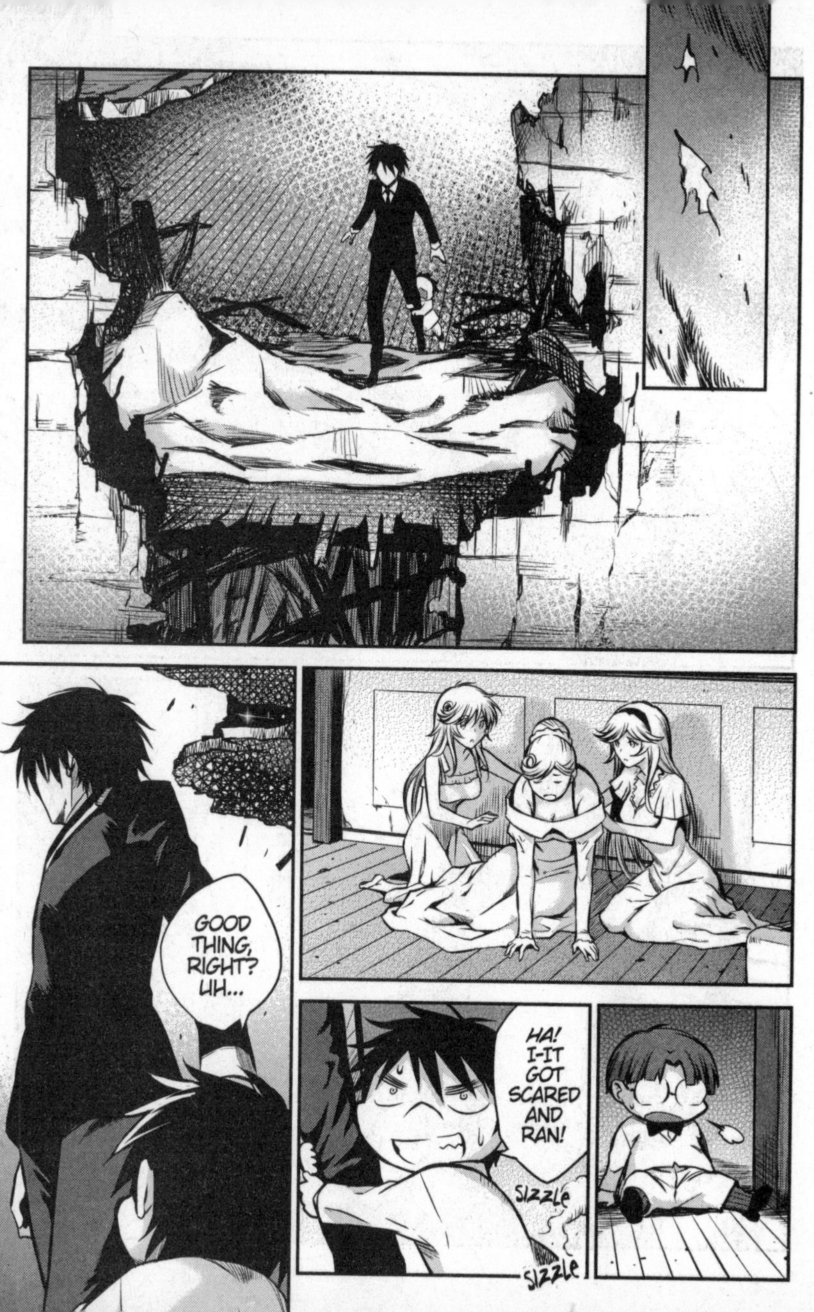
HA! I-IT GOT SCARED AND RAN!
SIZZLE
SIZZLE
GOOD THING, RIGHT? UH...

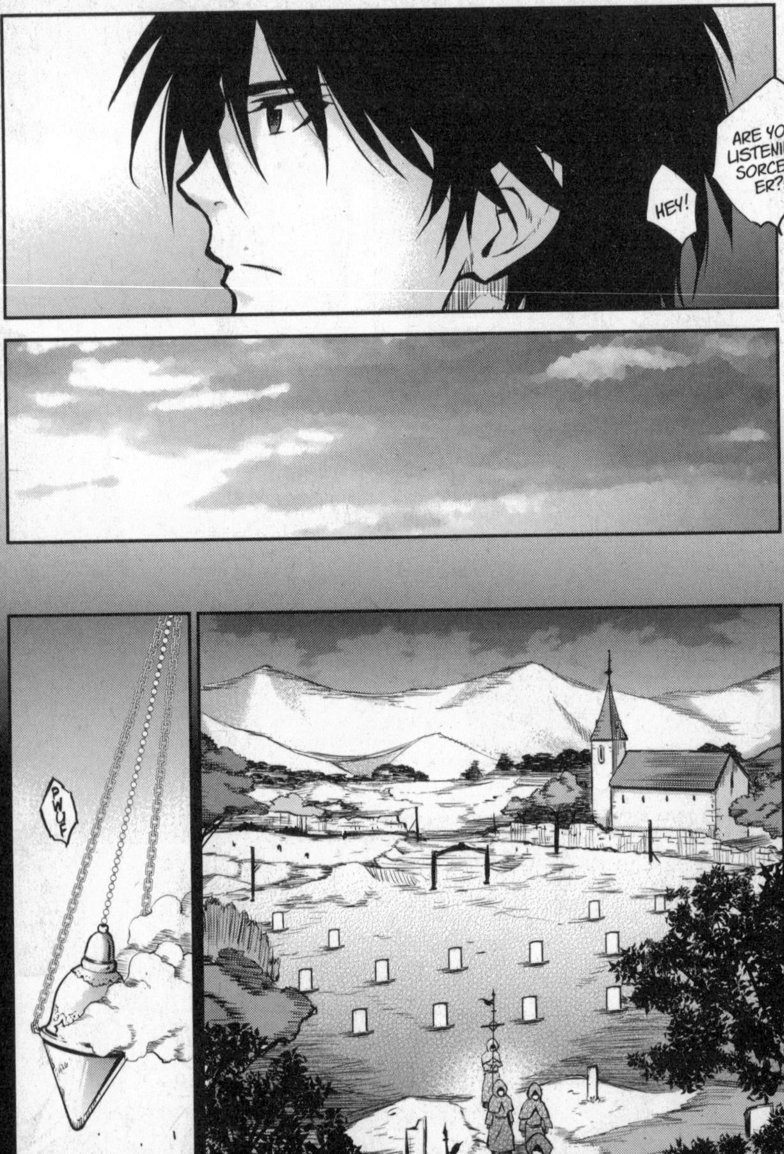
ARE YOU LISTENING, SORCERER?!
HEY!
PWUF

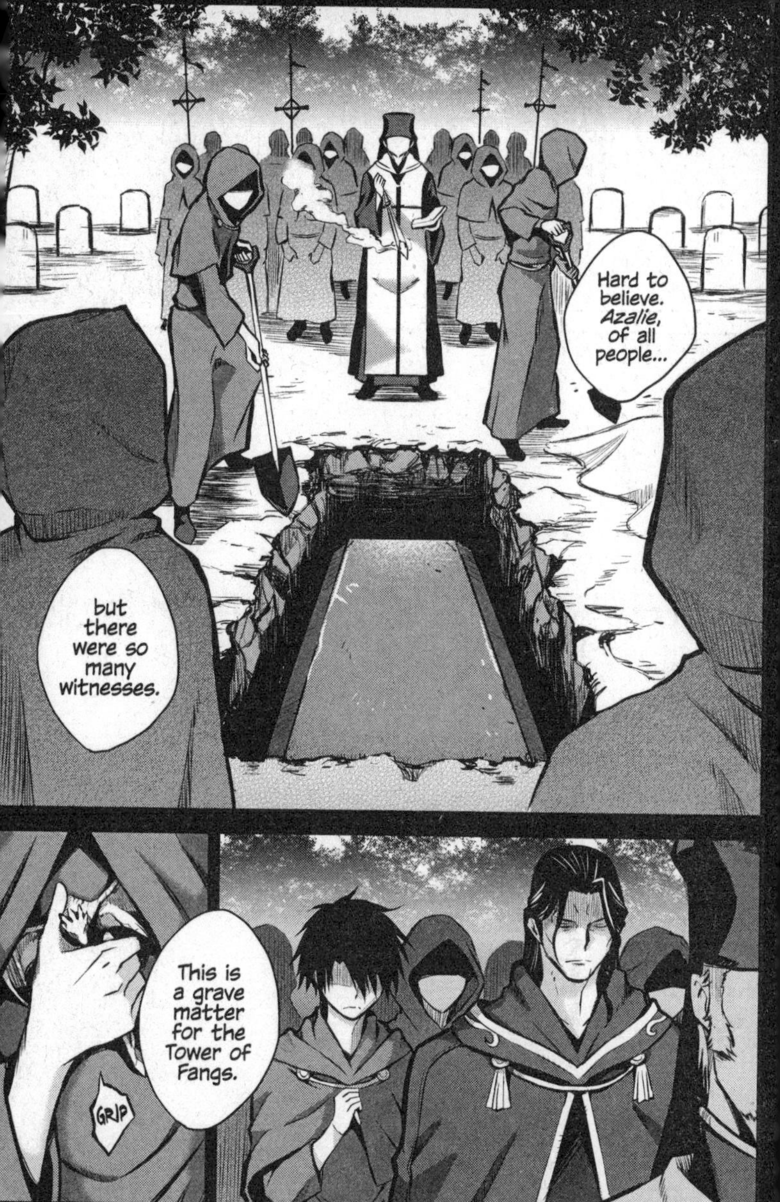
Hard to believe. Azalie, of all people...
but there were so many witnesses.
This is a grave matter for the Tower of Fangs.
GRIP

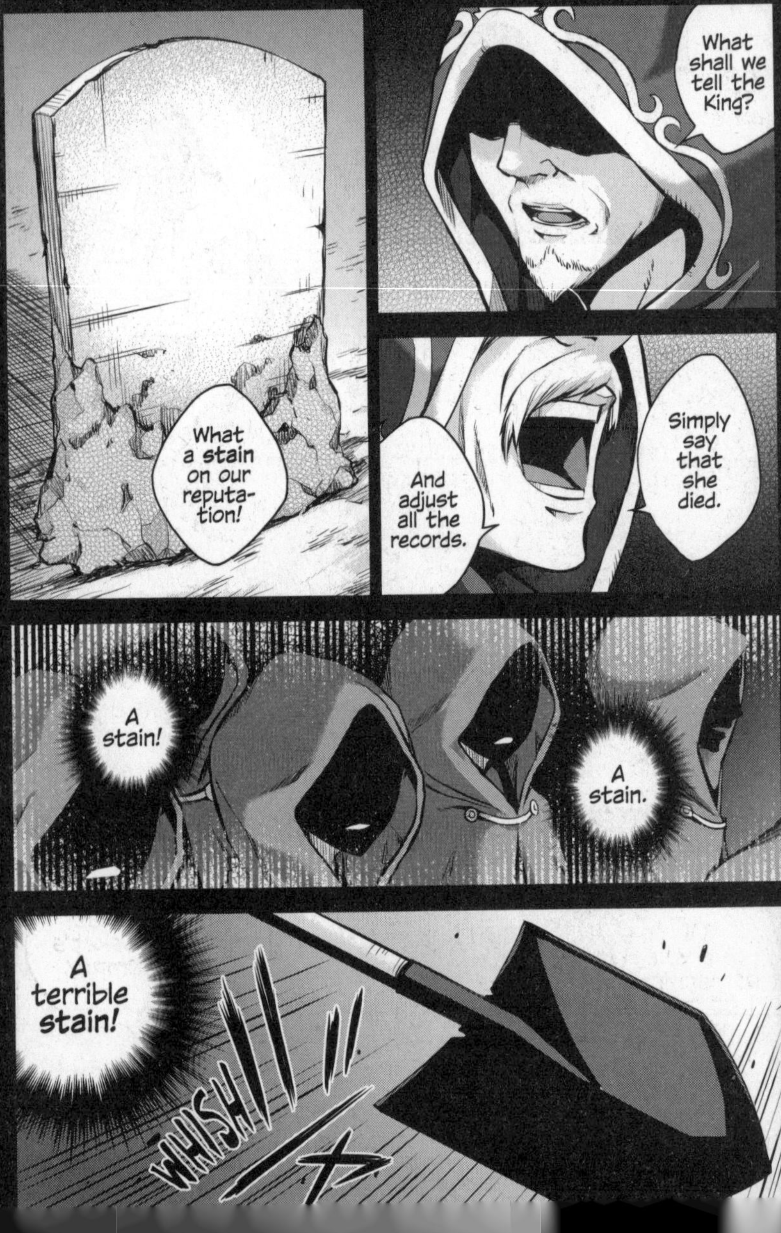
What shall we tell the King?
Simply say that she died.
And adjust all the records.
What a stain on our reputation!
A stain.
A stain!
A terrible stain!
WHISH!!

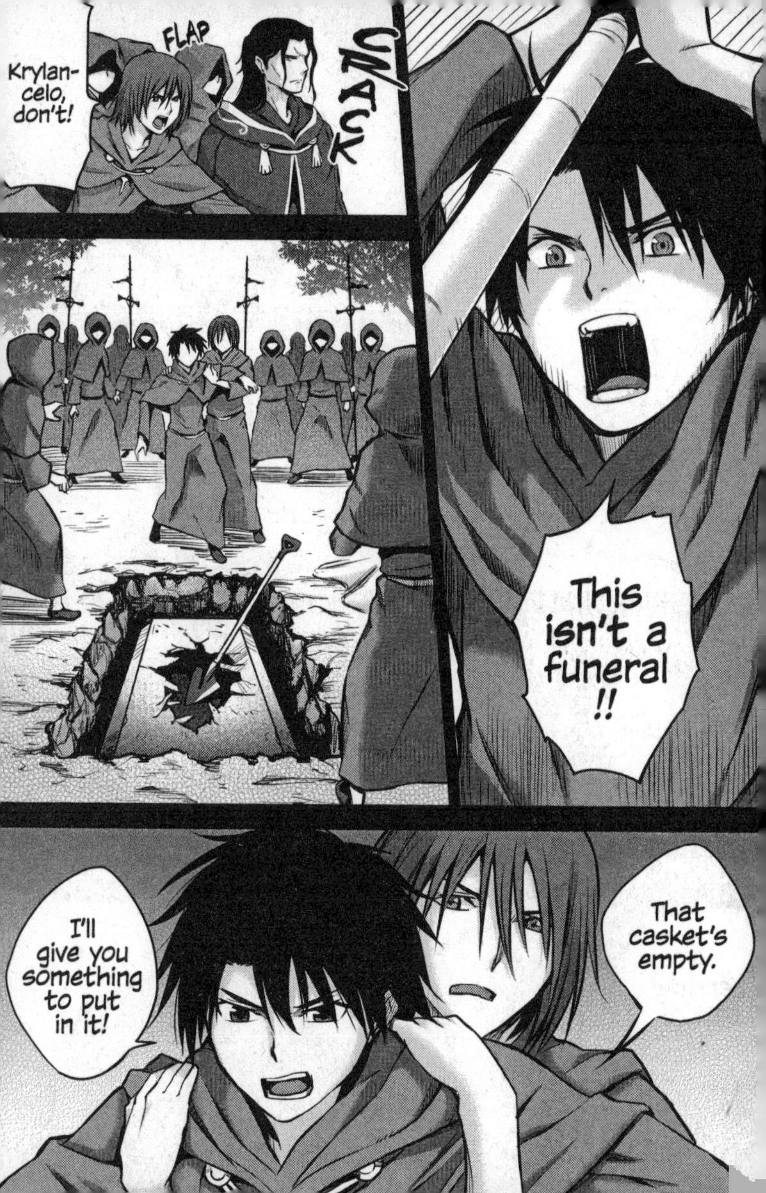
This isn't a funeral !!
CRACK
FLAP
Krylan-celo, don't!
That casket's empty.
I'll give you something to put in it!

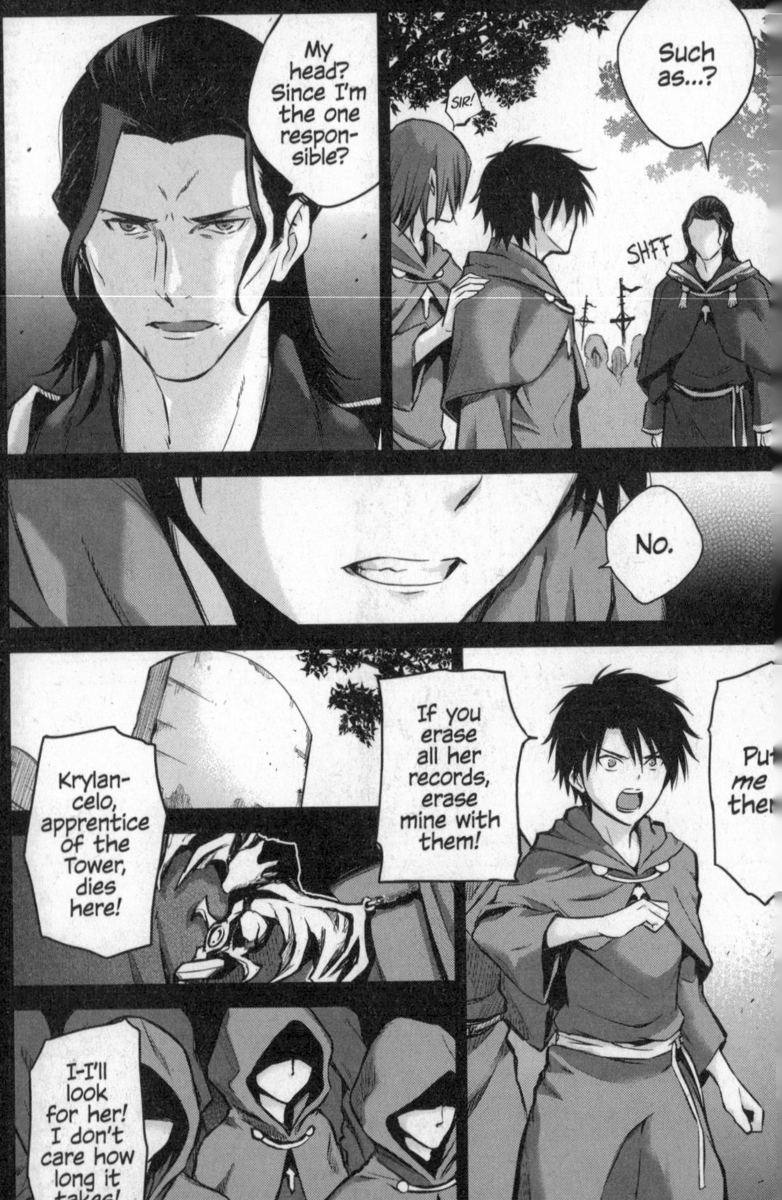
Such as...?
SIR!
SHFF
My head? Since I'm the one respon-sible?
No.
If you erase all her records, erase mine with them!
Krylan-celo, apprentice of the Tower, dies here!
I-I'll look for her! I don't care how long it takes!

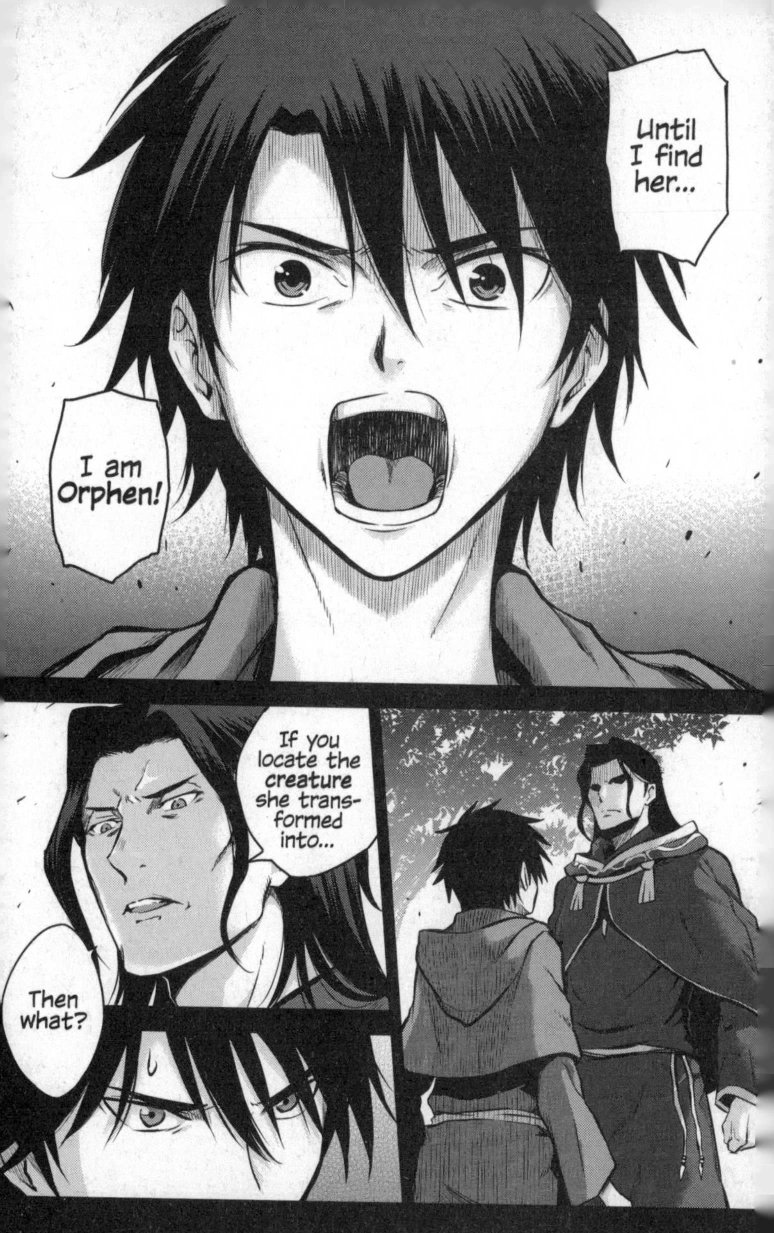
Until I find her...
I am Orphen!
If you locate the creature she trans-formed into...
Then what?

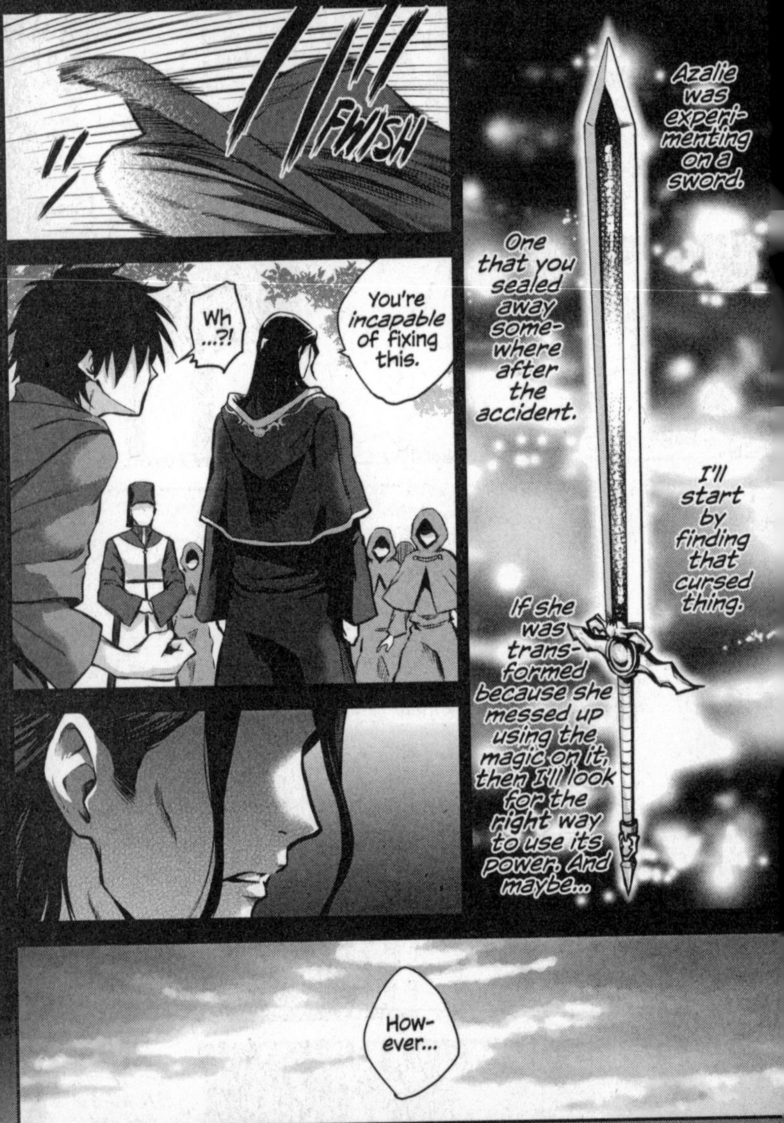
Azalie was experimenting on a sword.
One that you sealed away somewhere after the accident.
I'll start by finding that cursed thing.
If she was transformed because she messed up using the magic on it, then I'll look for the right way to use its power. And maybe...
FWISH
You're incapable of fixing this.
Wh ...?!
However...

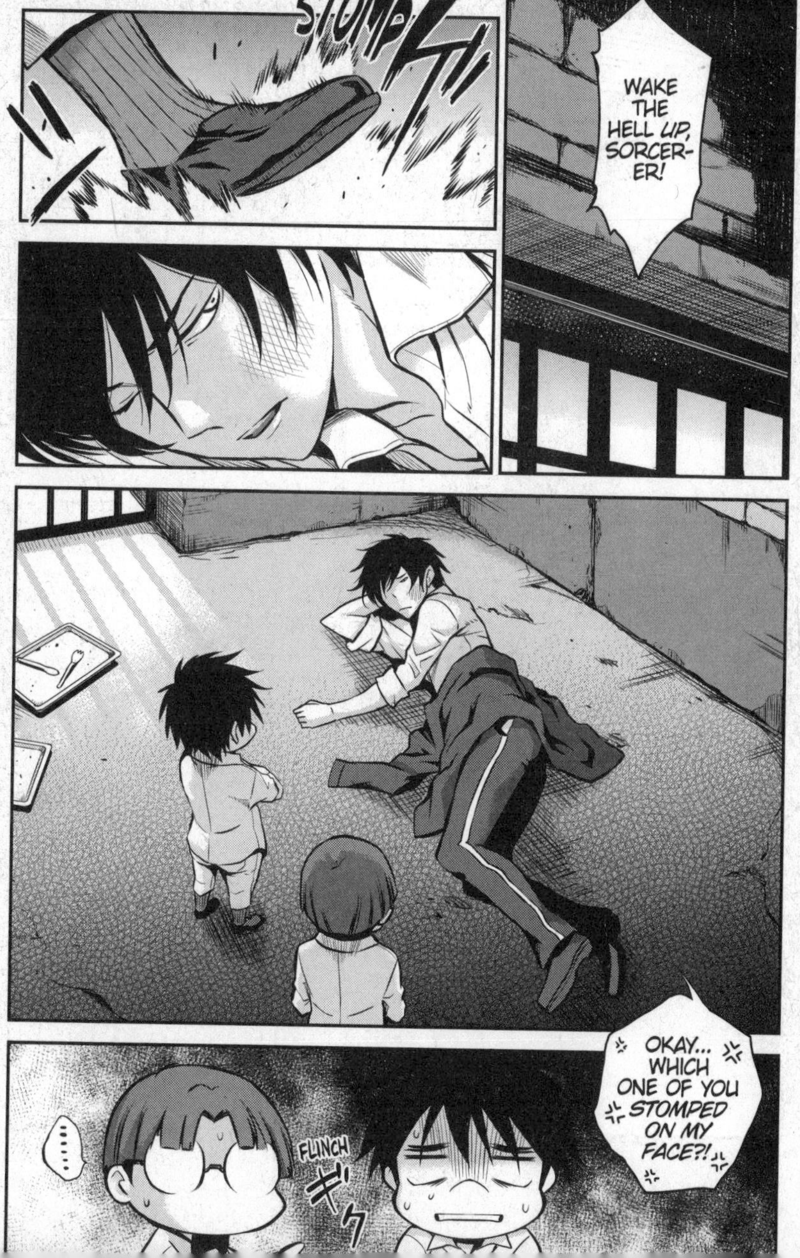
WAKE THE HELL UP, SORCERER-ER!
STOMP
OKAY... WHICH ONE OF YOU STOMPED ON MY FACE?!
FLINCH
ギク
......

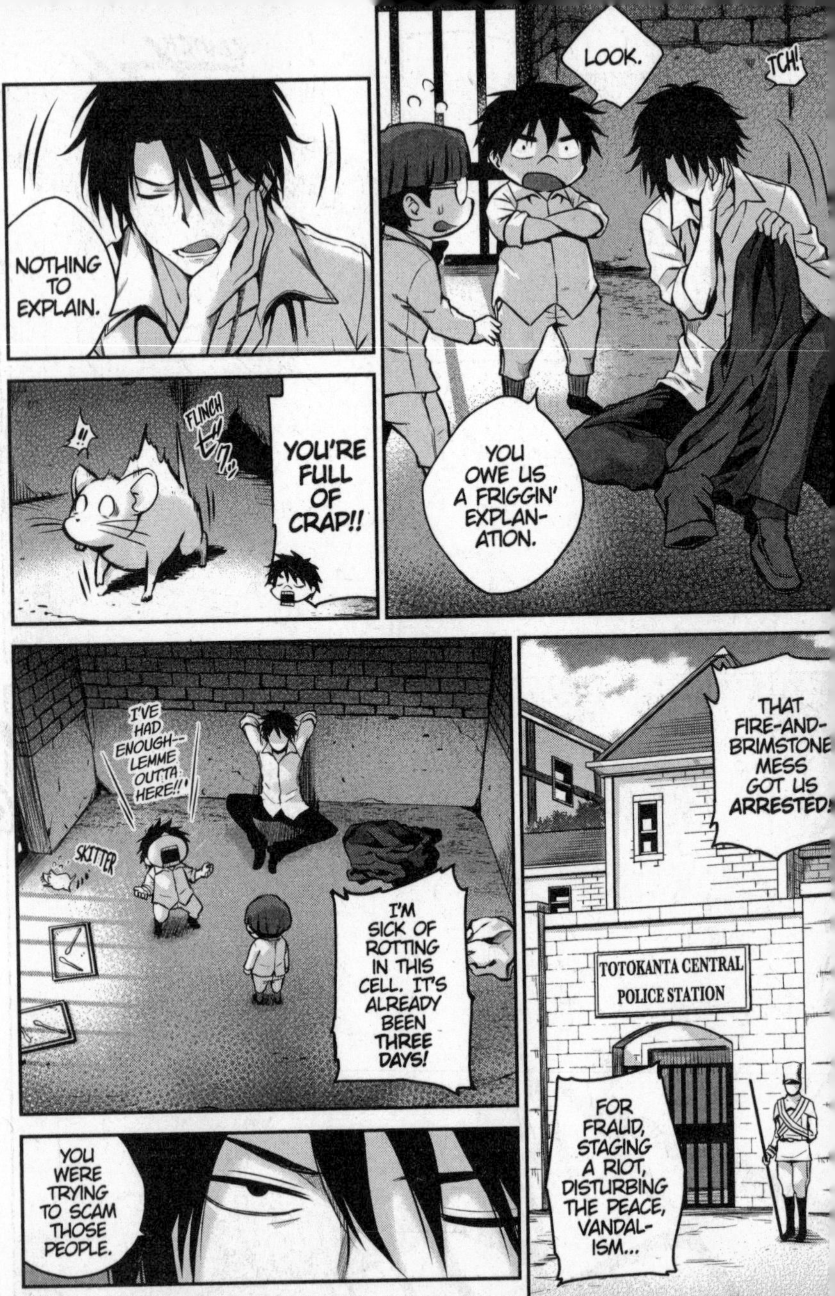
LOOK.
TCH!
YOU OWE US A FRIGGIN' EXPLANATION.
NOTHING TO EXPLAIN.
YOU'RE FULL OF CRAP!!
FLINCH
!!
THAT FIRE-AND-BRIMSTONE MESS GOT US ARRESTED!
TOTOKANTA CENTRAL POLICE STATION
FOR FRAUD, STAGING A RIOT, DISTURBING THE PEACE, VANDALISM...
I'M SICK OF ROTTING IN THIS CELL. IT'S ALREADY BEEN THREE DAYS!
I'VE HAD ENOUGH-- LEMME OUTTA HERE!!
SKITTER
YOU WERE TRYING TO SCAM THOSE PEOPLE.

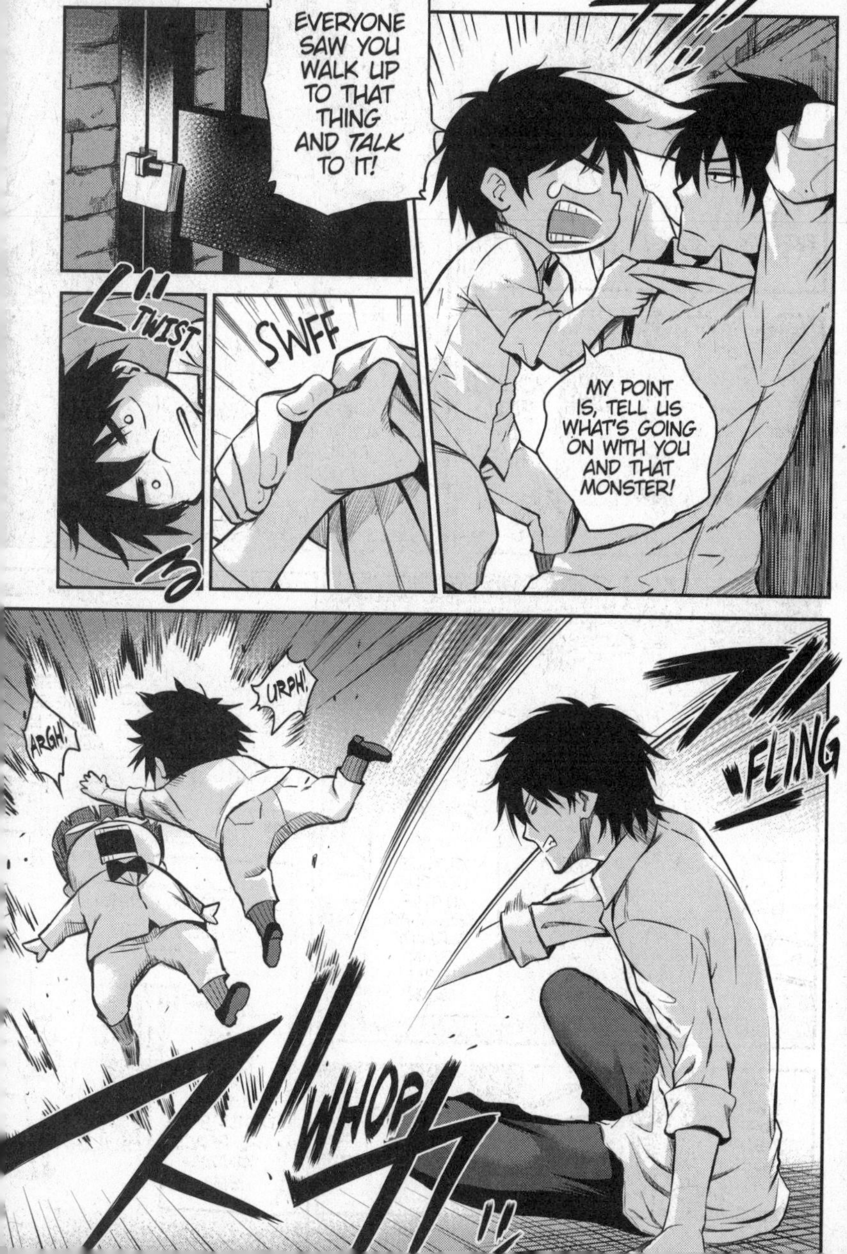
CLUTCH
MY POINT IS, TELL US WHAT'S GOING ON WITH YOU AND THAT MONSTER!
EVERYONE SAW YOU WALK UP TO THAT THING AND TALK TO IT!
SWFF
TWIST
FLING
URPH!
ARGH!
WHOP

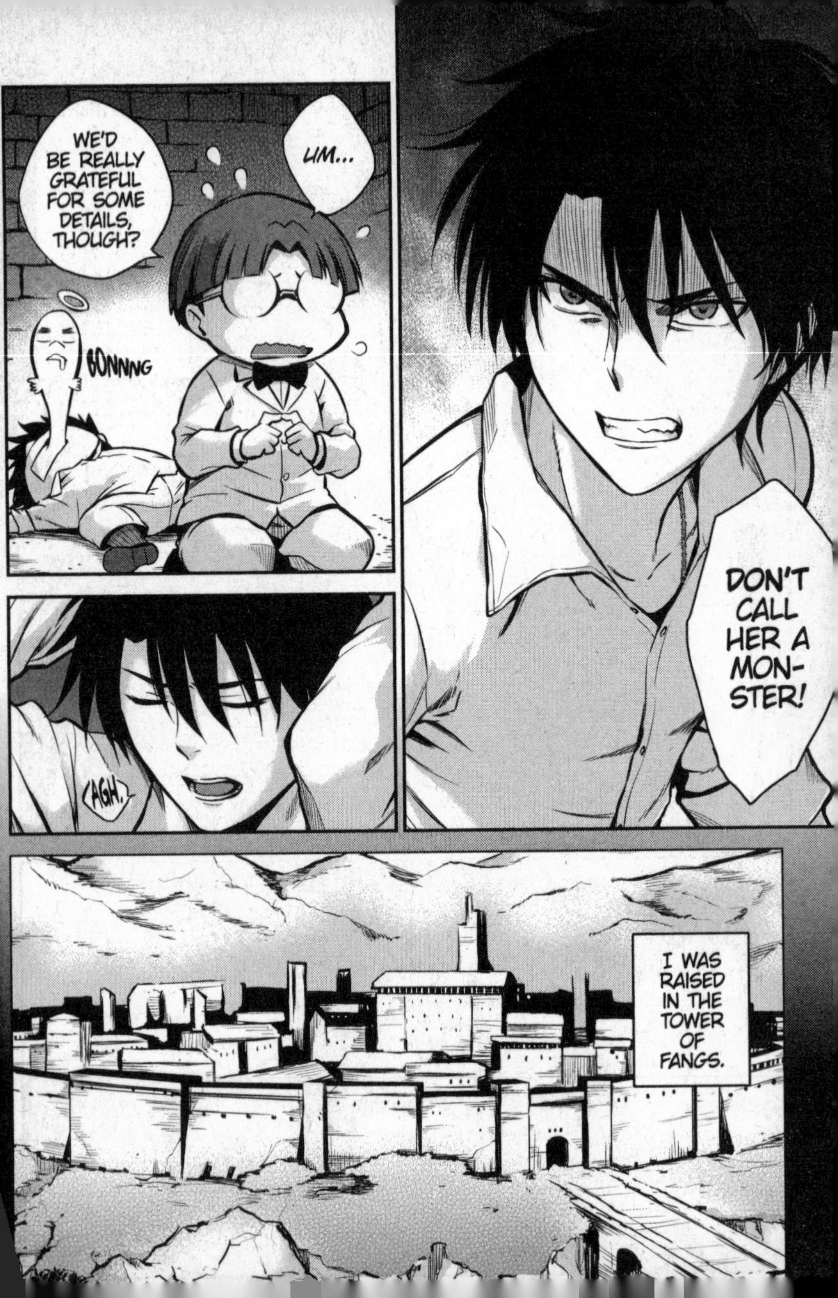

DON'T CALL HER A MON-STER!
UM...
WE'D BE REALLY GRATEFUL FOR SOME DETAILS, THOUGH?
BONNNG
AGH.
I WAS RAISED IN THE TOWER OF FANGS.

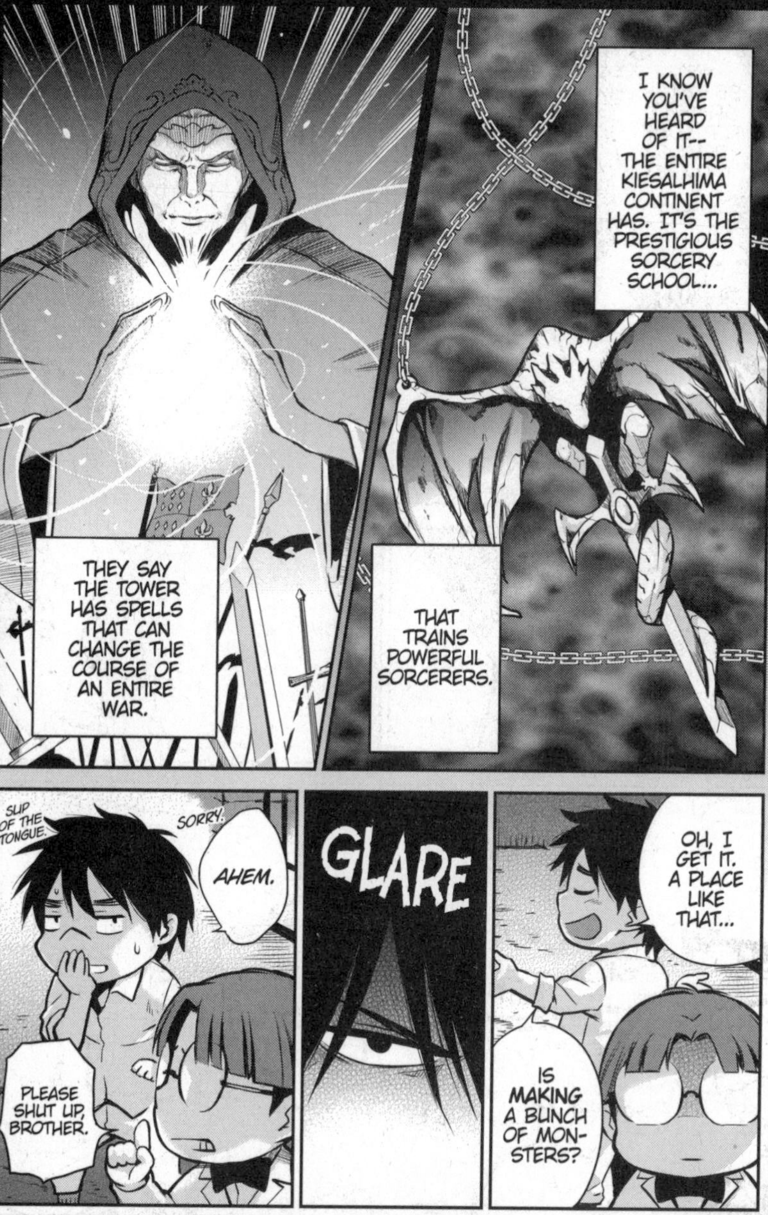
I KNOW YOU'VE HEARD OF IT-- THE ENTIRE KIESALHIMA CONTINENT HAS. IT'S THE PRESTIGIOUS SORCERY SCHOOL...
THAT TRAINS POWERFUL SORCERERS.
THEY SAY THE TOWER HAS SPELLS THAT CAN CHANGE THE COURSE OF AN ENTIRE WAR.
OH, I GET IT. A PLACE LIKE THAT...
IS MAKING A BUNCH OF MON-STERS?
GLARE
SORRY.
AHEM.
SLIP OF THE TONGUE.
PLEASE SHUT UP, BROTHER.

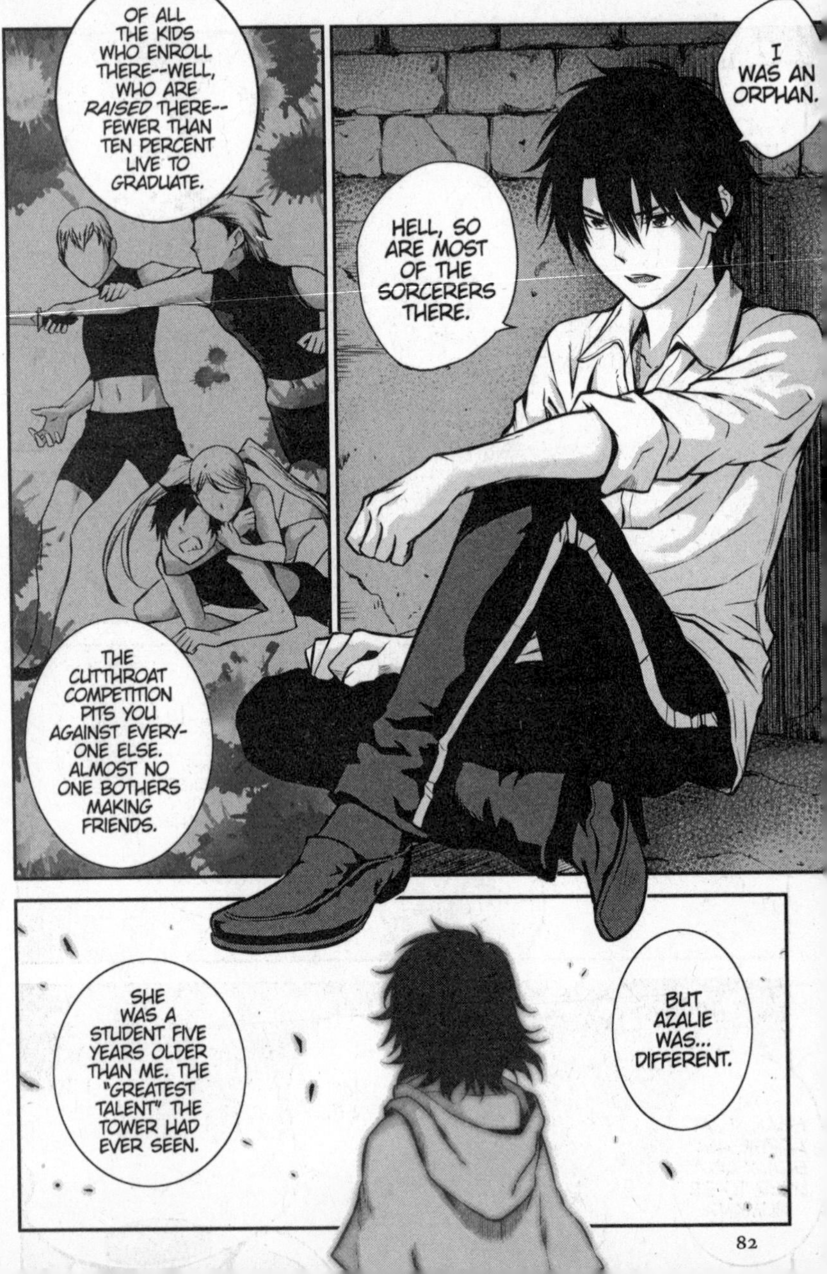
I WAS AN ORPHAN.
HELL, SO ARE MOST OF THE SORCERERS THERE.
OF ALL THE KIDS WHO ENROLL THERE--WELL, WHO ARE *RAISED* THERE--FEWER THAN TEN PERCENT LIVE TO GRADUATE.
THE CUTTHROAT COMPETITION PITS YOU AGAINST EVERY-ONE ELSE. ALMOST NO ONE BOTHERS MAKING FRIENDS.
BUT AZALIE WAS... DIFFERENT.
SHE WAS A STUDENT FIVE YEARS OLDER THAN ME. THE "GREATEST TALENT" THE TOWER HAD EVER SEEN.

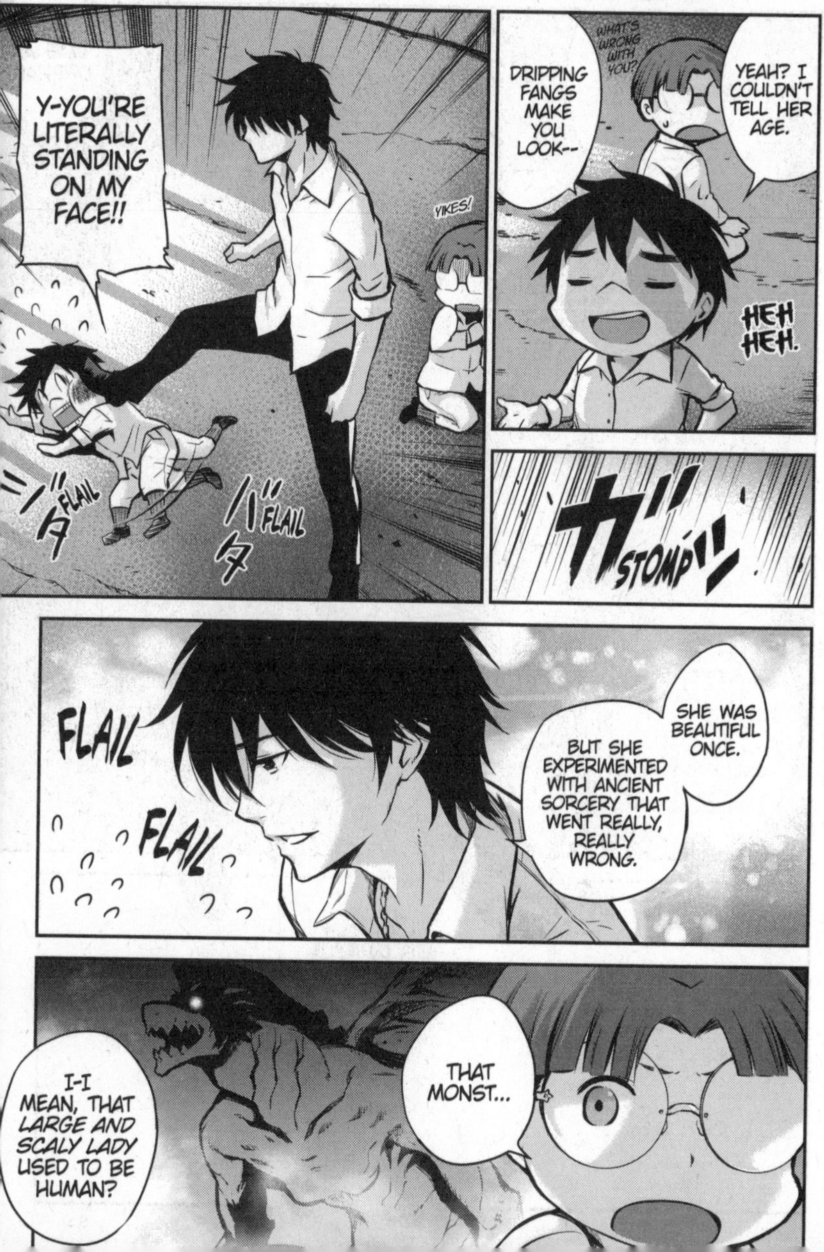
YEAH? I COULDN'T TELL HER AGE.
WHAT'S WRONG WITH YOU?
DRIPPING FANGS MAKE YOU LOOK--
HEH HEH.
ガッ
STOMP
YIKES!
Y-YOU'RE LITERALLY STANDING ON MY FACE!!
バタ FLAIL
ジタ FLAIL
SHE WAS BEAUTIFUL ONCE.
BUT SHE EXPERIMENTED WITH ANCIENT SORCERY THAT WENT REALLY, REALLY WRONG.
FLAIL
FLAIL
THAT MONST...
I-I MEAN, THAT *LARGE AND SCALY LADY* USED TO BE HUMAN?

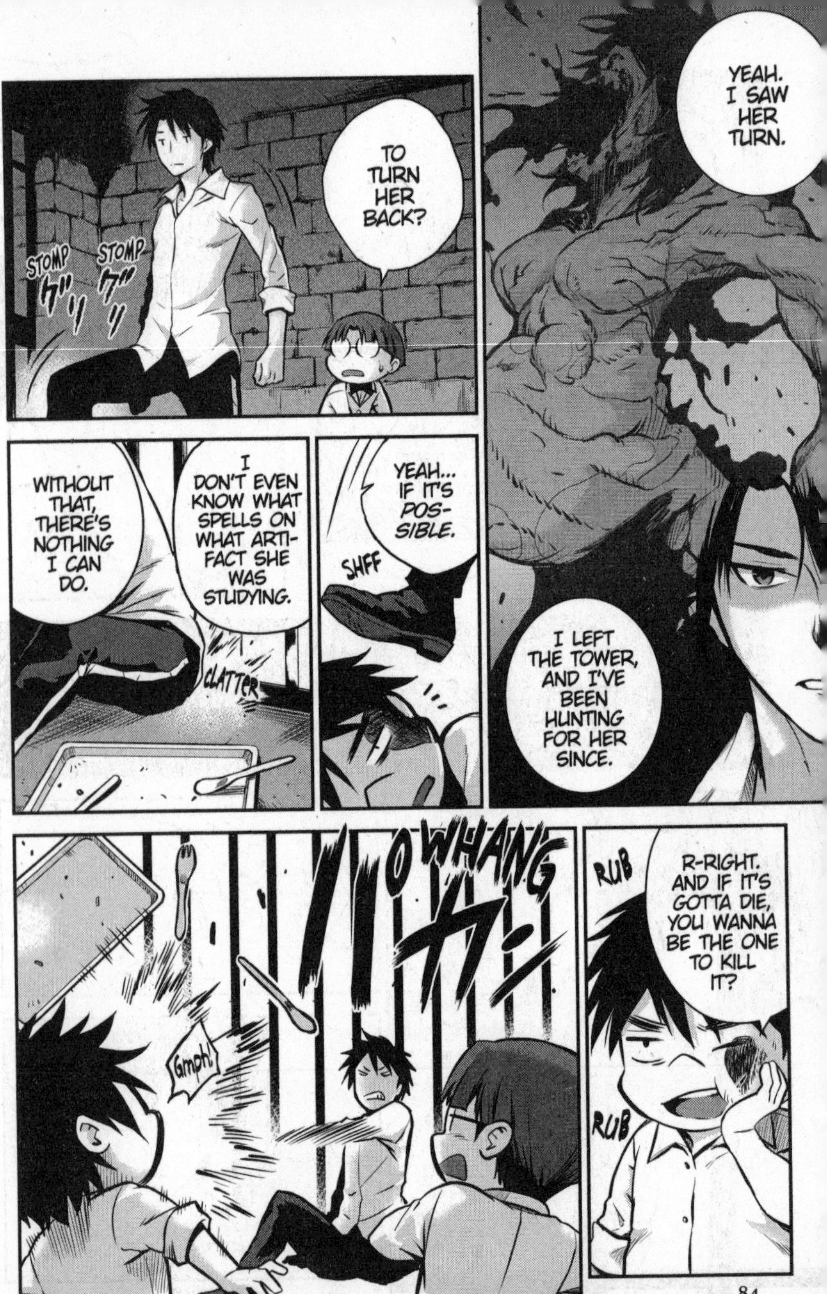
YEAH. I SAW HER TURN.
I LEFT THE TOWER, AND I'VE BEEN HUNTING FOR HER SINCE.
STOMP
STOMP
TO TURN HER BACK?
YEAH... IF IT'S POS-SIBLE.
SHFF
I DON'T EVEN KNOW WHAT SPELLS ON WHAT ARTI-FACT SHE WAS STUDYING.
WITHOUT THAT, THERE'S NOTHING I CAN DO.
CLATTER
RUB
R-RIGHT. AND IF IT'S GOTTA DIE, YOU WANNA BE THE ONE TO KILL IT?
RUB
WHANG
Gmph!

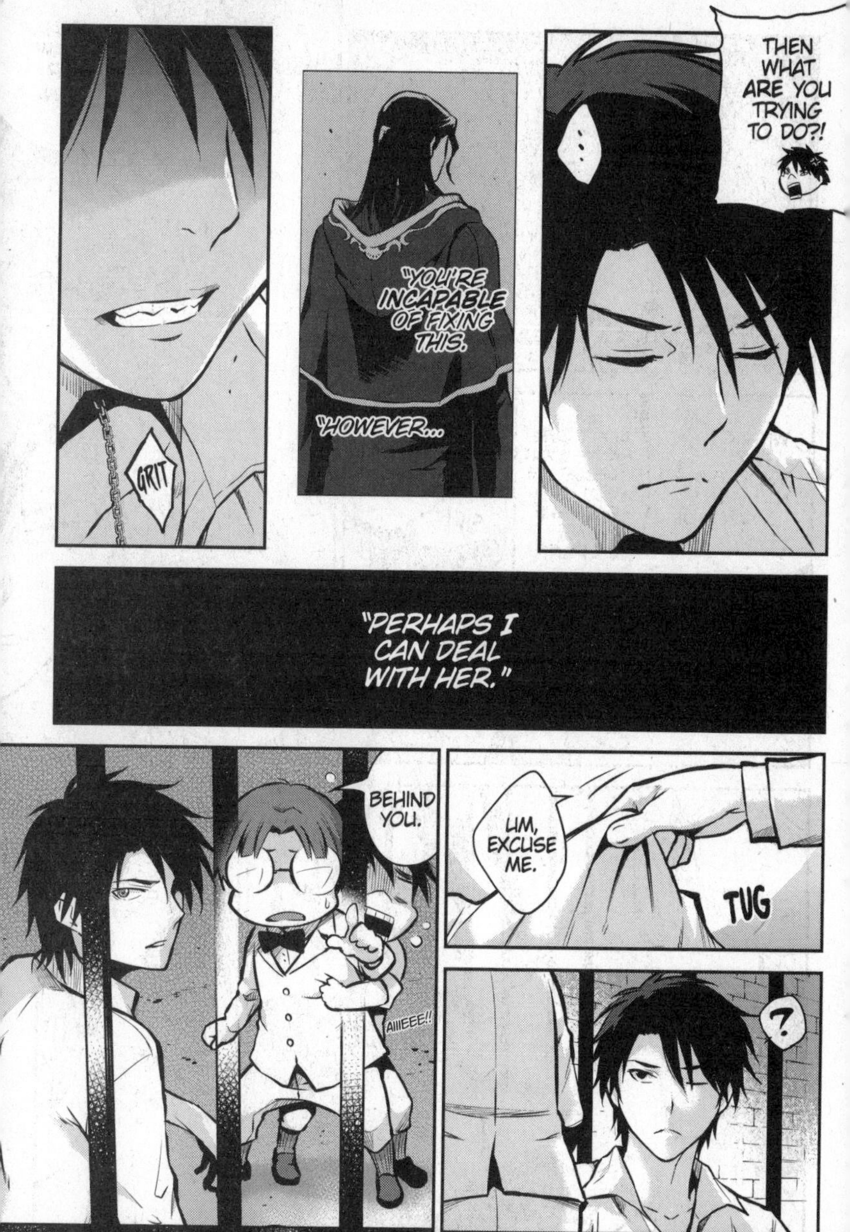
THEN WHAT ARE YOU TRYING TO DO?!
"YOU'RE INCAPABLE OF FIXING THIS.
"HOWEVER...
GRIT
"PERHAPS I CAN DEAL WITH HER."
UM, EXCUSE ME.
TUG
?
BEHIND YOU.
AIIIEEE!!

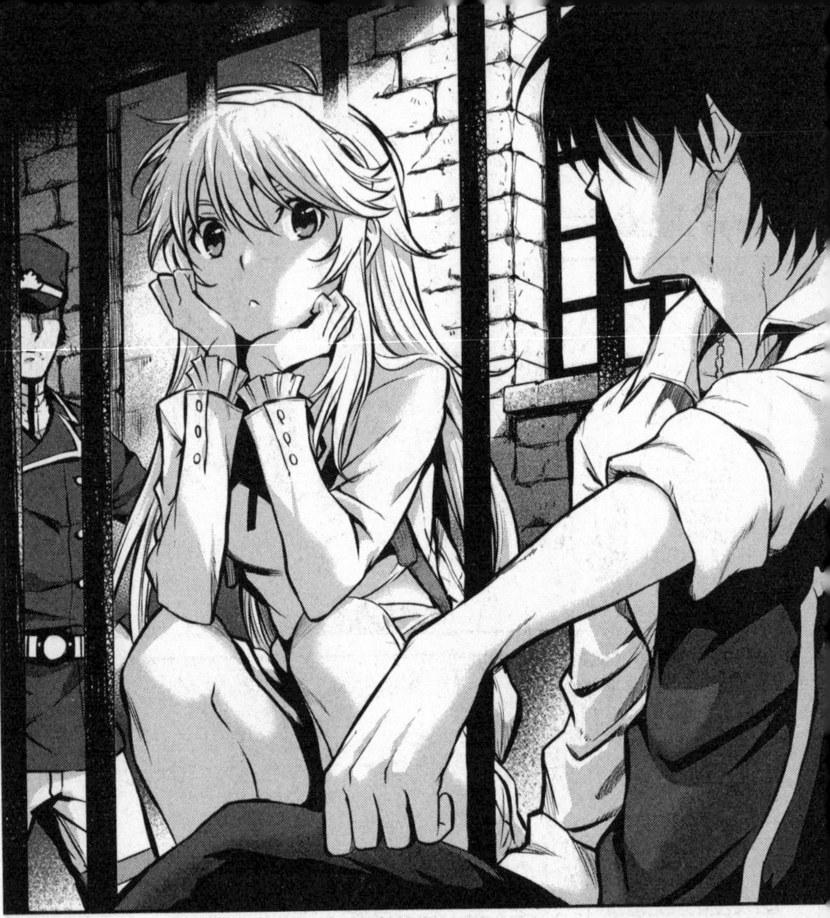

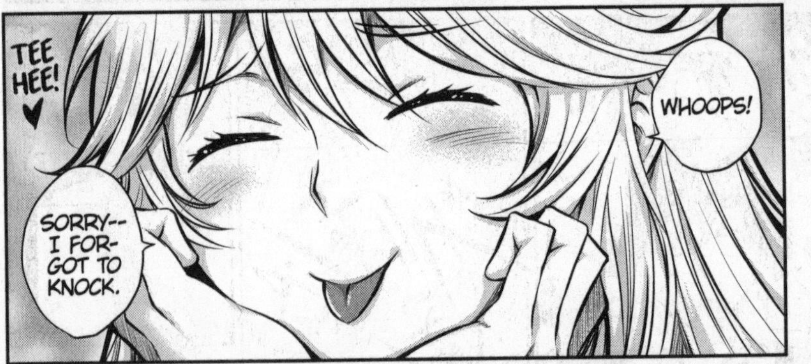
WHOOPS!
TEE HEE!
SORRY-- I FOR-GOT TO KNOCK.

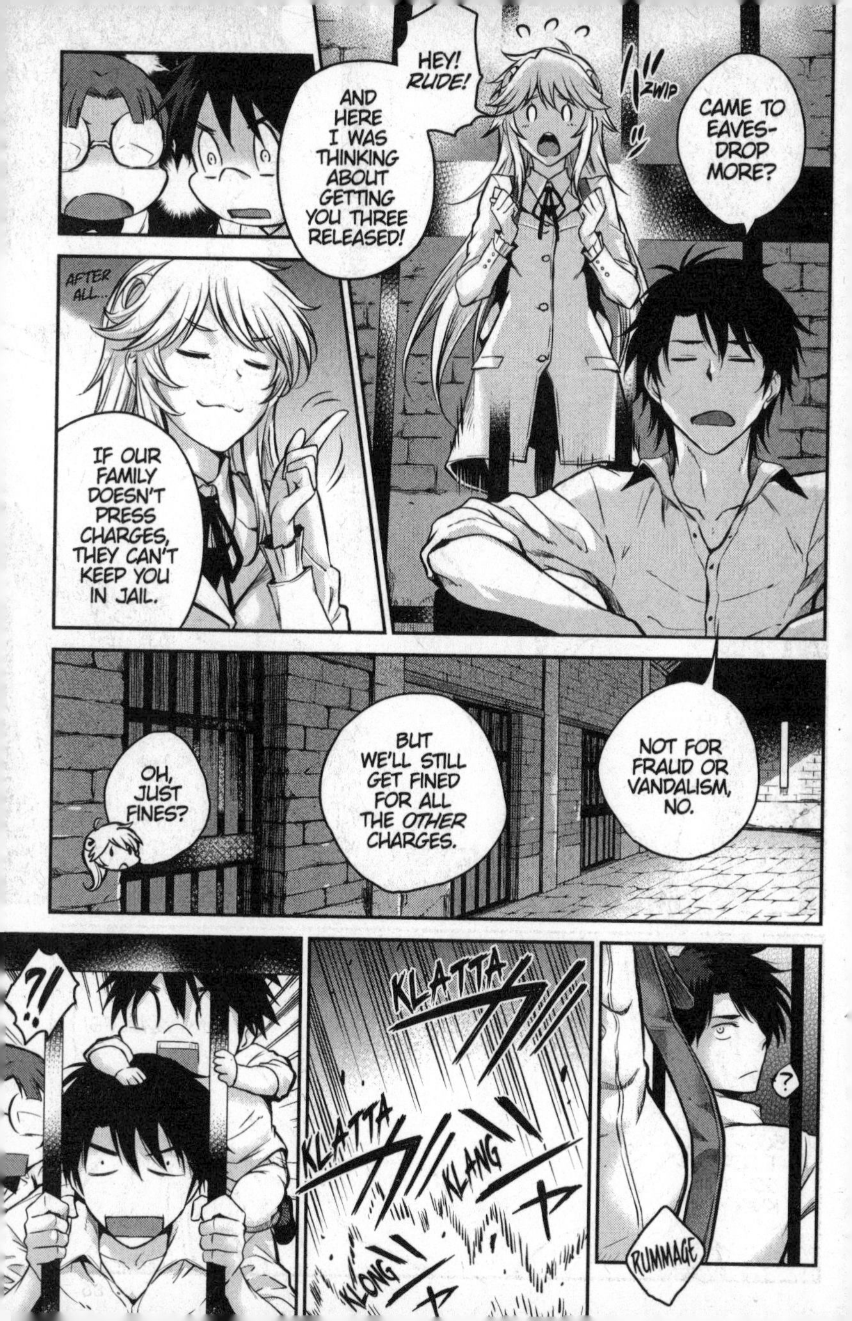
ZWIP
CAME TO EAVES-DROP MORE?
HEY! RUDE!
AND HERE I WAS THINKING ABOUT GETTING YOU THREE RELEASED!
AFTER ALL...
IF OUR FAMILY DOESN'T PRESS CHARGES, THEY CAN'T KEEP YOU IN JAIL.
NOT FOR FRAUD OR VANDALISM, NO.
BUT WE'LL STILL GET FINED FOR ALL THE OTHER CHARGES.
OH, JUST FINES?
?
RUMMAGE
KLATTA
KLATTA
KLANG
KLONG
?!

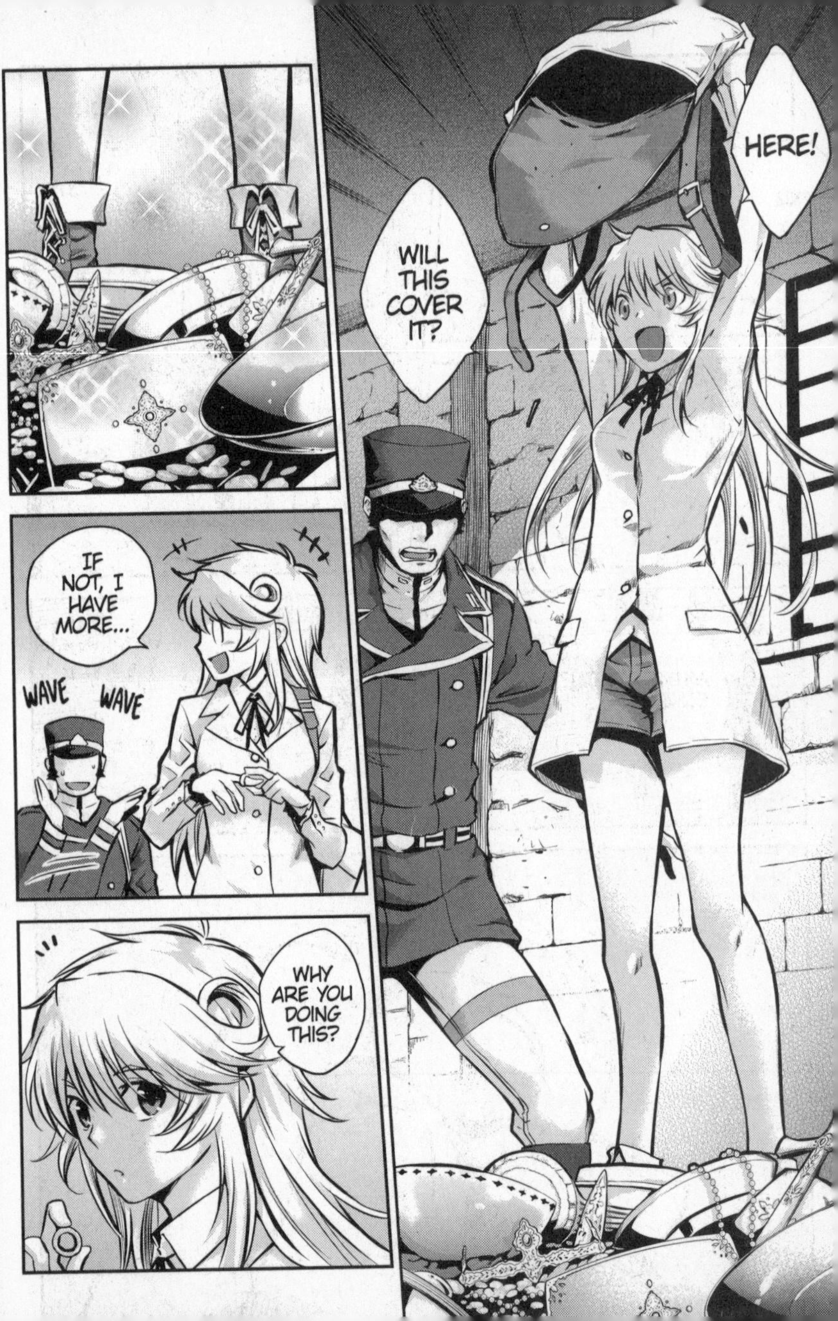
HERE!
WILL THIS COVER IT?
IF NOT, I HAVE MORE...
WAVE WAVE
WHY ARE YOU DOING THIS?

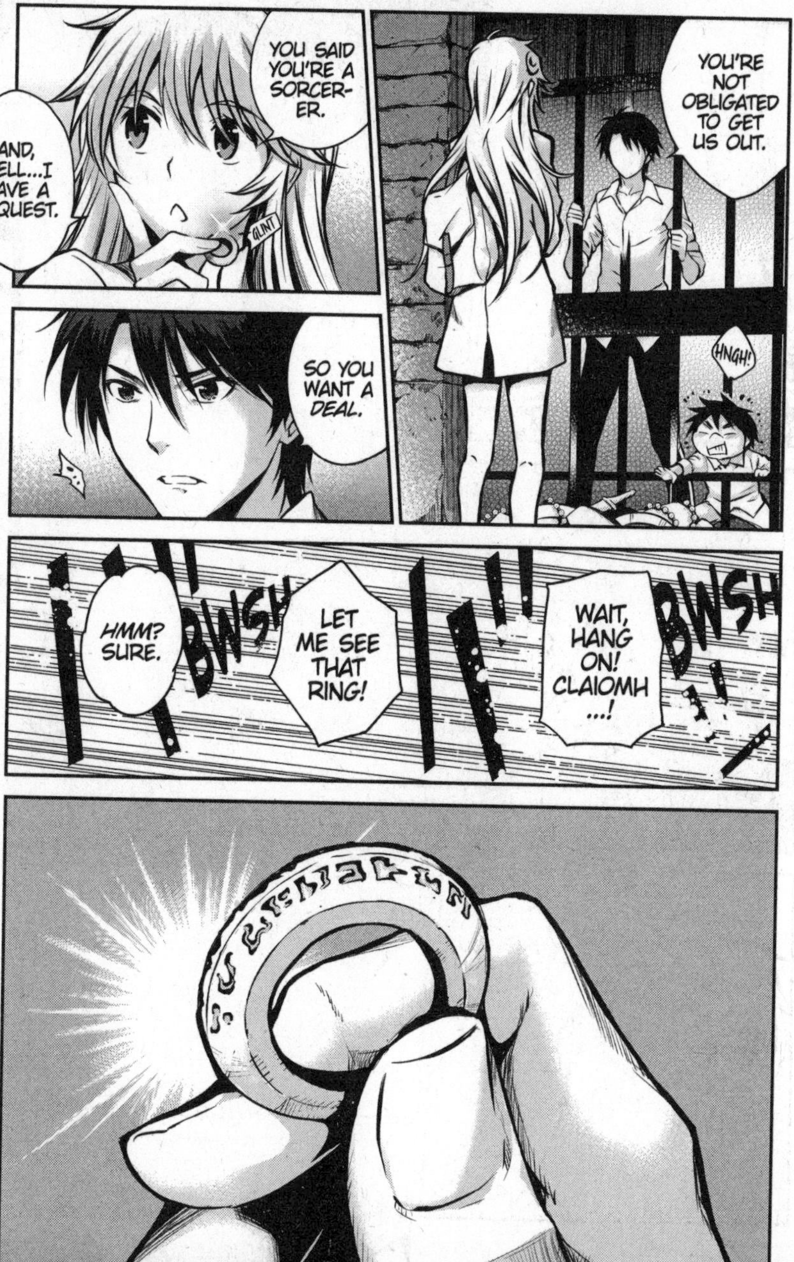
YOU'RE NOT OBLIGATED TO GET US OUT.
HNGH!
YOU SAID YOU'RE A SORCERER-ER.
AND, WELL...I HAVE A REQUEST.
GLINT
SO YOU WANT A DEAL.
BWSH
WAIT, HANG ON! CLAIOMH ...!
LET ME SEE THAT RING!
BWSH
HMM? SURE.

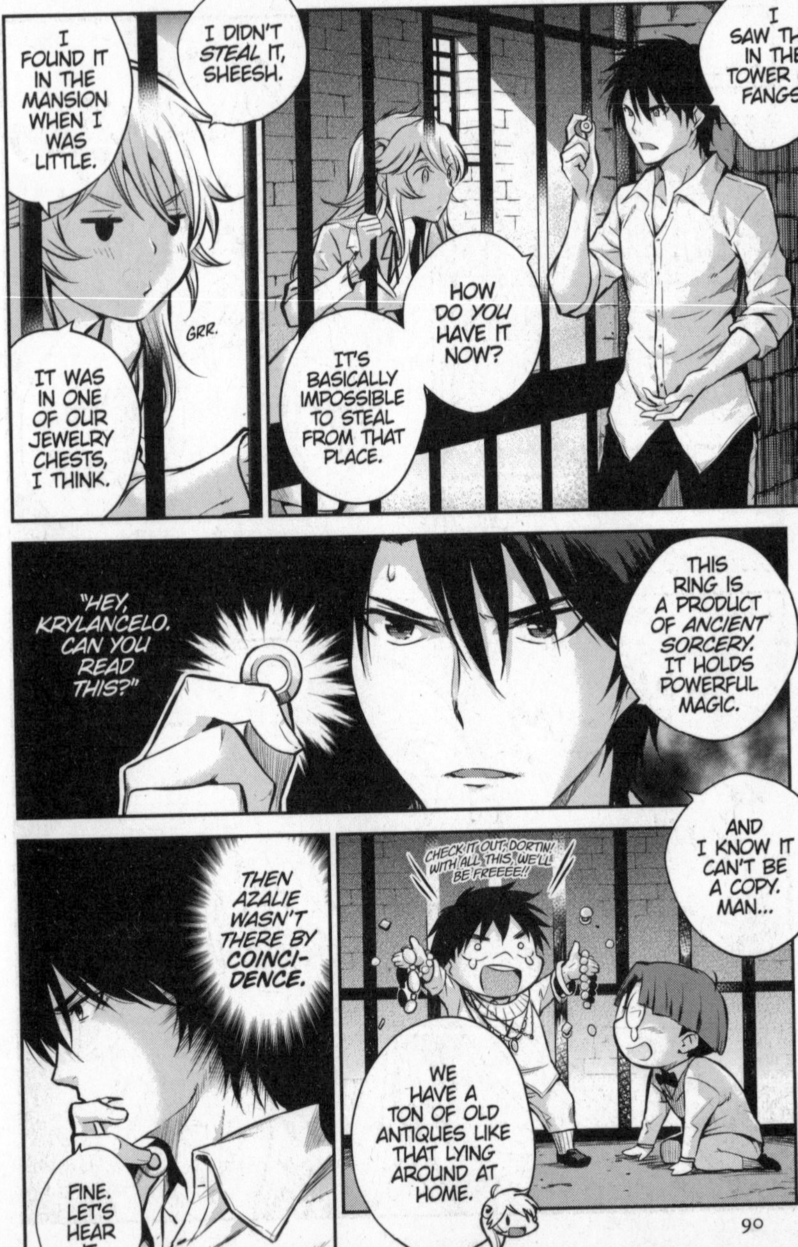
I SAW THIS IN THE TOWER OF FANGS!
HOW DO YOU HAVE IT NOW?
IT'S BASICALLY IMPOSSIBLE TO STEAL FROM THAT PLACE.
I DIDN'T *STEAL* IT, SHEESH.
I FOUND IT IN THE MANSION WHEN I WAS LITTLE.
GRR.
IT WAS IN ONE OF OUR JEWELRY CHESTS, I THINK.
THIS RING IS A PRODUCT OF *ANCIENT SORCERY.* IT HOLDS POWERFUL MAGIC.
"HEY, KRYLANCELO. CAN YOU READ THIS?"
AND I KNOW IT CAN'T BE A COPY. MAN...
CHECK IT OUT, DORTIN! WITH ALL THIS, WE'LL BE FREEEE!!
WE HAVE A TON OF OLD ANTIQUES LIKE THAT LYING AROUND AT HOME.
THEN AZALIE WASN'T THERE BY COINCIDENCE.
FINE. LET'S HEAR IT.

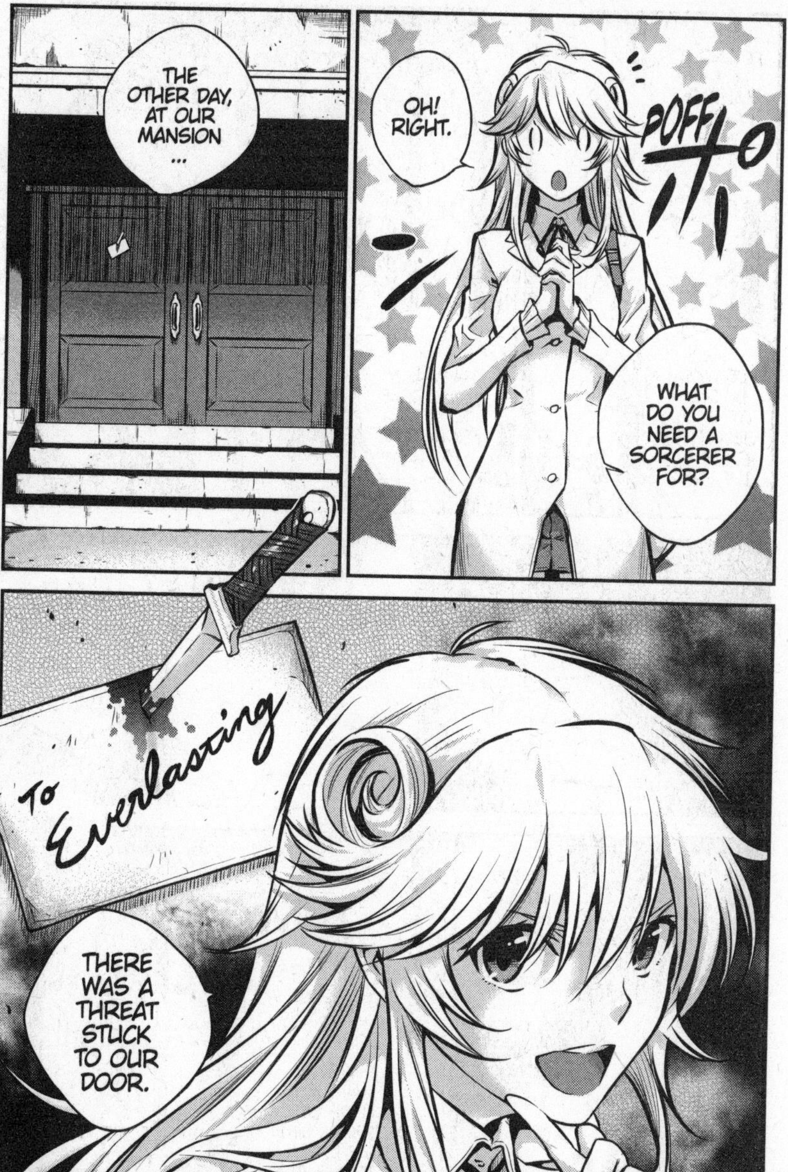
OH! RIGHT.
POFF
WHAT DO YOU NEED A SORCERER FOR?
THE OTHER DAY, AT OUR MANSION ...
To Everlasting
THERE WAS A THREAT STUCK TO OUR DOOR.

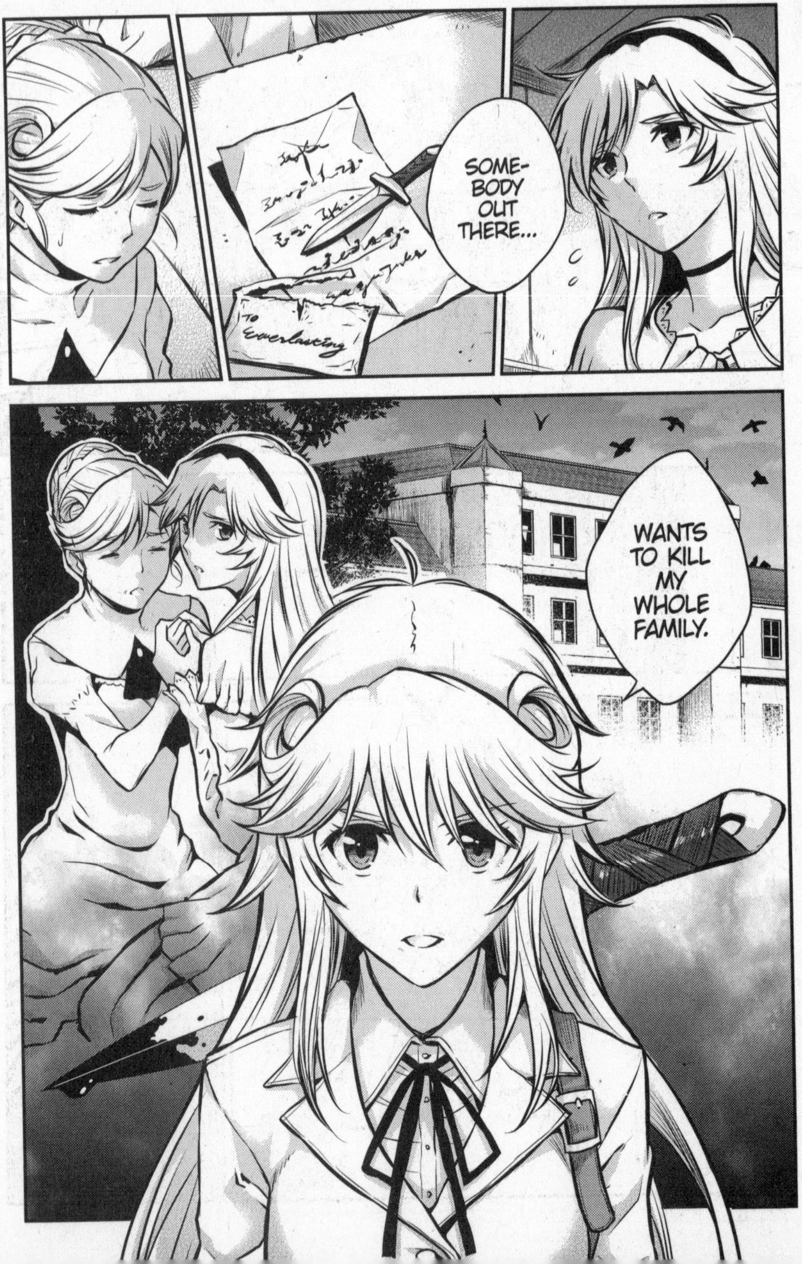
SOME-
BODY
OUT
THERE...
TO
Everlasting
WANTS TO KILL MY WHOLE FAMILY.

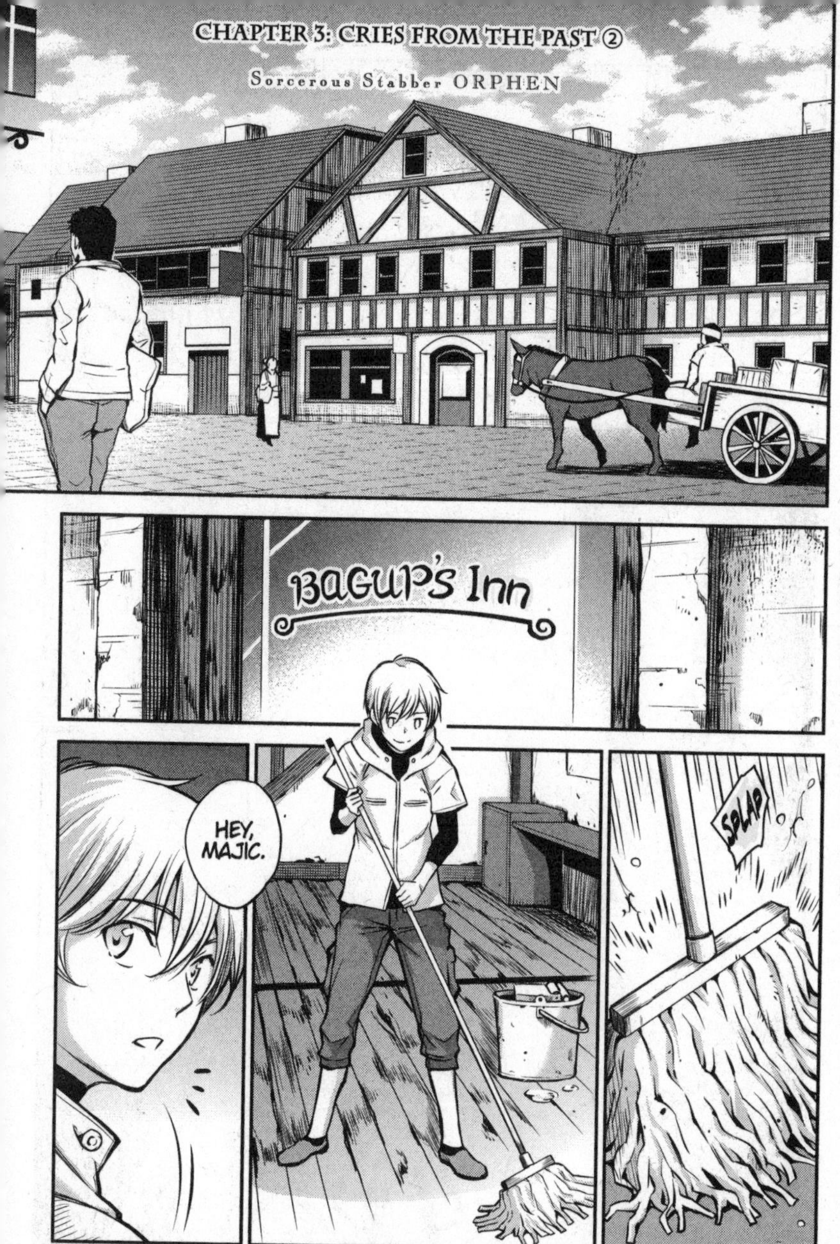
CHAPTER 3: CRIES FROM THE PAST ②
Sorcerous Stabber ORPHEN
BAGUP's Inn
SPLAP
HEY, MAJIC.

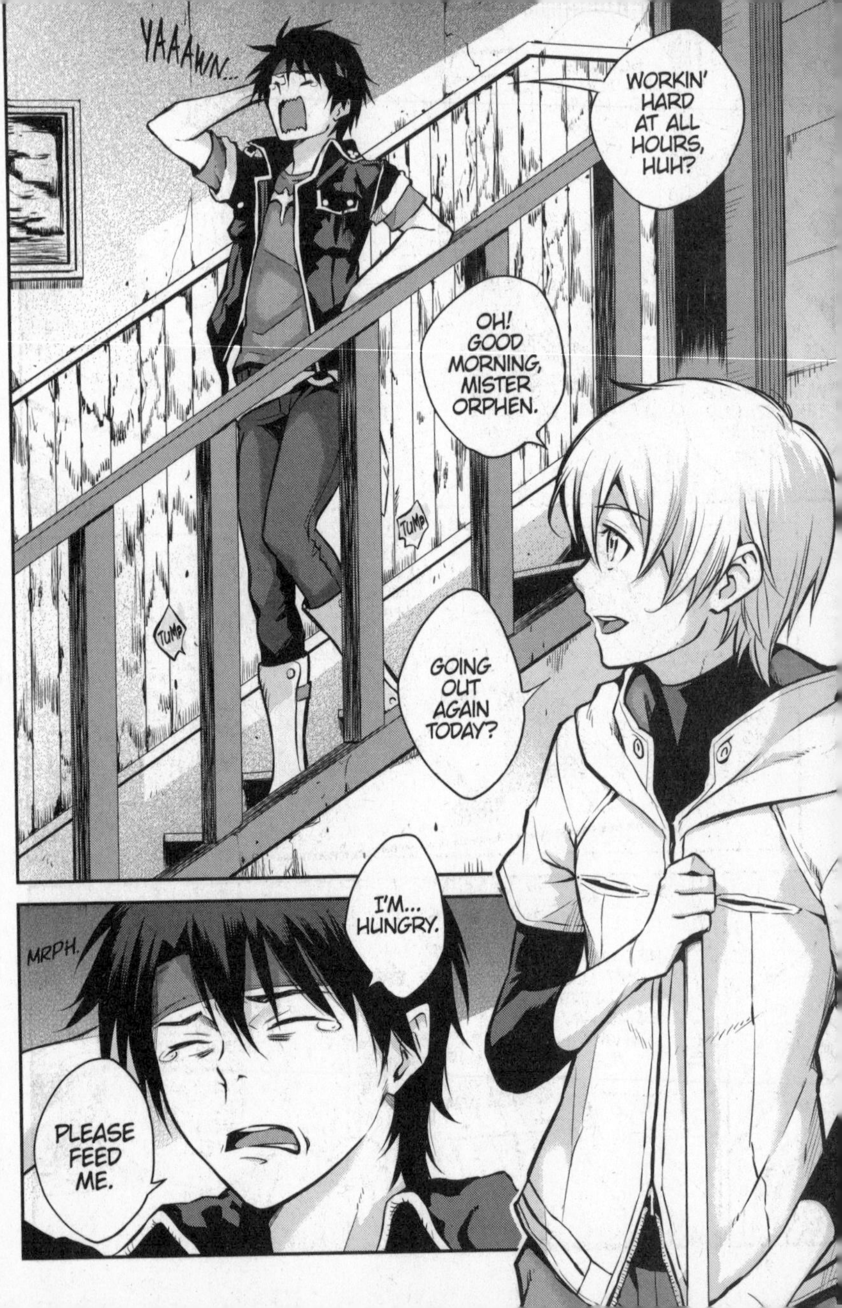
WORKIN' HARD AT ALL HOURS, HUH?
YAAAWN...
OH! GOOD MORNING, MISTER ORPHEN.
TUMP
TUMP
GOING OUT AGAIN TODAY?
I'M... HUNGRY.
MRPH.
PLEASE FEED ME.

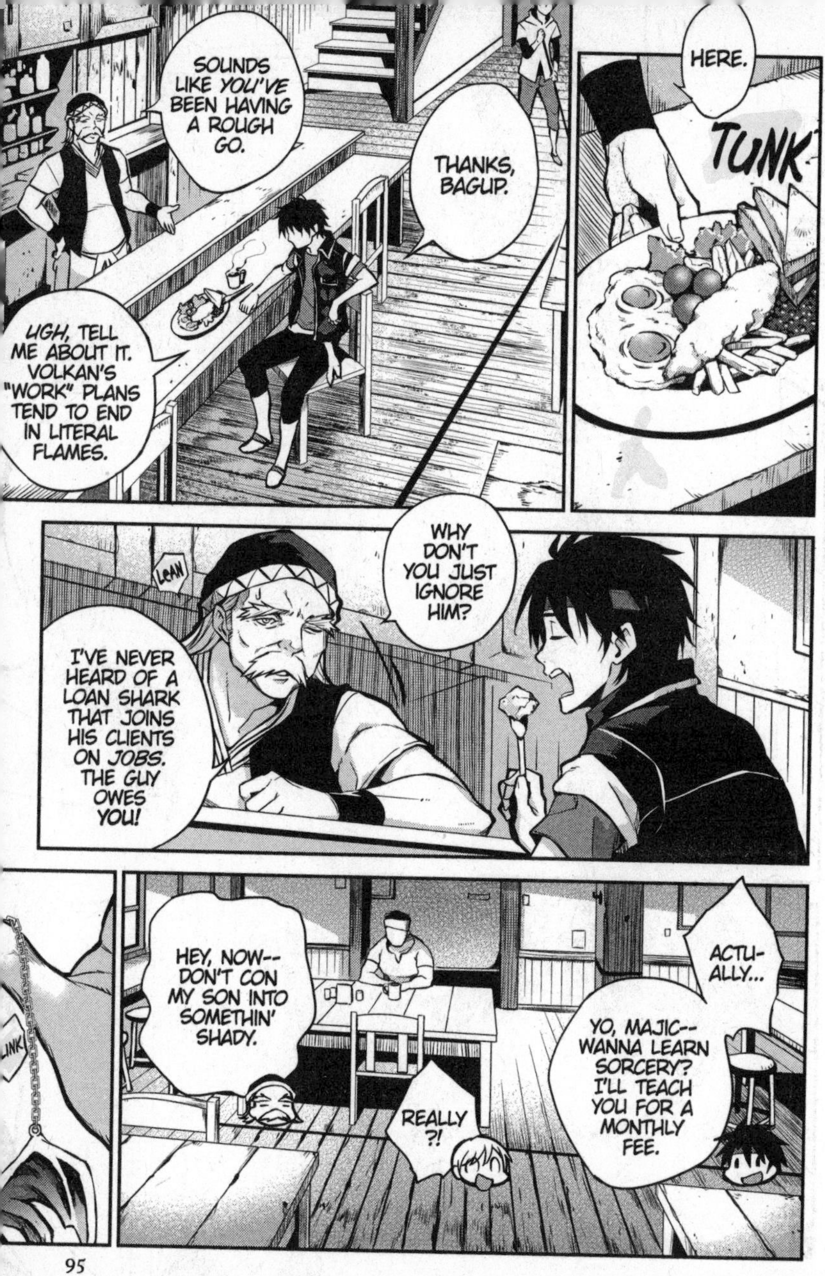
HERE.
TUNK
THANKS, BAGUP.
SOUNDS LIKE *YOU'VE* BEEN HAVING A ROUGH GO.
UGH, TELL ME ABOUT IT. VOLKAN'S "WORK" PLANS TEND TO END IN LITERAL FLAMES.
WHY DON'T YOU JUST IGNORE HIM?
LEAN
I'VE NEVER HEARD OF A LOAN SHARK THAT JOINS HIS CLIENTS ON *JOBS*. THE GUY OWES YOU!
ACTU-ALLY...
YO, MAJIC-- WANNA LEARN SORCERY? I'LL TEACH YOU FOR A MONTHLY FEE.
REALLY ?!
HEY, NOW-- DON'T CON MY SON INTO SOMETHIN' SHADY.
LINK

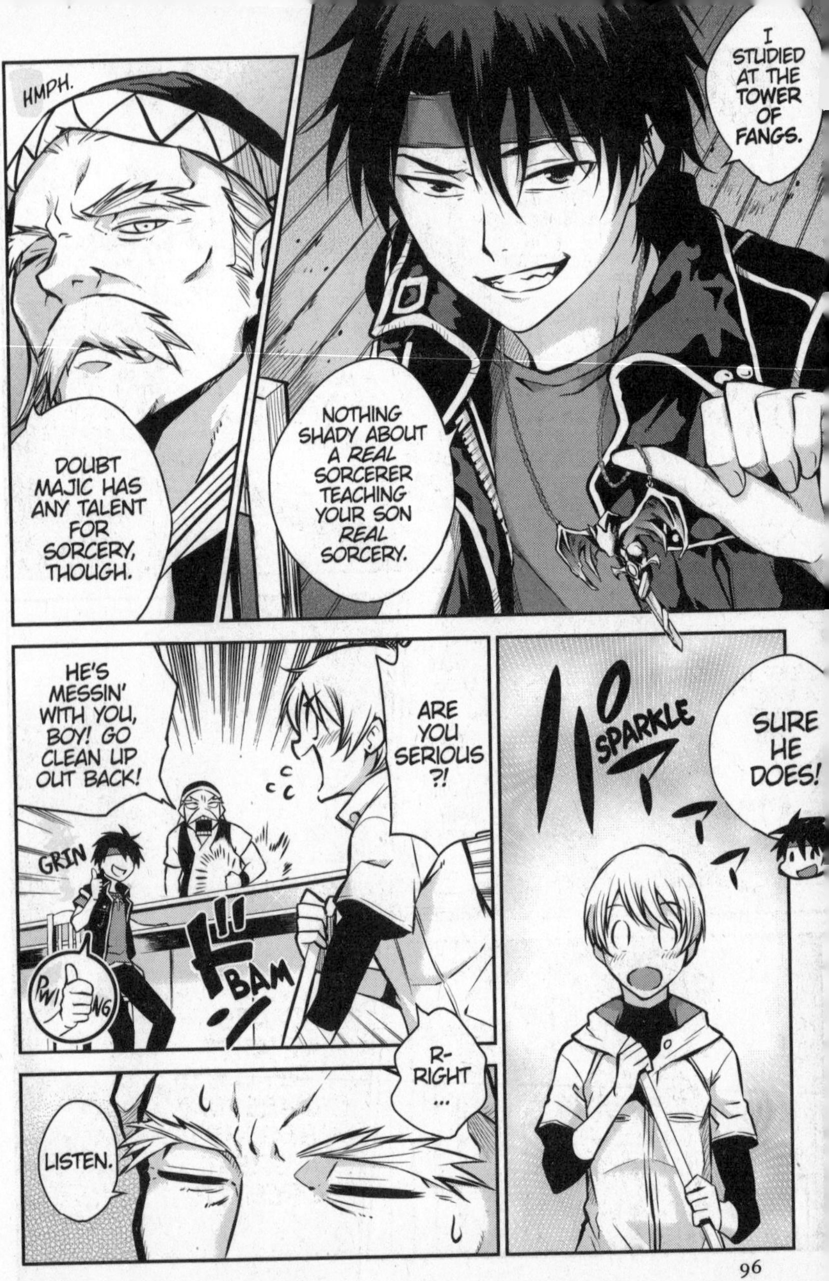
I STUDIED AT THE TOWER OF FANGS.
NOTHING SHADY ABOUT A *REAL* SORCERER TEACHING YOUR SON *REAL* SORCERY.
HMPH.
DOUBT MAJIC HAS ANY TALENT FOR SORCERY, THOUGH.
SPARKLE
SURE HE DOES!
ARE YOU SERIOUS?!
HE'S MESSIN' WITH YOU, BOY! GO CLEAN UP OUT BACK!
GRIN
BAM
PWING
R-RIGHT...
LISTEN.

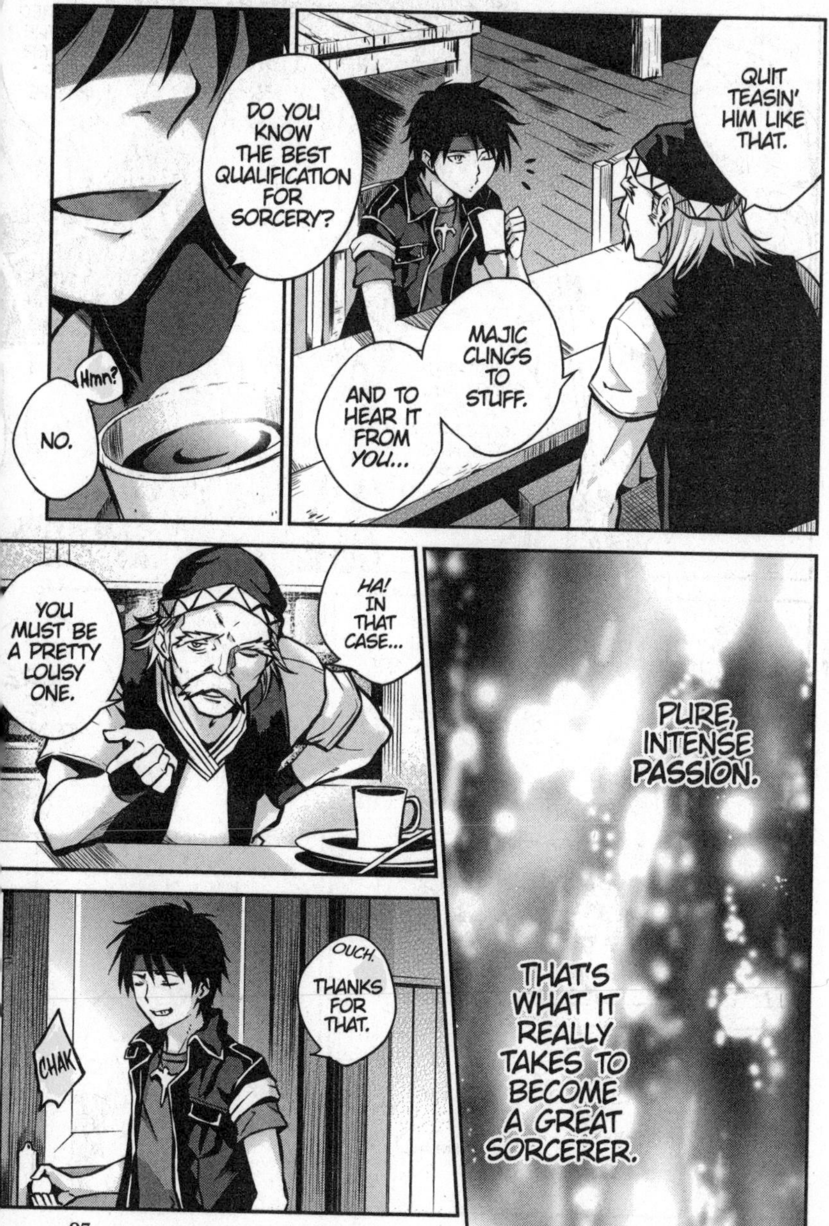

QUIT TEASIN' HIM LIKE THAT.
DO YOU KNOW THE BEST QUALIFICATION FOR SORCERY?
MAJIC CLINGS TO STUFF.
AND TO HEAR IT FROM YOU...
Hmn?
NO.
PURE, INTENSE PASSION.
THAT'S WHAT IT REALLY TAKES TO BECOME A GREAT SORCERER.
HA! IN THAT CASE...
YOU MUST BE A PRETTY LOUSY ONE.
OUCH.
THANKS FOR THAT.
CHAK

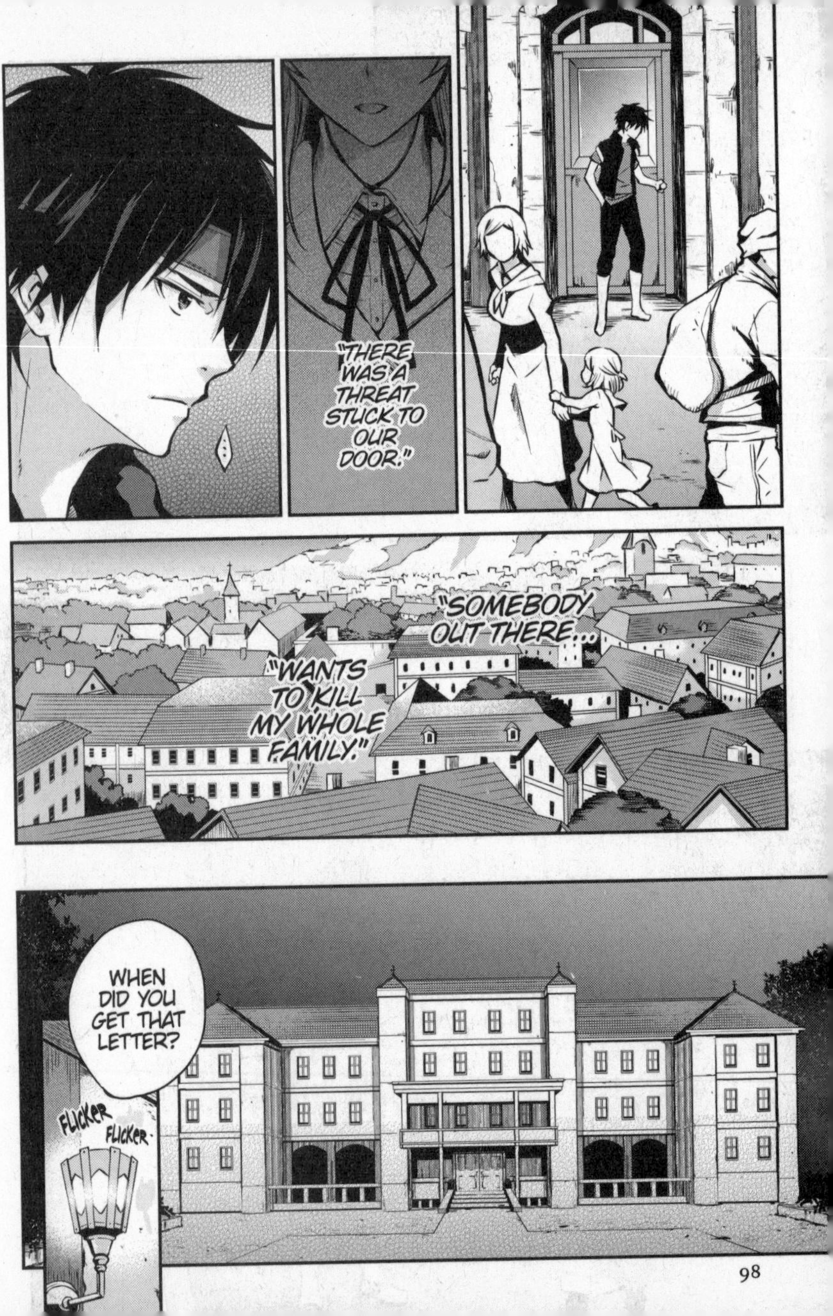
"THERE WAS A THREAT STUCK TO OUR DOOR."
"SOMEBODY OUT THERE...
"WANTS TO KILL MY WHOLE FAMILY."
WHEN DID YOU GET THAT LETTER?
FLICKER
FLICKER

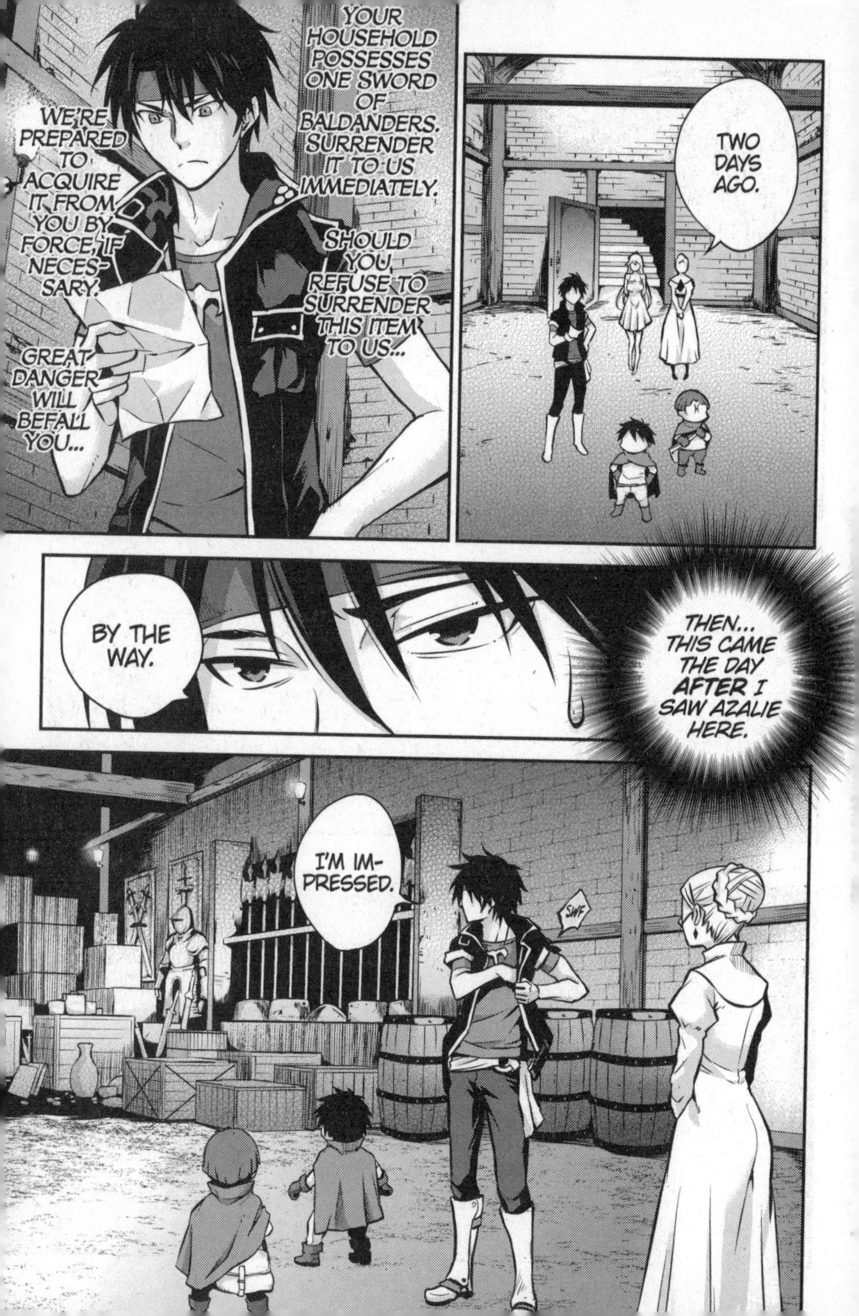
TWO DAYS AGO.
YOUR HOUSEHOLD POSSESSES ONE SWORD OF BALDANDERS. SURRENDER IT TO US IMMEDIATELY.
WE'RE PREPARED TO ACQUIRE IT FROM YOU BY FORCE, IF NECES-SARY.
SHOULD YOU REFUSE TO SURRENDER THIS ITEM TO US...
GREAT DANGER WILL BEFALL YOU...
THEN... THIS CAME THE DAY AFTER I SAW AZALIE HERE.
BY THE WAY.
SWF
I'M IM-PRESSED.

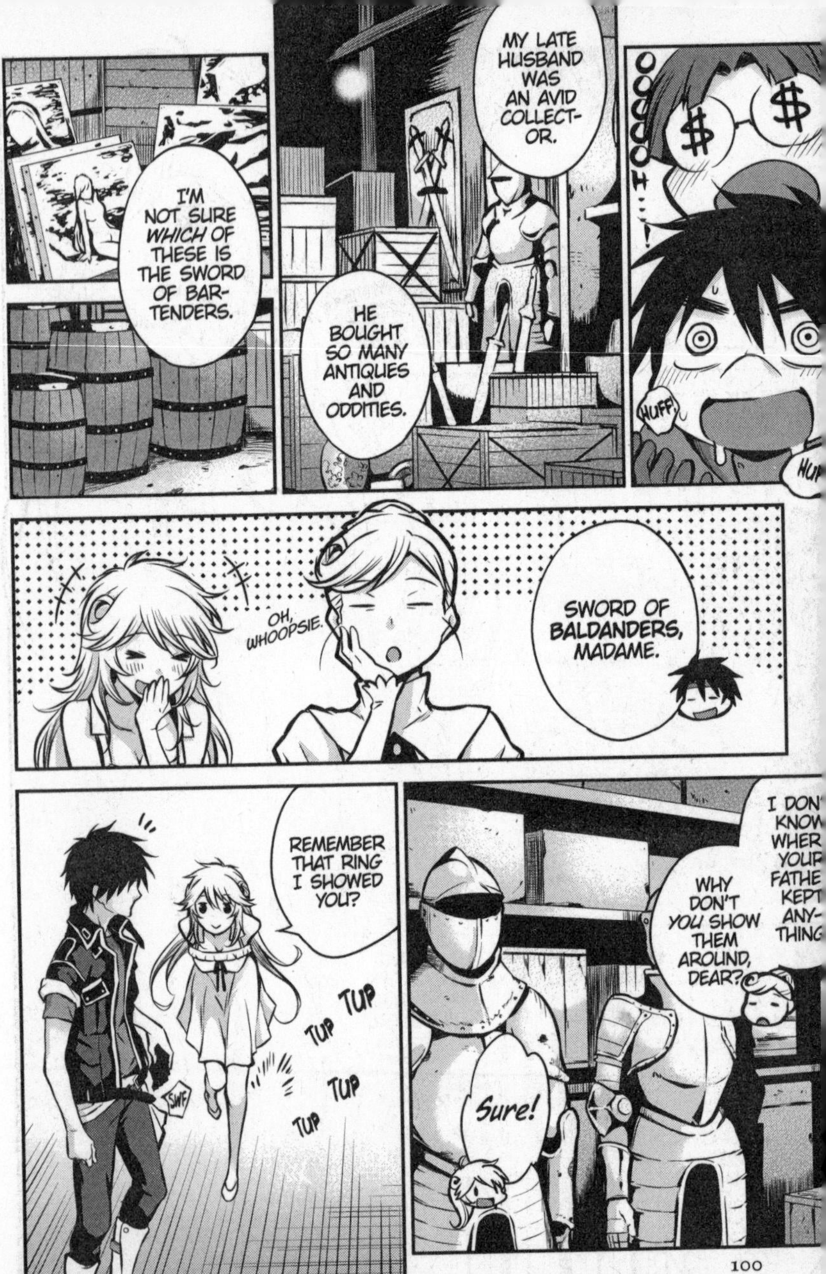
OOOOOOH...!
HUFF!
HUF
MY LATE HUSBAND WAS AN AVID COLLECT-OR.
HE BOUGHT SO MANY ANTIQUES AND ODDITIES.
I'M NOT SURE *WHICH* OF THESE IS THE SWORD OF BAR-TENDERS.
SWORD OF BALDANDERS, MADAME.
OH, WHOOPSIE.
I DON' KNOW WHER YOUR FATHE KEPT ANY-THING
WHY DON'T *YOU* SHOW THEM AROUND, DEAR?
Sure!
REMEMBER THAT RING I SHOWED YOU?
SWF
TUP TUP
TUP
TUP
TUP

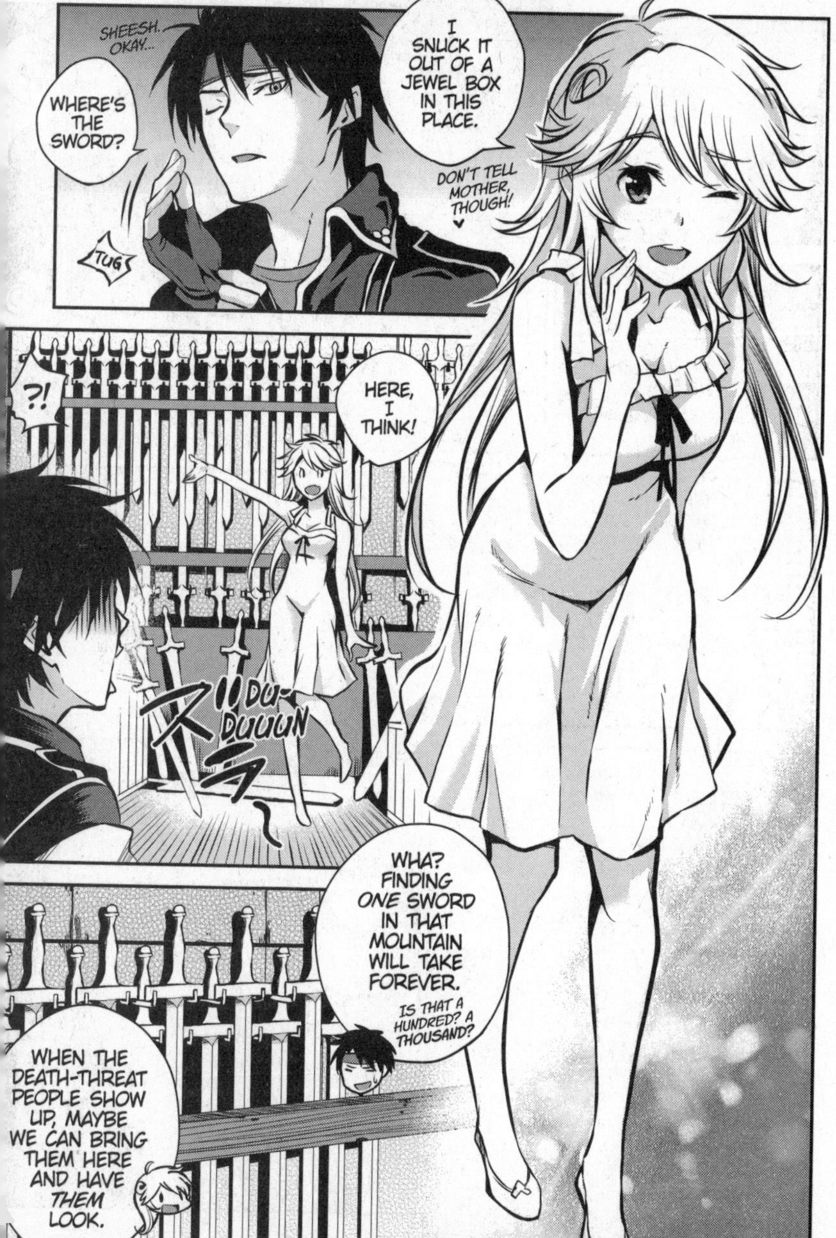
I SNUCK IT OUT OF A JEWEL BOX IN THIS PLACE.
DON'T TELL MOTHER, THOUGH! ♥
SHEESH. OKAY...
WHERE'S THE SWORD?
TUG
HERE, I THINK!
?!
DU-DUUUN
WHA? FINDING ONE SWORD IN THAT MOUNTAIN WILL TAKE FOREVER.
IS THAT A HUNDRED? A THOUSAND?
WHEN THE DEATH-THREAT PEOPLE SHOW UP, MAYBE WE CAN BRING THEM HERE AND HAVE THEM LOOK.

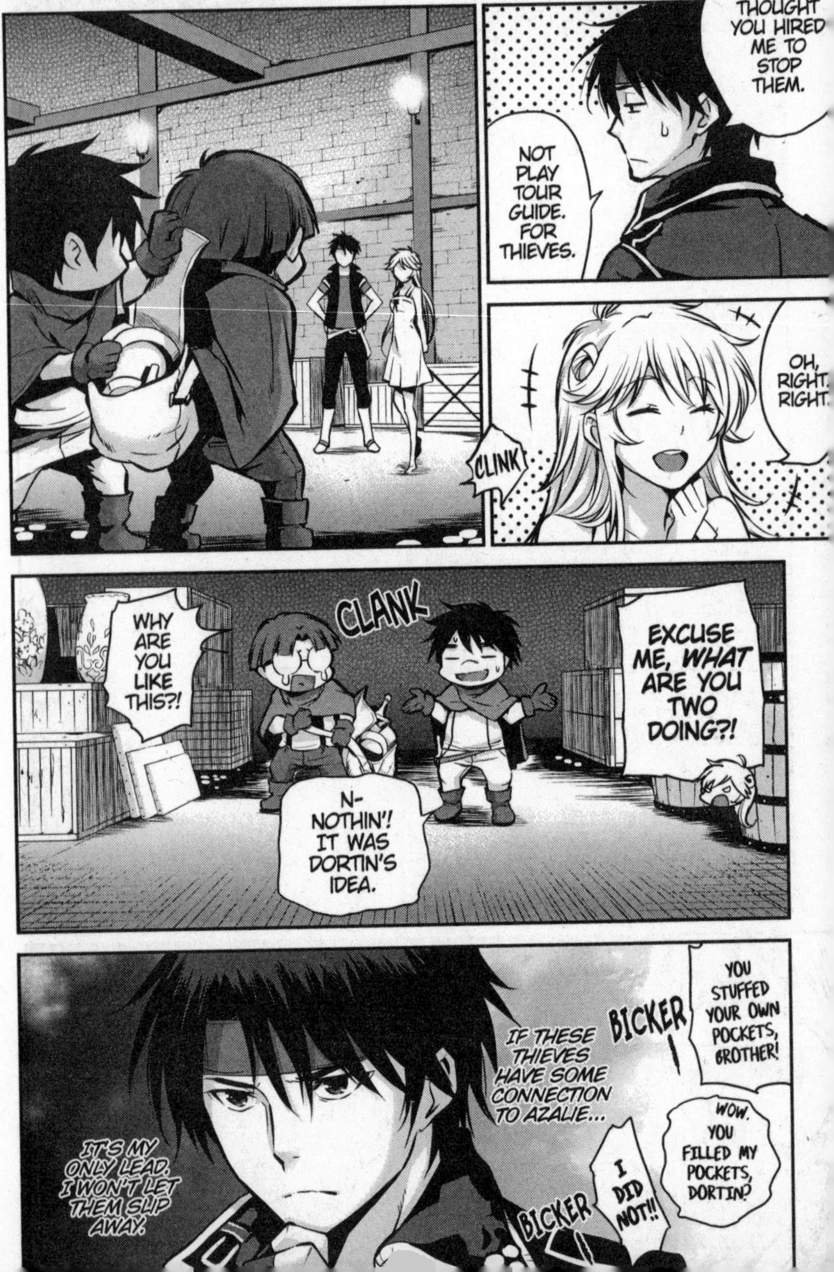
I THOUGHT YOU HIRED ME TO STOP THEM.
NOT PLAY TOUR GUIDE. FOR THIEVES.
OH, RIGHT. RIGHT.
CLINK
EXCUSE ME, WHAT ARE YOU TWO DOING?!
CLANK
WHY ARE YOU LIKE THIS?!
N- NOTHIN'! IT WAS DORTIN'S IDEA.
YOU STUFFED YOUR OWN POCKETS, BROTHER!
BICKER
IF THESE THIEVES HAVE SOME CONNECTION TO AZALIE...
WOW. YOU FILLED MY POCKETS, DORTIN?
I DID NOT!!
BICKER
IT'S MY ONLY LEAD. I WON'T LET THEM SLIP AWAY.

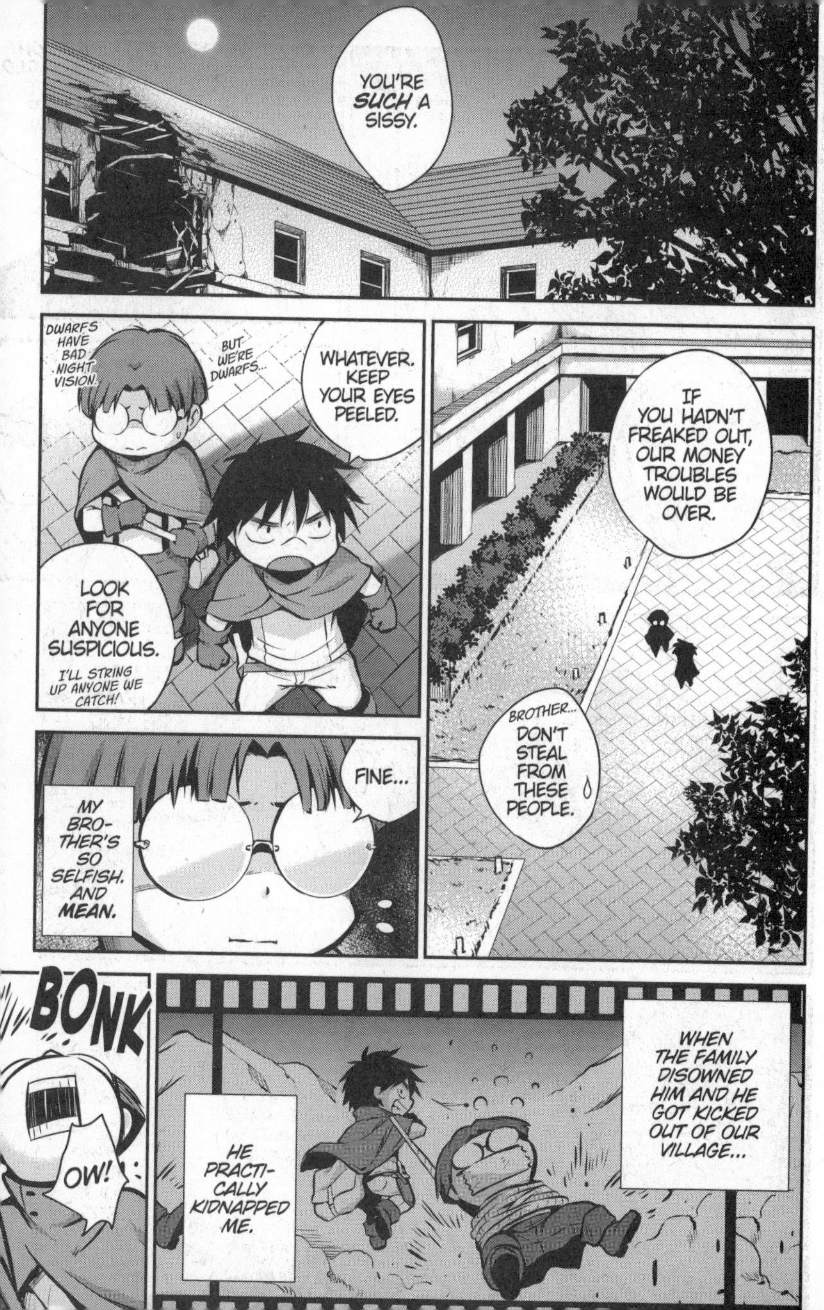
YOU'RE SUCH A SISSY.
IF YOU HADN'T FREAKED OUT, OUR MONEY TROUBLES WOULD BE OVER.
BROTHER... DON'T STEAL FROM THESE PEOPLE.
WHATEVER. KEEP YOUR EYES PEELED.
BUT WE'RE DWARFS...
DWARFS HAVE BAD NIGHT VISION.
LOOK FOR ANYONE SUSPICIOUS.
I'LL STRING UP ANYONE WE CATCH!
FINE...
MY BRO-THER'S SO SELFISH. AND MEAN.
WHEN THE FAMILY DISOWNED HIM AND HE GOT KICKED OUT OF OUR VILLAGE...
HE PRACTI-CALLY KIDNAPPED ME.
BONK
OW!

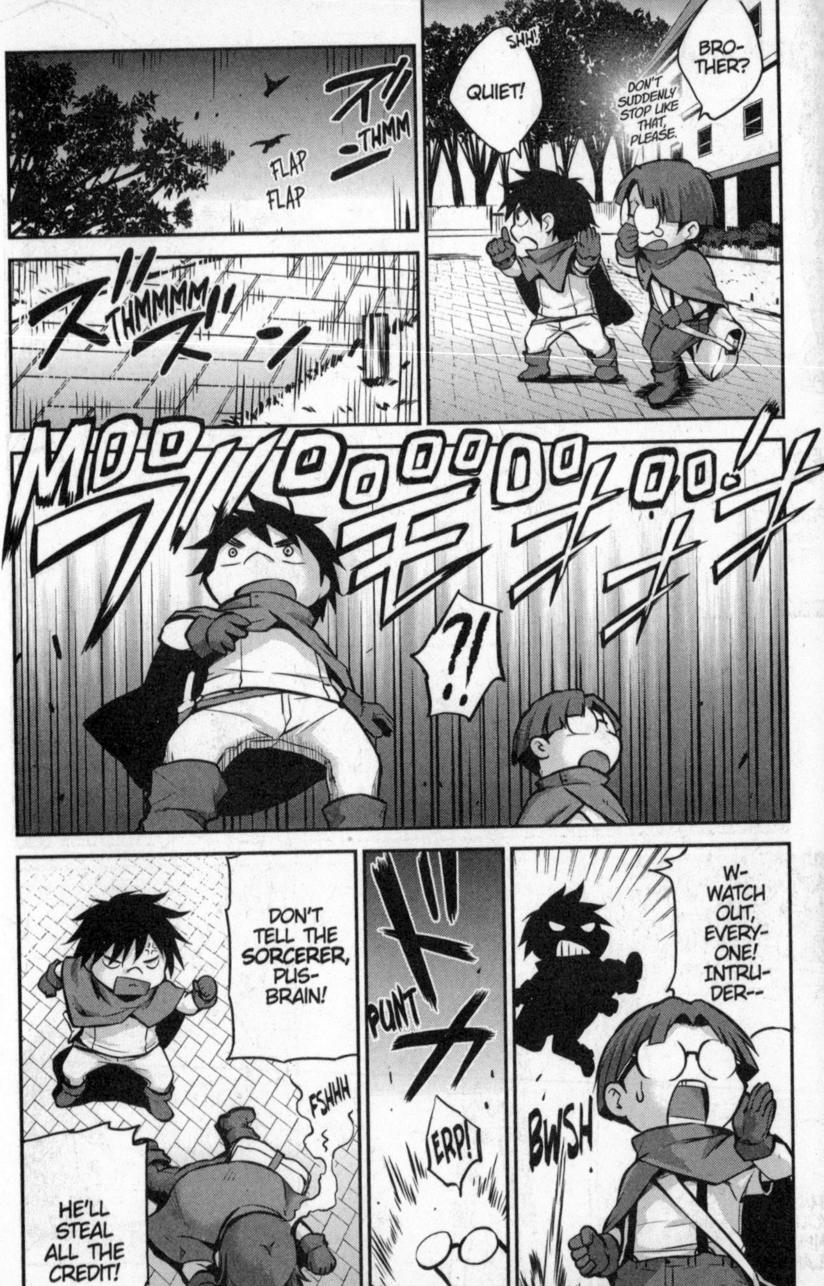
BRO-THER?
DON'T SUDDENLY STOP LIKE THAT, PLEASE.
SHH! QUIET!
THMM
FLAP FLAP
THMMMM
MOOOOOOOOOO!
?!!
W-WATCH OUT, EVERYONE! INTRU-DER--
BWSH
PUNT
ERP!
DON'T TELL THE SORCERER, PUS-BRAIN!
FSHHH
HE'LL STEAL ALL THE CREDIT!

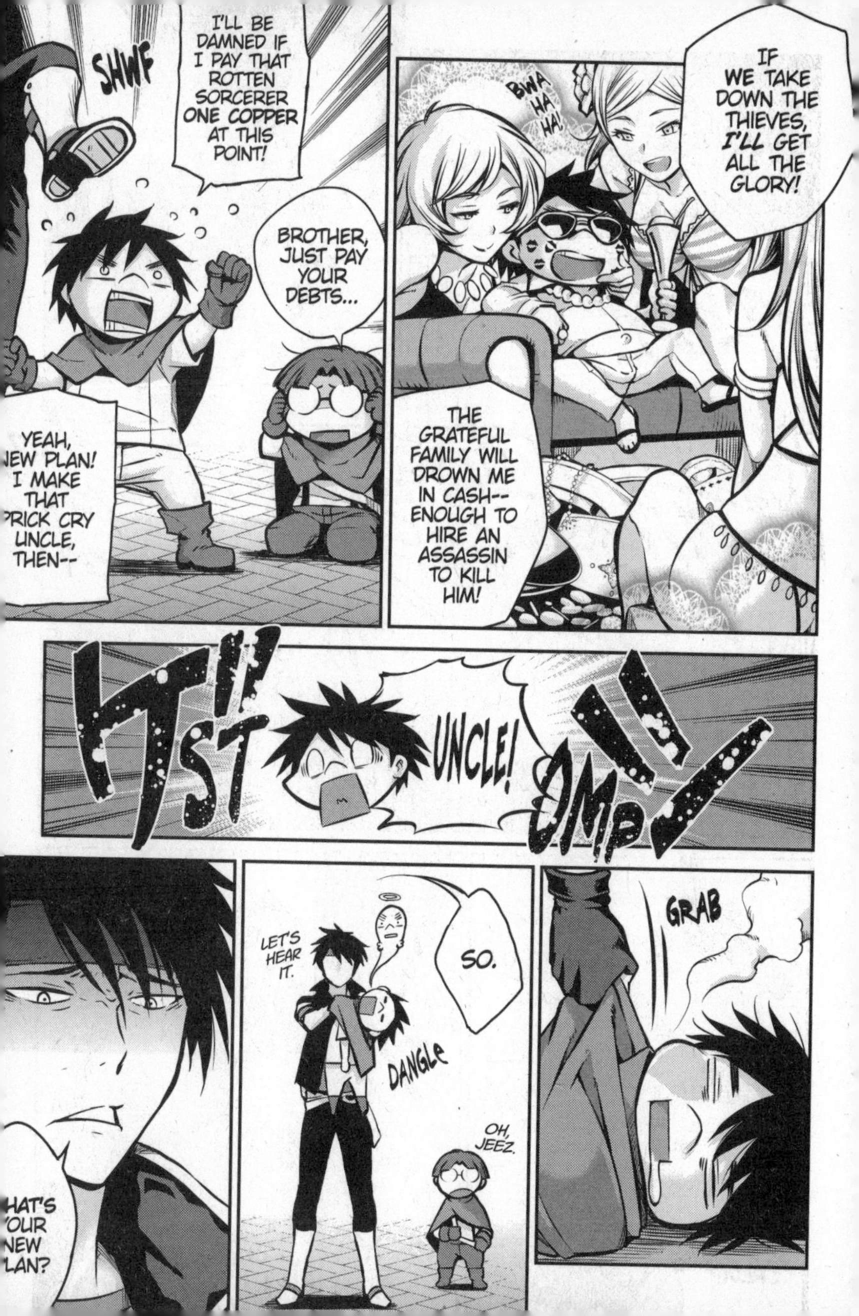
IF WE TAKE DOWN THE THIEVES, I'LL GET ALL THE GLORY!
BWA HA HA!
THE GRATEFUL FAMILY WILL DROWN ME IN CASH-- ENOUGH TO HIRE AN ASSASSIN TO KILL HIM!
SHWF
I'LL BE DAMNED IF I PAY THAT ROTTEN SORCERER ONE COPPER AT THIS POINT!
BROTHER, JUST PAY YOUR DEBTS...
YEAH, NEW PLAN! I MAKE THAT PRICK CRY UNCLE, THEN--
UNCLE!
GRAB
SO.
LET'S HEAR IT.
DANGLE
OH, JEEZ.
WHAT'S YOUR NEW PLAN?

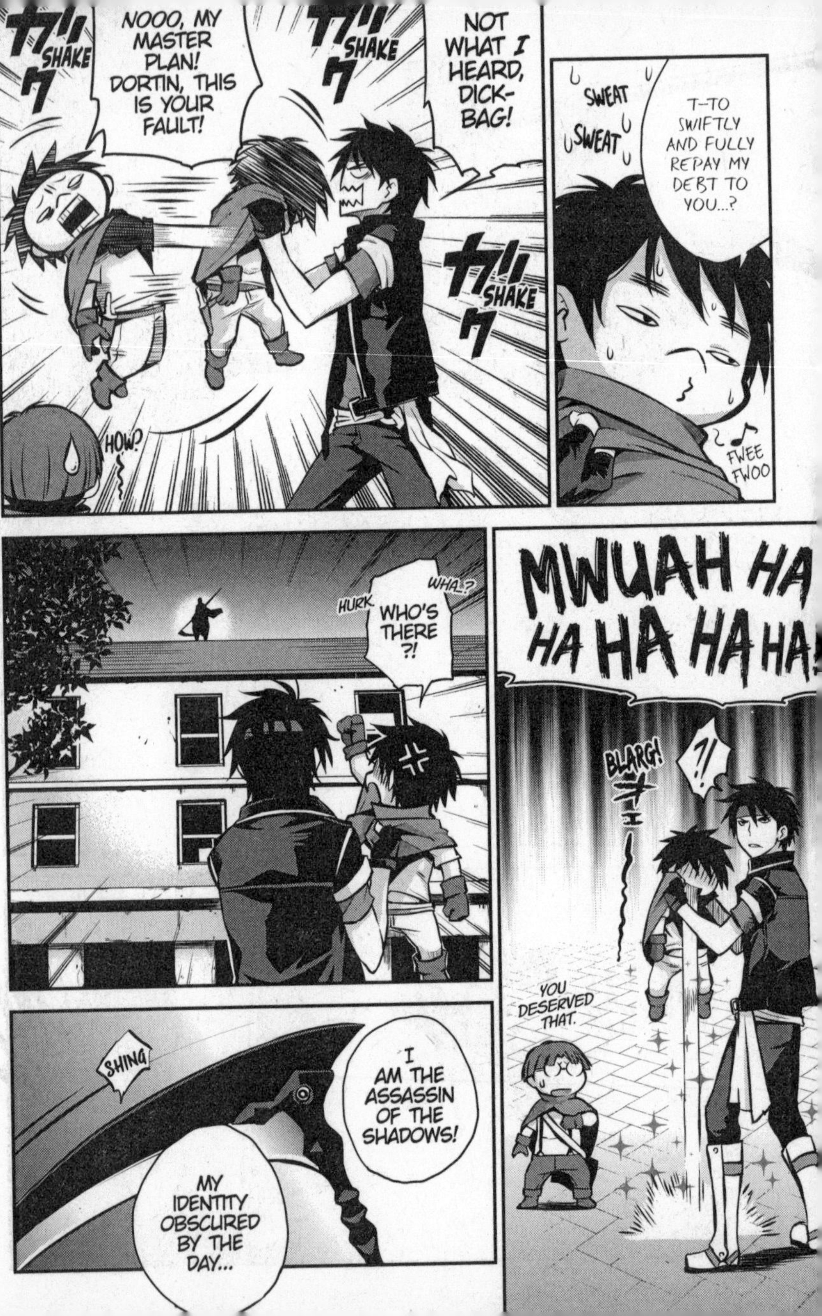
SWEAT
SWEAT
T-TO SWIFTLY AND FULLY REPAY MY DEBT TO YOU...?
FWEE FWOO
NOT WHAT I HEARD, DICK-BAG!
SHAKE
NOOO, MY MASTER PLAN! DORTIN, THIS IS YOUR FAULT!
SHAKE
SHAKE
HOW?
MWUAH HA HA HA HA HA!
?!
BLARG!
YOU DESERVED THAT.
WHA..?
WHO'S THERE ?!
HURK
I AM THE ASSASSIN OF THE SHADOWS!
SHING
MY IDENTITY OBSCURED BY THE DAY...

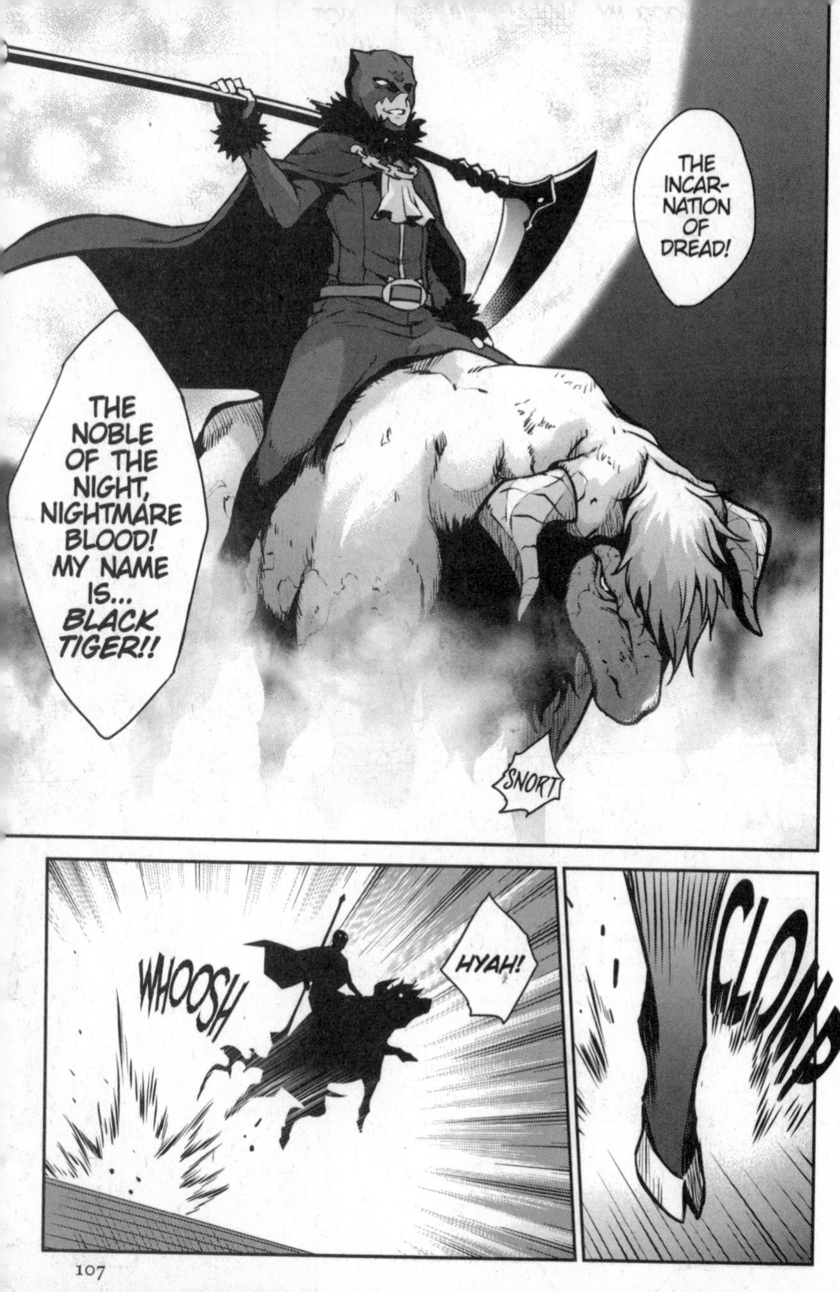
THE INCARNATION OF DREAD!
THE NOBLE OF THE NIGHT, NIGHTMARE BLOOD! MY NAME IS... BLACK TIGER!!
SNORT
CLOMP
HYAH!
WHOOSH

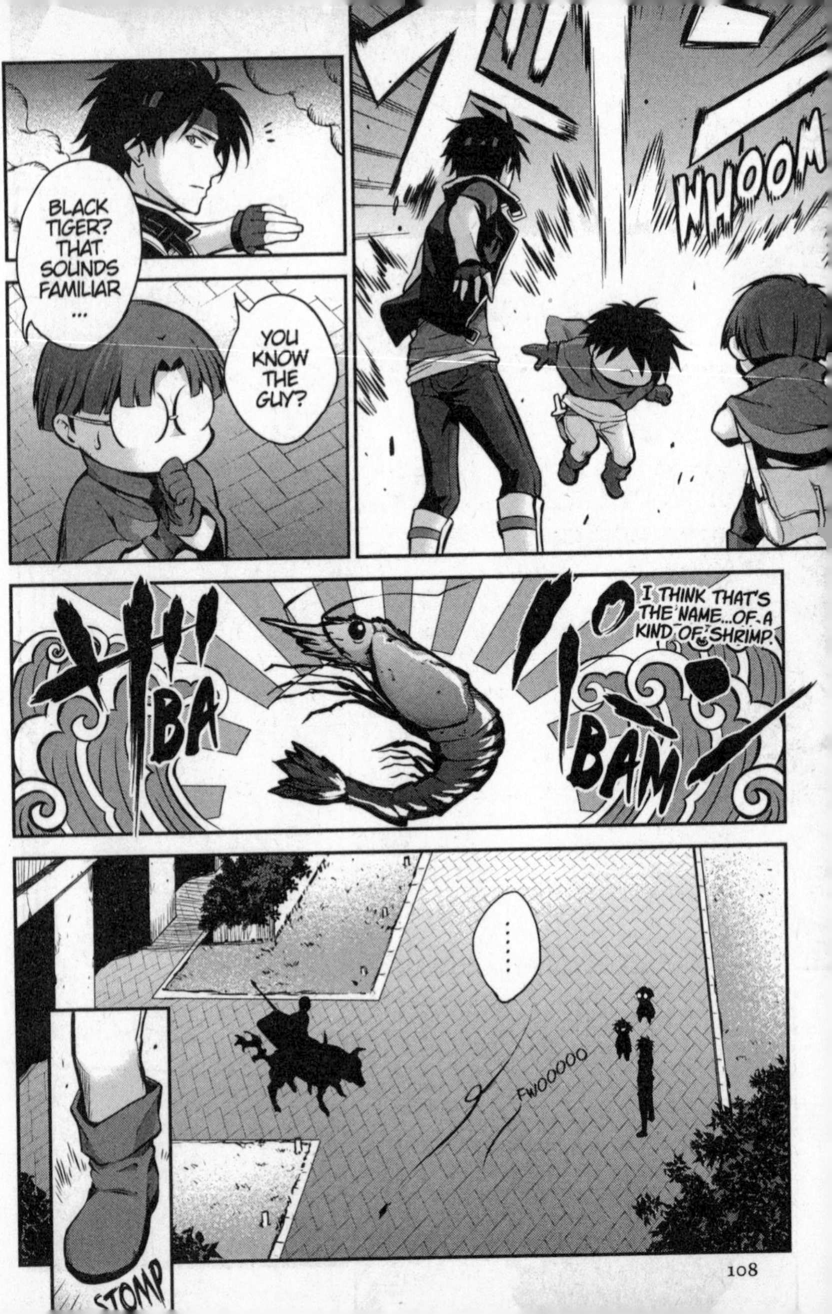
WHOOM
BLACK TIGER? THAT SOUNDS FAMILIAR ...
YOU KNOW THE GUY?
I THINK THAT'S THE NAME...OF A KIND OF SHRIMP.
BA
BAM
......
FWOOOOO
STOMP

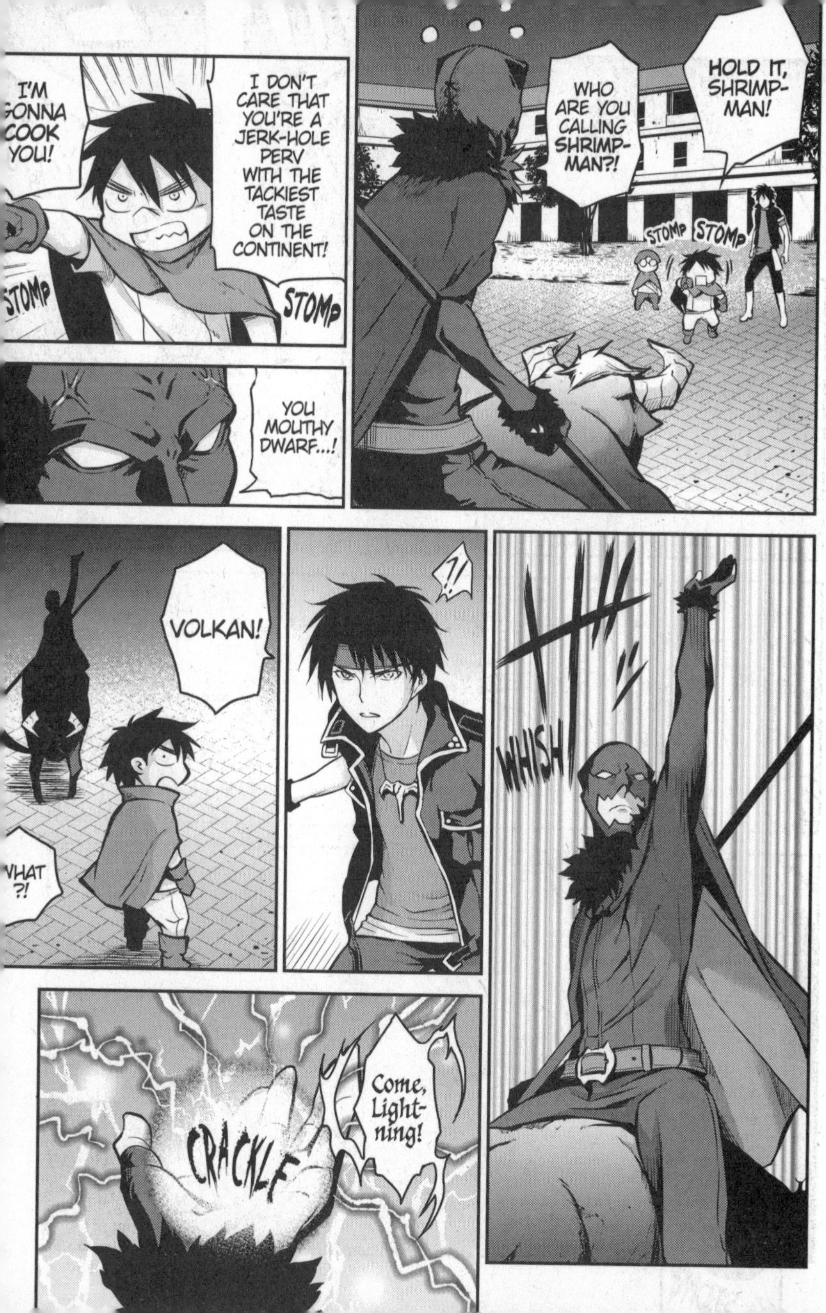
HOLD IT, SHRIMP-MAN!
WHO ARE YOU CALLING SHRIMP-MAN?!
STOMP STOMP
I DON'T CARE THAT YOU'RE A JERK-HOLE PERV WITH THE TACKIEST TASTE ON THE CONTINENT!
I'M GONNA COOK YOU!
STOMP
STOMP
YOU MOUTHY DWARF...!
WHISH
?!
VOLKAN!
WHAT?!
Come, Lightning!
CRACKLE

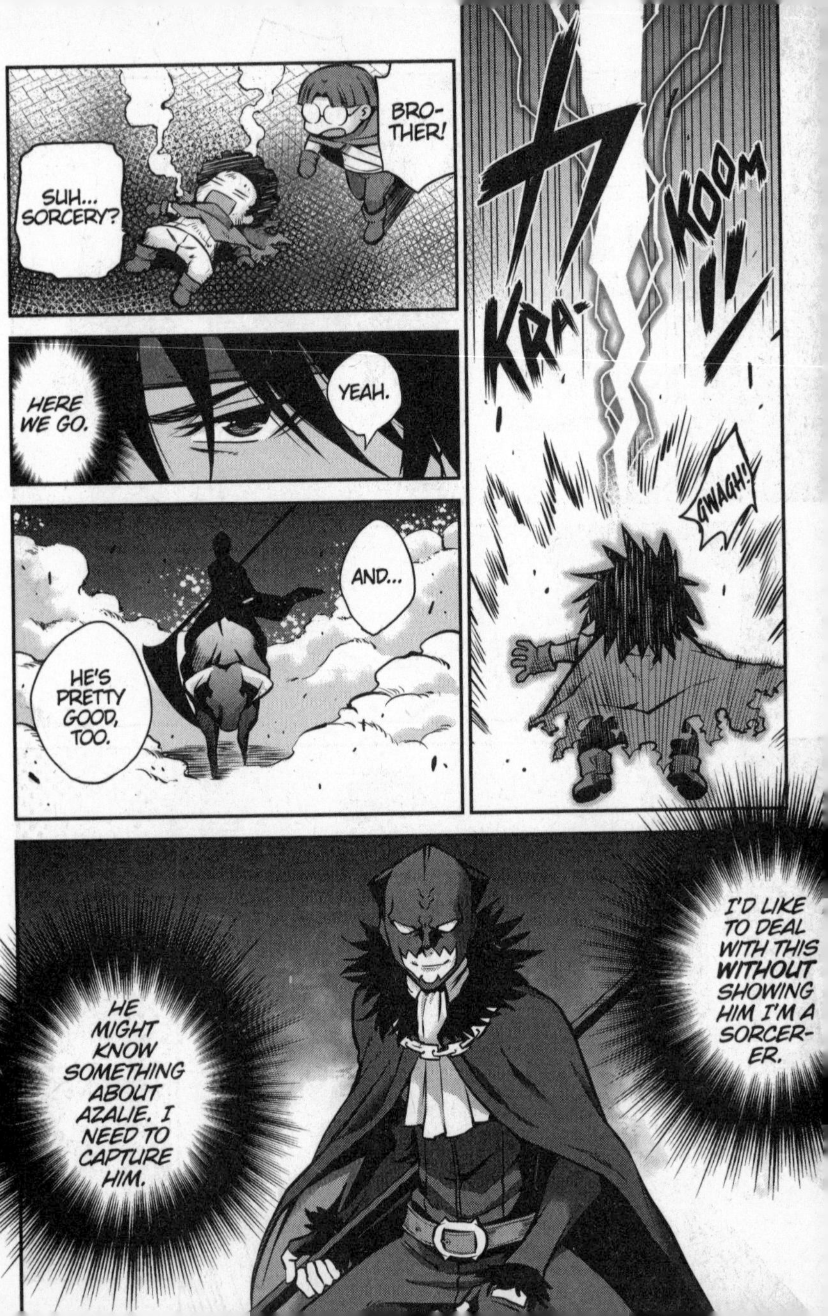
KRA-KOOM!!
GWAGH!
BRO-THER!
SUH... SORCERY?
YEAH.
HERE WE GO.
AND...
HE'S PRETTY GOOD, TOO.
I'D LIKE TO DEAL WITH THIS WITHOUT SHOWING HIM I'M A SORCER-ER.
HE MIGHT KNOW SOMETHING ABOUT AZALIE. I NEED TO CAPTURE HIM.

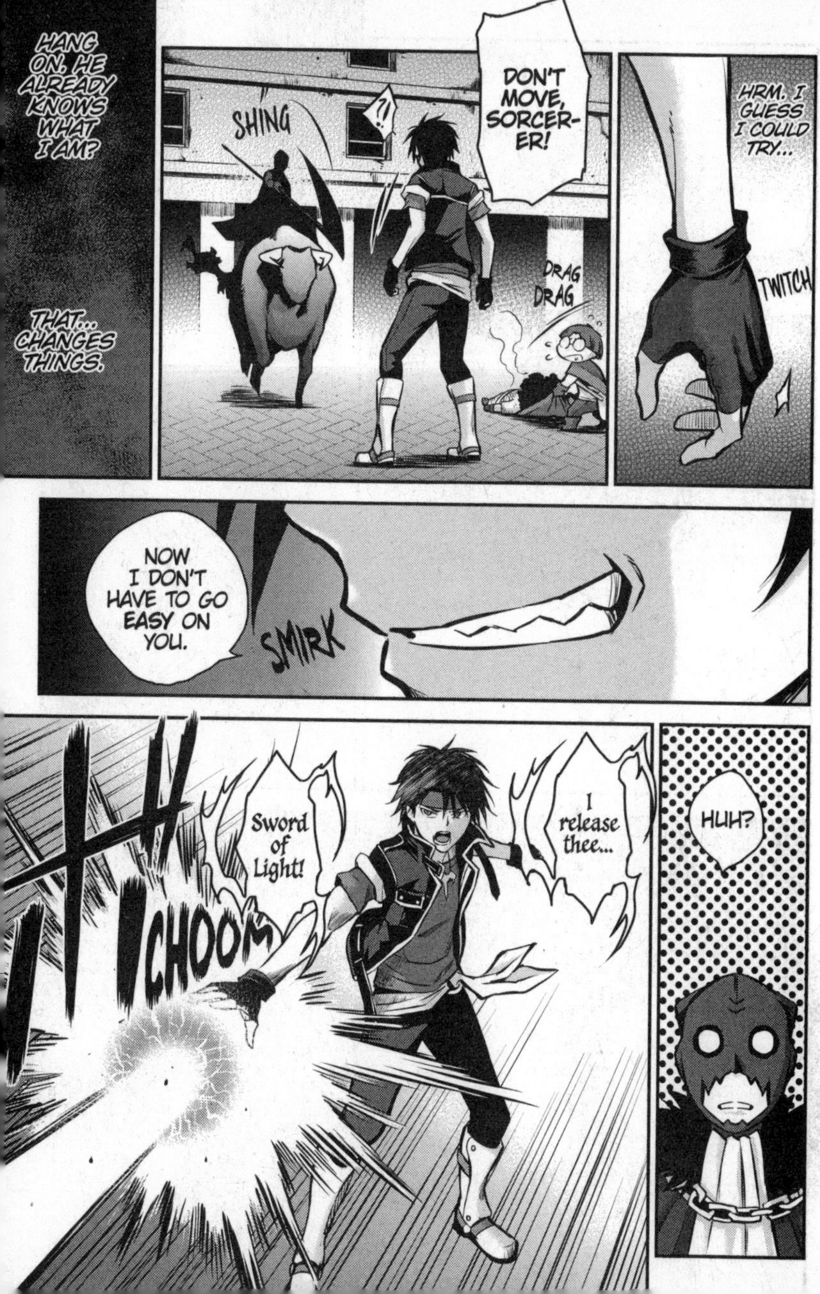
HRM. I GUESS I COULD TRY...
TWITCH
DON'T MOVE, SORCERER!
?!
SHING
DRAG DRAG
HANG ON. HE ALREADY KNOWS WHAT I AM?
THAT... CHANGES THINGS.
NOW I DON'T HAVE TO GO EASY ON YOU.
SMIRK
HUH?
I release thee...
Sword of Light!
CHOOM

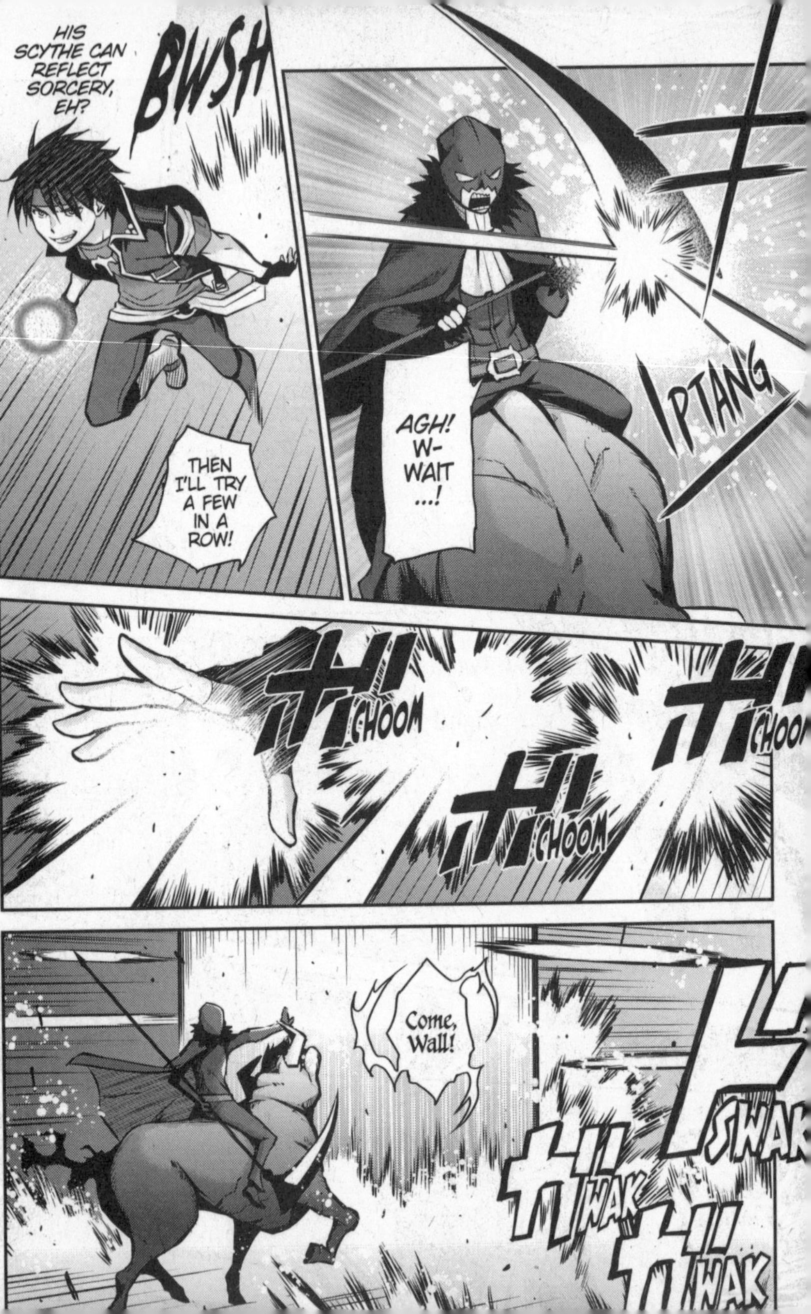

IPTANG
AGH! W-WAIT ...!
BWSH
HIS SCYTHE CAN REFLECT SORCERY, EH?
THEN I'LL TRY A FEW IN A ROW!
CHOO
CHOOM
CHOOM
SWAK
Come, Wall!
WAK
WAK

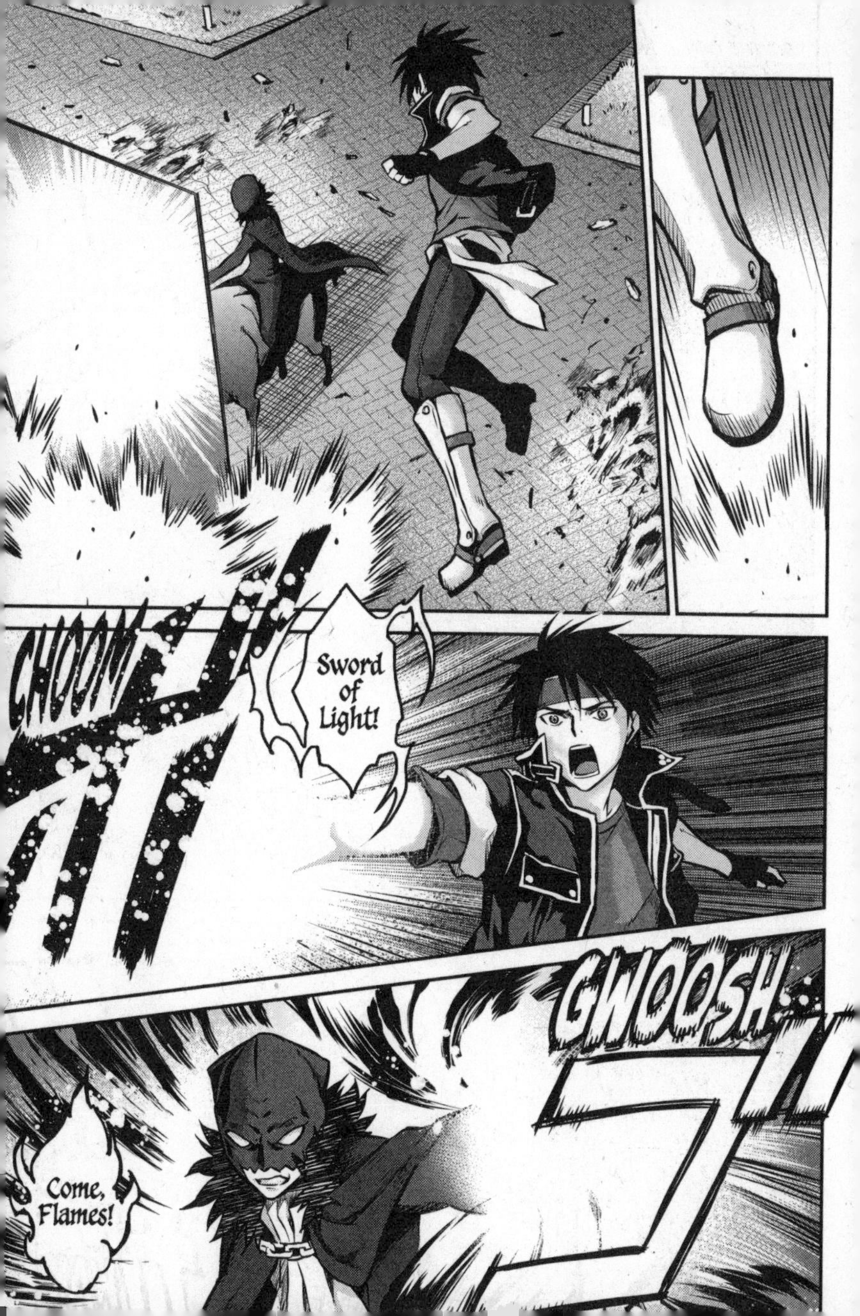
Sword of Light!
CHOOM
GWOOSH
Come, Flames!

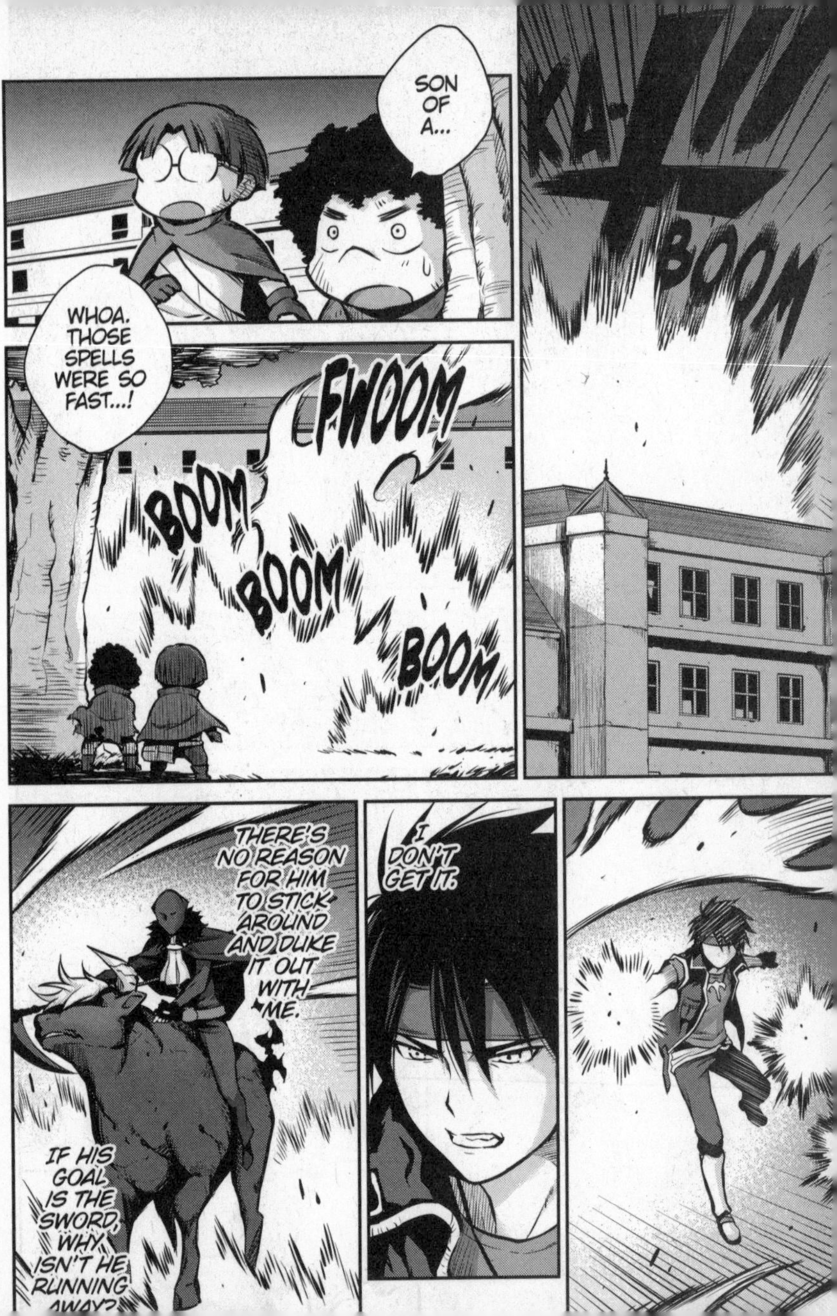
BOOM
SON OF A...
WHOA. THOSE SPELLS WERE SO FAST...!
FWOOM
BOOM
BOOM
BOOM
I DON'T GET IT.
THERE'S NO REASON FOR HIM TO STICK AROUND AND DUKE IT OUT WITH ME.
IF HIS GOAL IS THE SWORD, WHY ISN'T HE RUNNING AWAY?

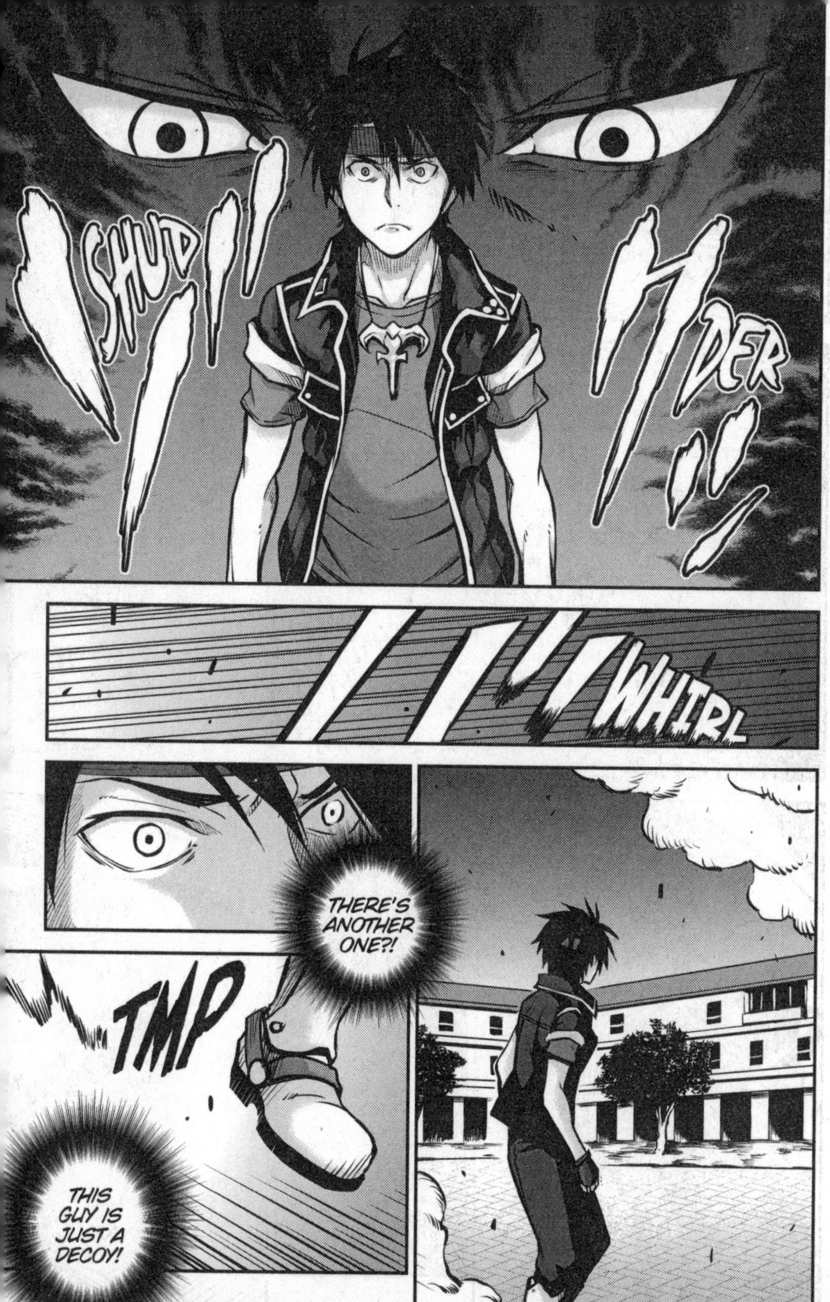
SHUD
DER
WHIRL
THERE'S ANOTHER ONE?!
TMP
THIS GUY IS JUST A DECOY!

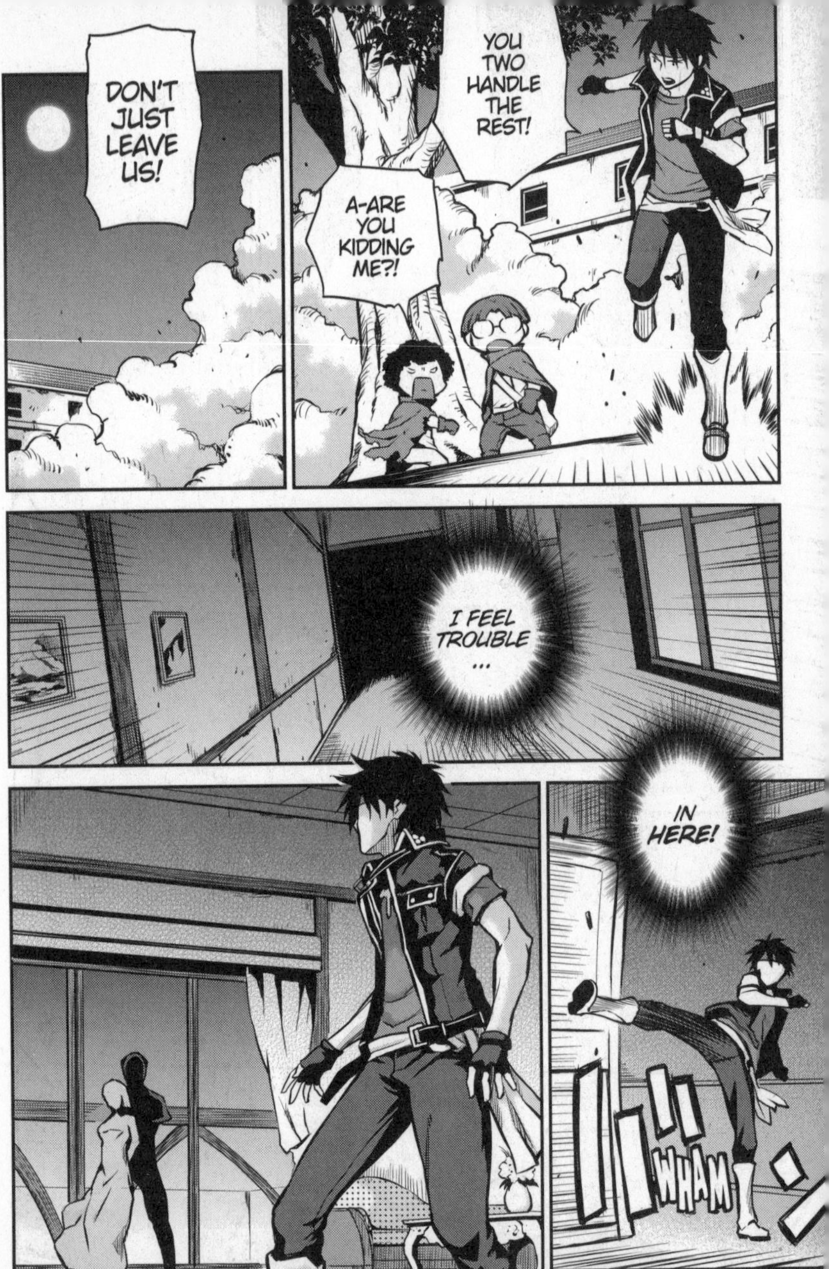
YOU TWO HANDLE THE REST!
A-ARE YOU KIDDING ME?!
DON'T JUST LEAVE US!
I FEEL TROUBLE ...
IN HERE!
WHAM

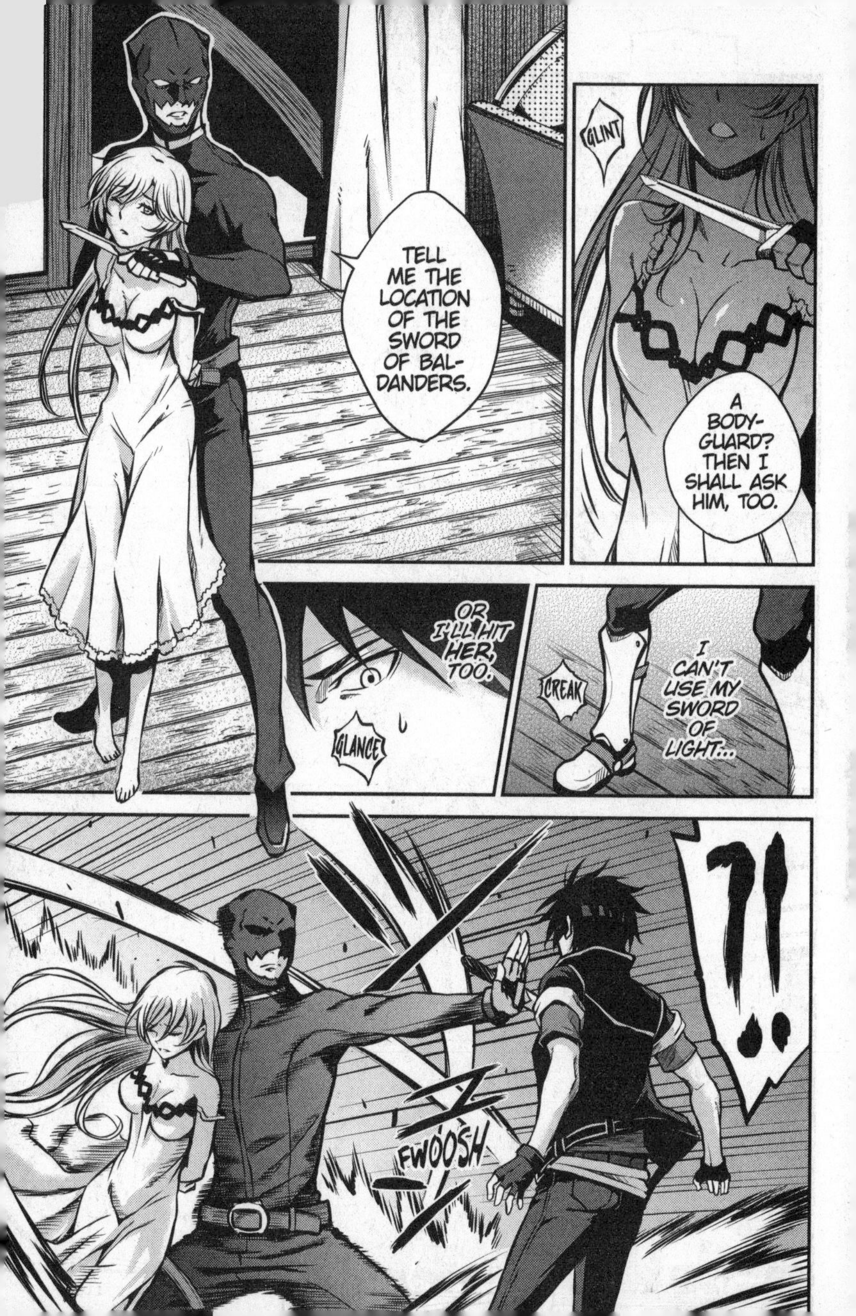
GLINT
A BODY-GUARD? THEN I SHALL ASK HIM, TOO.
CREAK
I CAN'T USE MY SWORD OF LIGHT...
OR I'LL HIT HER, TOO.
GLANCE
TELL ME THE LOCATION OF THE SWORD OF BAL-DANDERS.
?!
FWOOSH

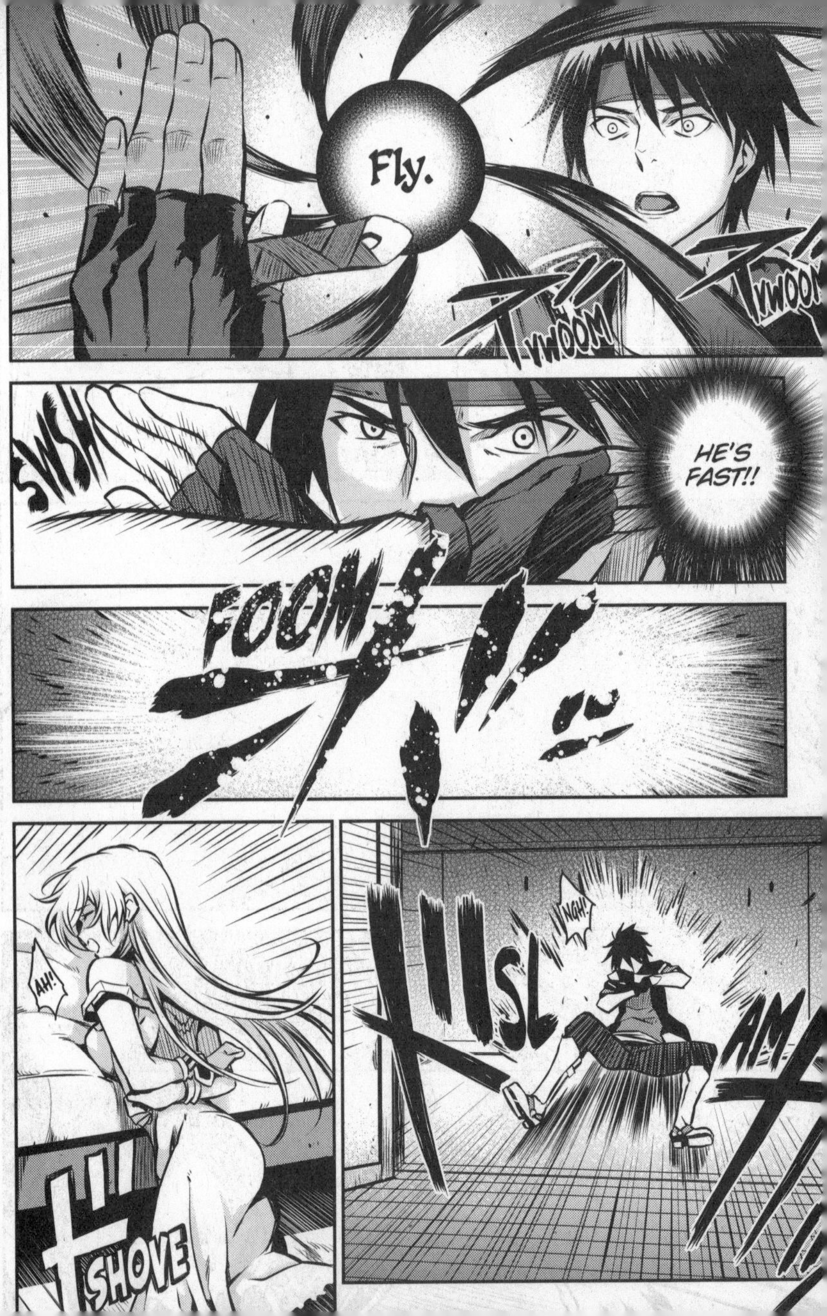
VWOOM
VWOOM
Fly.
HE'S FAST!!
SWSH
FOOM!!
NGH!
SLAM
AH!
SHOVE

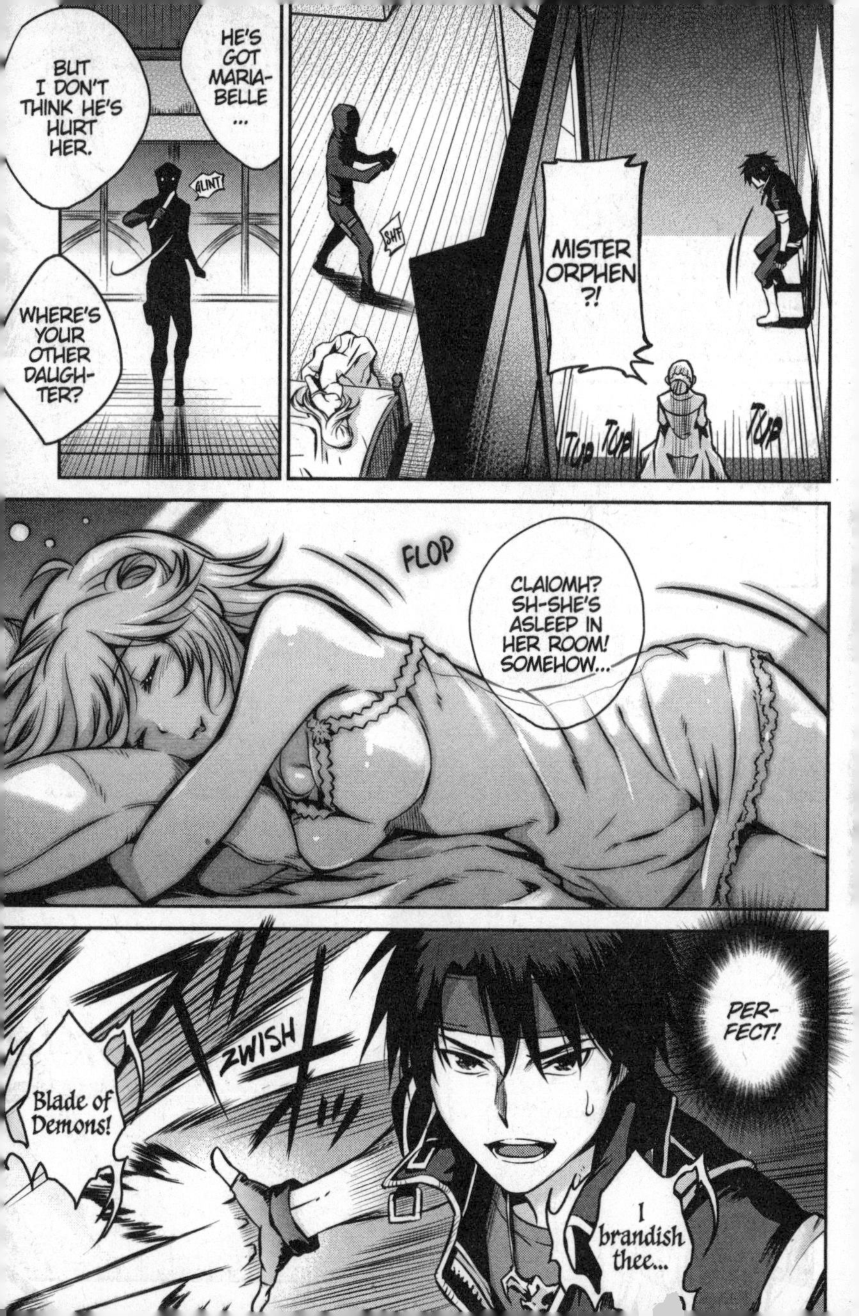
MISTER ORPHEN?!
TUP TUP TUP
SHF
HE'S GOT MARIA-BELLE...
BUT I DON'T THINK HE'S HURT HER.
GLINT!
WHERE'S YOUR OTHER DAUGH-TER?
FLOP
CLAIOMH? SH-SHE'S ASLEEP IN HER ROOM! SOMEHOW...
PER-FECT!
ZWISH
Blade of Demons!
I brandish thee...

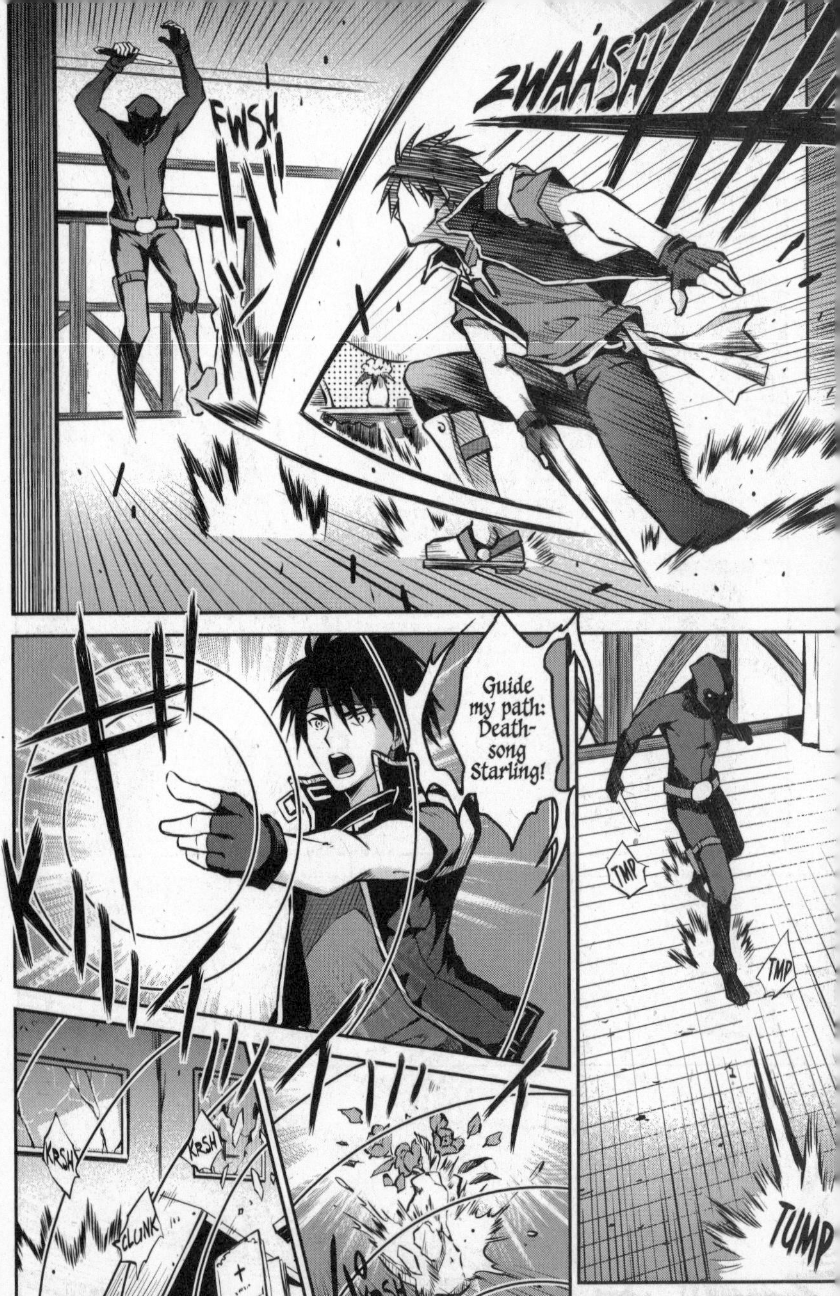
ZWAASH
FWSH
TMP
TMP
TUMP
Guide my path: Death-song Starling!
KRSH
KRSH
CLUNK
KRSH

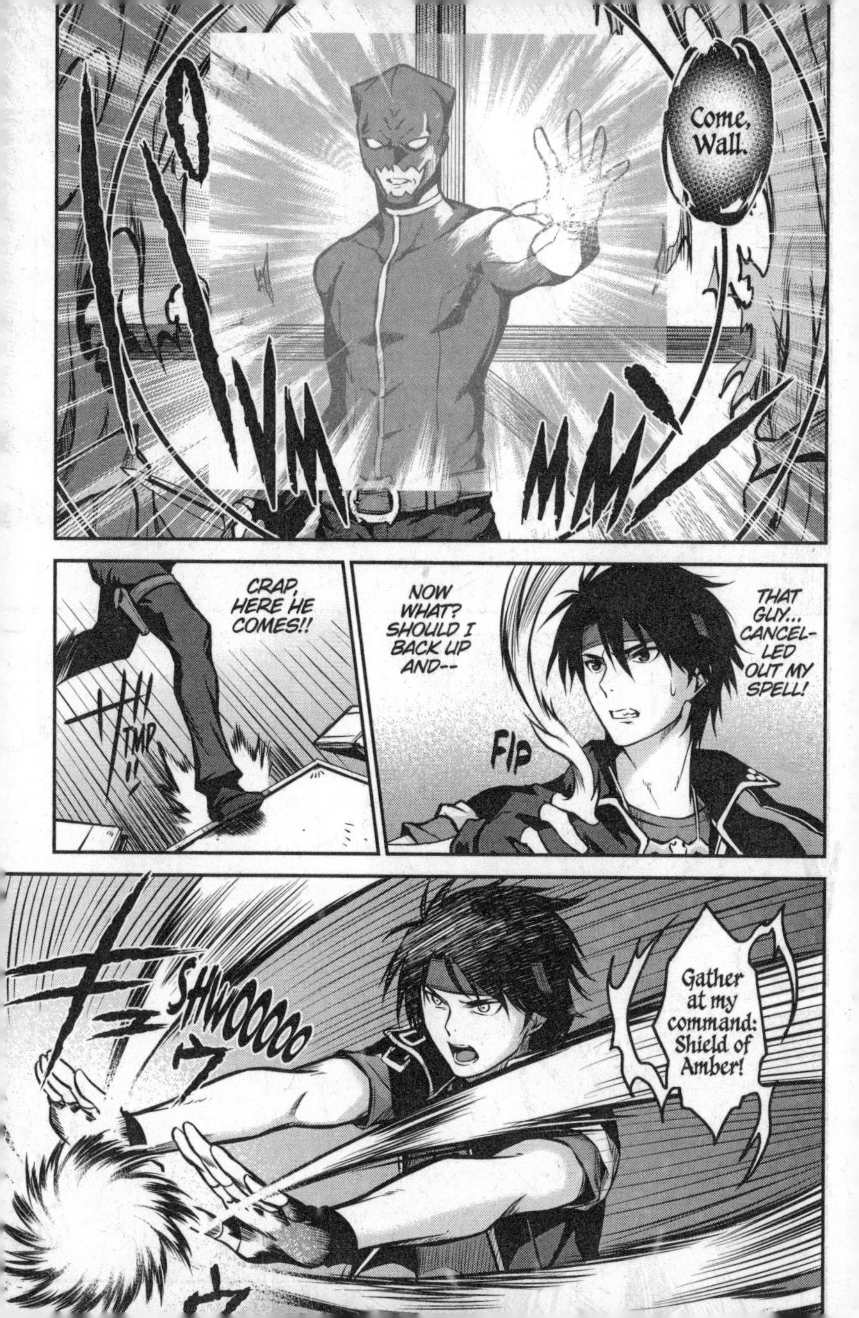
Come, Wall.
THAT GUY... CANCEL-LED OUT MY SPELL!
FLP
NOW WHAT? SHOULD I BACK UP AND--
CRAP, HERE HE COMES!!
TMP!!
Gather at my command: Shield of Amber!
SHWOOOOOO

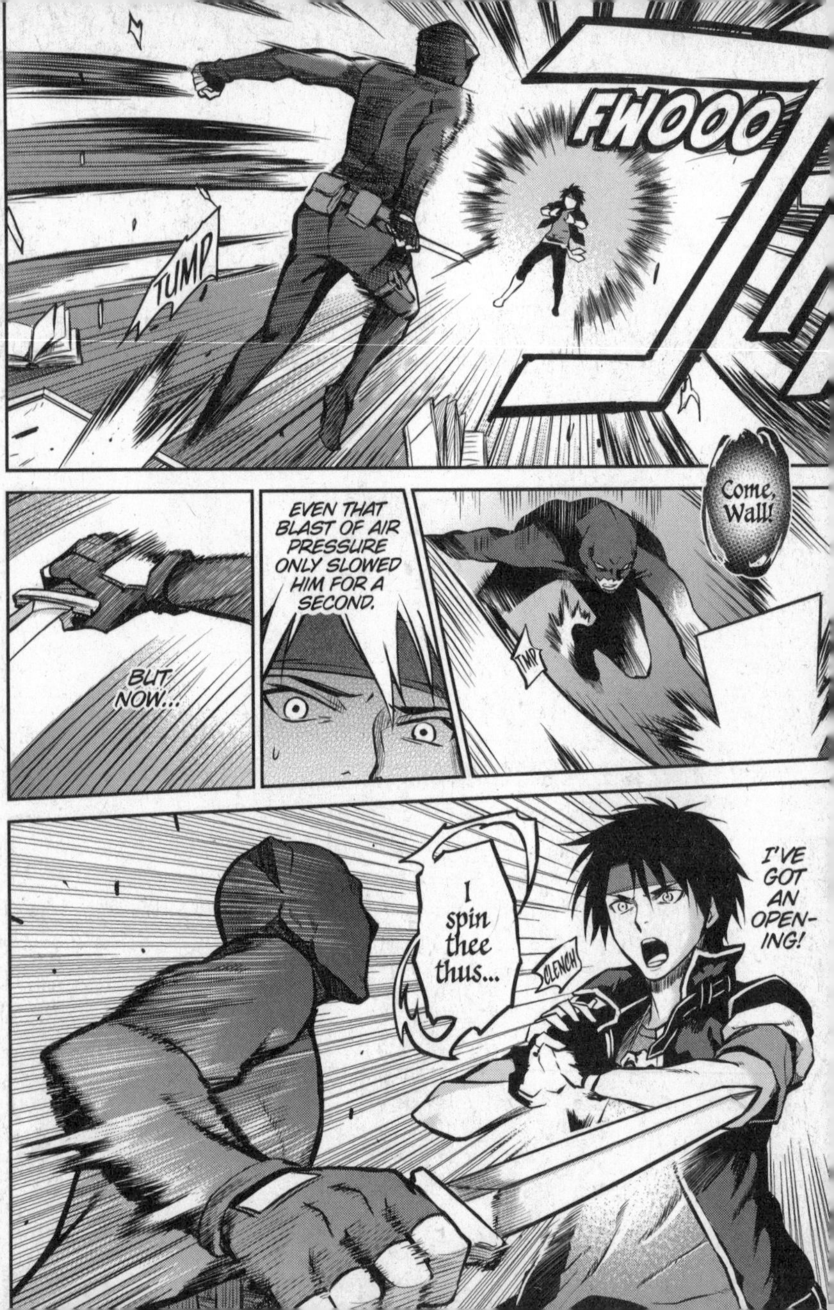
FWOOO
TUMP
Come, Wall!
TMP
EVEN THAT BLAST OF AIR PRESSURE ONLY SLOWED HIM FOR A SECOND.
BUT NOW...
I'VE GOT AN OPEN-ING!
CLENCH
I spin thee thus...

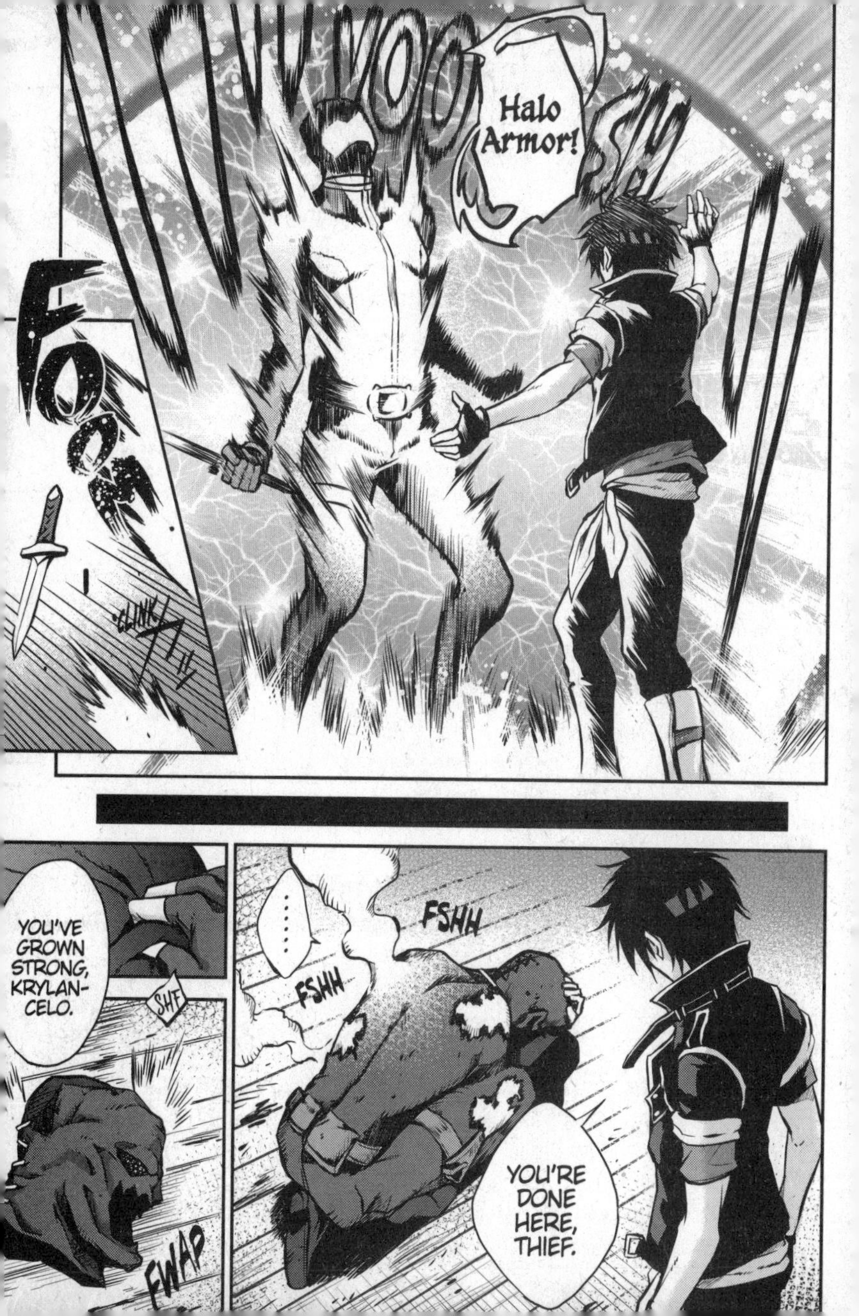
Halo Armor!
FOOM
CLINK
......
FSHH
FSHH
YOU'RE DONE HERE, THIEF.
YOU'VE GROWN STRONG, KRYLANCELO.
SHF
FWAP

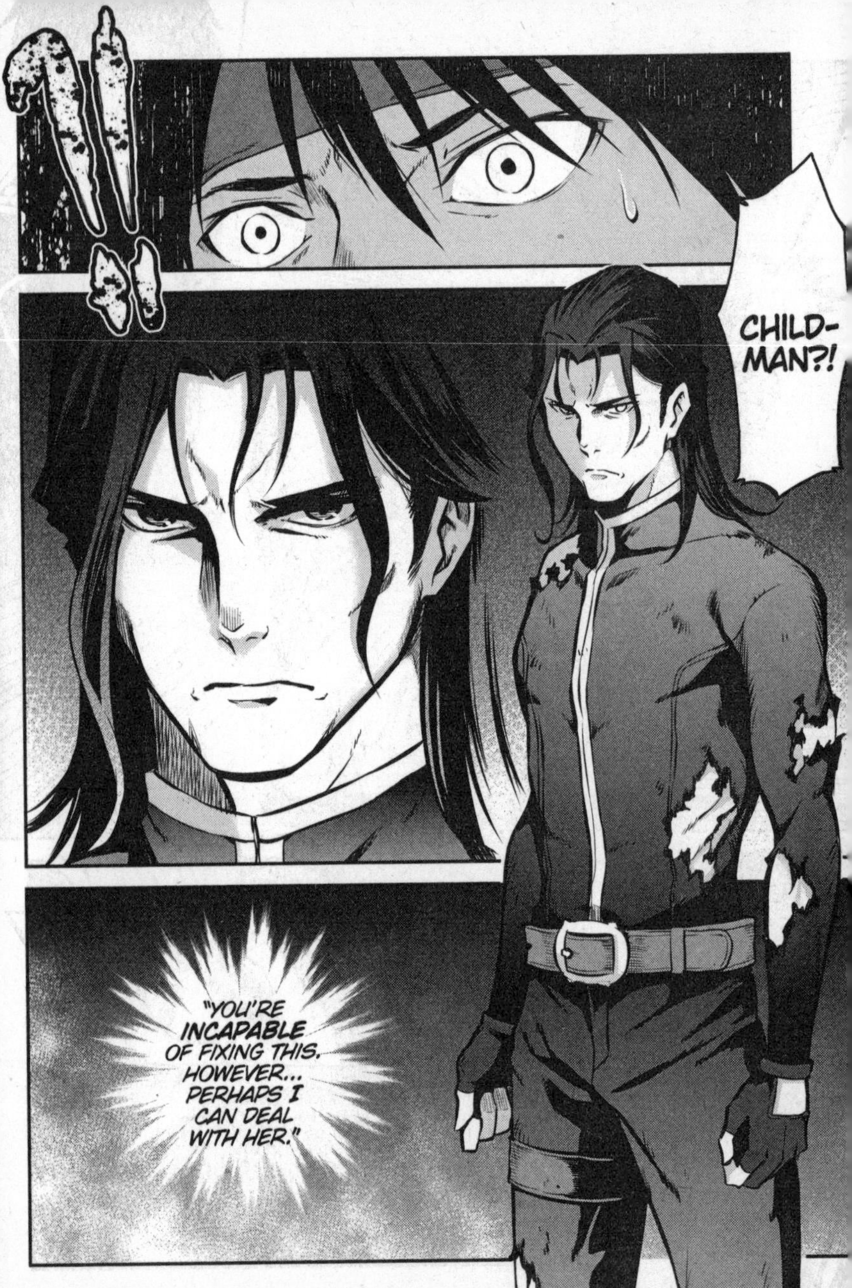
CHILD-MAN?!
"YOU'RE INCAPABLE OF FIXING THIS. HOWEVER... PERHAPS I CAN DEAL WITH HER."

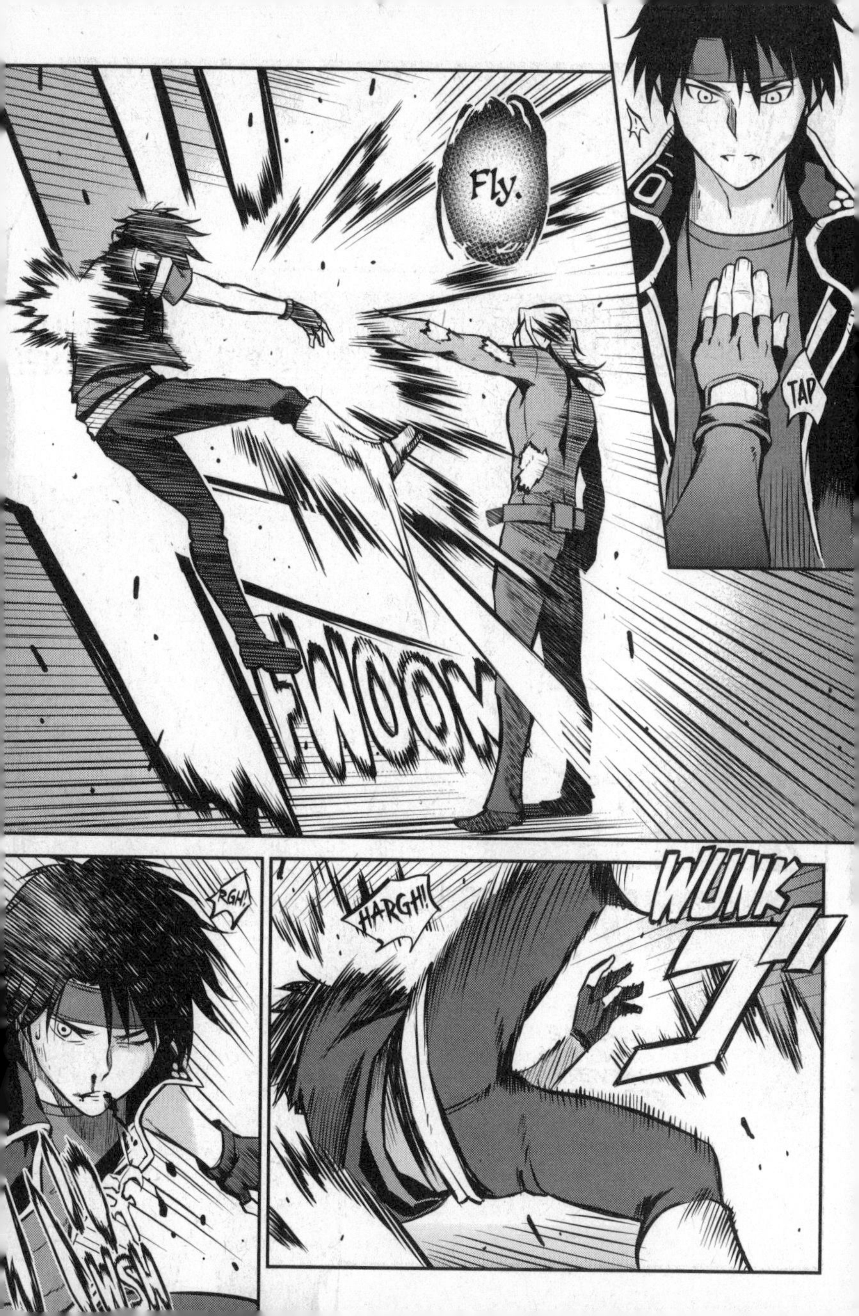
TAP
Fly.
FWOOM
WUNK
HARGH!
RGH!

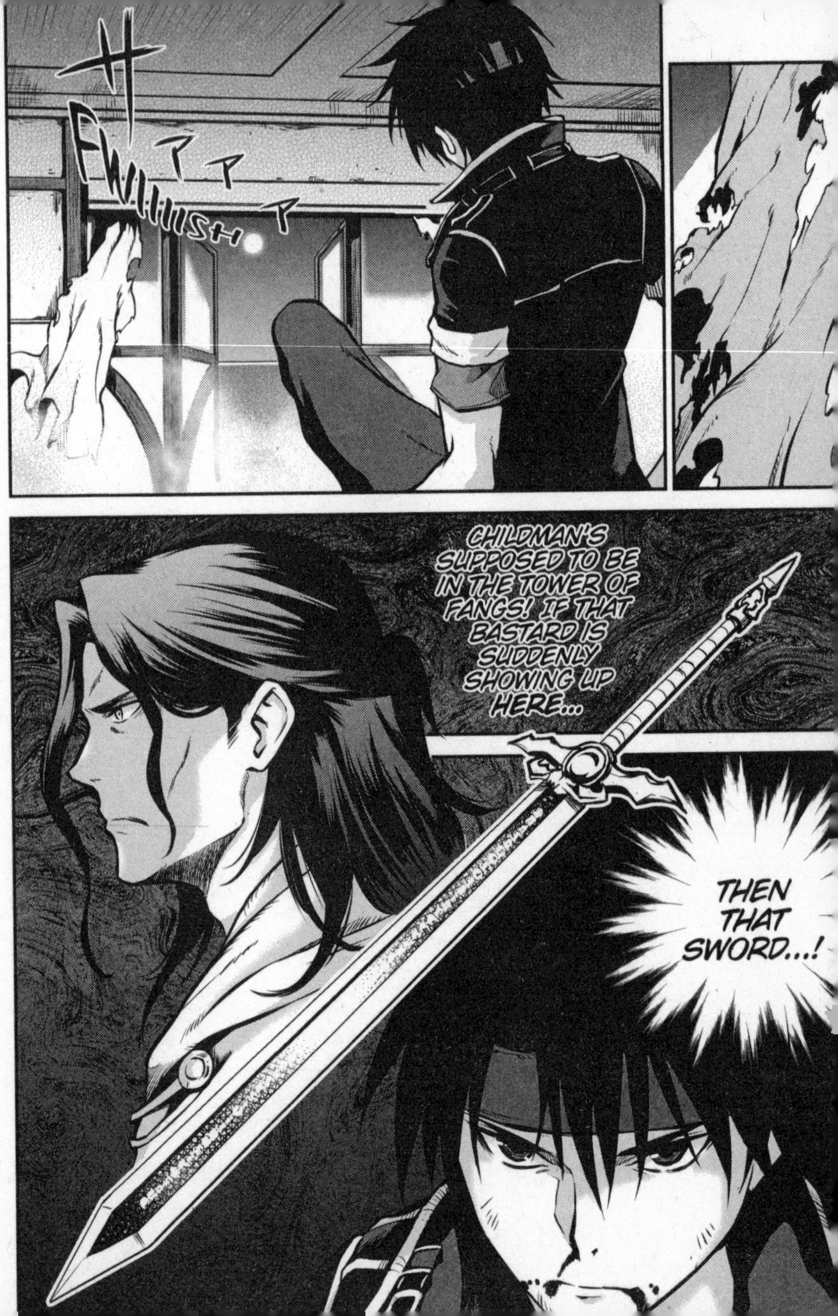
FWIIIISH
CHILDMAN'S SUPPOSED TO BE IN THE TOWER OF FANGS! IF THAT BASTARD IS SUDDENLY SHOWING UP HERE...
THEN THAT SWORD...!

Sorcerous Stabber ORPHEN

CHARACTER DESIGNS ②: CLAIOMH

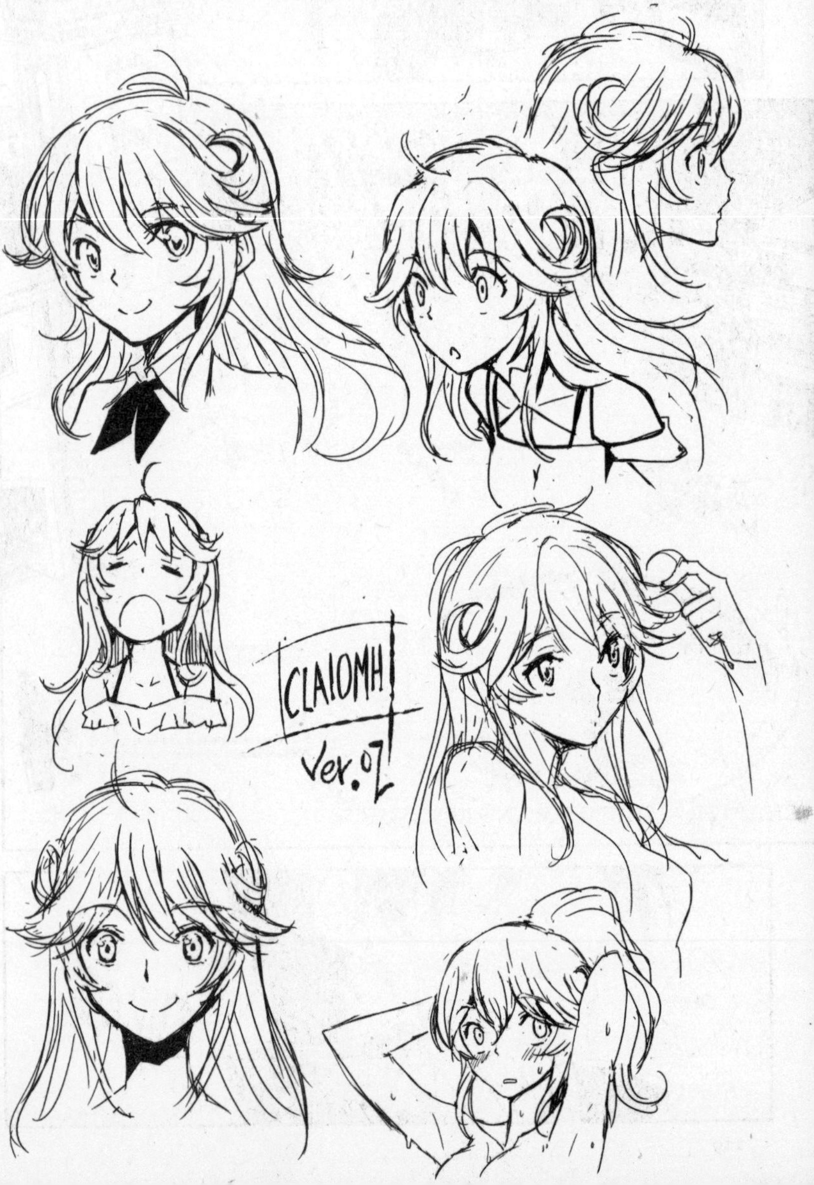
CLAIOMH
Ver.02

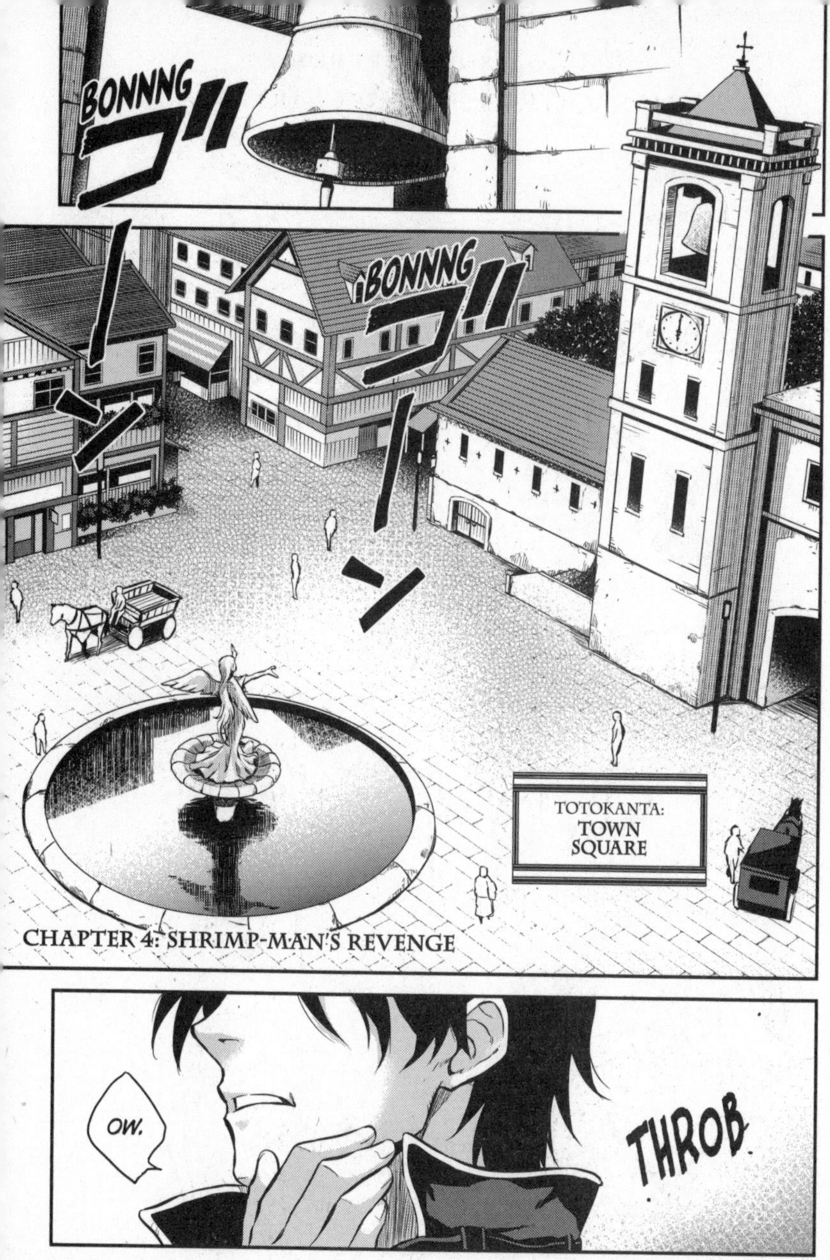
BONNNG
ゴーン
BONNNG
ゴーン
TOTOKANTA: TOWN SQUARE
CHAPTER 4: SHRIMP-MAN'S REVENGE
OW.
THROB

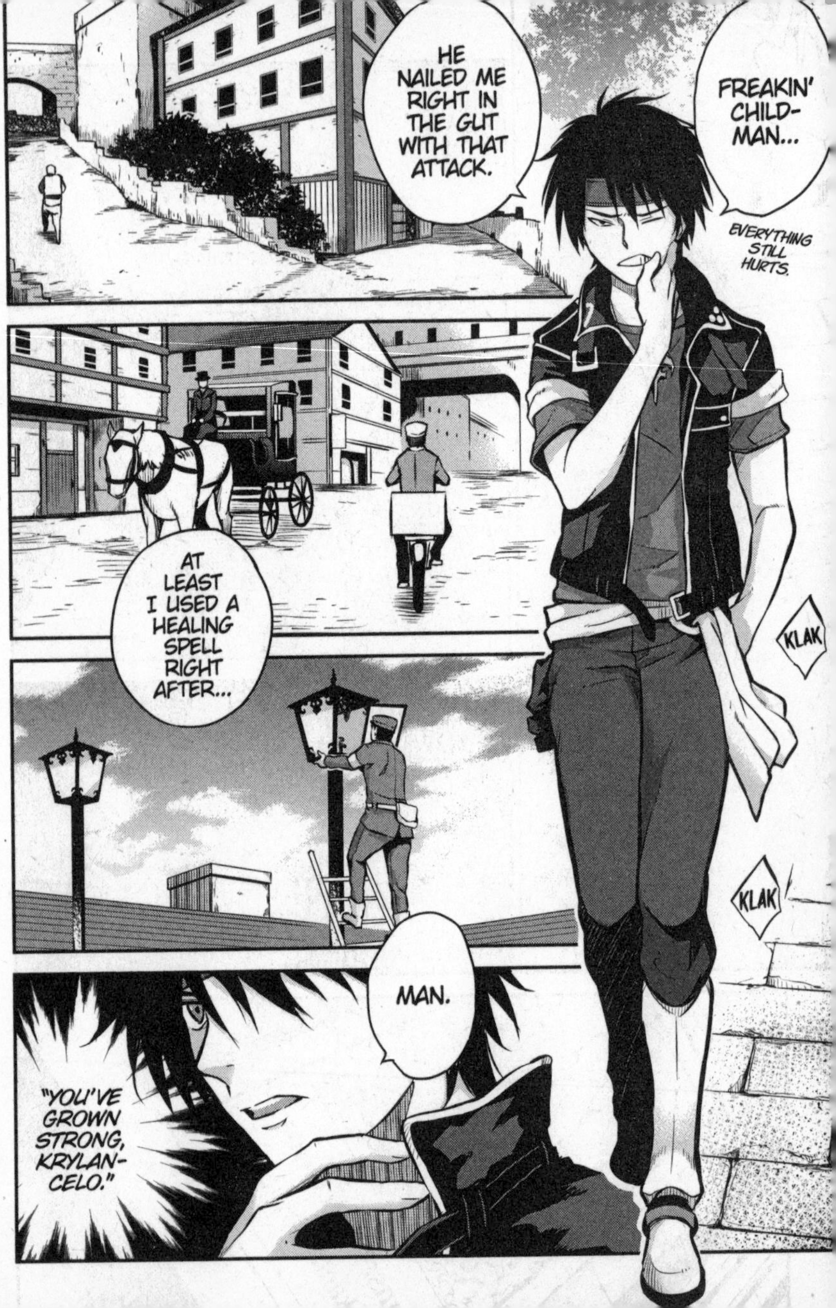
FREAKIN' CHILD-MAN...
EVERYTHING STILL HURTS.
KLAK
KLAK
HE NAILED ME RIGHT IN THE GUT WITH THAT ATTACK.
AT LEAST I USED A HEALING SPELL RIGHT AFTER...
MAN.
"YOU'VE GROWN STRONG, KRYLAN-CELO."

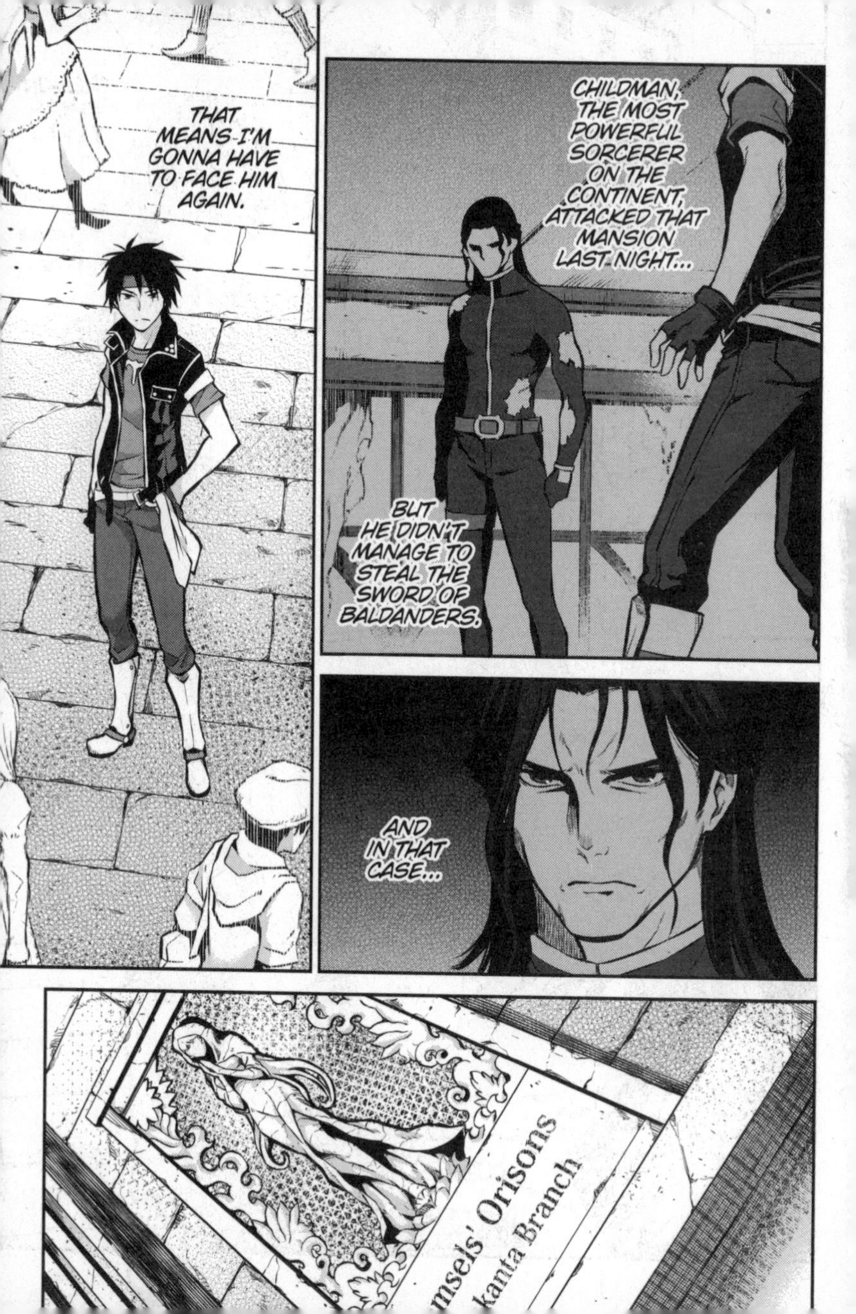
CHILDMAN, THE MOST POWERFUL SORCERER ON THE CONTINENT, ATTACKED THAT MANSION LAST NIGHT...
BUT HE DIDN'T MANAGE TO STEAL THE SWORD OF BALDANDERS.
AND IN THAT CASE...
THAT MEANS I'M GONNA HAVE TO FACE HIM AGAIN.
msels' Orisons
kanta Branch

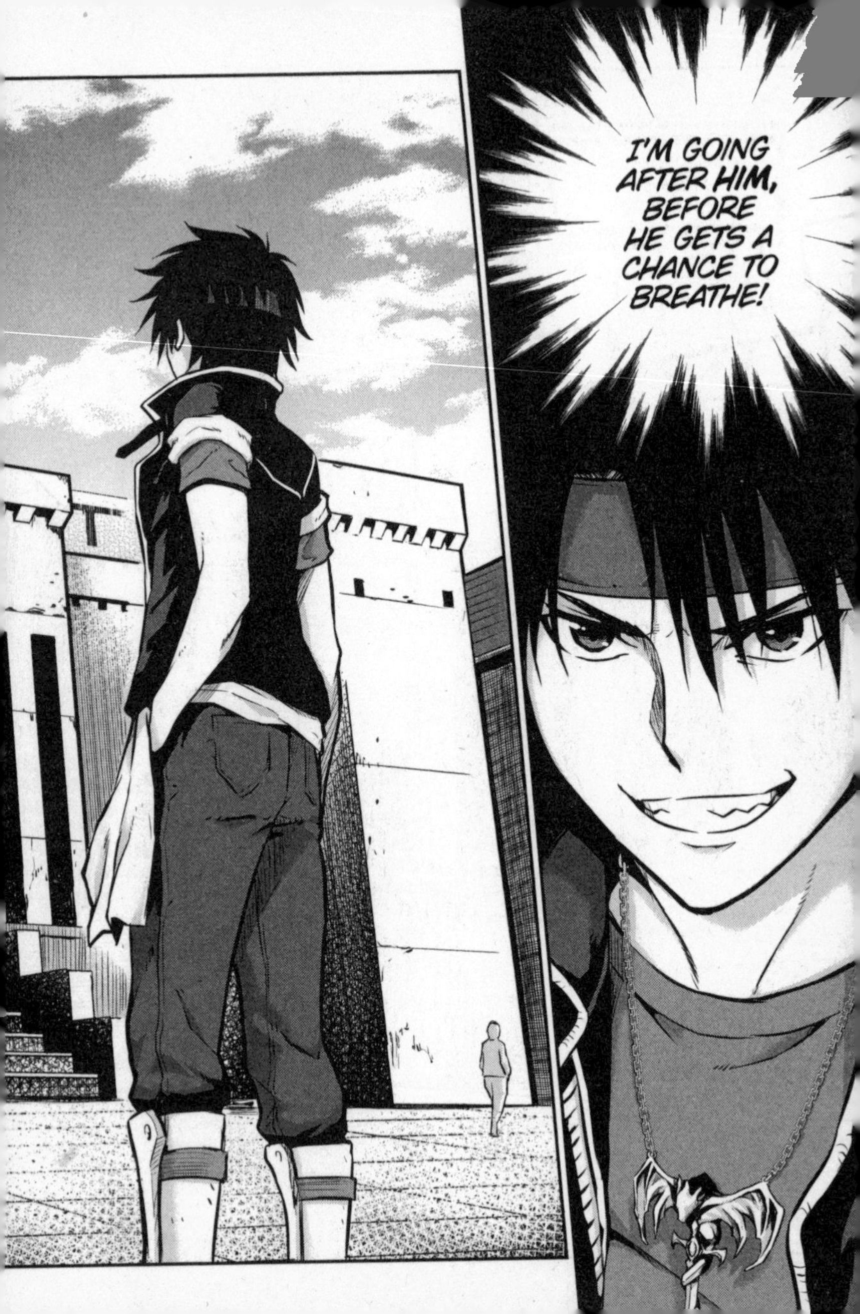
I'M GOING AFTER HIM, BEFORE HE GETS A CHANCE TO BREATHE!

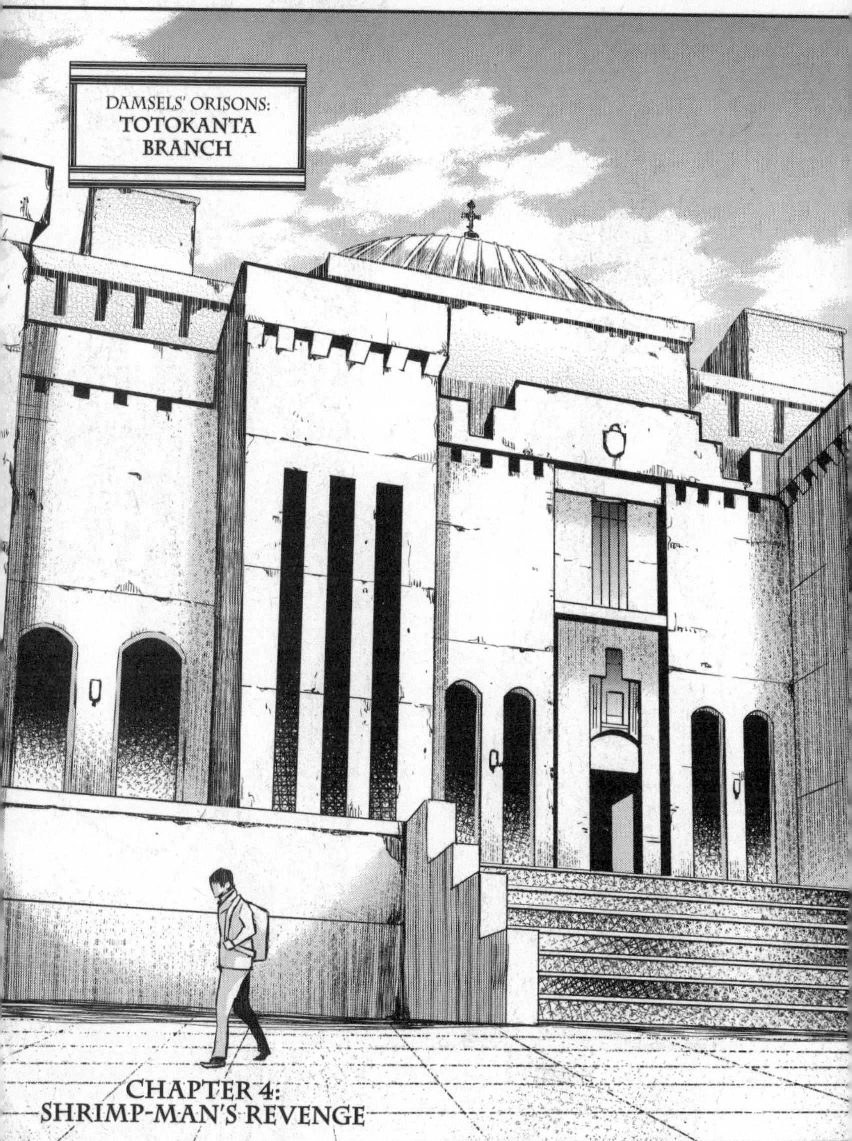
DAMSELS' ORISONS: TOTOKANTA BRANCH
CHAPTER 4: SHRIMP-MAN'S REVENGE
Sorcerous Stabber ORPHEN

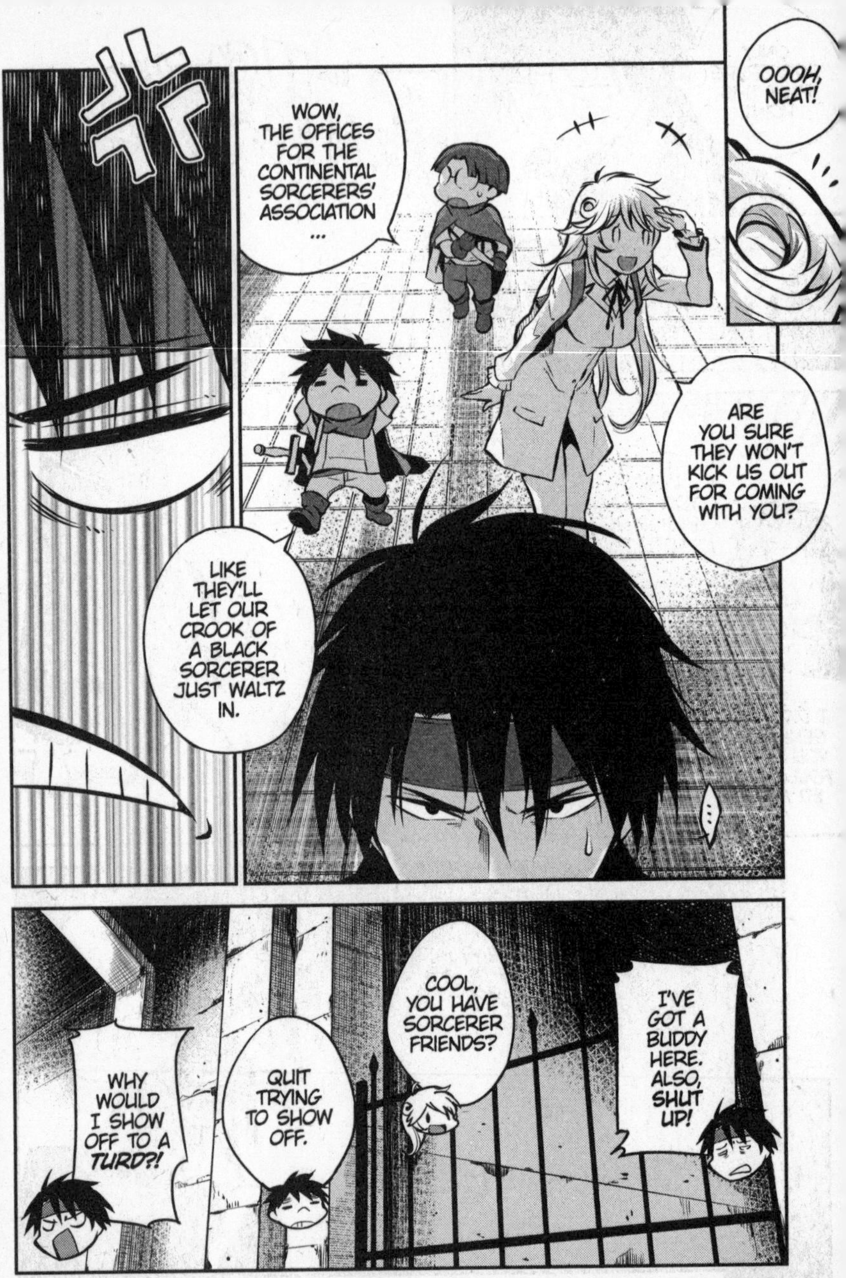

OOOH, NEAT!
WOW, THE OFFICES FOR THE CONTINENTAL SORCERERS' ASSOCIATION ...
ARE YOU SURE THEY WON'T KICK US OUT FOR COMING WITH YOU?
LIKE THEY'LL LET OUR CROOK OF A BLACK SORCERER JUST WALTZ IN.
I'VE GOT A BUDDY HERE. ALSO, SHUT UP!
COOL, YOU HAVE SORCERER FRIENDS?
QUIT TRYING TO SHOW OFF.
WHY WOULD I SHOW OFF TO A *TURD?!*

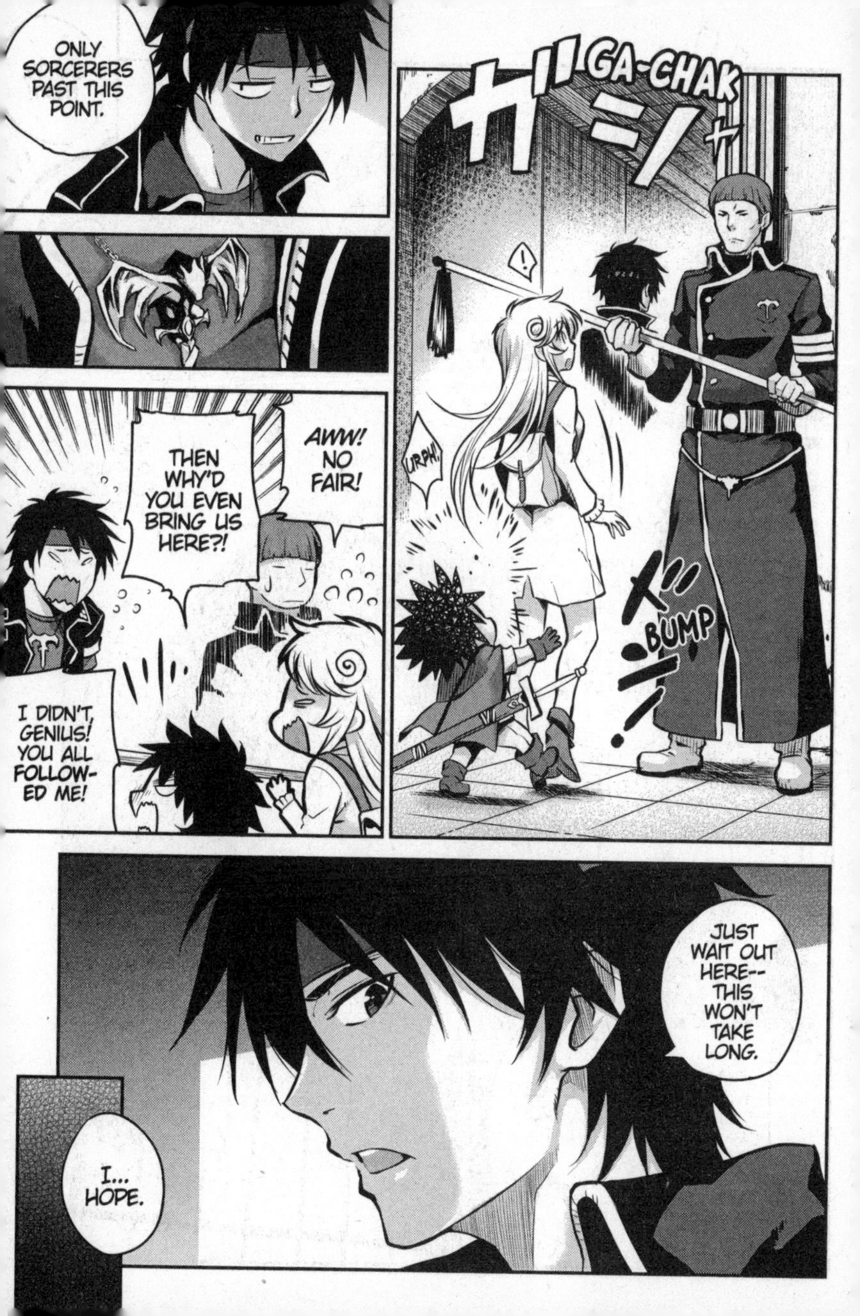
GA-CHAK
!
URPH!
BUMP
ONLY SORCERERS PAST THIS POINT.
AWW! NO FAIR!
THEN WHY'D YOU EVEN BRING US HERE?!
I DIDN'T, GENIUS! YOU ALL FOLLOWED ME!
JUST WAIT OUT HERE--THIS WON'T TAKE LONG.
I... HOPE.

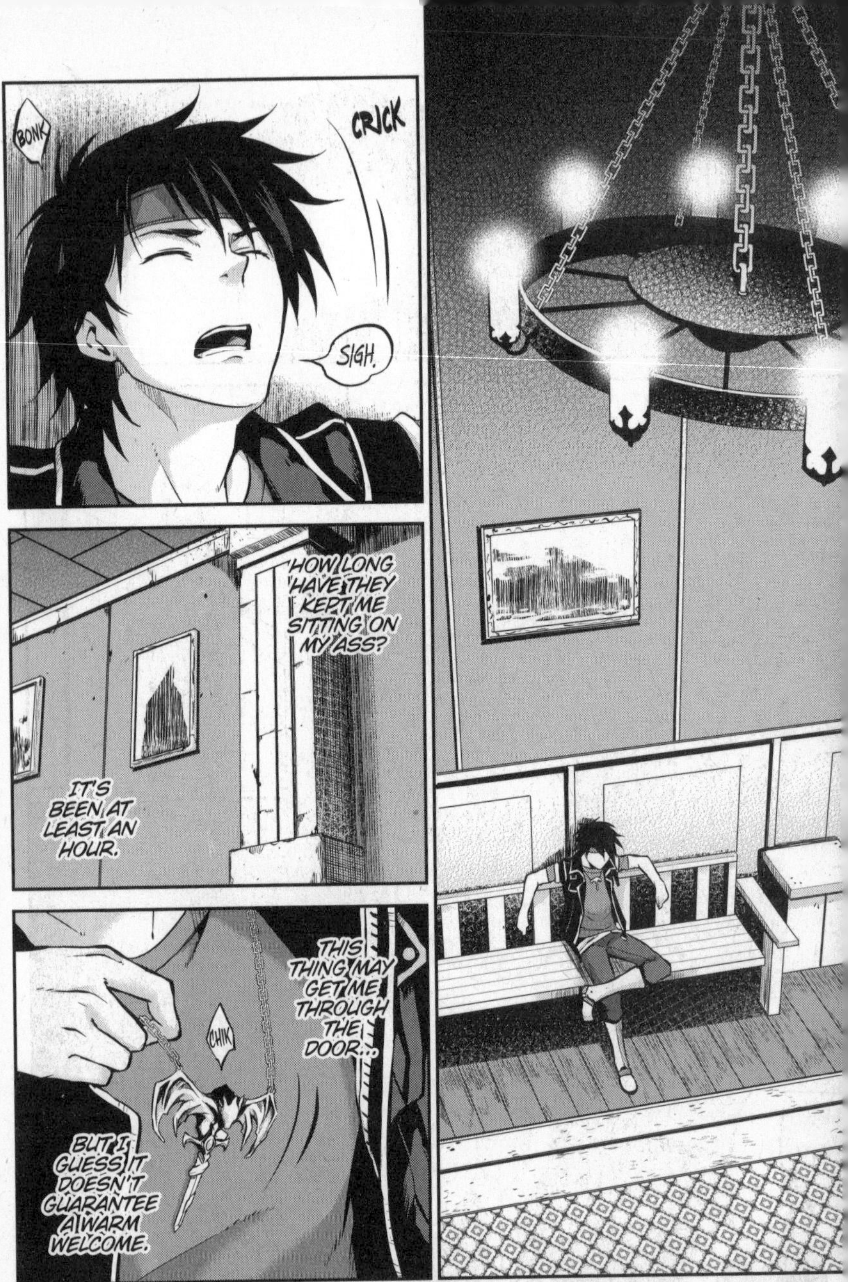
CRICK
BONK
SIGH.
HOW LONG HAVE THEY KEPT ME SITTING ON MY ASS?
IT'S BEEN AT LEAST AN HOUR.
THIS THING MAY GET ME THROUGH THE DOOR...
CHIK
BUT I GUESS IT DOESN'T GUARANTEE A WARM WELCOME.

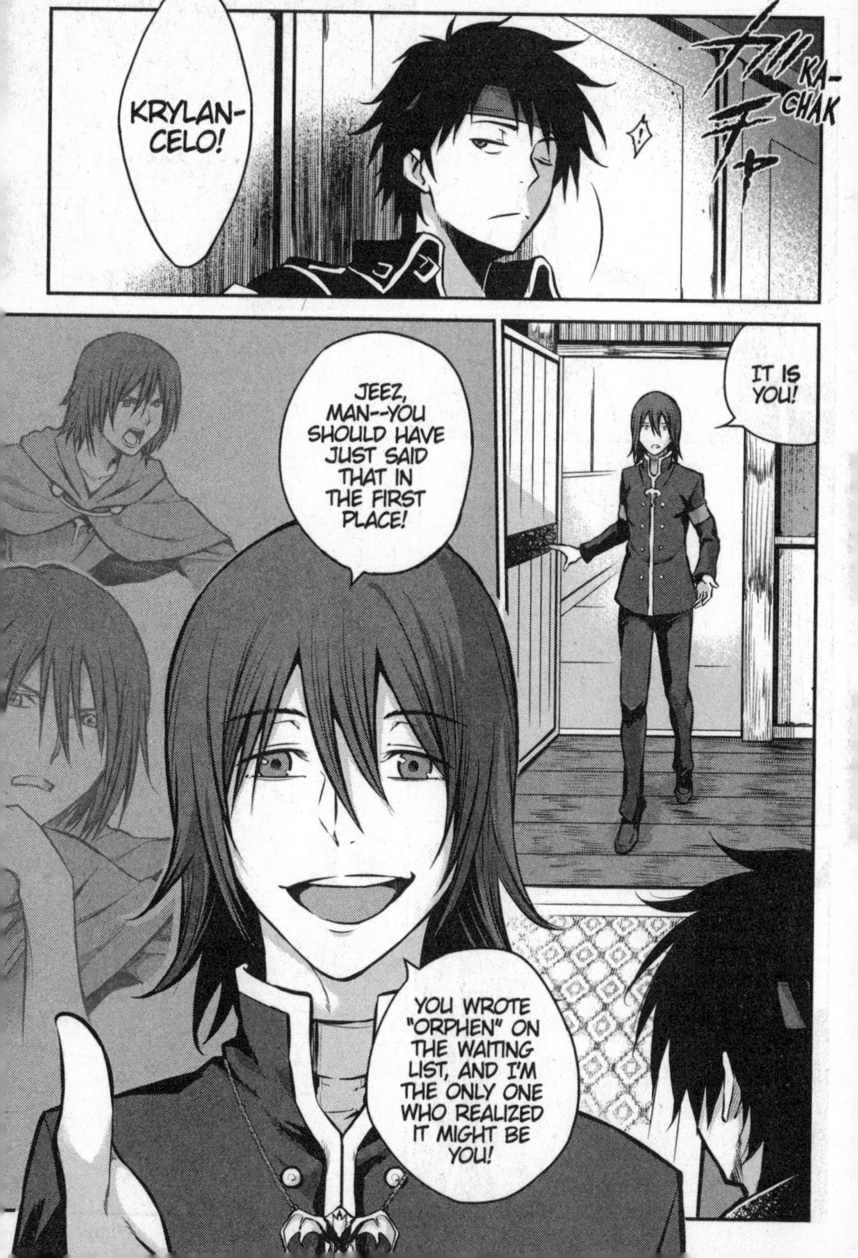
KA-CHAK
KRYLAN-CELO!
IT IS YOU!
JEEZ, MAN--YOU SHOULD HAVE JUST SAID THAT IN THE FIRST PLACE!
YOU WROTE "ORPHEN" ON THE WAITING LIST, AND I'M THE ONLY ONE WHO REALIZED IT MIGHT BE YOU!

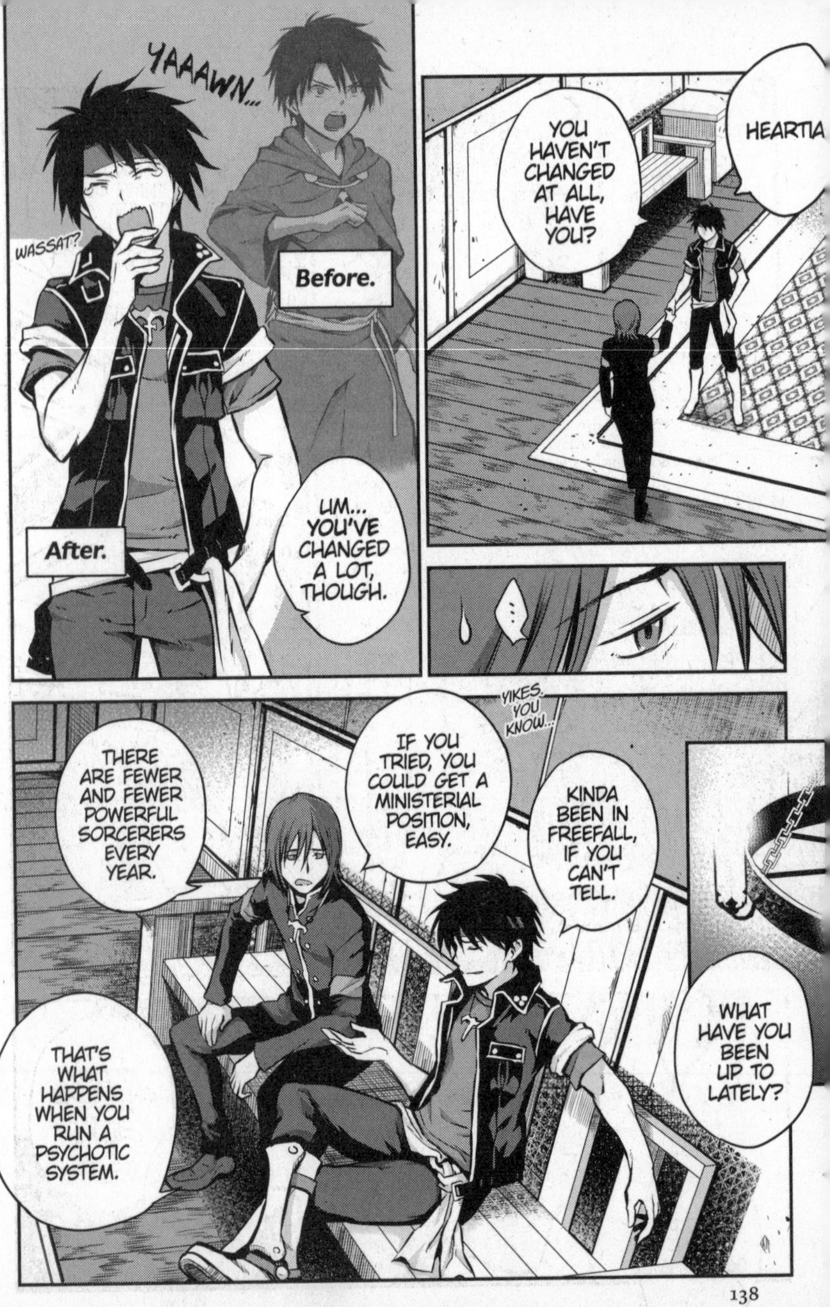
HEARTIA
YOU HAVEN'T CHANGED AT ALL, HAVE YOU?
...
YAAAWN...
Before.
WASSAT?
UM... YOU'VE CHANGED A LOT, THOUGH.
After.
WHAT HAVE YOU BEEN UP TO LATELY?
YIKES. YOU KNOW...
KINDA BEEN IN FREEFALL, IF YOU CAN'T TELL.
IF YOU TRIED, YOU COULD GET A MINISTERIAL POSITION, EASY.
THERE ARE FEWER AND FEWER POWERFUL SORCERERS EVERY YEAR.
THAT'S WHAT HAPPENS WHEN YOU RUN A PSYCHOTIC SYSTEM.

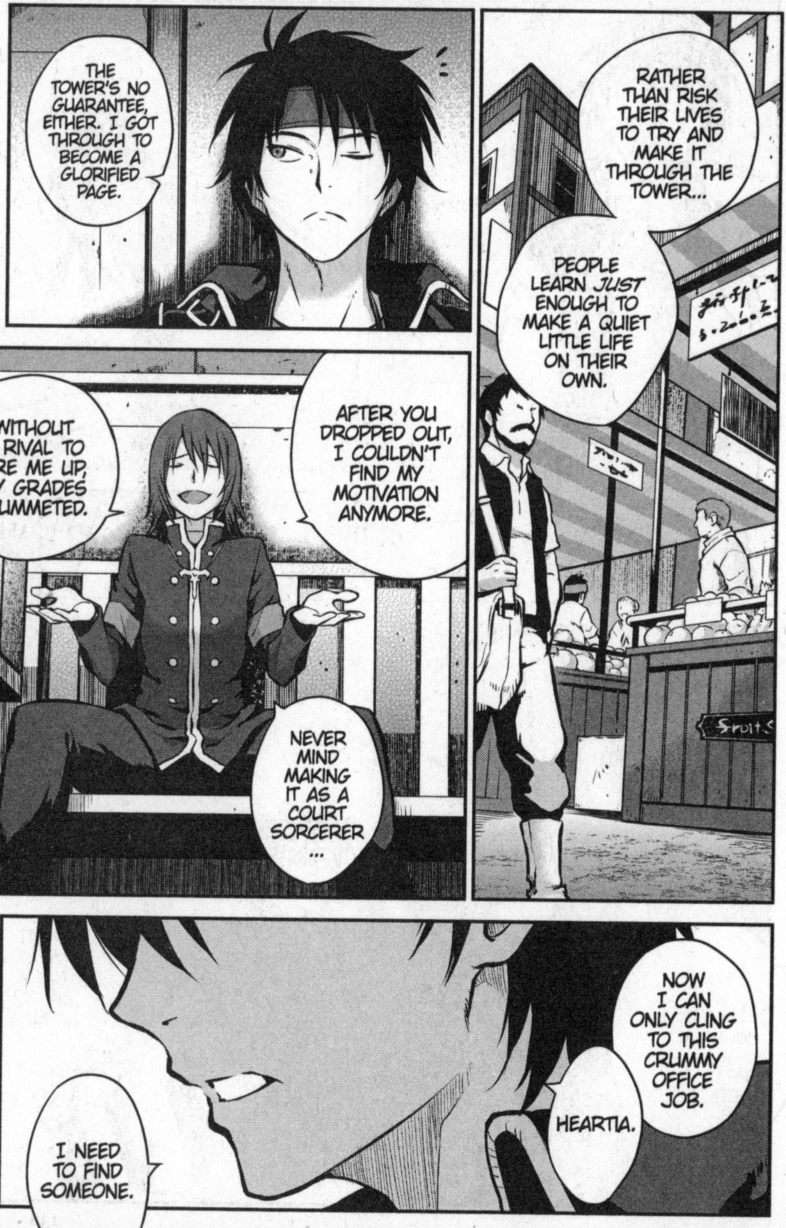
RATHER THAN RISK THEIR LIVES TO TRY AND MAKE IT THROUGH THE TOWER...
PEOPLE LEARN *JUST* ENOUGH TO MAKE A QUIET LITTLE LIFE ON THEIR OWN.
THE TOWER'S NO GUARANTEE, EITHER. I GOT THROUGH TO BECOME A GLORIFIED PAGE.
AFTER YOU DROPPED OUT, I COULDN'T FIND MY MOTIVATION ANYMORE.
WITHOUT A RIVAL TO FIRE ME UP, MY GRADES PLUMMETED.
NEVER MIND MAKING IT AS A COURT SORCERER...
NOW I CAN ONLY CLING TO THIS CRUMMY OFFICE JOB.
HEARTIA.
I NEED TO FIND SOMEONE.

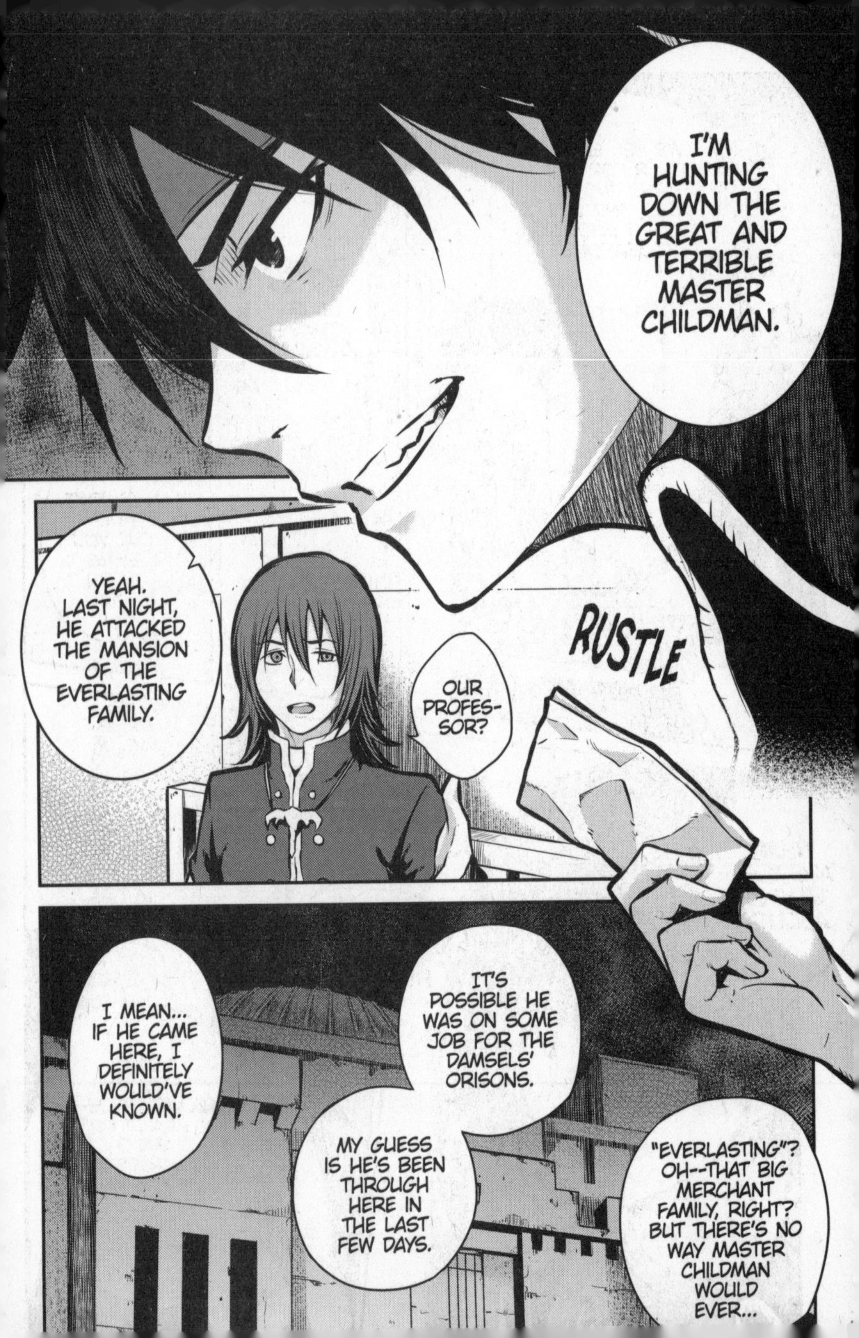
I'M HUNTING DOWN THE GREAT AND TERRIBLE MASTER CHILDMAN.
RUSTLE
OUR PROFES-SOR?
YEAH. LAST NIGHT, HE ATTACKED THE MANSION OF THE EVERLASTING FAMILY.
"EVERLASTING"? OH--THAT BIG MERCHANT FAMILY, RIGHT? BUT THERE'S NO WAY MASTER CHILDMAN WOULD EVER...
IT'S POSSIBLE HE WAS ON SOME JOB FOR THE DAMSELS' ORISONS.
MY GUESS IS HE'S BEEN THROUGH HERE IN THE LAST FEW DAYS.
I MEAN... IF HE CAME HERE, I DEFINITELY WOULD'VE KNOWN.

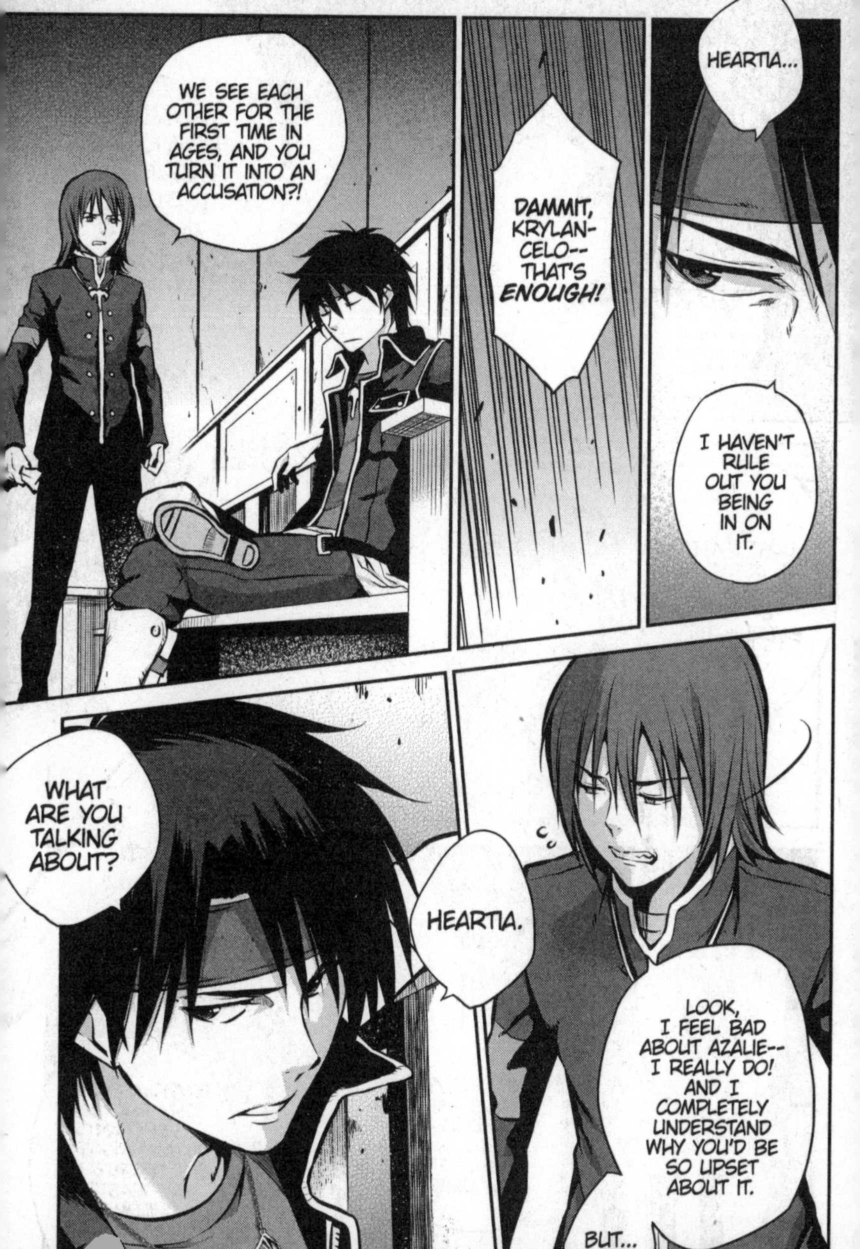
HEARTIA...
I HAVEN'T RULE OUT YOU BEING IN ON IT.
DAMMIT, KRYLAN-CELO-- THAT'S *ENOUGH!*
WE SEE EACH OTHER FOR THE FIRST TIME IN AGES, AND YOU TURN IT INTO AN ACCUSATION?!
HEARTIA.
LOOK, I FEEL BAD ABOUT AZALIE-- I REALLY DO! AND I COMPLETELY UNDERSTAND WHY YOU'D BE SO UPSET ABOUT IT.
BUT...
WHAT ARE YOU TALKING ABOUT?

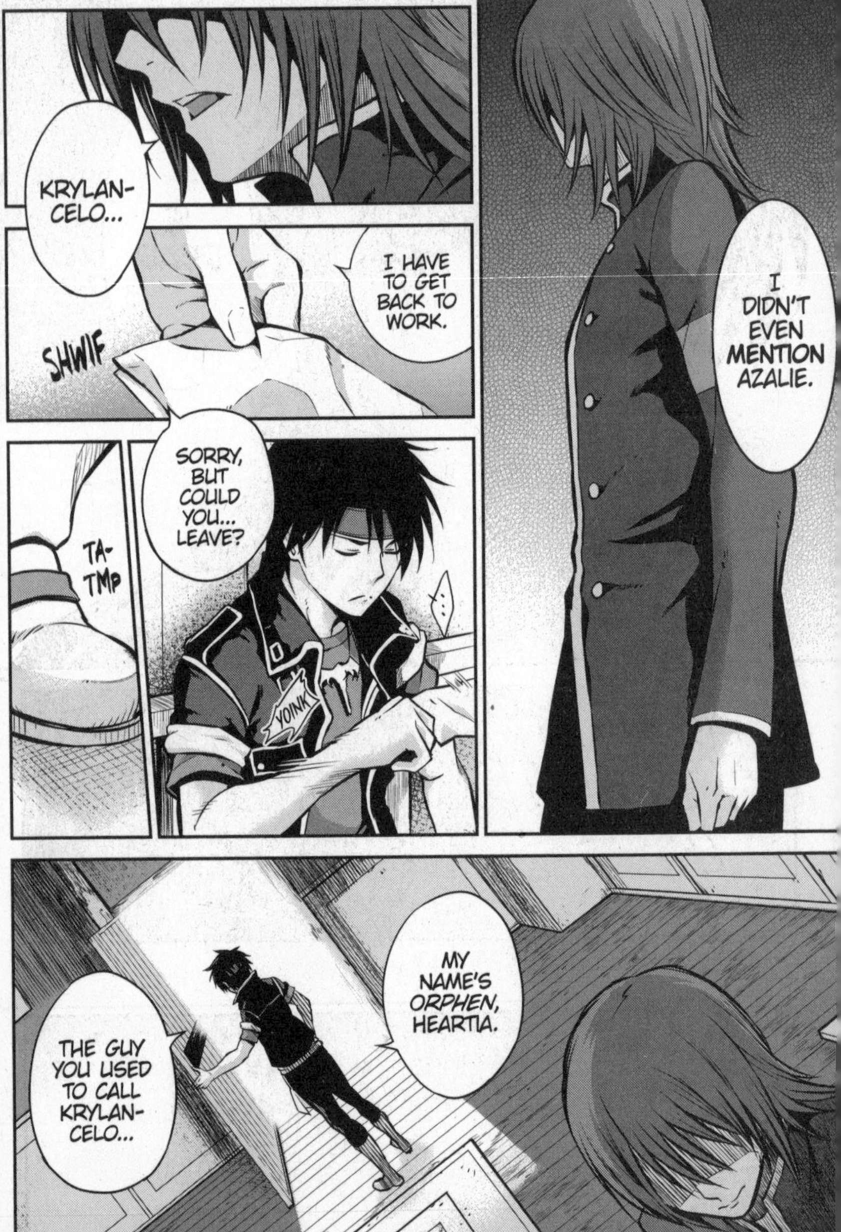
I DIDN'T EVEN MENTION AZALIE.
KRYLAN-CELO...
I HAVE TO GET BACK TO WORK.
SHWIF
SORRY, BUT COULD YOU... LEAVE?
YOINK
TA-TMP
MY NAME'S *ORPHEN*, HEARTIA.
THE GUY YOU USED TO CALL KRYLAN-CELO...

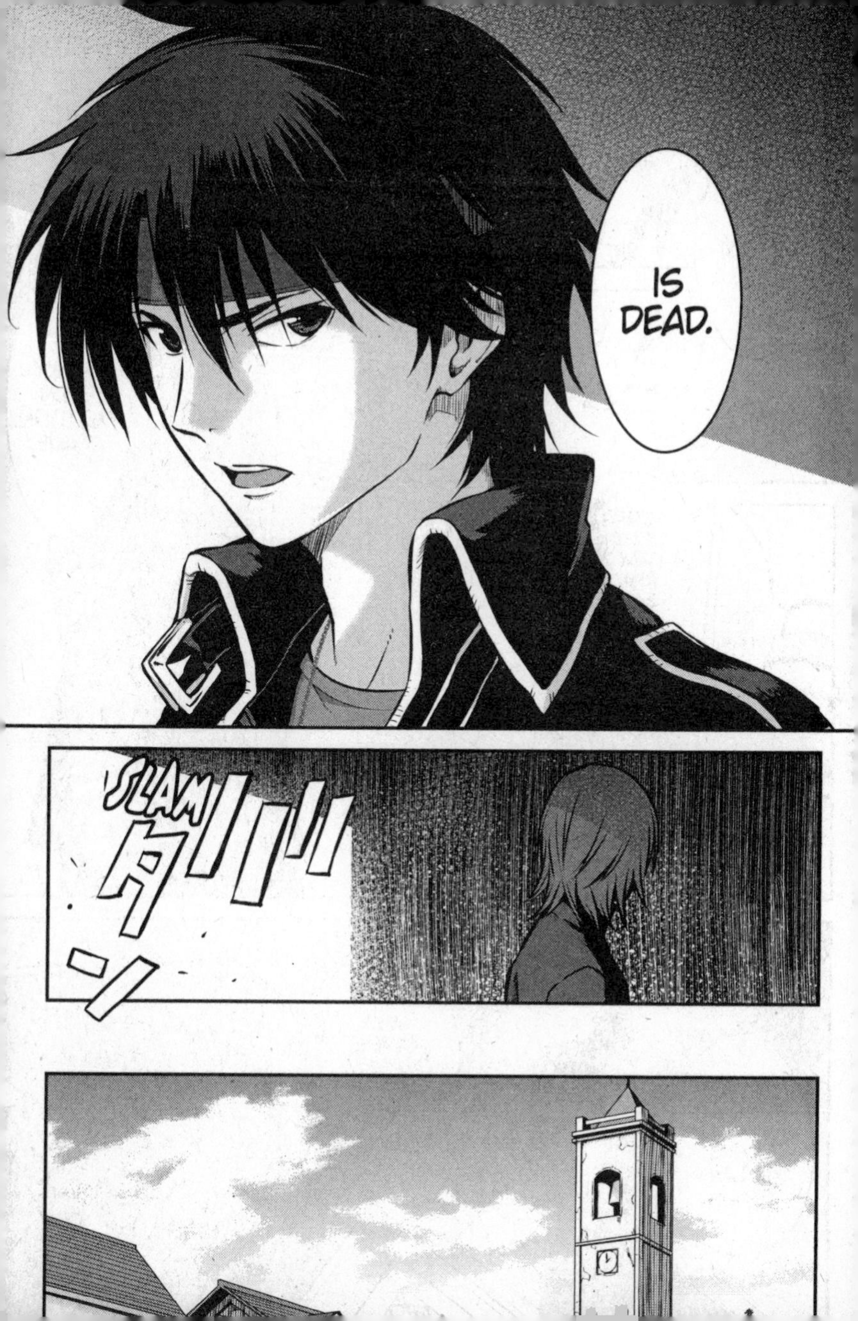
IS
DEAD.
SLAM

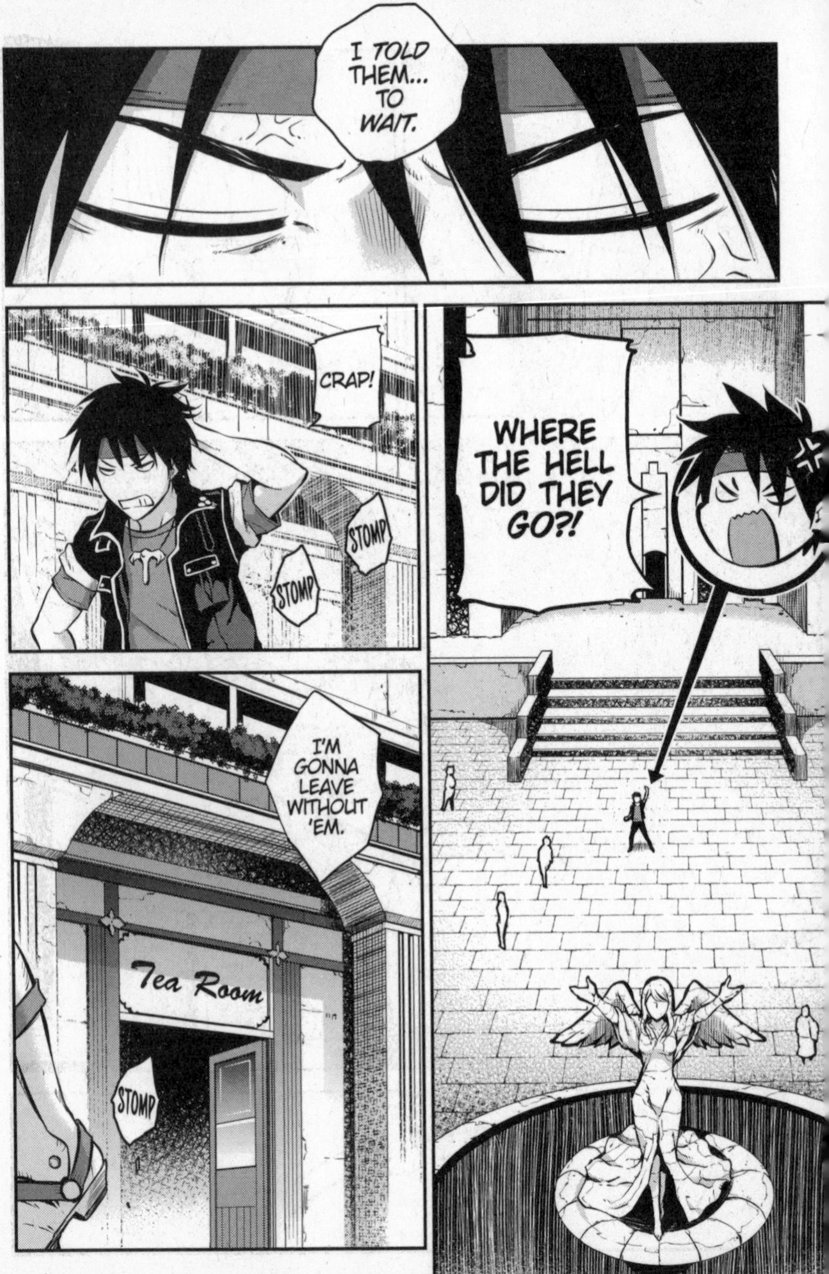
I TOLD THEM... TO WAIT.
WHERE THE HELL DID THEY GO?!
CRAP!
STOMP
STOMP
I'M GONNA LEAVE WITHOUT 'EM.
Tea Room
STOMP

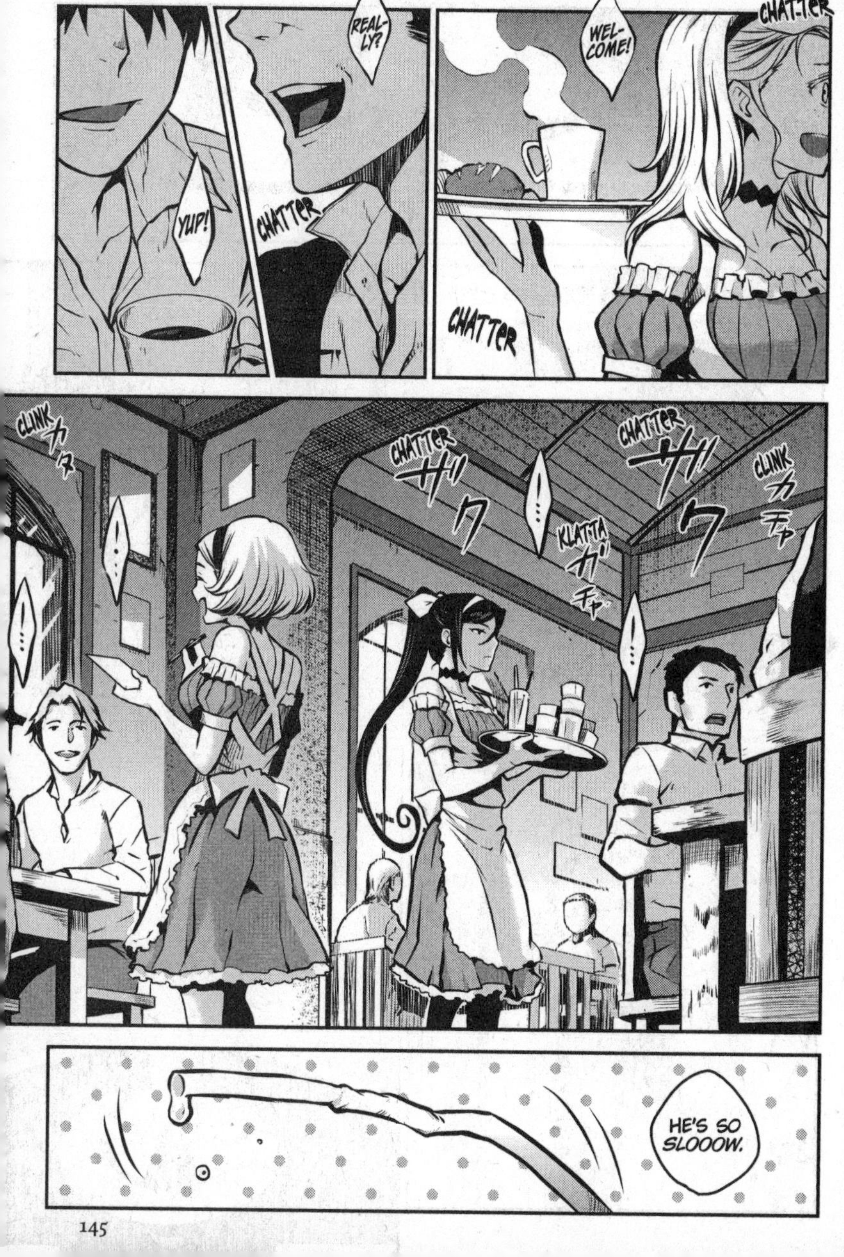

CHAT-TER
WEL-COME!
CHATTER
REAL-LY?
CHATTER
YUP!
CLINK
カチャ
CHATTER
KLATTA
ガチャ
!...
CHATTER
!...
!...
CLINK
カタ
!...
HE'S SO SLOOOW.

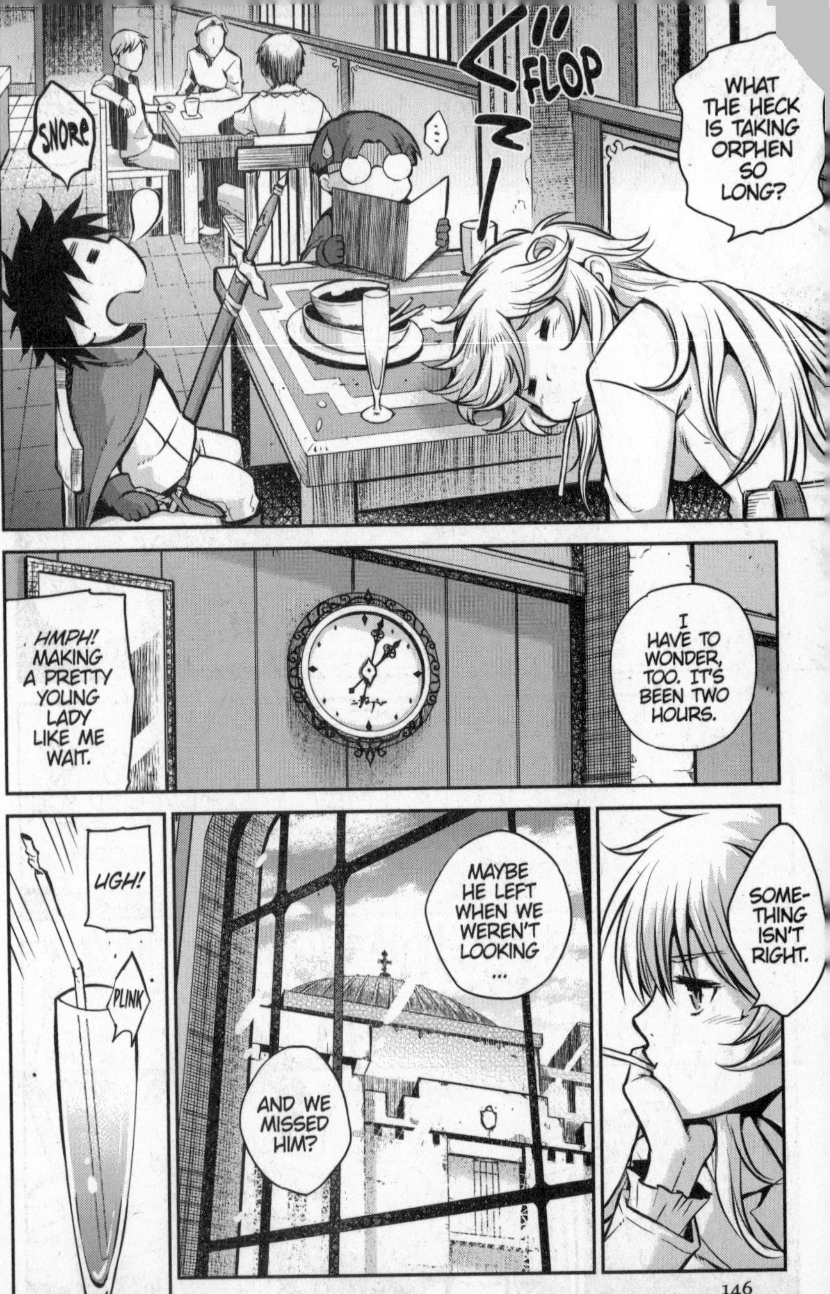
WHAT THE HECK IS TAKING ORPHEN SO LONG?
FLOP
...
SNORE
I HAVE TO WONDER, TOO. IT'S BEEN TWO HOURS.
HMPH! MAKING A PRETTY YOUNG LADY LIKE ME WAIT.
SOME-THING ISN'T RIGHT.
MAYBE HE LEFT WHEN WE WEREN'T LOOKING ...
AND WE MISSED HIM?
UGH!
PLINK

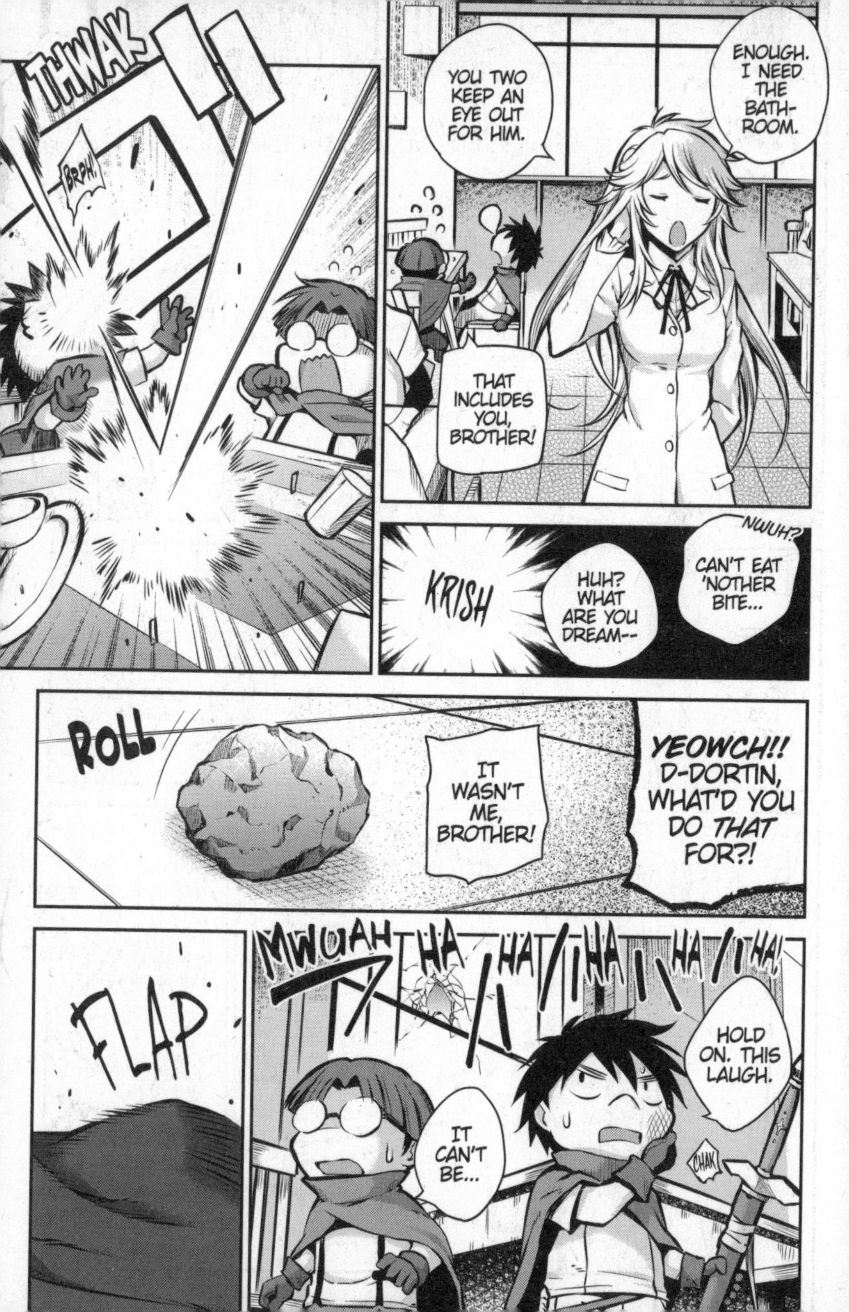
ENOUGH. I NEED THE BATH-ROOM.
YOU TWO KEEP AN EYE OUT FOR HIM.
THAT INCLUDES YOU, BROTHER!
NWUH?
CAN'T EAT 'NOTHER BITE...
HUH? WHAT ARE YOU DREAM--
KRISH
THWAK
BRPH
YEOWCH!! D-DORTIN, WHAT'D YOU DO *THAT* FOR?!
IT WASN'T ME, BROTHER!
ROLL
MWUGAH HA HA HA HA HA HA!
HOLD ON. THIS LAUGH.
CHAK
IT CAN'T BE...
FLAP

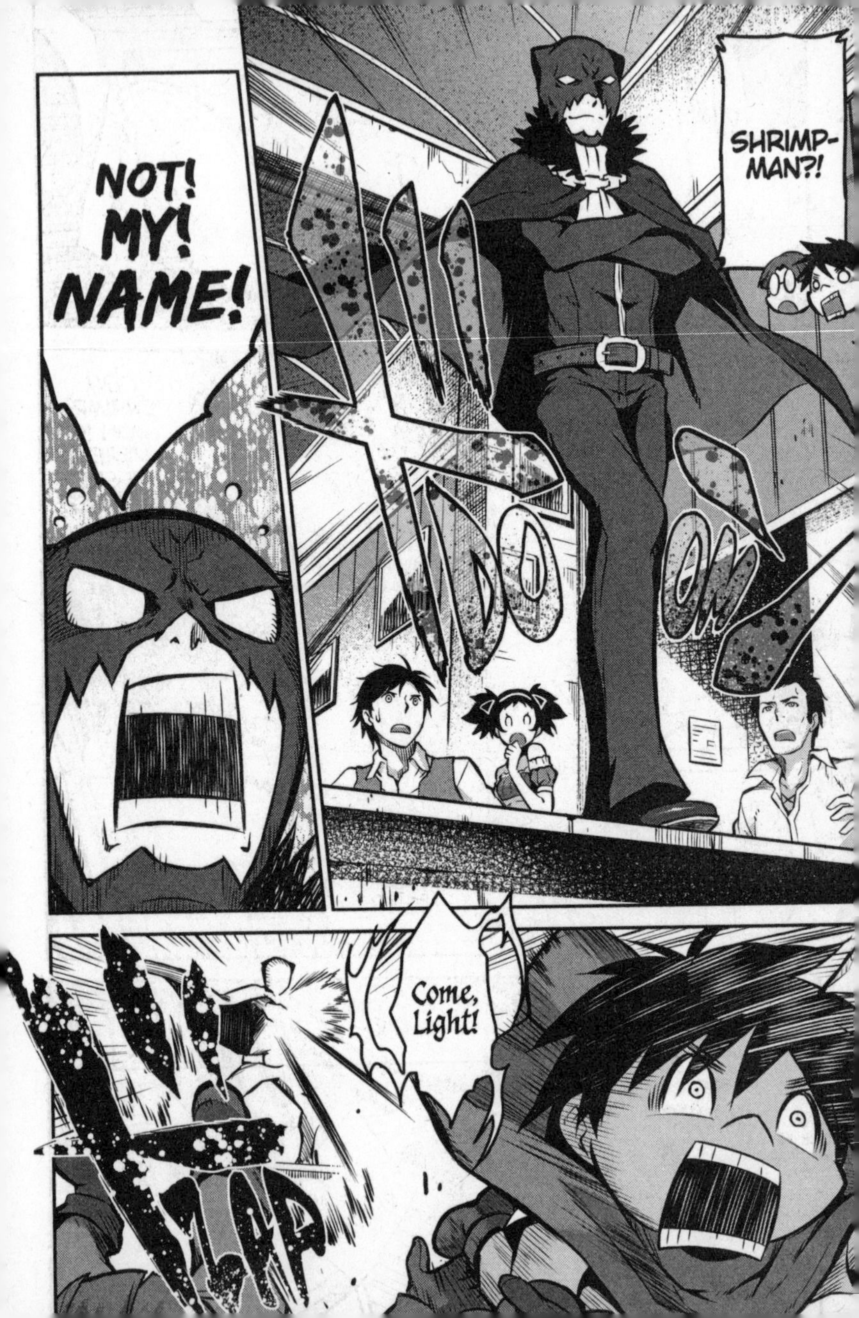
SHRIMP-MAN?!
NOT! MY! NAME!
Come, Light!

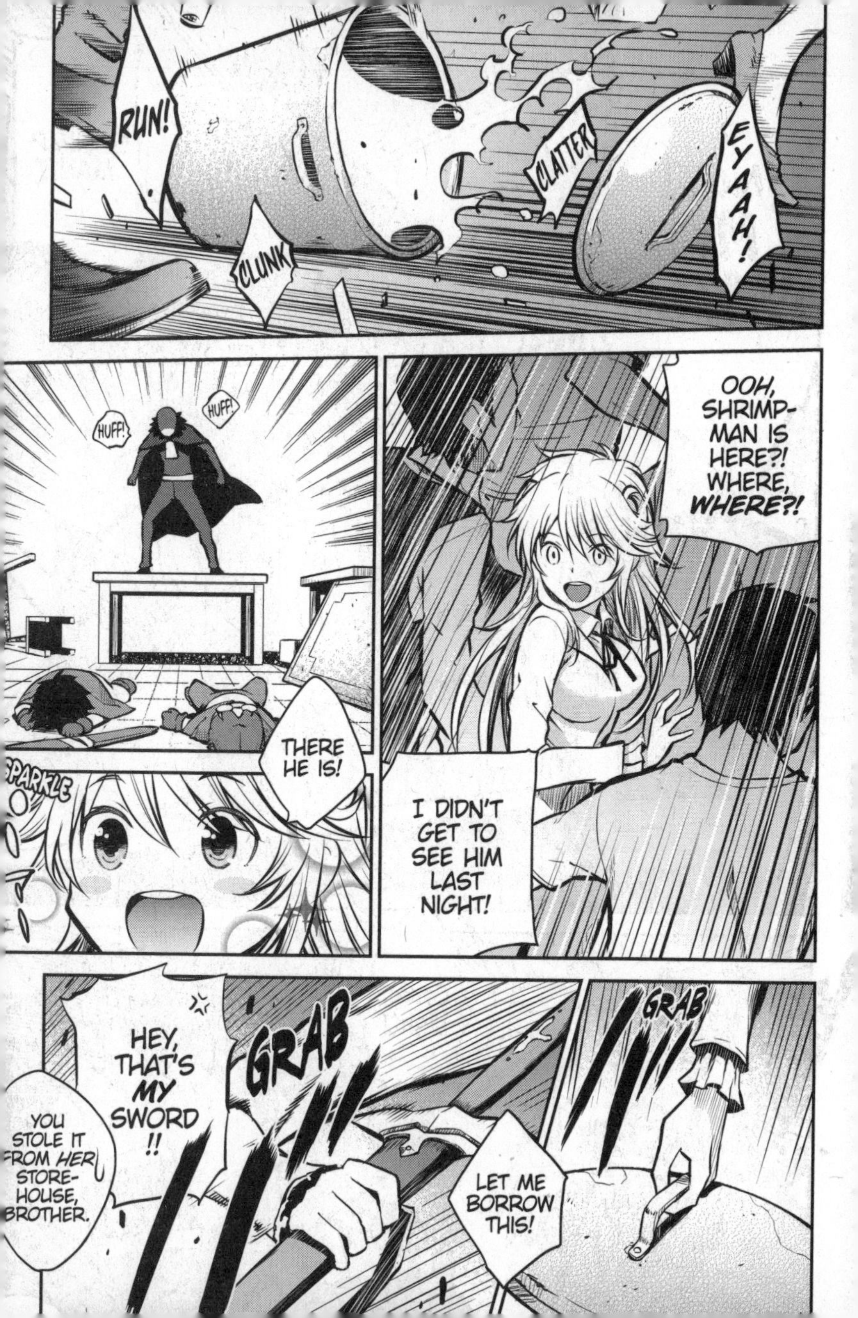
EYAAH!
CLATTER
RUN!
CLUNK
OOH, SHRIMP-MAN IS HERE?! WHERE, *WHERE?!*
I DIDN'T GET TO SEE HIM LAST NIGHT!
HUFF!
HUFF!
THERE HE IS!
SPARKLE
GRAB
LET ME BORROW THIS!
HEY, THAT'S *MY* SWORD!!
GRAB
YOU STOLE IT FROM *HER* STORE-HOUSE, BROTHER.

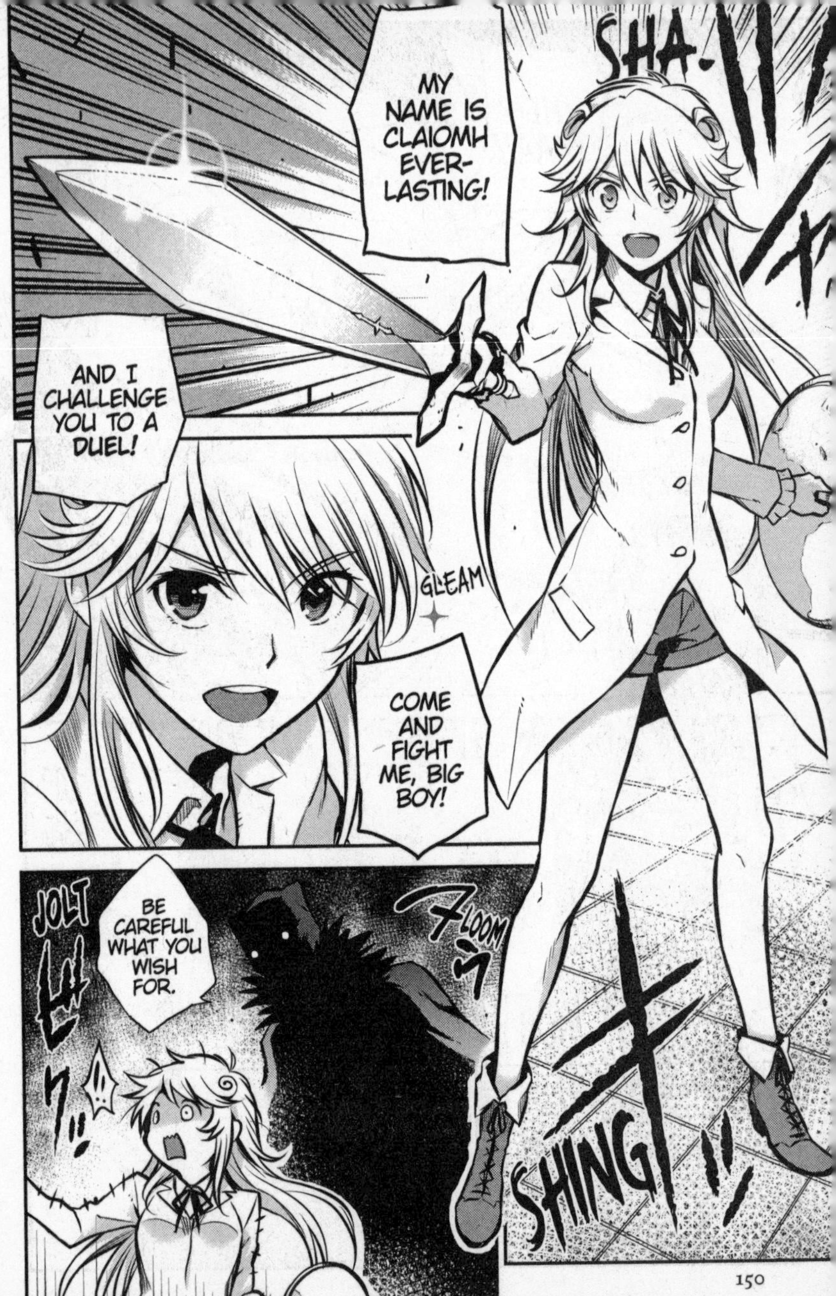
SHA-!!
MY NAME IS CLAIOMH EVER-LASTING!
AND I CHALLENGE YOU TO A DUEL!
GLEAM
COME AND FIGHT ME, BIG BOY!
SHING!!
FLOOM
BE CAREFUL WHAT YOU WISH FOR.
JOLT
!!

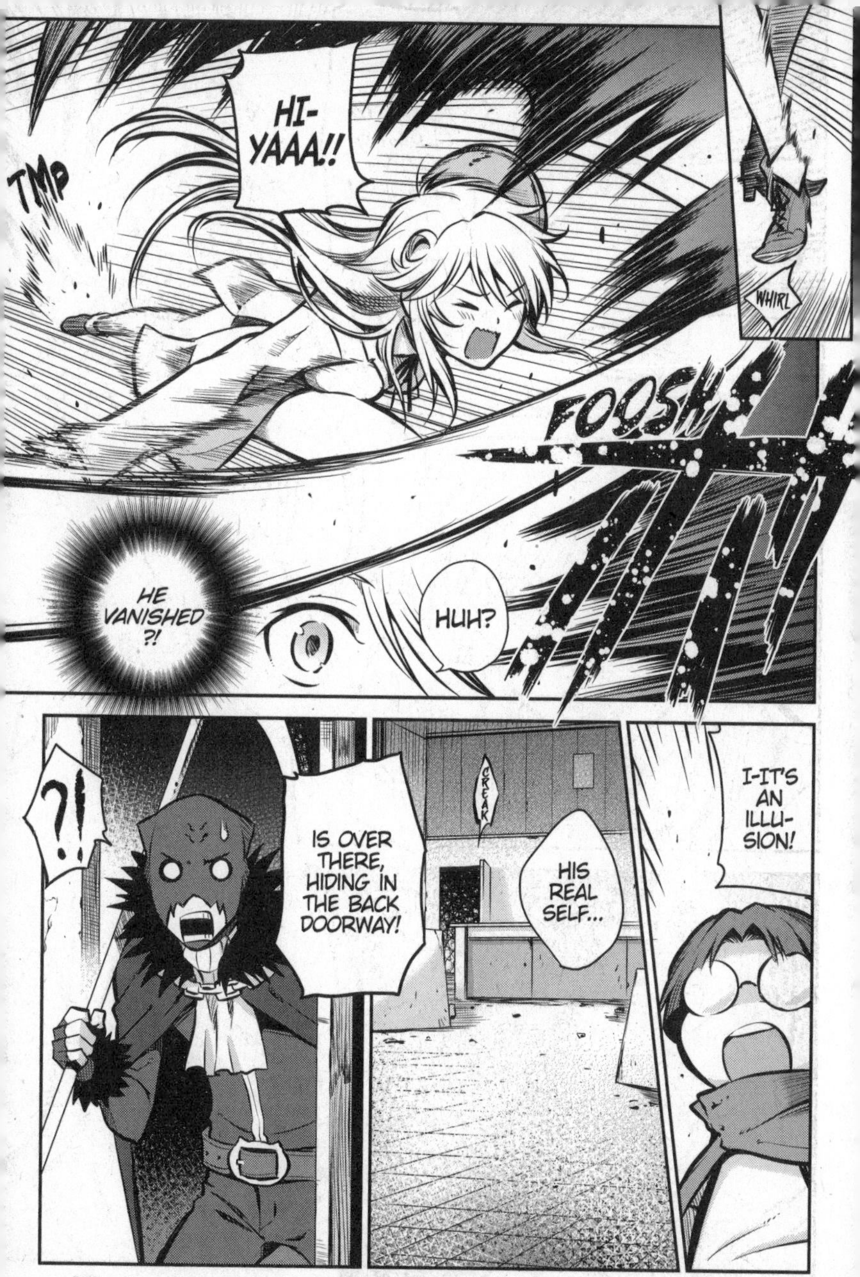
WHIRL
HI-YAAA!!
TMP
FOOSH
HUH?
HE VANISHED?!
I-IT'S AN ILLUSION!
HIS REAL SELF...
CREAK
IS OVER THERE, HIDING IN THE BACK DOORWAY!
?!

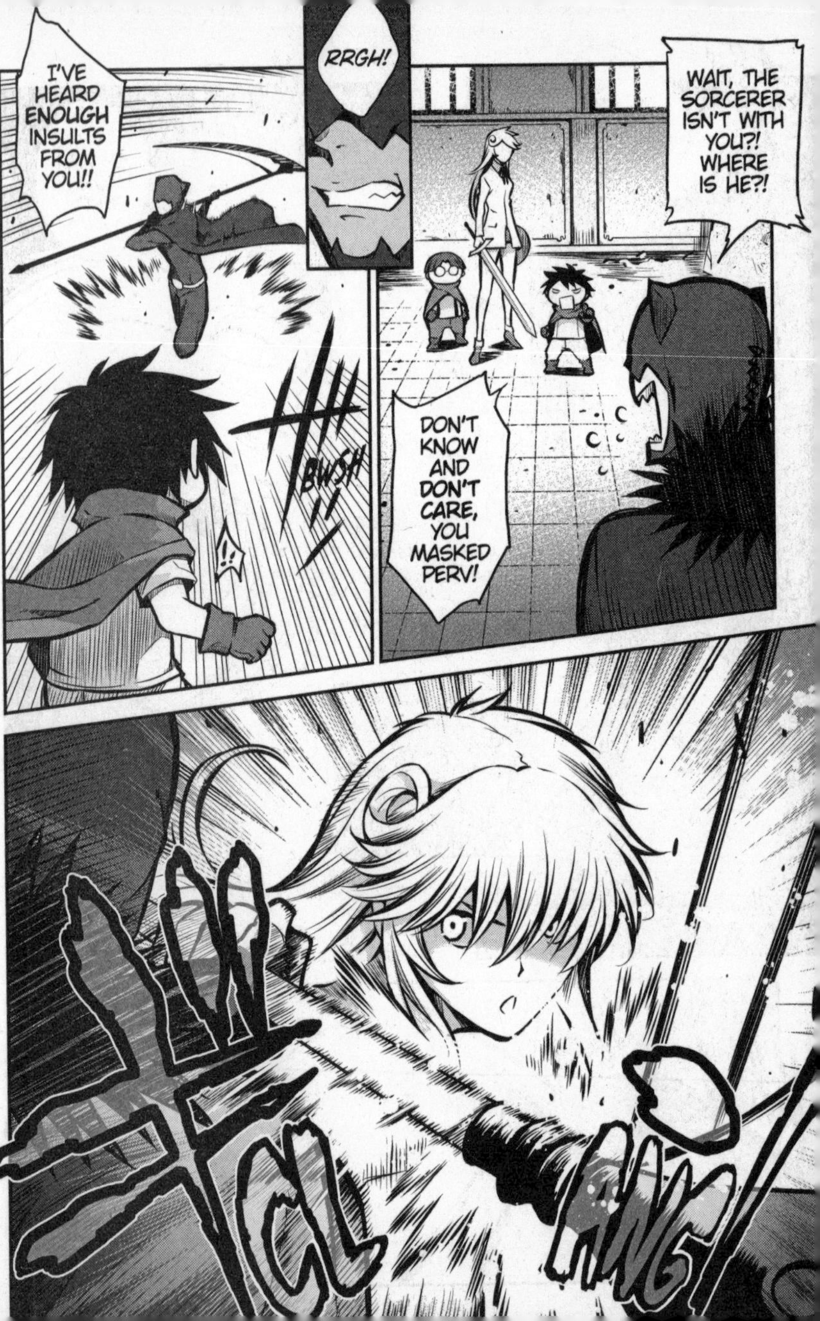
WAIT, THE SORCERER ISN'T WITH YOU?! WHERE IS HE?!
DON'T KNOW AND DON'T CARE, YOU MASKED PERV!
RRGH!
I'VE HEARD ENOUGH INSULTS FROM YOU!!
BWSH!!
!!
CLANG!

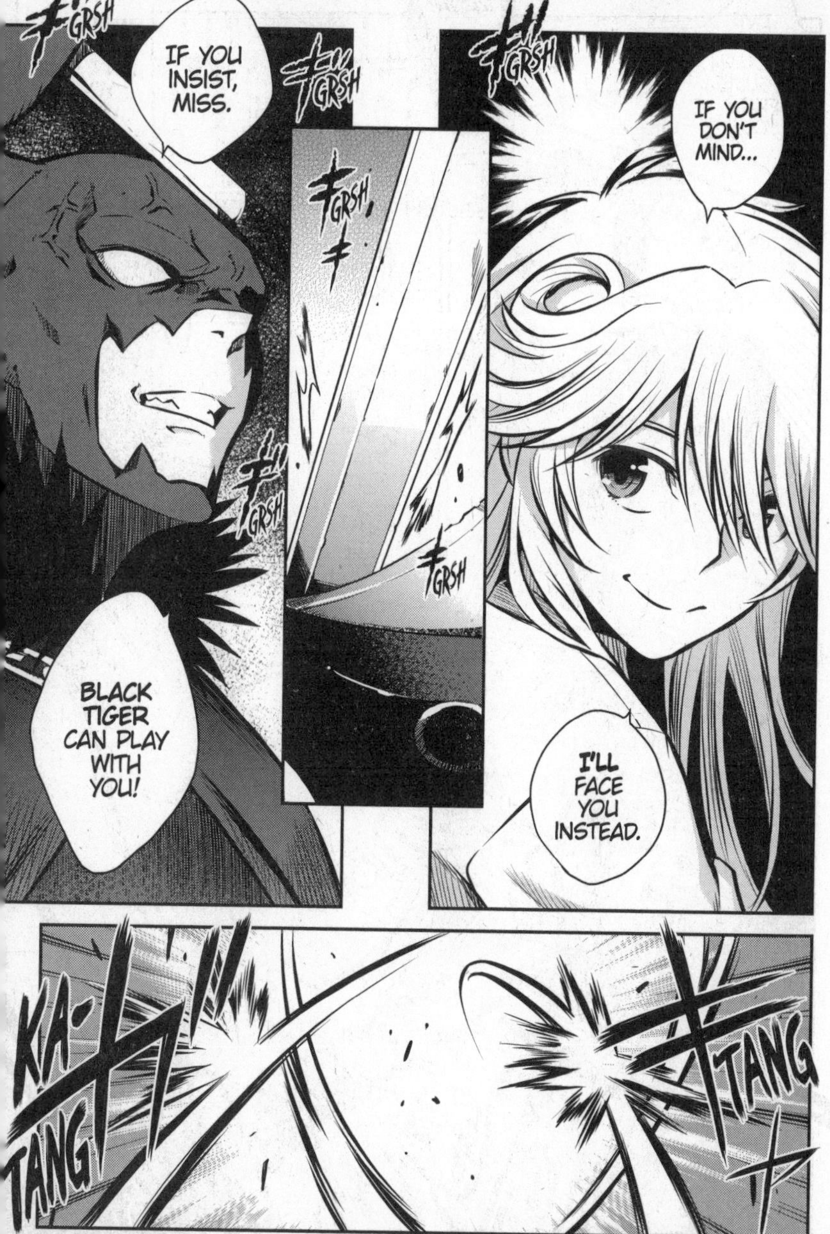
GRSH
IF YOU DON'T MIND...
I'LL FACE YOU INSTEAD.
GRSH
GRSH
GRSH
GRSH
GRSH
IF YOU INSIST, MISS.
BLACK TIGER CAN PLAY WITH YOU!
TANG
KA-TANG!

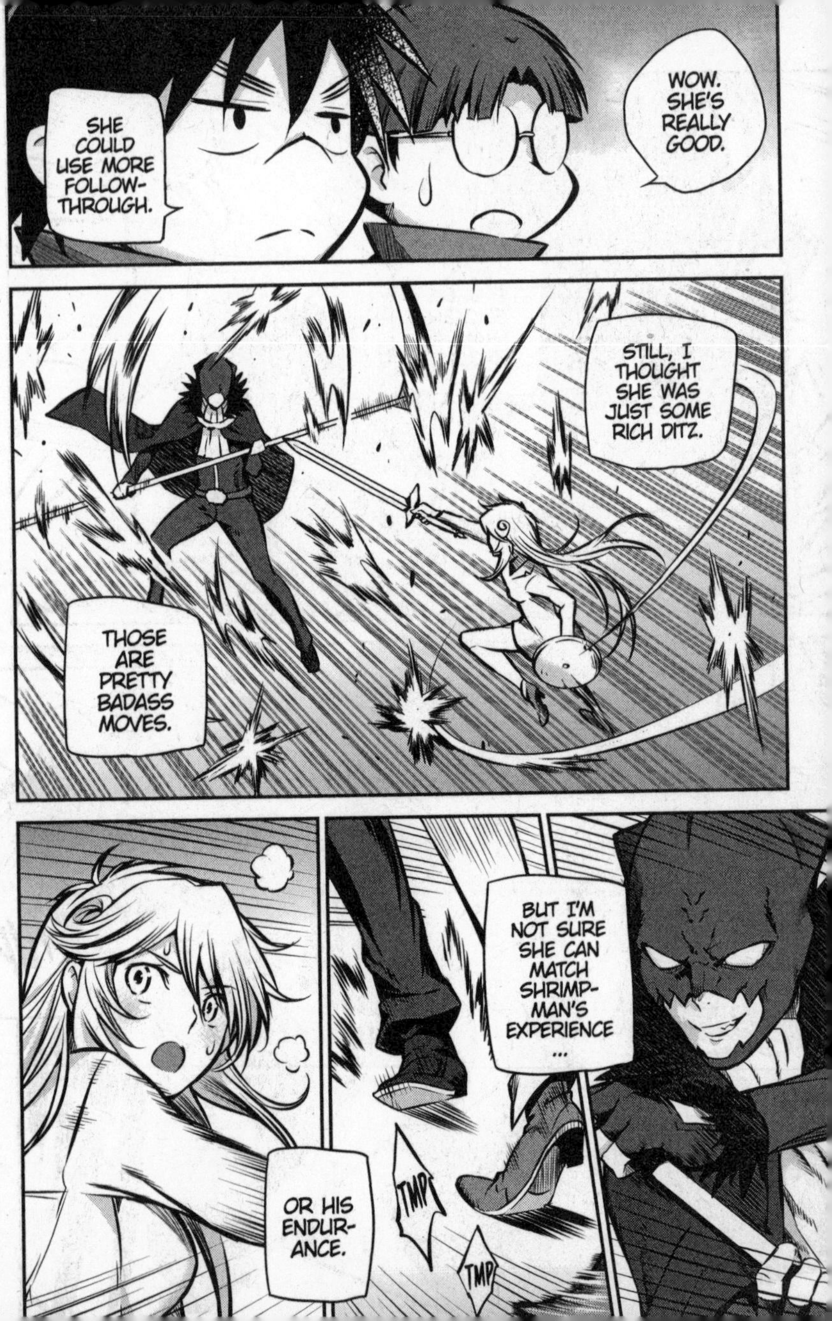
WOW. SHE'S REALLY GOOD.
SHE COULD USE MORE FOLLOW-THROUGH.
STILL, I THOUGHT SHE WAS JUST SOME RICH DITZ.
THOSE ARE PRETTY BADASS MOVES.
BUT I'M NOT SURE SHE CAN MATCH SHRIMP-MAN'S EXPERIENCE ...
OR HIS ENDURANCE.
TMP
TMP

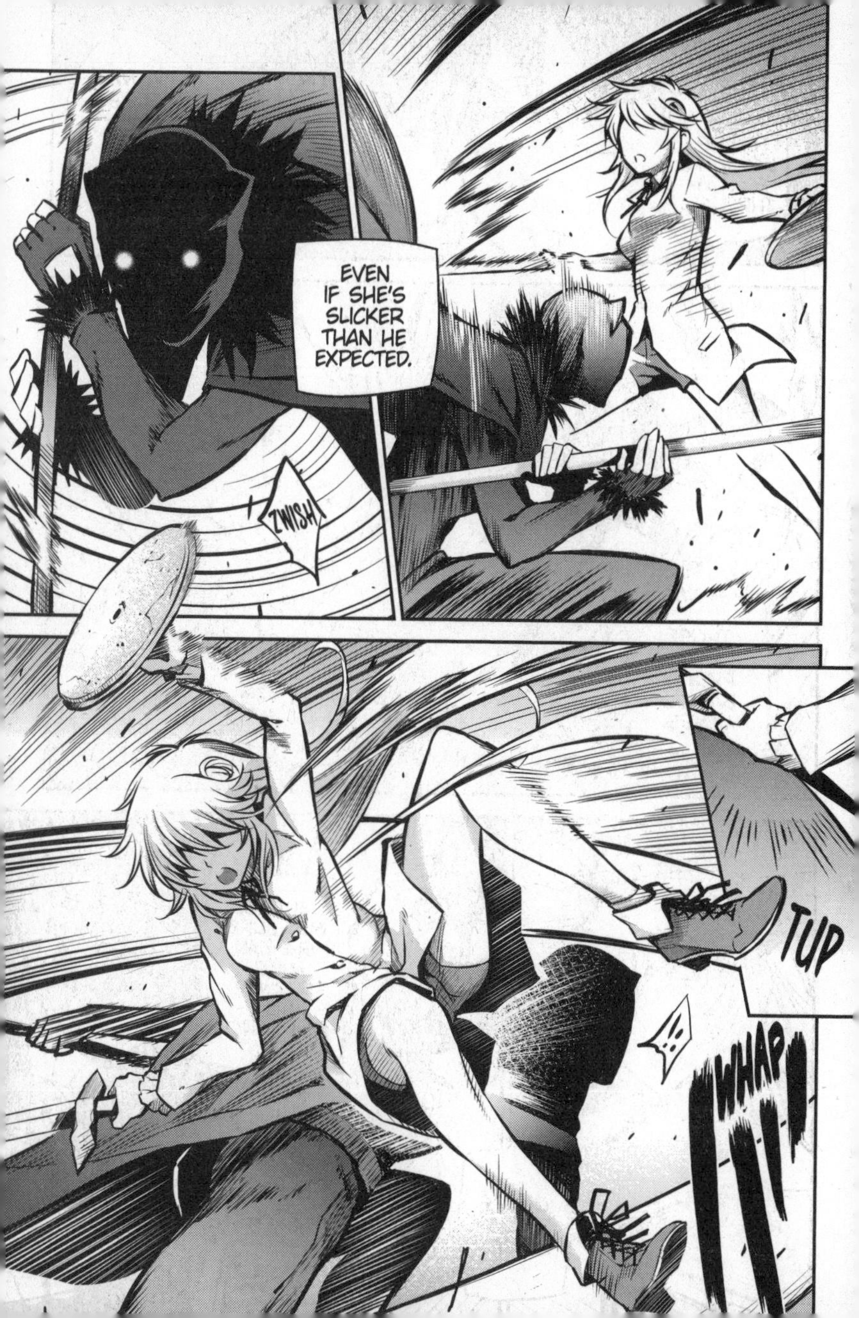
EVEN IF SHE'S SLICKER THAN HE EXPECTED.
ZWISH
TUP
..!
WHAP

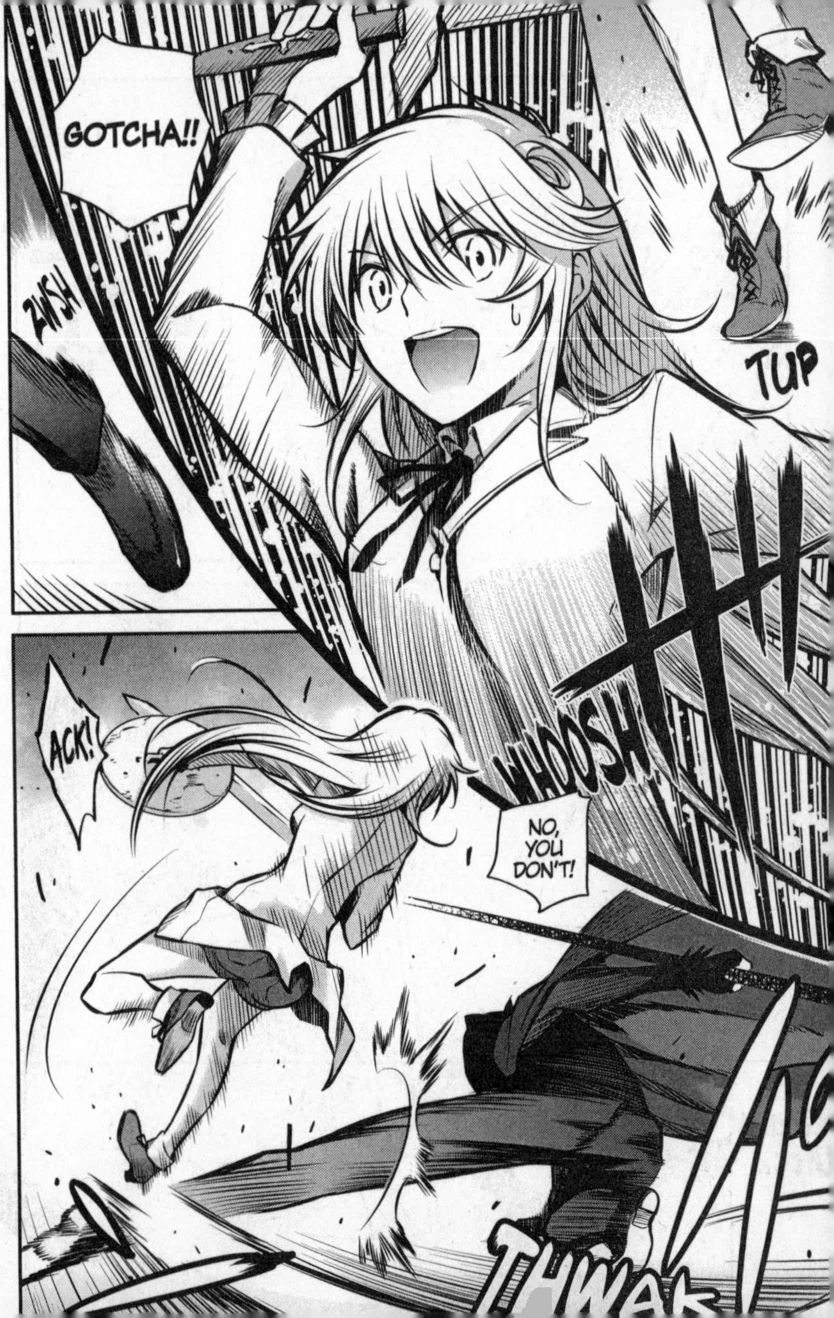
GOTCHA!!
ZWSH
TUP
WHOOSH
ACK!
NO, YOU DON'T!
THWAK

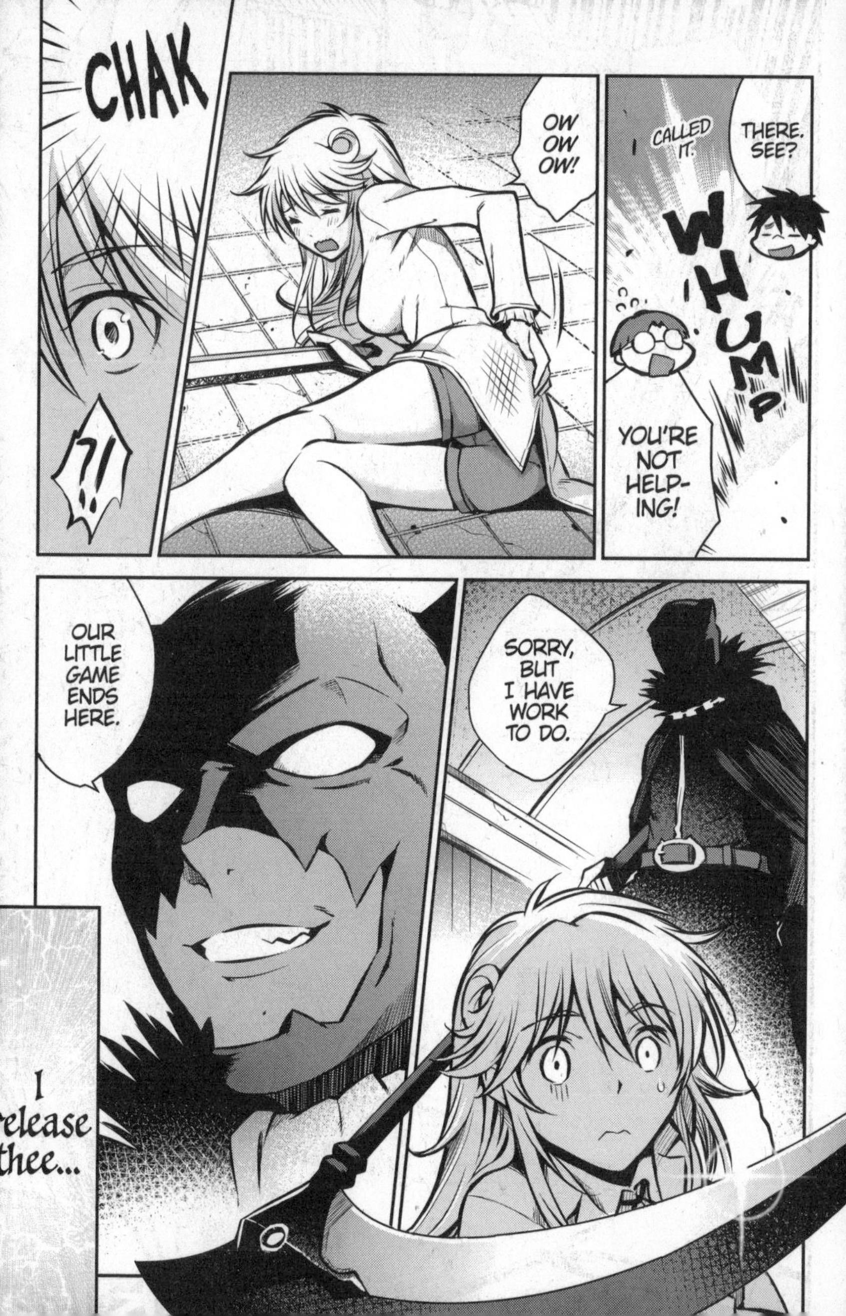
THERE. SEE?
CALLED IT.
WHUMP
YOU'RE NOT HELPING!
OW OW OW!
CHAK
?!
SORRY, BUT I HAVE WORK TO DO.
OUR LITTLE GAME ENDS HERE.
I release thee...

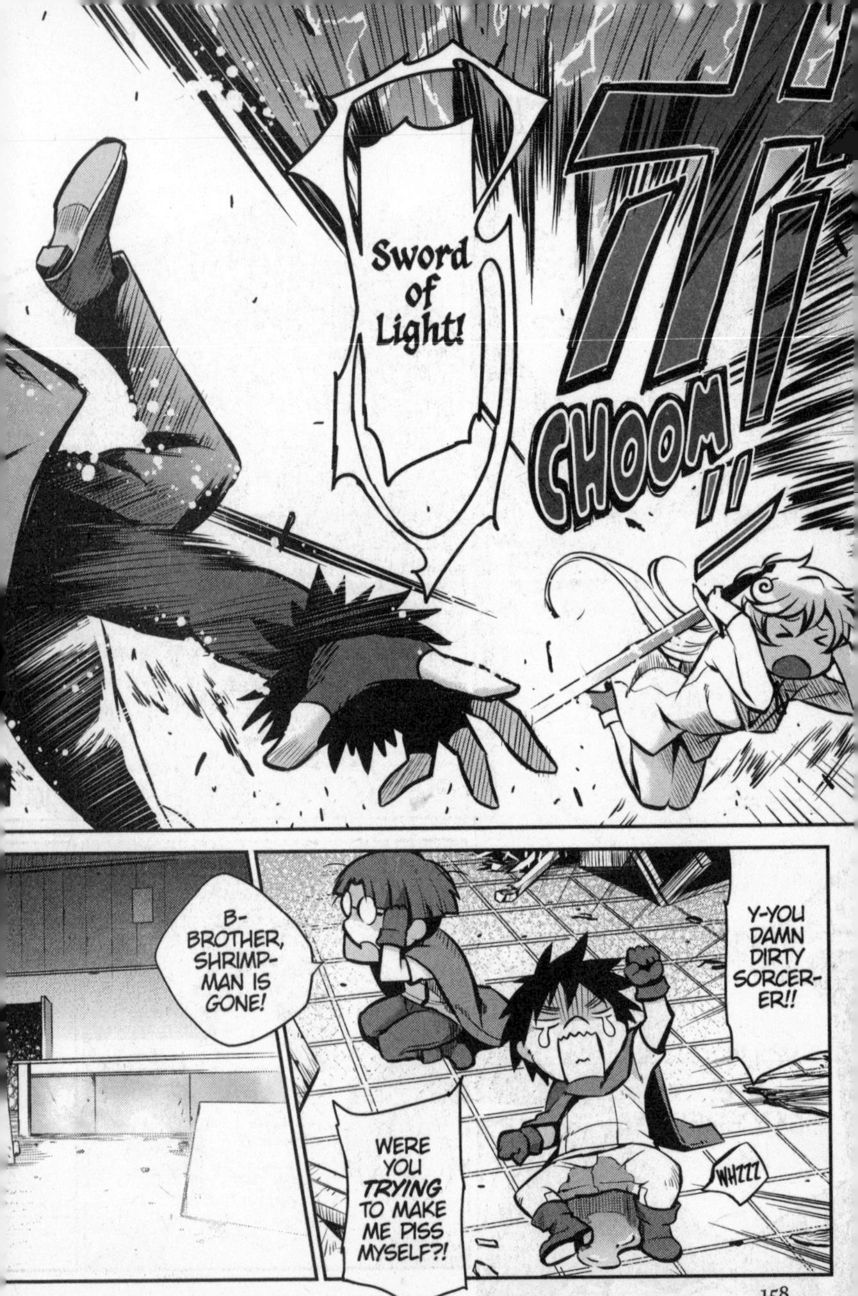
Sword of Light!
CHOOM!!
Y-YOU DAMN DIRTY SORCERER!!
B-BROTHER, SHRIMP-MAN IS GONE!
WHZZZ
WERE YOU *TRYING* TO MAKE ME PISS MYSELF?!

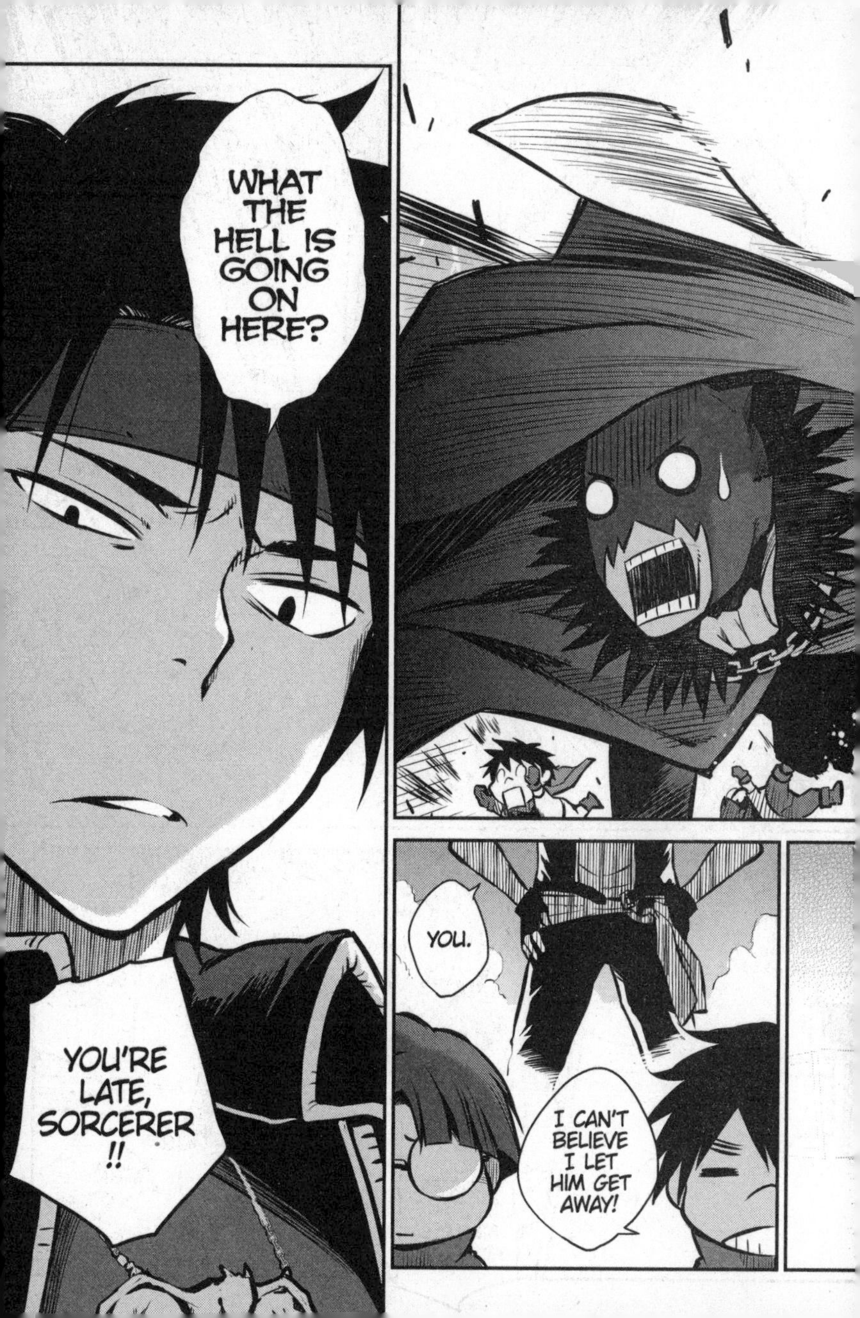
YOU.
I CAN'T BELIEVE I LET HIM GET AWAY!
WHAT THE HELL IS GOING ON HERE?
YOU'RE LATE, SORCERER!!

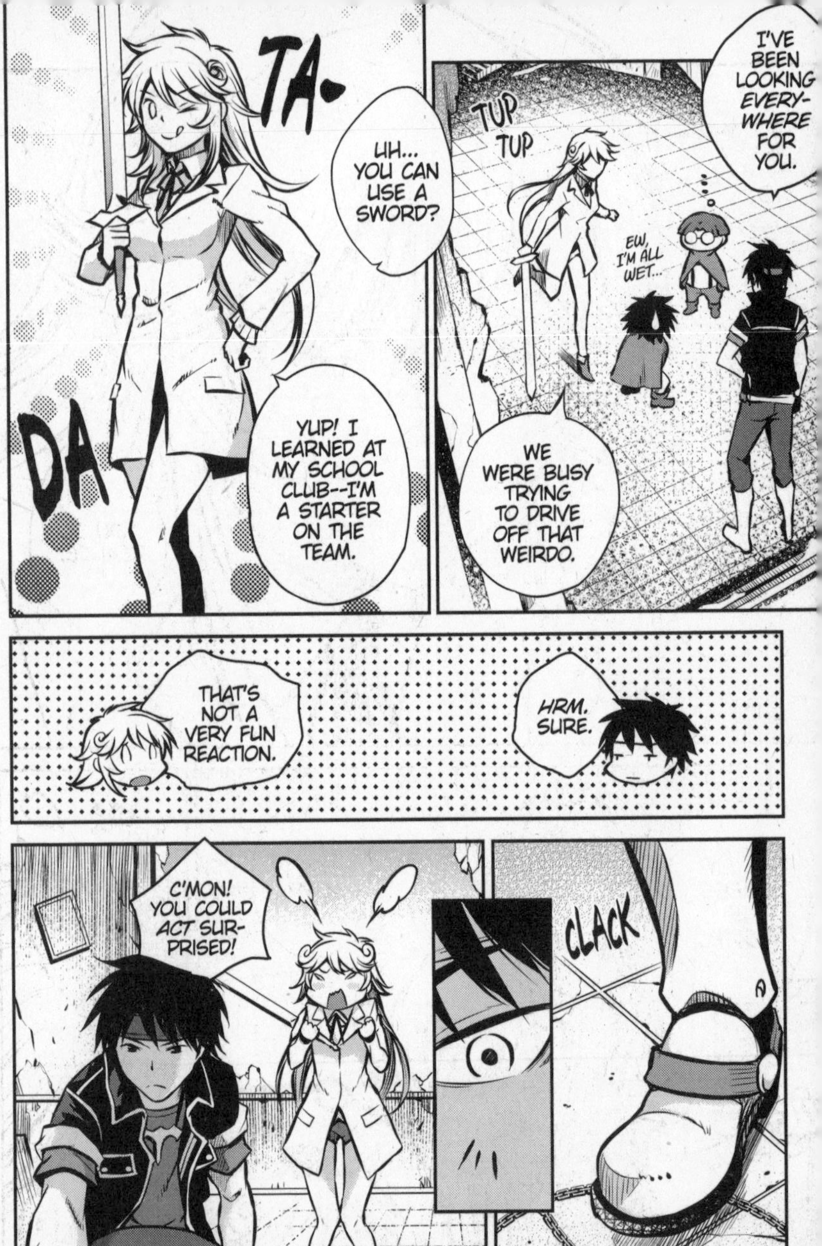
I'VE BEEN LOOKING EVERYWHERE FOR YOU.
TUP TUP
EW, I'M ALL WET...
WE WERE BUSY TRYING TO DRIVE OFF THAT WEIRDO.
TA-
UH... YOU CAN USE A SWORD?
YUP! I LEARNED AT MY SCHOOL CLUB--I'M A STARTER ON THE TEAM.
DA
HRM. SURE.
THAT'S NOT A VERY FUN REACTION.
CLACK
...
C'MON! YOU COULD ACT SURPRISED!

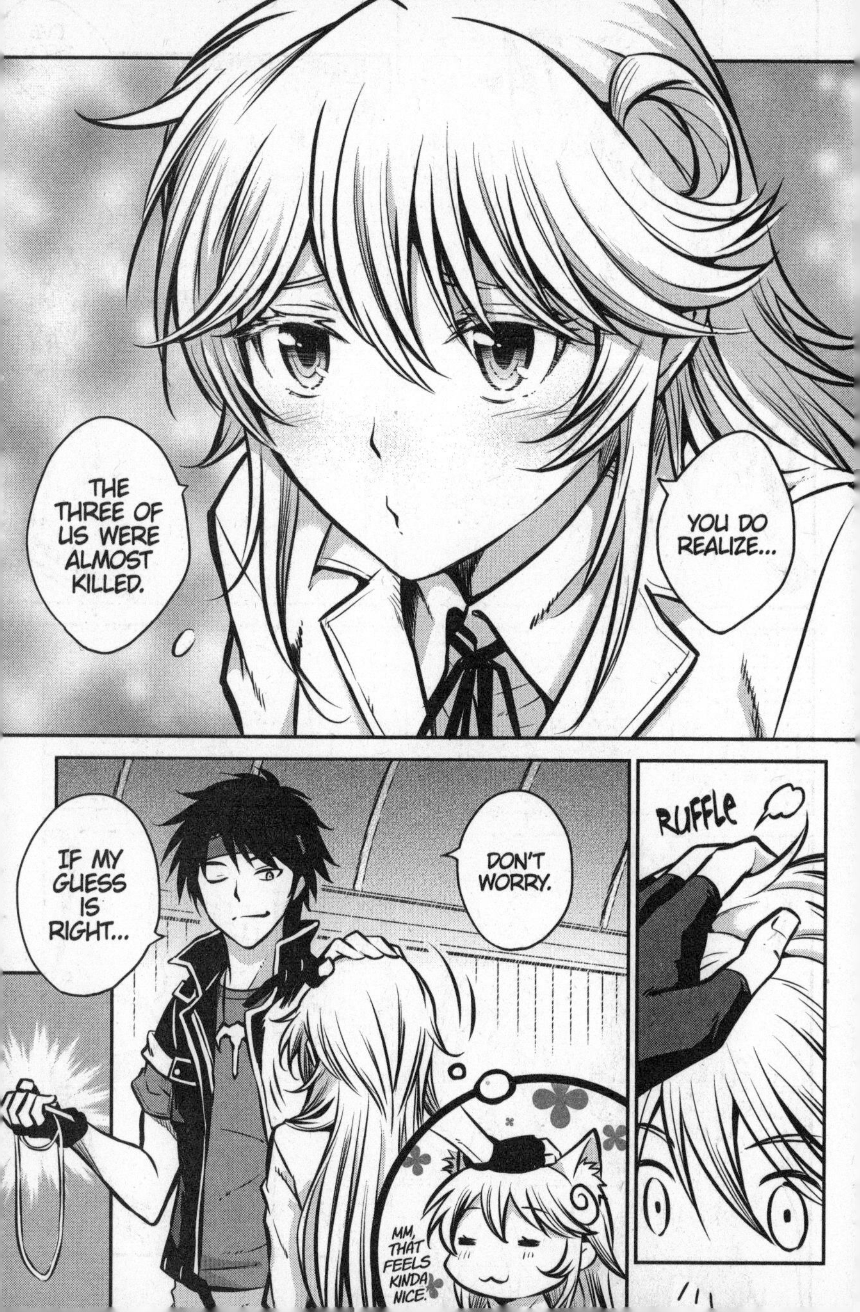
YOU DO REALIZE...
THE THREE OF US WERE ALMOST KILLED.
RUFFLE
DON'T WORRY.
IF MY GUESS IS RIGHT...
MM, THAT FEELS KINDA NICE.

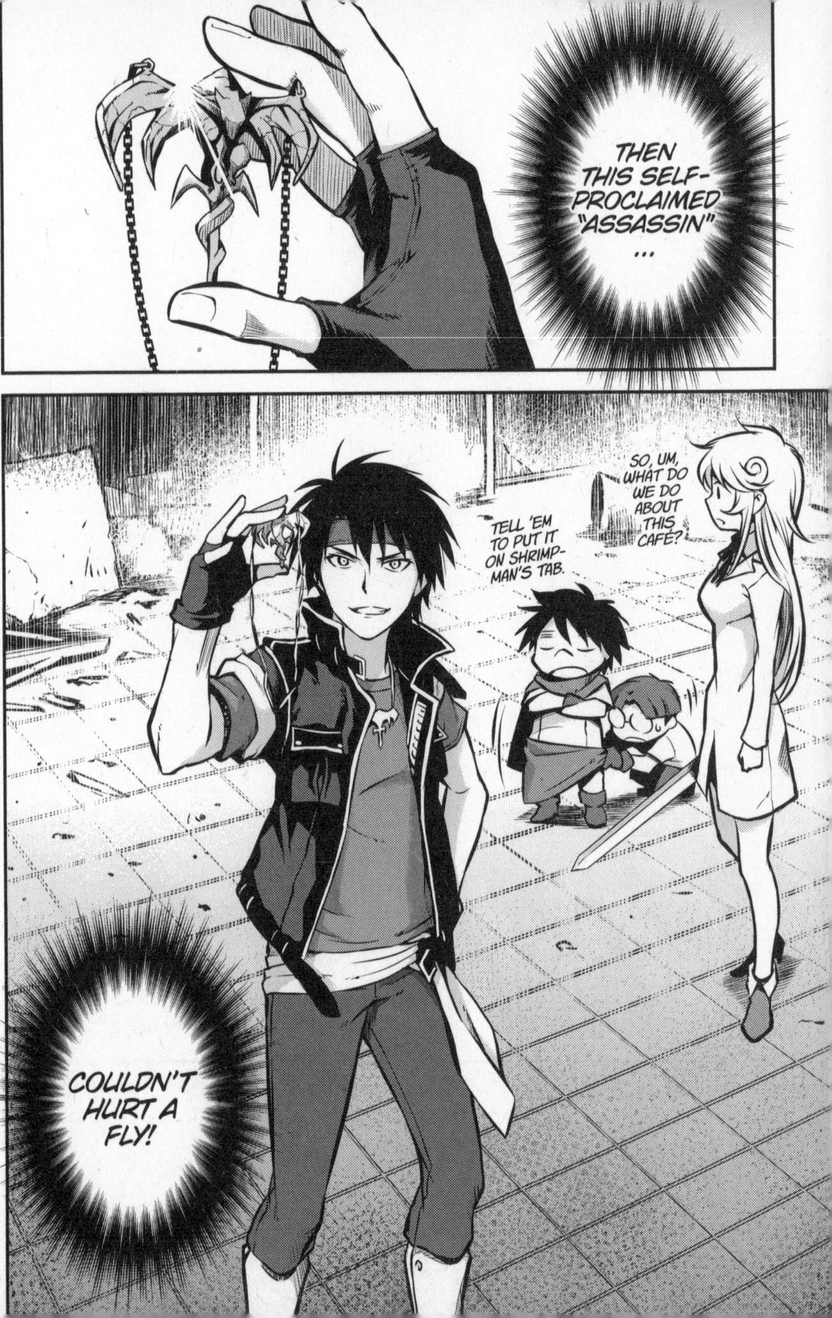
THEN THIS SELF-PROCLAIMED "ASSASSIN" ...
SO, UM, WHAT DO WE DO ABOUT THIS CAFÉ?
TELL 'EM TO PUT IT ON SHRIMP-MAN'S TAB.
COULDN'T HURT A FLY!

TO BE CONTINUED

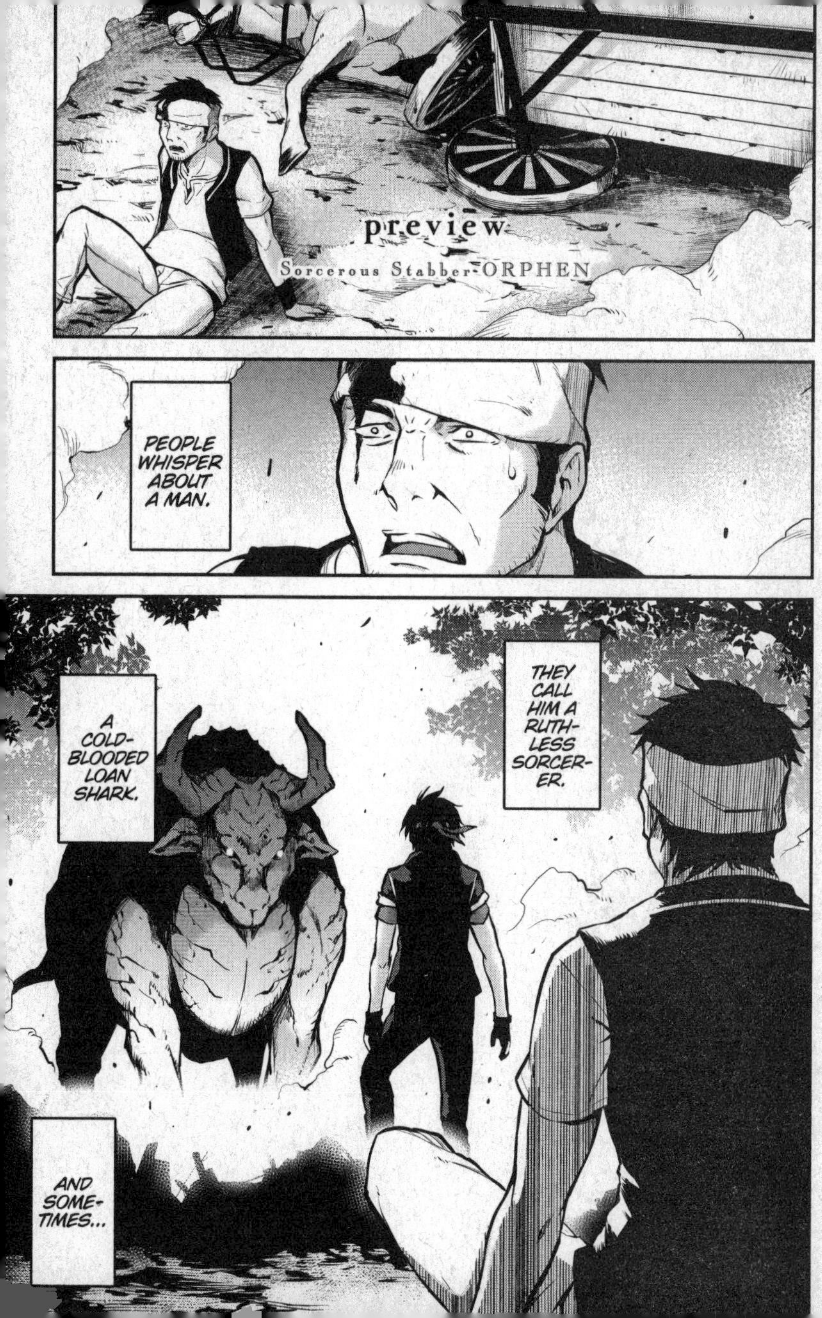
preview
Sorcerous Stabber ORPHEN
PEOPLE WHISPER ABOUT A MAN.
THEY CALL HIM A RUTHLESS SORCERER.
A COLD-BLOODED LOAN SHARK.
AND SOMETIMES...

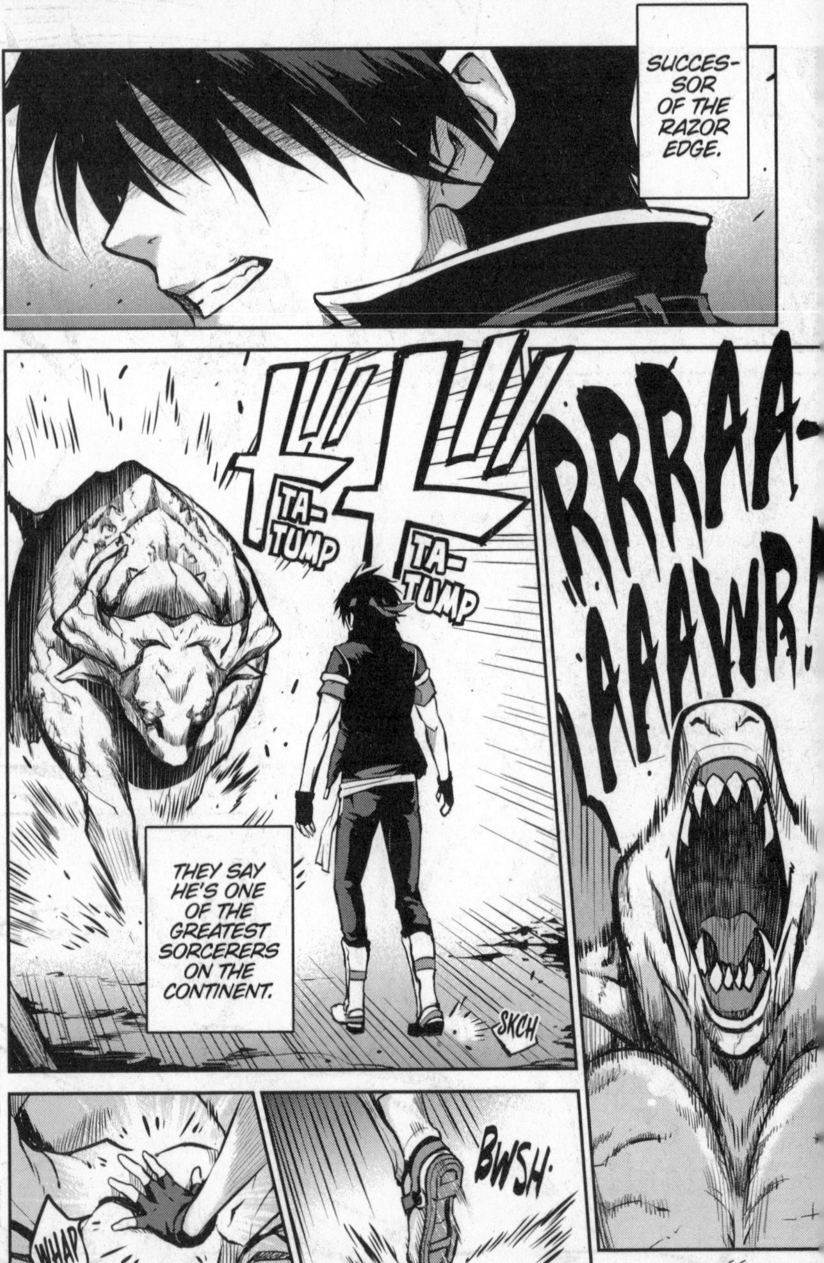
SUCCES-
SOR
OF THE
RAZOR
EDGE.
RRRAA-
AAAWR!
TA-
TUMP
TA-
TUMP
THEY SAY HE'S ONE OF THE GREATEST SORCERERS ON THE CONTINENT.
SKCH
BWSH
WHAP

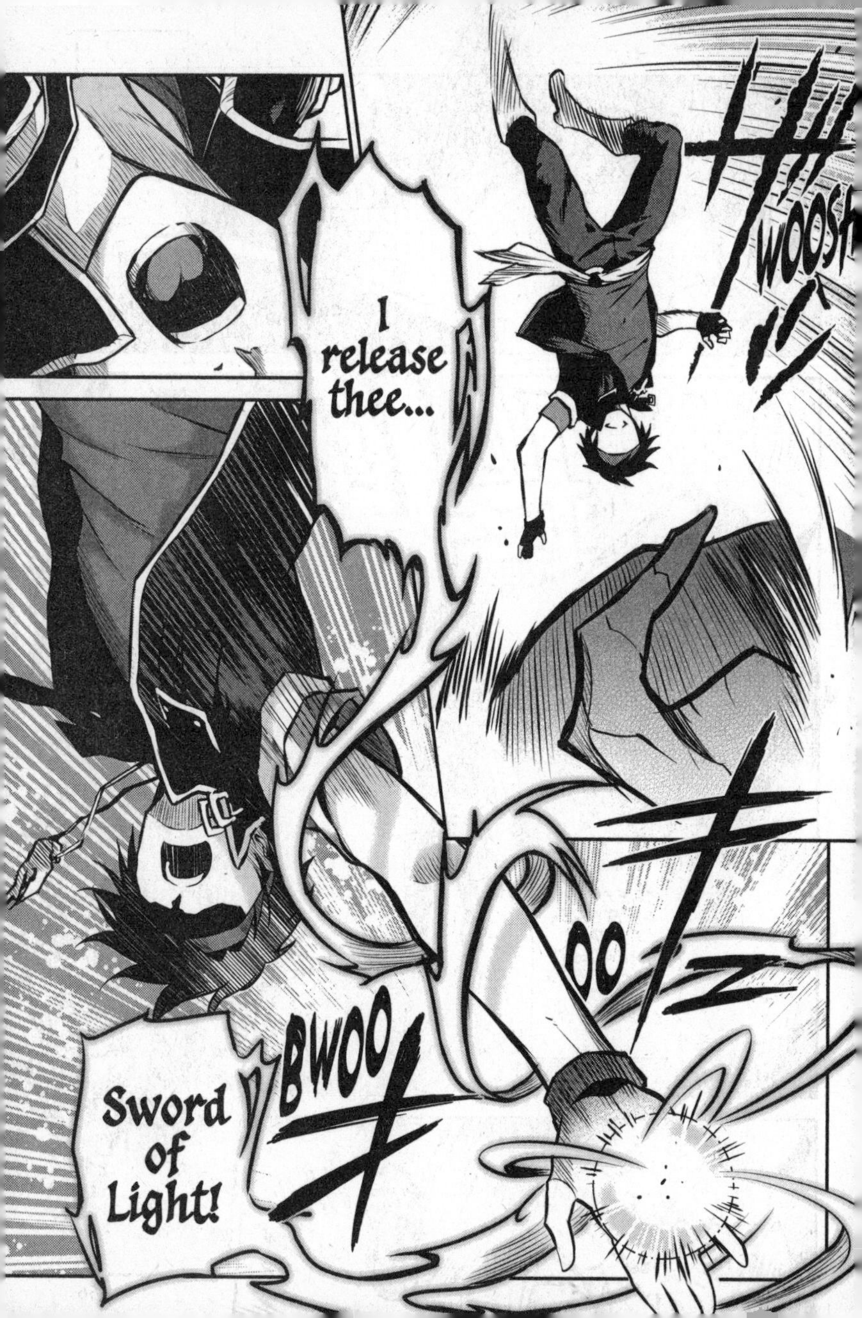
WOOSH!!
I release thee...
Sword of Light!
BWOO
OO

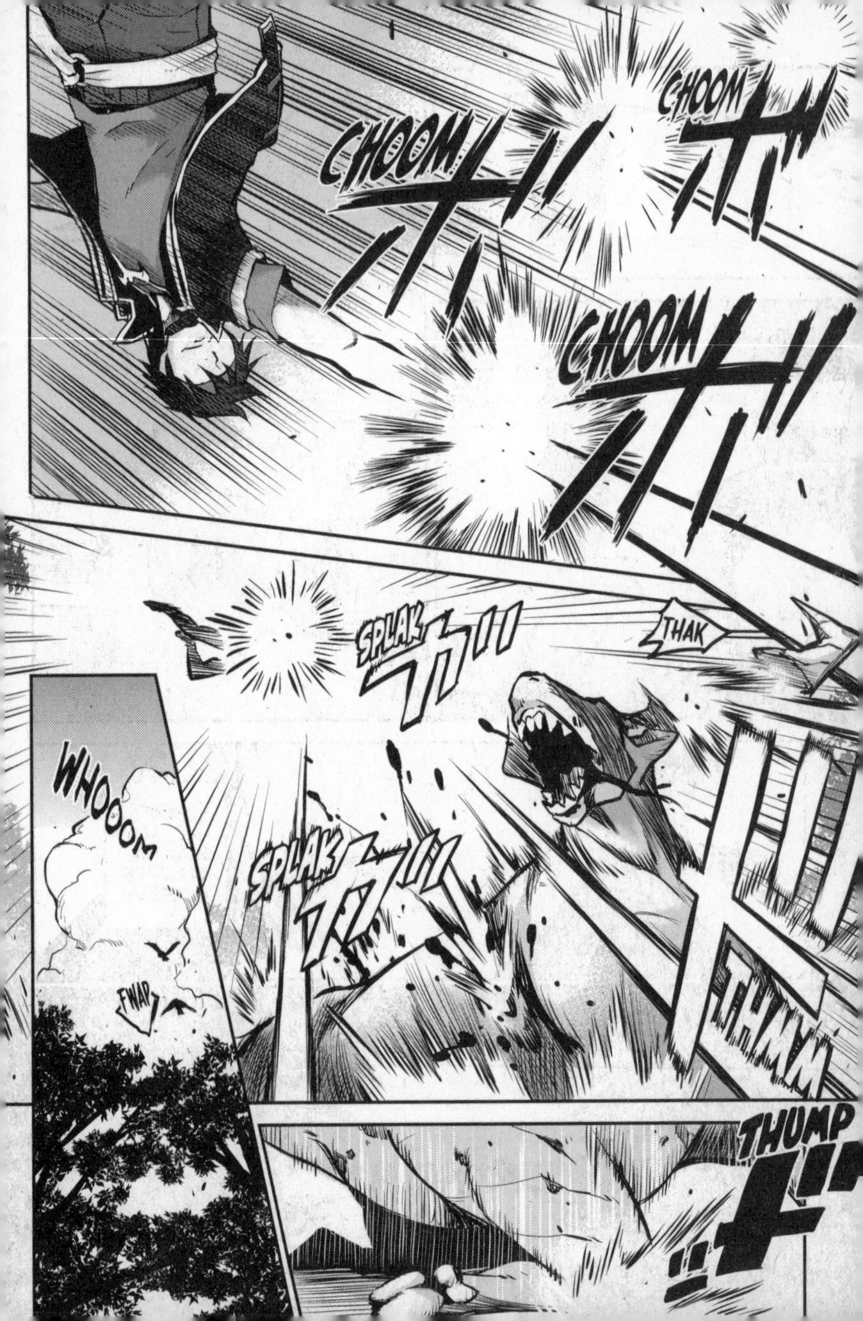
CHOOM
CHOOM
CHOOM
THAK
SPLAK
THNK
SPLAK
WHOOOM
FWAP
THUMP

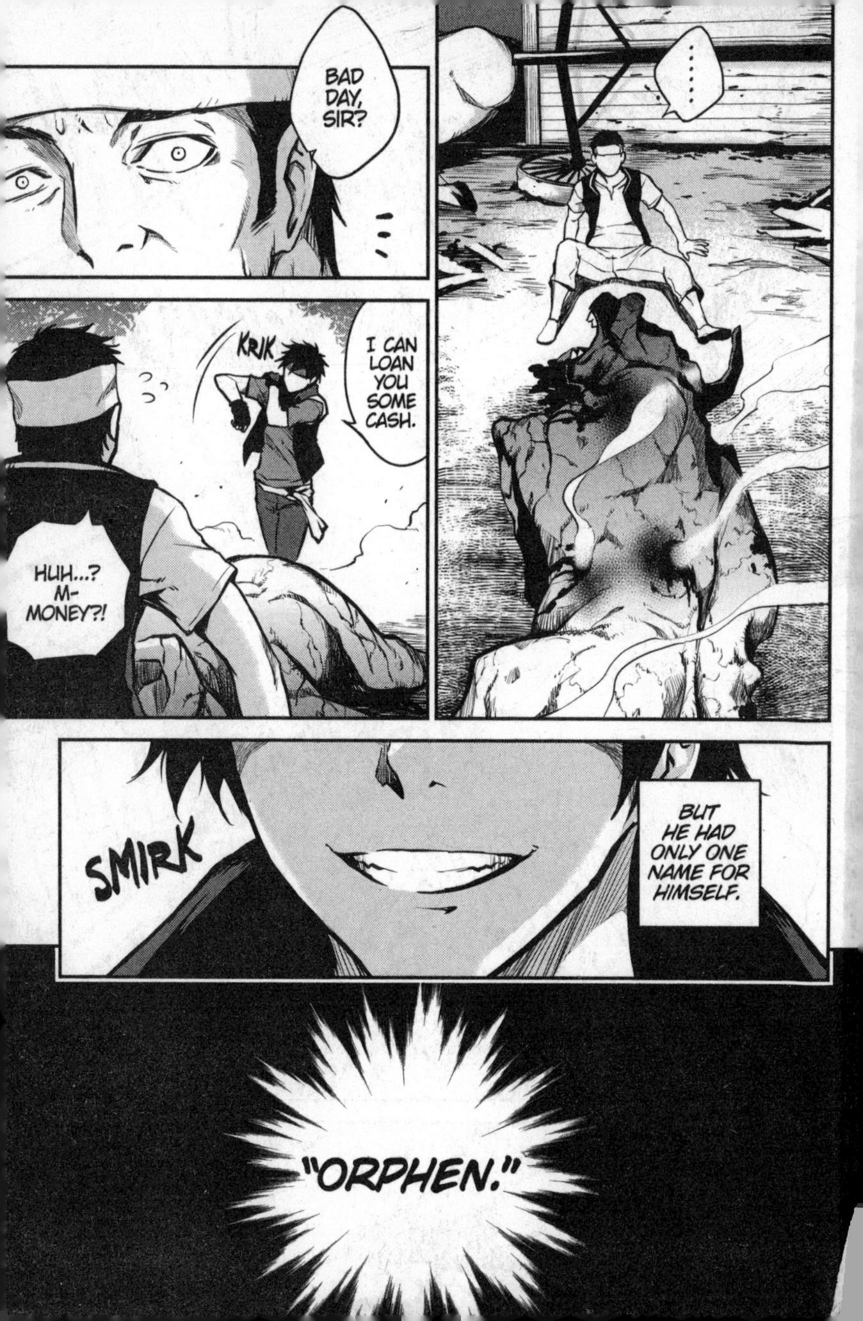
......
BAD DAY, SIR?
KRIK
I CAN LOAN YOU SOME CASH.
HUH...? M-MONEY?!
BUT HE HAD ONLY ONE NAME FOR HIMSELF.
SMIRK
"ORPHEN."

SEVEN SEAS ENTERTAINMENT PRESENTS

SORCEROUS STABBER ORPHEN

Heed My Call, Beast! Part 1

story by YOSHINOBU AKITA / art by MURAJI

TRANSLATION
Adrienne Beck

ADAPTATION
Lianne Sentar

LETTERING AND RETOUCH
Ray Steeves

COVER DESIGN
KC Fabellon

PROOFREADER
Janet Houck
Danielle King

EDITOR
J.P. Sullivan

PRODUCTION MANAGER
Lissa Pattillo

MANAGING EDITOR
Julie Davis

EDITOR-IN-CHIEF
Adam Arnold

PUBLISHER
Jason DeAngelis

SORCEROUS STABBER ORPHEN: HEED MY CALL, BEAST! Part 1
© 2017 Yoshinobu Akita, TO BOOKS
© MURAJI 2017
First published in Japan in 2017 by KADOKAWA CORPORATION, Tokyo.
English translation rights arranged with KADOKAWA CORPORATION, Tokyo.

No portion of this book may be reproduced or transmitted in any form without written permission from the copyright holders. This is a work of fiction. Names, characters, places, and incidents are the products of the author's imagination or are used fictitiously. Any resemblance to actual events, locales, or persons, living or dead, is entirely coincidental.

Seven Seas press and purchase enquiries can be sent to Marketing Manager Lianne Sentar at press@gomanga.com. Information regarding the distribution and purchase of digital editions is available from Digital Manager CK Russell at digital@gomanga.com.

Seven Seas and the Seven Seas logo are trademarks of Seven Seas Entertainment. All rights reserved.

ISBN: 978-1-642750-74-4
Printed in Canada
First Printing: May 2019

10 9 8 7 6 5 4 3 2 1

DISCARD

JUN 1 1 2019

FOLLOW US ONLINE: *www.sevenseasentertainment.com*

READING DIRECTIONS

This book reads from ***right to left***, Japanese style. If this is your first time reading manga, you start reading from the top right panel on each page and take it from there. If you get lost, just follow the numbered diagram here. It may seem backwards at first, but you'll get the hang of it! Have fun!!

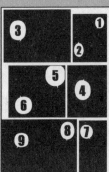